PRAISE FOR FIONA McIN

'Skilful storytelling and co
that leap from the page.' BOOKS+PUBLISHING

'Elegantly written, yet with no shortage
of satisfying thrills.' APPLE BOOKS

'Flawless.'
AUSTRALIAN WOMEN'S WEEKLY

'Will keep you second-guessing until the very end.'
BETTER READING

'McIntosh's riveting, page-turner style makes this book
an ideal poolside summer holiday read.'
SYDNEY MORNING HERALD

'Will have you hooked from page one . . .
a fast-paced romance filled with secrets, adventure,
and plenty of twists.' WEEKENDER

'A blockbuster of a book that you won't
want to put down.' BRYCE COURTENAY

'She's so prolific, you wonder how
Fiona McIntosh does it.' THE AGE

'A fast-paced and enchanting page-turner.'
KIRKUS REVIEWS

'Fiona McIntosh is an extraordinary storyteller.'
BOOK'D OUT

BLOOD PACT

Fiona McIntosh is an internationally and million-copy bestselling author of novels for adults and children across several genres. Alongside her highly successful historical fiction titles, for which she has been nominated at the Australian Book Industry Awards for commercial fiction book of the year, her popular Detective Jack Hawksworth series will soon be released across the UK. Several of her historical titles as well as the 'world of Hawksworth' crime novels have been optioned for the screen. Her debut children's picture book, *Harry and Gran*, will be published in 2025. Fiona roams the world for her research and lives between Adelaide in South Australia and Wiltshire in England.

BOOKS BY FIONA McINTOSH
AVAILABLE FROM PENGUIN RANDOM HOUSE

Fields of Gold
The Lavender Keeper
The French Promise
Nightingale
The Tailor's Girl
The Last Dance
The Perfumer's Secret
The Chocolate Tin
The Tea Gardens
The Pearl Thief
The Diamond Hunter
The Champagne War
The Spy's Wife
The Orphans
The Sugar Palace
The Fallen Woman

In the DCI Jack Hawksworth series:

Bye Bye Baby
Beautiful Death
Mirror Man
Dead Tide
Foul Play

FIONA McINTOSH

BLOOD PACT

PENGUIN BOOKS

UK | USA | Canada | Ireland | Australia
India | New Zealand | South Africa | China

Penguin Books is part of the Penguin Random House group of companies
whose addresses can be found at global.penguinrandomhouse.com

First published by Penguin Books, 2025

Cover image by Miguel Sobreira/Arcangel
Cover design by Louisa Maggio Design © Penguin Random House Australia Pty Ltd
Typeset in Bembo Std by Midland Typesetters, Australia

Printed and bound in Australia by Griffin Press, an accredited
ISO AS/NZS 14001 Environmental Management Systems printer

 A catalogue record for this
book is available from the
National Library of Australia

ISBN 978 1 76134 360 5

penguin.com.au

*We at Penguin Random House Australia acknowledge that Aboriginal and Torres Strait Islander
peoples are the Traditional Custodians and the first storytellers of the lands on which we live and work.
We honour Aboriginal and Torres Strait Islander peoples' continuous connection to Country, waters,
skies and communities. We celebrate Aboriginal and Torres Strait Islander stories, traditions and living
cultures; and we pay our respects to Elders past and present.*

To all the people who donate the gift of life –
you are wonderful.

PROLOGUE

She hadn't meant to kill anyone.

It was Liv's first time. She was embarrassed that she'd left it this long. She could track who received it, but she wouldn't. That would be creepy.

She grabbed her ID tag and slung it around her neck before putting on the olive-green Barbour-style coat she'd bought at Jigsaw. When she'd decided she needed this coat, there had been none left in the country; she'd finally found one in Northern Ireland, of all places. She had never regretted the ninety pounds or the postage.

Liv negotiated the myriad corridors of the sprawling rabbit warren, a single-storey building on an industrial estate, and once again counted her blessings for the purchase as she exited the facility's revolving doors into the bitterly cold car park.

If she had a good run, she could be at the centre in about five minutes, and then if she allowed half an hour to lose her virginity – that thought made her smile – she could be back in time to grab a baked potato with trashy trimmings as her reward; it was today's special in the canteen.

At the Blood Donor Centre the nurse welcomed her warmly, a contrast to the cold smells of antiseptic, plastic and metal that hit her on arrival. 'Oh, 'ello, a brave soul. Come on in from the cold, my lover. You're in luck. It's just slowed down.'

Liv glanced around. The only other person she could see was a second nurse, packing plastic bags of blood: some a rich scarlet, others so dark they could be brown. 'Is it just me?'

'For now,' the nurse said with a grin. Her badge said *Gail P.* 'Run off our feet all morning and the last fella just left.'

'Good to hear. How many?'

'Lost count. Maybe nearing three dozen,' the other nurse said, as Gail reached for Liv's form.

'Did you fill it in earlier?'

Liv nodded. 'I've confessed all my sins, medical and lifestyle, and travel and, er . . . romantic, not that there's been much of the latter.'

'Right,' Gail said, checking through the paperwork. 'Sorry to make you repeat yourself, but you'll get used to it. I need your full name, please, then your date of birth and your address.'

Liv dutifully recited all the information as George Michael sang about the previous Christmas on the radio they'd turned up full blast – probably because it was so slow they thought they were done with collections for the day. The other nurse was bopping along, and the tinsel wound around her name badge danced with her.

'All right, my lover,' Gail said in that familiar West Country way. She attached Liv's form to a clipboard. 'I see this is your first time?'

'A virgin!' the second nurse crowed.

'Yes. I'm glad I'm finally doing this. Oh, you're Gayle too,' Liv said, noticing the name on the dancing woman's badge.

'Yes, spelt differently but there's confusion, obviously, so we have Gail P and Gayle G.'

'Have you stayed hydrated this morning?' Gail asked, leading Liv over to a blue vinyl recliner chair.

'Yes. Do I really have to drink another pint of water?'

'Protocol, my love,' she said, handing Liv an A4 folder. 'And here's your delightful reading material.'

Liv groaned.

'I know. Go on, flick through it. It's necessary. I'll get your water while you read.'

Liv obediently turned the laminated pages of safety information, scanning but not really reading them. Gail returned with a plastic cup and Liv began to drink, closing the folder and looking around the room. A number of brightly coloured posters told her how many products could be made from her blood, how many people she might be helping today, how her donation was the gift of life, along with several testimonials from donors and recipients alike. Everyone on the posters was smiling. One suggested she consider becoming a tissue donor. Working at Filton's massive blood centre, she was frequently reminded of just how brilliant blood donations were and how many people a single donation could help, yet it had taken her this long to finally do it. Oh well, she was here now.

'Do we drink all this to replenish the liquid being taken?' Liv asked as the nurse returned to take her cup.

Gail nodded. 'It also stops you fainting afterwards.'

'I'm going to faint?' Liv repeated, sounding mortified.

Gail snorted. 'No, love. It's a precaution. We make sure you leave us feeling great, I promise.' She snapped on a pair of fresh gloves. 'Right, more questions. Are you feeling well today? Haven't had any illness recently?'

Liv shook her head.

'Have you been out of the country in the last six months?'

'Nope. I wish.'

'No lucky fellow in your life?'

Liv shrugged with a sad expression.

'He'll find you.'

'Hope so. Sometimes I think I'm pathetic, but to be honest all I want is a quiet life and a nice man to settle down with and have a family.'

'Why is that pathetic?' Gail sounded astonished. 'Nothing wrong with that.'

'Oh, these days I feel like every woman my age has to be striving for a career, the perfect lifestyle, a glamorous home, you know.'

Gail made a sound of disdain.

'But I'll be happy with someone who loves me and I love back.'

'Stick to that plan. It's all that matters,' the older woman assured her. 'So, we're going to check name, date of birth and address again, please. I know it's tedious, but it prevents any mishaps,' she said.

Liv obliged with the details.

'Thank you. So now the finger prick. Don't be scared – you won't feel a thing. You're a leftie?'

Liv nodded.

'Okay, we'll use your right hand,' she said and wiped Liv's middle finger with an alcohol swab. She made a swift prick to Liv's finger and squeezed a small drop of blood from the site, which she wiped away and then repeated to elicit a bright, richly scarlet droplet that she drew into a pipette.

Liv watched her drop the blood sample into one of two vials of coloured liquid. 'What's that solution you're putting it into?' She knew very well what it was from her work as a lab assistant, but she wanted to see how much the nurses knew about their routine. She was ready with an answer if asked: it would feel awkward now to mention Filton and face the inevitable question of why she hadn't already donated.

'This is copper sulphate. The gals are green and the guys are blue. Don't ask me to explain why – it's all a bit technical.'

Liv laughed, the answer running through her head: women's solution had a specific gravity of 1.053 and the men's 1.055. 'And why do we do that?'

'We need your drop of blood to sink. If it fails to do that, I won't be drawing blood from you today. I'm a little tired and caffeine-deprived to explain the complexity of this.' She grinned and turned on a timer. 'But let me try because you're interested and we're grateful for your gift. If the specific gravity of your blood is higher than the solution, which is what we want, it will sink and assure me that you have adequate levels of haemoglobin to safely donate.' She tapped Liv's arm gently. 'Now we wait.'

Liv was impressed by Gail's layman's explanation.

It was an obedient drop of blood.

'There we go,' Gail said triumphantly. 'So get comfy while I fetch what we need.'

The HemaFlow Scale, which would gently rock Liv's blood to prevent it from coagulating, was already on the floor at her side. Gail returned with a plastic basket containing a blood donation pack, swabs, sample vials and assorted paraphernalia.

'Do you know your blood type?'

Liv shook her head, unsure of why she was fibbing. Still, Gail, despite her fatigue, seemed to enjoy leading her through the process.

'You're A positive, for future reference. I hope you'll become a regular. You and about half the population belong to the A group.'

'A plus,' Liv said. 'I hope my parents are proud.'

Gail laughed and put the blood pack onto the scales. 'I'll just recline the seat and adjust this armrest. Comfortable?'

Liv nodded.

Gail wound a blood pressure cuff around Liv's upper arm and pumped it up. 'Make a fist for me,' she said. 'Open and close a couple of times.' She studied Liv's inner elbow. 'Well, we have a lovely vein right here,' she said, ripping open an alcohol swab and wiping the area. She picked up the 16-gauge retractable needle. 'Sharp scratch,' she warned, and inserted the needle as Liv looked away, barely feeling the expert intrusion. 'All done,' she said cheerfully, taping the attached tubes in place on Liv's arm. 'I'm just going to take some samples for testing,' she said, snapping on and off various vials that she filled with Liv's blood before attaching the bag. 'Try to relax.' She switched on the HemaFlow machine, and the first small stream of blood began to settle into the bag. 'I'm just going to get everything checked and ready for sending – I'll be back in a few, okay?'

Not quite five minutes later, the alarm on Liv's machine sounded and the donation of nearly 500 millilitres of her blood was complete.

Gail switched off the alarm. 'Feeling light-headed?'

'No.' Liv smiled with relief.

'Good, but you need to sit for another fifteen minutes. Those are the rules,' she said. 'I'll get you a hot cuppa. Do you take sugar?'

Liv nodded. 'Half a spoon.'

'Let me just get all this off you,' Gail said, removing the needle and pressing a swab on the entry site. 'Press on that for a couple of minutes.' She removed the tape and bundled up the blood pack, then cleared away all the equipment before checking under Liv's swab for bleeding. 'All good. Are you allergic to plasters?'

'No,' Liv answered, and a large plaster was opened and applied to the tiny wound.

'Keep this on for the rest of the day, eh?' Gail advised before applying a small pressure dressing. 'I'll get that cuppa.'

She returned with a plastic cup of tea and a selection of snacks. 'I'm sorry, it's vending machine tea, but the Club Orange biscuits make up for it.' She grinned. 'Eat something now. It helps. And then here's a safety information card with a helpline you can call if you feel unwell. You've got another ten minutes and then Gayle G will see you out – I'm about to go on a break. Thanks for your donation, especially at this time of year, and Merry Christmas to you.'

'Thanks. Same to you.'

Gail turned as she was leaving. 'Hope to see you in about four months . . . maybe wearing an engagement ring?' she said, holding up her left hand.

The women shared a laugh.

As Liv left the donor centre, hoping there might still be some baked potatoes in the canteen, her parcel of A+ blood – which had the potential to save lives in 43 per cent of the population – was being carefully packaged up with the other donations for the day. They would be taken to Filton within the hour for processing and would be moving through her own lab by the time she finished eating.

She felt cheered by her first donation, unaware that her blood was already on its journey to killing someone.

Sally was on autopilot without realising it. It happened a lot, and not just to her – her colleagues at North London's Barnet Hospital might not admit to it publicly but, between them, on these extra-long shifts, with many unpaid overtime hours, they understood the mind drifted and muscle memory often took over.

She'd not expected to do a double shift. The only reason she felt obliged to agree – apart from the short staffing and desperate need of the patients – was the extra money, plus the fact that both her children were staying with her parents this week for school holidays. They loved being spoiled by their grandparents, and she didn't have to worry about not getting home as promised. Still, she did feel guilty about Rob missing out on their private time.

'Aw, really?' he whined when she rang. 'You promised no more of these, sweetheart.'

'I know, but it's good money and they're in trouble here. It's shorter. Just six hours.'

'Not short on top of the eight or nine hours you've already done.'

'This is the last time. Means we can get Amy the birthday present she wants without having to argue about how much it costs.'

'I know that's how you look at it, but it's robbing Peter to pay Paul, as my old dad used to say.'

'Well,' she said with a sigh, not relishing the hard yards ahead, 'it's the only way I can look at it. A happy daughter on her birthday, rather than one who feels she's not as good as the others at school. No contest, right?'

'If you say so.'

'I'll make it up to you.'

'How?'

'The only way I know, my love.' She laughed.

'Then hurry home!'

They rang off. And now here she was, five and a half hours into that final six-hour slog. The phrase *Dead on my feet* kept going through her head but she was so close now, ready to start the final round of the ward, when the urgent call came through from her colleague, Janine.

'Sally? Oh, thank heavens. I was told you were pulling a long one.'

'Why do you sound so relieved?' She yawned silently.

'We've got a group and hold in A&E. The surgeon was called and she's ordered a transfusion.'

Shit! she thought silently, stifling another yawn. A group and hold meant a blood test to group the blood and have the supply readied in the lab. 'Which patient?'

'Er . . . his name is William Parker.'

Sally's back was aching; the pinch of sciatica was surely just one more patient-lift away and then her days off would mean limping around awkwardly. 'Janine,' she said, using one hand to support herself against the wall, 'I don't have a William on my ward.'

'I know. It's the other children's ward, not yours.'

'Oh,' she said, surprised. 'Then why am I being asked?'

She heard her senior sigh. She was likely tired too. 'Because I've never met another nurse in my time who draws blood from a child as ably as you do. This boy, seven, had his tonsillectomy a week ago but he presented at A&E yesterday, bleeding from one side. They got it all under control but the family's back again tonight – more haemorrhaging, same side.'

'Not unusual.'

'Except he's tachycardic and, worse, I've just heard back that his haemoglobin is at seventy. As I said, A&E contacted the paediatric surgeon – you know Emily Harley – and she's placed an urgent order for a crossmatch. We're taking all precautions.'

'So do it in A&E.' She didn't mean to sound uncaring, but it seemed counterproductive not to follow the surgeon's advice right away.

'We already did.'

'And?' She yawned, trying not to open her mouth, which just made her eyes glisten with tears.

'It clotted.' Janine sounded dismayed.

'Unusable?'

'Yeah, I'm afraid so. It has to be done again and the little fellow was already traumatised to be back in A&E and all its chaos. He's been taken up to the ward to settle down, perhaps even sleep, and so we need you to work your magic. The others don't have your light touch. The mum's given permission. Once we verify every-thing, the blood will be sent down and the night shift on that ward can do the transfusion.'

Sally gave a snort of disgust. 'The others really should learn how to do it without frightening the little ones.'

'I know. Please, Sally. This is a young life in danger, and I'm too tired to debate the inconvenience and unfairness . . . and I know you're probably even more fatigued than I am. It's probably faster to just go down the hallway and do it than argue.'

'Right.' She blew out a breath.

'Let me give you the details again.'

'No, I heard it the first time. William Parker. I'll do it now. You know I'm nearly off a second shift?' Sally looked at her watch. 'In under twenty minutes, and I am not staying a second over.'

'Nor do I expect you to. Five minutes is all you'll need and then you can go. The others can cover you.' The senior nurse thanked her profusely.

Sally checked at her station and told the other two nurses what she had been asked to do. They both made faces of sympathy. 'It's all quiet on ours,' one assured her.

'Back in a jiffy,' Sally said, dragging her heavy feet down the corridor towards the other children's ward.

Tonsillectomies weren't so common any more. Sally's mother, who had been a nurse in the 1960s and 70s, had told her they were done as a matter of course back then, the moment a child started to show a propensity for sore throats. Today it was only standard practice to remove tonsils and adenoids if there would otherwise be an unpleasant childhood of constant illness.

She stifled another deep yawn as she arrived at the nurse's station. 'What's up?' asked Annie, the rostered nurse. 'Why are you here, Sally?'

'Emergency crossmatch sample for your tonsillectomy.'

'Oh. Okay, but which—' But before she could finish, a colleague was calling her anxiously from the swinging doors.

'Annie, can you help, please? I think we have a fainter.'

Annie looked back. 'You okay, Sally? It's all quiet in there. Do you need me to—'

'No, you carry on. I'll be in and out. Janine will call you shortly, okay?'

Annie nodded and hurried after her colleague.

Sally stepped quietly into the ward, dark other than a small nightlight. Six children of varying ages were sleeping, and she could see two made-up cots, presumably for parents, both empty. She sighed. Just her luck. They were probably in the canteen or down the hall at the vending machine. Well, she couldn't wait, and Emergency couldn't either.

She saw the name William and tonsillectomy on the sign above one bed and, barely rousing the child, she worked her magic, drawing the blood sample swiftly and disappearing again in minutes.

Sally took the blood to the lab with the request form. 'They need an urgent crossmatch transfusion,' she said, writing down the ward. 'I did the blood draw; all is correct.' She signed the form.

The laboratory technician nodded. 'Of course. They're always urgent.'

'No, really. Straight away, Alec,' she said in a tired voice. 'It's a child.'

'Doing it now, Sally,' he said, mimicking her tone.

She returned to her own ward and rang Janine. 'Right, it's done, and the lab will send the blood down immediately. You'd better get them all organised now for the transfusion.'

'I'll ring Jess and Annie now. Night-night, Sally, and thanks. You've just saved another life and my arse.'

Sally smiled, just so glad to be going home.

Except she hadn't just saved a life.

She'd just killed seven-year-old Billy Parker, who had returned twice to the hospital for unusual bleeding and was now showing physiological signs of stress. William Smithson, meanwhile, was in normal post-op care for a tonsillectomy.

William Smithson was blood type A positive.

William Parker was blood type B negative.

The bag of A positive was retrieved. It had been donated by Liv – the virgin blood donor – on 23 December.

Janine had duly called Annie. 'Blood's on its way for William Parker. Get it into him immediately. The surgeon is also on her way in, but she's about an hour away; do not wait.'

They didn't. At his bedside, they checked paperwork that the blood was drawn and crossmatched for William Parker. No blood type was mentioned; all that detail was held at the lab with Alec. The blood was transfused into Billy's arm while his anxious mother watched.

'Why does he need this?' she asked.

'It's been ordered by Billy's surgeon and it's just a precaution.' Annie smiled. 'Billy's doing well; the bleeding has been subsiding since he came on the ward.'

'I was told before the op that Will might need one too,' the other mother in the ward said softly. 'I think it's just a top-up if they're bleeding a bit much.'

Billy's mother looked reassured. 'He's been so lethargic up until now, but I agree he's looking brighter.'

Billy grinned back at her, tearing his fascinated gaze from the tube in his arm.

'He'll really perk up after this,' Annie said, smiling. 'He'll be home tomorrow and kicking a ball around next week, won't you, matey?'

Billy looked at his mum. 'Will you tell Dad how brave I've been?'

'Of course,' she said, and all three women chuckled at his sweetness. 'He's going to be so proud of you. I'll phone him as soon as we finish.'

'Nearly done,' Annie said. 'You go to sleep now, Billy. You've had a big day and we'll see you when you wake up. Mrs Parker, you should rest too. Call me if you need me. Mrs Smithson, would you like a cuppa?'

The nurse and the other mother left the ward as Billy's mother closed her eyes next to her dozing son.

Within ten minutes of the transfusion beginning, Billy's blood pressure began to drop precipitously. He was unresponsive after sixteen minutes, and as frightened emergency buttons were pressed and alarms sounded, Billy, already weakened from surgery, suffered cardiac arrest and could not be resuscitated.

1

As Lou widened her eyes with mischievous pleasure and blew him a kiss over the heads of other customers in the gelato bar, Jack smiled at her delight. It had been a very good holiday, despite its brevity, and the building warmth of their relationship had more than countered the chilly weather.

They'd spent four days in Venice, with its misty mornings and damp days, roaming its narrow cobbled lanes. He loved this city in winter; its ancient buildings became even more muted and the Grand Canal looked like a watercolour painting.

They were now so used to traversing the maze of the old city that they could get back to St Mark's Square without any assistance, and from any corner of the city – even if it appeared unfamiliar. He had to resist giving too much of a history lesson, but then Lou had studied art history and loved it. They were combining both of their loves with this trip – and, really, with this relationship, which had moved quickly from the first flush of meeting to something that felt solid, full of substance and potential.

Jack felt slightly scared when he looked at Lou. He kept thinking about how much he didn't want to lose her – to an operation he was involved in, to some criminal who might decide to make his personal life a misery or, perhaps more predictably, to the long and demanding hours of his job. It was no nine to five. And it wasn't friendly. He couldn't discuss much of it with her, and wouldn't anyway, not after her reaction, just over a year earlier, when Operation Stonecrop had brought fear and danger into her life through him.

Meeting Lou had been a chance occurrence: he'd been holding up her drunk, semiconscious flatmate at the door of their apartment building as she skipped down the stairs in pyjamas, her hair looped up in a bun with a pencil, and a warm smile on her face. She didn't seem to care that he'd caught her so informally, and her casual friendliness, with a promise of cheekiness, had taken him by surprise. He now knew that his handsomely suited, but dishevelled, look that night had caught her unawares, too. Jack, even now, could feel the intensity of that first moment, its scorching pleasure, and he hoped that would never change. The last time he'd felt anything to match such a powerful desire for someone was six or seven years earlier, and he didn't want to remember that time.

It was full of pain.

But this was full of fun.

Long may it reign, he thought as she edged another couple of people closer to the front of the queue. He was lurking at the back of the gelato bar; they'd been told not to miss this ice cream on any account so he would remain patient. He wandered out of the shadows into the sunshine of a Venetian winter, and caught his reflection in the shop window: the thin rays highlighted the tiny brushstrokes of grey at his ears. Not a lot, but enough that he realised he wasn't getting enough times like these; life was all work and no play. He needed to do something about that. He raked long, blunt fingers through his dark hair, thinking about the trim he would need before he next walked into the office.

Another wave of people surged past him, speaking in various languages. What had happened to seasonal travel? He felt just a little churlish at discovering there were so many people on the move in one of his favourite cities. He was in their way. Another big group were just pushing through, following a woman with a red umbrella and looking longingly at the gelato bar, despite its being winter.

Tour groups gave him hives, but he understood the attraction. How else were holidaymakers to get their culture fix and be able to say yes, we saw this, and here's the photo to prove it, while leaving time for what they really wanted to do on holiday – relax, eat, sleep long and lazily, and be in a new and exotic destination that didn't resemble their daily grind.

He was certainly appreciating it, after months of working cold cases. After the adrenaline-pumping ops of the past, he was glad of the almost dull routine of these older cases, the bonus being that they had more friendly hours and he could spend more time with Lou. She deserved as much spoiling as he could give. And it was lovely to be kitted out in jeans and sweatshirts, with a casual jacket, rather than the obligatory suit or sports jacket with neat chinos and collared shirt. He could get used to this.

There she was . . . at last!

'I hope it's worth it.' He grinned.

'I've already licked yours.' She laughed, flicking back a long tail of golden hair that had come loose from its clip and fallen across her face. It gave her a wanton look he liked. Lou, oblivious to his yearning, handed him a cone with a scoop of green gelato the colour of artichoke. He hoped it was a different flavour.

'It will blow your mind,' she promised with an arch expression. 'The world's best pistachio.'

'And your flavour?'

'Tangerine,' she said. 'It's like you, Mr Hawksworth . . . all fresh and spritzy.'

He laughed aloud. 'I look like tangerine gelato?'

'I didn't say that. I would have bought mint chocolate chip in that case, to go with your minty sweatshirt and dark hair. No, this gelato tastes the way you make me feel.'

'Fresh and spritzy . . . I'll take that.' He put his arm around her shoulders. With or without the extraordinary pistachio gelato – she hadn't lied – he couldn't think of a moment in the past few years when he'd been happier. 'I was thinking of lunch on the top of the Hotel Cipriani.'

She cut him a dubious look. 'Really?'

'Do you have a better idea?'

'Yeah, walk down a random alley and sit down at the first restaurant that doesn't look touristy or dodgy.'

He shrugged. 'They're all touristy.'

'I don't want anywhere posh. I want to hold your hand and steal spaghetti off your plate, and not feel embarrassed to order an outrageous dessert.'

He laughed. 'Another reason to love you.'

'That you don't need to impress me with fancy places?'

Jack hugged her closer. 'No, that you want to hold my hand while you eat.' He leaned down and kissed her, knowing he would annoy the approaching tour group but to hell with it. Life felt good. He was in love.

His phone rang. He gave Lou an apologetic glance as he pulled it from his pocket. Carol Rowland. His heart sank momentarily but he didn't answer, let it ring out.

'Not important?' Lou asked.

'They know I'm on leave.'

'Who was it?'

'My boss.'

'I think you should have answered it,' she said as they broke into the glorious square of St Mark's, where two small string quartets were vying to attract customers to their respective grand cafés. Pigeons lifted and resettled constantly in a madly moving flock.

'If she calls again, I'll answer,' he said. He didn't want to ruin this romantic time, but if Carol was ringing, knowing he was away, then something was up. She would definitely ring again . . . and soon. 'Now, do you want to try somewhere in San Marco?' he asked, sweeping his hand in an arc.

'No, Jack, this really is for the tourists, although I admit the music is delightful. But look at the queues. I swear Venice becomes more crowded each time I visit.'

They strolled to the opposite corner and ducked down a familiar lane, but then deliberately took unfamiliar turns until they found a streetside restaurant where a couple was vacating a table.

'Here,' Lou said, squeezing in with her back to the window. 'Perfect.'

They were near a heater too. The house specialty, risi e bisi, was delicious, and just as they began sharing a tiramisu, his phone rang again.

'Sorry,' he mouthed.

'Take it. The rest of this is mine, though,' she warned.

He laughed and swung away from the table to talk. 'Hawksworth.'

'Jack.'

'Ma'am.'

'I apologise for interrupting your break.'

'It must be important.'

'It is. When are you back?'

'Two more nights. Back Friday.' He heard her give a soft hiss. 'Do I need to change my flights?'

'No,' she said, after a pause. She sounded emphatic, as though she was trying to convince herself. 'Enjoy your time. I'll see you Saturday, then?'

'Of course. I'm guessing I'm not going back to cold cases?'

'No. I had a drink with the Deputy Assistant Commissioner at CTC,' she said. 'And I've offered you up to him.'

He blinked. *Counter Terrorism Command?* 'All right. Why?'

'Don't worry about that now. Get on with your holiday, and I'll brief you when you get in. Bye, Jack.'

He stared at the phone after Carol rang off.

'Everything okay?' Lou asked, dramatically spooning the last mouthful of tiramisu into her mouth without a shred of guilt in her expression.

He shook his head. 'Not sure.' Then he looked down at the empty plate and gave a wicked smile. 'What I am sure about is that you're going to have to pay for that selfish gluttony.'

She raised her eyebrows. 'Is that so?'

'Yes, I'm going to take you back to the hotel and—'

'Coffee?' the waiter interrupted. He began to expertly clear the dishes.

'Yes, please. Two,' Lou said, laughing at Jack's face as he disguised his next words by clearing his throat. 'And Jack . . .' she began, waiting for the young man to depart. 'I'm too full to pay my debt. You'll have to wait.'

'I can't help it if you're a glutton.'

She tipped her head back and laughed joyously.

'But it's another reason to love you.'

'How I love my food, you mean?' she asked.

He nodded.

'So that's two reasons to love me that you've mentioned this afternoon.' A playful tension suddenly wrapped around them. 'Is three the charm?'

He studied her, thoughts swirling. Just before the silence became awkward, he smiled tenderly. 'No, I love everything about you. They don't need to be numbered.'

She nodded. 'Good. So . . .?' Playful turned to more serious. She covered his hand with hers. 'You know about my past relationships, and you've told me about yours.'

'Very grown-up, aren't we?' He laughed but she didn't. 'And?' Now he frowned.

'I don't want to be just another one in the line. I'm thirty-five, too old now to invest in the wrong guy. You feel like the very best fit I've ever met, but maybe you're someone who can't imagine beyond the first year or two.' She waited. 'I'm not accusing you of anything, Jack. I just want to be honest. So here it is. I'm crazy about you, and I don't get crazy about people. I prefer animals, to be frank, but I'm frightened to let myself go any deeper with you in case you don't feel the same way.' He opened his mouth to speak but she continued before he could. 'And I'm not suggesting you have to be in love with me, but I am with you. I don't want to become a casualty if you're reluctant to look too far ahead. I'd rather you had the space right now to say so, because I'm in a dangerous quicksand.'

The coffees arrived before he could respond, creating a momentary brittle silence.

Lou sighed. 'Talk about a mood buster. I'm sorry, I shouldn't have—'

'No, no, I'm glad you've said what you have. And you're right, I'm nervous to speak of love because I've had my fair share of disasters.'

She leaned forward with an earnest expression. 'Hey, irrespective of me, it's probably time you accepted that what happened with Anne was never your fault, if I've listened correctly. She marked you and deliberately pretended to be someone else.'

He nodded thoughtfully. That wound was only just healing . . .
scar tissue covering it.

'I'm being very selfish, but I have to protect myself. I'm not a
kid and being someone's date or holiday companion isn't enough.
You've changed my world, and I can see a life with you in it, but
I can't go for years wondering about a future. Now—'

'Marry me,' he said quietly, cutting across her words.

'What?' She said it far too loudly, her voice taut with shock. She
sat back, looking perplexed. 'I didn't mean for you—'

'I know. Will you marry me, Lou?' He got off his chair to kneel,
smiling at her.

'Stop!' she said, looking around wildly as people began to stare
and point excitedly, realising what was happening.

'Is that a no?' He looked wounded. 'Don't break my heart.'

'And you won't break mine?' she all but whispered.

He shook his head slowly, skewering her with his gaze to empha-
sise his sincerity.

'Then yes. Yes, a thousand times over!'

He made a show of struggling up from his knees, to laughter all
around, and then bent to kiss her tenderly. 'I love you with all my
heart . . . all of me.' Then he whispered, 'As I'll show you later
when your tonne of tiramisu has settled.'

She gurgled laughter through her tears. 'I love you back, Jack
. . . almost as much as that tiramisu. It's a tight contest.'

He kissed her again to applause all around, and when they parted
he murmured, 'Let's go find a ring in Venice.'

'Well, you look very . . .'

Jack waited for his boss to find the right word. She was in one of
her favoured silk shirts, of which she had an endless supply. Today
it was a soft lilac. Her new softer, shaggier haircut suited her too,

as did the lighter colour; it made her appear younger. He would've liked to say so but didn't think it would be appropriate.

'Er, glowy,' Rowland finished. 'Venice suited, obviously.'

'It did,' he replied. 'It even had me proposing to my girlfriend.'

She stared at him in astonishment. 'Wow, not much shocks me, Jack, but I had you down for a permanent bachelor. And the lucky lady's name is . . .?'

'Lou. Louise Barclay.'

'My sincere congratulations.'

'Thank you. I must admit I also thought marriage might pass me by. But . . . I know she's the one.'

'Then I'm even sorrier to burst that happy bubble by dragging you in today.'

He shook his head to say it was all right. 'What's going on, ma'am?'

She pushed a file across the desk and reached for her cup of coffee. He noted a new machine in her office. She'd upgraded to pod coffee since they'd last sat down like this. At least it smelled like real coffee.

Rowland began to talk him through the information. 'There have been curious, isolated crimes, mostly in the middle of the country, but they have stretched to the south coast. It began in August 2009 with needles in strawberries.'

'I remember this – it raged for a while, and then stopped. All over the news.'

'Mmm, yes, strange and cruel. At first the police thought it was Tesco being targeted, but then Sainsbury's and Waitrose suffered the same.'

Jack frowned. 'From Somerset to Sussex, am I right?'

'Correct. No leads. No CCTV footage, no witnesses of any kind. To be honest, no one was putting the incidents together to begin with. And then it all stopped almost as soon as it began.

Internally it was considered to have been some nutjob with a grievance. We didn't have the tech at that time to be across all the events. And fortunately no one was hurt, though a lot of people were scared and the strawberry growers were in limbo for a few months.'

He nodded. They'd come a long way with computer technology since 2009.

'Anyway, it ended after four incidents. Then just over a year ago, women noticed that their lips were blistering. Most thought it must be herpes – cold sores, you know – and went to the chemist to find ointment. It was a canny chemist at Boots, who happened to be the relief chemist for different branches, who began to notice a higher-than-normal incidence of the problem. She was the one who contacted police and suggested they should be looking at the make-up counter; it was her idea to check lipsticks. An internal investigation showed that the lipstick testers of their house brand had been tampered with.'

Jack shook his head in dismay. 'How hideous.'

'Nasty, but not life-threatening . . . just a bloody nuisance to stir vexation in the part of the population who wear that brand of lipstick. The time lag meant the strawberries weren't popping into the collective mind to link them with this new nuisance crime. The lipstick scare stopped once Boots had recalled all testers and put out new ones nationally.'

Jack flicked a page in the file and sighed. 'I'm reading baby formula here.'

Rowland nodded. 'Nearly a year ago. Now it gets more twisted. An infant became ill in Hounslow – again, nothing life-threatening but she was unwell enough to go to hospital – and, although tests were not conclusive, it is strongly believed that her formula was laced with something. The can had been punctured. The parents were cleared of all wrongdoing, especially as the contamination was found in another three cans in the same branch of the chemist. Only the top quarter of the formula had been contaminated, so the sampling was tiny. Nevertheless, all cans were removed nationally. And they didn't find another from all those removed that had the same puncture hole. Some sort of syringe with a needle, they thought. Some sort of herbicide – it's all in the file.'

Jack frowned, turning the page. 'And then mushrooms?'

Carol nodded. 'They were three months ago, in Gloucester. A couple got quite ill from eating poisonous mushrooms. And a few days earlier, two friends at a casual dinner in a small place called Hotwells, in Bristol, became sick and one died. The one who died had eaten poisonous mushrooms.'

'Shit.'

Rowland grimaced. 'Yes, that sums it up.'

'Did they connect the two events?'

'Nothing connects them other than toxic mushrooms that have no place at the dinner table. Both households were counties apart, and both claim they bought their mushrooms at local shops.'

'The same sort of poisonous mushroom?' Jack asked.

'Yes. One from a well-known supermarket. The other from a local greengrocer.'

'So there are some who believe it's the same person planting them and others aren't so sure.'

'Precisely. No one's sure of anything.'

Jack shook his head. 'I can understand both points of view.'

She shrugged. 'So can I, but Jack, what if they're *all* linked? The strawberries, the lipstick, the formula and the mushrooms? What if it's one perpetrator?'

He watched Carol carefully. She seemed to be waiting for an answer. 'Then it's domestic terrorism over a long time and on a national scale.' He could understand now why she was having him absorbed into Counter Terrorism Command.

She nodded. 'And no one wants to make such a sweeping conclusion but, for argument's sake, if this is one party, then it feels as though they've been testing themselves and Britain's ability to respond.'

'Or waiting to see if we're joining the dots?'

'That's my fear . . . that we haven't.'

He rolled the theory around in his mind. 'If it is the same perpetrator, they're escalating the level of harm.'

Carol didn't answer but gave a grateful sigh; he'd grasped the gravity of the situation.

'How can I help, ma'am?'

'I want you to lead a taskforce to first establish whether this could be the work of one perpetrator and, if so, to hunt them down. Because like you, the head of CTC and I believe it's escalating. We are under pressure to produce this perpetrator. What began as mischief has morphed into fear-mongering, but if death is now acceptable to this person, then I suspect we're looking at an even larger scale. We don't even know how big the stakes might be.'

Jack nodded. 'When do I start?'

'As soon as possible. The head of CTC will expect you. Find this bastard, Jack, please, and quickly.' She made it sound so straightforward.

He stood and gave her a nod of confidence before moving to the door.

'And, um,' she added, 'I do hope I am invited to the wedding?'

He smiled. 'Of course, ma'am.'

2

The pain was now centralised. It lived within. To everyone else Hannah looked normal and acted normal – if normal meant not breaking down into gulping sobs without warning, or thinking of the simplest, least gory way to join Billy.

People around her probably thought she'd 'got over it'. Even her parents, who used to watch her every move with darting eyes and worried expressions, were increasingly cheerful around her, willing her to look to the future. That said, her brother Ben had expressed more fury than even Jonathan. While her husband had turned quiet, seemingly focused on 'supporting her through the ordeal of grief', as her father had succinctly put it, it was her brother who had matched her rage and even her despair. He was one of those men born to be a father and the way he was with his children – funny, gentle but firm, affectionate yet rough-and-tumble when the children wanted to wrestle or ride on his shoulders – attracted adoring looks from other mums, who perhaps watched their husbands gathering with the other fathers to talk about the FA Cup or work. When Ben was with his children, he was one hundred per cent present, Hannah believed, and even though his response to her son's death was perhaps not what was required, she had wished on occasion that Jonathan had showed more of his pain, rather than bottling it up in some sort of protective role towards her.

Ben had been initially so enraged and had talked about how to punish the people responsible, echoing her own thoughts of justice, but his passion had cooled and dissipated. He seemed to have got past his nephew's death. Suddenly family Christmas was back on the agenda. Her brother and sister returned to talking openly about their children rather than hiding their milestones or accomplishments. Ben had even found a six-bedroom house in Cornwall for rent, which was being mooted for the return to the annual family getaway in the spring.

Getting on with life.

Moving forward.

One step at a time.

Starting again.

All those placations that were reassuring for the person saying them, but not for the sufferer. To her, nothing was the same or ever would be. Her life had irrevocably changed from light to dark. It might never move forward. Or it had felt that way for so long that she'd presumed it would never restart.

But that unhelpful adage that *Time heals* held some truth. Recently she had discovered herself behaving differently. It was subtle, but she'd noticed it. Not looking into his room each day, not losing hours and hours to memories of life with Billy, working full-time again, feeling like cooking again.

Small steps.

Nothing could change the fact that the life she'd created for herself, which she had loved, had been yanked away. Starting again meant being a new version of herself, which intrinsically meant no longer being a mother . . . although she could never consider herself as not being a mother, she was now without her child . . . without her own flesh. Half of herself missing.

You can have more children.

That was her most hated placation. How dare anyone suggest she bear up and have a replacement. And anyway, with whom? Jonathan was gone. Besides, no new baby would be Billy, her sweet-natured, giggling son with his pink-cheeked face and eyes that lovely shade of greyish green like his father's, which she had also loved deeply. Her child had trusted her, and she had let him down.

And his father had moved on too.

Not dead, but he might as well be.

Billy's passing had killed their marriage as effectively as the wrong blood had killed Billy, sweeping through and gathering him up. She wished it had taken her with him. She had not been on Death's list, though, more's the pity, but then neither had Billy. It was an accident alone that had claimed him. Death had simply answered Fate's call and become the obliging collector. 'Just doing my job, madam,' she could imagine Death saying with an apologetic shrug.

It wasn't fate, though. Billy had died due to human error.

That human's name was Sally. And Sally was a nurse, although not any more. A nurse's job was to protect life and care for those who were sick. But Sally, like many in the medical profession, had been overworked and, on that particular day three years ago, had been on the end of a double shift. Tired and expected to be in several places at once, as she claimed in her testimony in the coronial inquiry, she had been asked to help prepare a crossmatch transfusion for a child.

According to the coroner's findings, Sally had observed all the correct protocols – *well done, Sally* – except she had made one tiny, catastrophic error. She'd crossmatched the wrong child.

I hate you, Sally!

That single mistake had cost Billy his future, which might have included a loving partner, children . . . a long life.

The coroner might have found that error and acknowledged its result – *how gracious* – but it wouldn't bring seven-year-old Billy back. Where did that leave two broken parents?

I know you're sorry, Sally, but fuck you!

I know the hospital was deeply apologetic and claimed new systems would be put in place. Fuck all of you!

I know children are dying all over the world for all sorts of reasons, but this was my only child . . . my precious son. Don't compare his death with others.

The coronial explanation was meant to somehow give closure to their son's senseless death, and she and Jonathan had gone home and packed up Billy's room, and their marriage along with it. Neither of them could face grieving together any longer. Grieving alone, as selfish as it was, seemed easier, Hannah thought, especially contemplating her own death, as she had once. Looking after each other and trying to remain positive became too burdensome on top of Billy's absence, who had filled their life with so much joy.

Jonathan's time in the army may have helped him stay strong for her but she wanted nothing and no one if she couldn't have Billy; her husband's love was not enough. And so Jonathan had moved out. It seemed to her he had also moved on from the darkness, glimpsing some sort of chance for life after death, while she refused to leave her pool of grief.

The last she'd heard, Jonathan was living with a woman called Shelley McPherson in Scotland. He'd had the grace to visit and explain in person. She probably shouldn't have been surprised; Jonathan had always been a thoughtful, sensitive guy. It's why she'd loved him, and Billy had inherited much of that sensitivity.

Her husband looked different on that visit; he'd been lean and muscled during their time together, with a moustache, but now sported a clean-shaven look. Shelley must have insisted. He'd lost a lot of weight following Billy's death – all that angry running and cycling – but now looked better for the few extra kilos he'd put on.

'Do you still do those triathlons?' she'd asked.

He shook his head with a grimace. 'No, I don't do that any more. I needed to then, as it kept my mind empty. Although Shelley is encouraging me to take up trail running. I'm not interested in competition . . . just the personal challenge. I do a lot of weights now instead.'

'It shows,' she said, trying to muster a smile. She couldn't think of anything else to say. 'Well, I'm happy to see you, Jon.'

He nodded, looking self-conscious. Why was it that he seemed awkward with the one person he'd always been comfortable around? 'I felt it was time we saw each other and, I suppose, that we said goodbye properly. Last time was so . . .'

'I know,' she said, 'although this is an odd goodbye, with you talking about your new passions.' She'd hoped it would be delivered more lightly, to lift the moment, but it came out sounding accusatory.

'I . . . it wasn't my plan. I didn't expect to find someone else, to be honest, Han.'

She simply nodded. 'It's certainly not in my plans to replace you.'

'I haven't replaced you! But there's no point in us going through the rest of our lives miserable and lonely. No one benefits from that. And Billy wouldn't w—'

'Fair enough,' she cut in. 'In truth, I do feel I'm emerging from the deepest, maddest, angriest grief. I'm definitely better, Jon, so you don't have to worry about me as you did before.'

He regarded her carefully. 'Are you still looking for revenge?'

She shook her head. She wished she could tell him the whole truth, but she couldn't bear how he might think of her. 'Revenge, I've realised, will not bring me peace.'

'No?'

'I know it's all I used to talk about. But I just don't know who takes the blame . . . the nurse who drew the blood, the lab guy who chose the blood, the nurse who did the transfusion . . . or the national health system for being so tight it can't pay enough people to do their shifts awake and alert. Do I blame the blood bank for sending that blood . . . the person who donated it?'

He was shaking his head as though he didn't know what to say.

Hannah continued. 'I think we both agreed a long time ago that we blame everyone, don't we? I blame the surgeon for ordering the transfusion. I even blame our GP for referring us to a surgeon to look at Billy's tonsils.'

'Hannah. She was doing her job, taking the right precaution for our son.'

She turned away. 'As if I need reminding. No, I'm just trying to explain the breadth of the accountability that I once allowed to roam free. It's not reasonable, I see that now, but, hey, if I could blow up that fucking hospital I would.' She breathed out in an effort to calm herself and smiled – for him. 'Sorry. I just wish I could be at the stage you're at. You've found some level of peace. I need to get there too, and maybe, after all of this time of hate and despair, I'm on my way. I am teaching myself to put one foot in front of the other, to stay busy and distracted, to engage with others and life in general. It's hard . . . but it works.'

Jon nodded, eyes sad. 'I loved him as much as you did. And I loved you as much as him.'

'I know. I miss us – the three of us – and how we used to be.'

'So do I. But you won't let us have what's left any more.'

'Jon, you've accepted a new life,' she said, hating the accusing tone. She hadn't wanted to make him feel guilty and yet couldn't help herself.

His eyes flashed with anger. 'You *made* me find one. Shelley came into my life unexpectedly and it felt good to actually feel something again. I've been so numb. I don't think I realised how I'd begun to disappear – I'm sure you know what I mean.'

'I do.' She really did understand; she didn't blame him. Her voice softened. 'You need to know that I'm pleased one of us has made it out of the grave.'

'Don't say that.'

'You're right, I shouldn't. That's how I used to feel – that I might as well be shrivelling up next to him – but I don't want to die any more. I don't want to make anyone pay any more. I just want change so it never happens to any other parents.'

He nodded. 'Good, Han. There's nothing to be gained by living years in total misery. I didn't go looking for it, but when Shelley offered me a chance at laughter and happiness again, I grabbed it. But it doesn't mean I will ever forget us . . . or him. He's my boy, you're my girl, and always will be.'

He reached for her, and she briefly wept in his arms, for the last time.

'Go be happy, Jon . . . for both of us.'

He searched her face. 'Do you mean that?'

Hannah nodded, but with a desperately sad smile. 'Of course I do. I am going to use you as my inspiration and try to repair the broken pieces of my life. It won't look or feel the same, but I'll find some glue to hold it. We aren't bad people. Neither of us deserved to lose him, lose each other.'

'Maybe I was bad in another life.'

She pushed gently away from him, and shook her head. 'Not you. Me, maybe. Let me carry all the poison, Jon. You go off and live for all of us.'

Jon kissed the top of her head. 'You'd like her, you know —
Shelley.'

'I'm sure I would . . . if she wasn't with my husband.' She held
up a hand. 'Don't. You needn't justify anything. The problem
is mine . . . I just have to teach myself how to be Hannah alone
again.'

'If I could fix it somehow — no matter what it cost me — I would.'

'I know,' she said, touching his face briefly.

'Just stay open to people — new people coming into your life.
Promise me.'

'Someone might have, but . . .'

His expression brightened and then he frowned in soft confusion.
'That's great, Han. Just having a companion is healing: someone to
have dinner with, go to the movies with. It doesn't have to turn
serious too fast . . . or at all.'

She nodded. 'I don't respond very often, or at all at times.'

'He knows about . . .?'

She nodded.

'Then he's giving you space. That's so good. I'm glad you told me.'

Hannah gave a wry smile. 'Does it make your heart feel lighter
that maybe I won't be all alone?'

'It does,' he answered. 'I don't like to think of you sitting here
alone, with grief as your only company. Billy's in my mind every
day, but Shelley, a different job, a new life in Scotland . . . it helps.
There are still days when I need to be alone — that's when trail
running helps and I can let Billy back in fully.'

She laid a hand on his chest. 'I'm glad he's still with you.'

He covered her hand with his. 'Always. As you will be. But
I am uplifted to hear about . . .?'

'Tom.'

Jon nodded. 'Give him every chance, Han. So long as he understands — and he seems to — that this is a burden for life.'

She nodded. 'Well, good luck to you and Shelley.'

He leaned in to kiss her cheek. 'I'll ring you now and then . . . if that's still okay?'

She smiled. 'I want you to. You look good, Jonathan Parker. Don't feel guilty.'

'Thanks. Even in grief you're still beautiful.' He kissed her again, lingering slightly to hug her. 'Bye, Han.'

'Take care, you.'

And as she waved goodbye, she tried not to think of the secret she was hiding from the man she loved, or the fact that Tom did not exist.

Hannah's thoughts had roamed to Shelley – what did she look like? She probably had blonde hair . . . Jonathan was a sucker for a pretty blonde – but were interrupted by a sad chuckle from the group. She dragged her attention back to the room.

She was at her regular support group, which connected parents who had lost children. She used to attend frequently but she was now turning up once a month. That was enough. It was hard grieving alone, but seeing other grieving mothers tended to enhance her torment. And those who appeared to be coming to terms with the loss were borderline irritating, what with their compassion and sympathetic smiles of understanding . . .

If only they knew how she had tried to help herself. Every time she thought about it, she steered her thoughts away again, horrified. That was the past. This was Hannah on the mend. It was gruelling. It required her to follow routine, day after day, and realise another week had passed, another month, and Christmas had come and gone . . . again.

Time healed. She had to trust that. Maybe some luck had been thrown her way, out of pity for taking her son, and that was why no one had discovered her secret. No one who could make her pay, anyway.

She looked around the circle. There were a couple of newbies today. A woman had introduced herself and spoken briefly, breaking down almost as soon as she began and excusing herself. Another parent, a father this time, had just begun. She wasn't really concentrating but she gathered he'd lost two babies to SIDS. She tuned out again, unsure that she could keep coming to these meetings. The regular members encouraged everyone to keep supporting each other but she didn't think she had enough will to look after others.

She stood to make herself a cup of coffee, mostly to get away from the circle. She would slip out as soon as she could. She boiled the kettle, giving an apologetic smile for the noise it made, and then turned her back on the group. She didn't even want it, but it gave her something to do while she edged closer to the exit.

By the time she'd stirred in some milk, the guy had finished speaking. She decided to add sugar, tearing the top off a small packet. She sighed. She could probably slip away now, as others began talking and were fully distracted.

'Hi,' a voice murmured.

She looked around, surprised to have company. It was the father who had been speaking.

'Oh, hi. You were brave,' she whispered. It seemed like the right thing to say.

He shrugged. 'I don't know why I'm here. It won't change anything.' He had an accent, she noted.

She nodded. 'Mmm, that's the catch.'

One corner of his mouth lifted in a sort of sympathetic grin. 'I'm Jim.'

'Hannah.'

'Nice to meet you.'

'I was just leaving, actually.'

He glanced at her untouched coffee. 'Fancy a better quality one of those? There's a café around the corner doing pretty good espresso.'

'Erm . . . I'm still married in my mind and—'

'Hannah?'

She paused.

'It's just coffee. Friends in grief, that's all. So, want to get out of this depressing place?'

She was reminded of Jonathan's advice. 'Sure,' she said with a shrug. Anywhere was better than here.

Without looking back, they tiptoed away and out of the local hall. She pulled her scarf closely around her and zipped up her puffer coat. He was wearing just a hoodie, no gloves or scarf.

'Aren't you freezing?' she asked.

'I think I left my coat on the train coming in. I'll have to track it through lost property.'

'Oh, that's a bummer. Will you be all right?'

He nodded; he didn't seem troubled, although his hands were jammed into his pockets. She recognised the brand. Paul Smith was not cheap.

'Do you live around Dartmouth Park?' she asked.

He shook his head. 'No, just here for the group. There aren't many around. My wife and I started married life in Golders Green, but she's gone back to Norfolk and I'm renting while I build a townhouse at Crouch End.'

'I'm in Gospel Oak.'

He opened the door to the café for her. 'Here we are. Mmm, smell that?'

She looked slightly baffled.

'Well-drawn espresso,' he explained. 'You get a table. I'll get the coffees. Flat white?'

'Fine,' she answered, not really that interested in coffee. She usually drank Gold Blend at home, or Costa when she was getting a takeaway.

She watched him talking to the next person in the queue and then engaging with the server who took his order. He even had a word or two with the barista, who looked too busy to talk. It seemed he was friendly to all. He returned with two coffees that lacked the usual image in foam. Is that what a flat white meant?

'Thanks. Jim, did you say?'

He nodded. 'James Clydesdale.'

'Very Scottish. But you sound . . . Australian?'

'Yeah.' He took a sip and sighed with pleasure. 'The family is descended from convicts.'

'Oh,' she said. 'That's an opener.'

He laughed. 'It's a thing there. I don't mind. I'm proud of my ancestors. I mean, they were sent to a penal colony for petty theft . . . My great-great-whatever stole a couple of loaves of bread, and his wife, who he met on the convict ship out to Australia, was arrested for taking a small piece of lace from the woman she worked for.' He pointed a finger in the air. 'Which, our family mythology has it, had been thrown away.'

Hannah smiled. She had never thought herself a sharp judge of character, preferring to accept people as they presented themselves and discover them as she got to know them, but Jim seemed to have an openness to his gaze. It probably arose from his easy, friendly manner and she felt he was someone she could trust. This was a novel feeling, given she'd given up her faith in people generally. 'I don't know Australia,' she said.

'It's hard to know unless you live there. It's huge.'

'I just hear that everything in nature there is trying to kill you.'

He gave a soft snort of amusement. 'It's not untrue but, at the same time, snakes aren't lying in wait in the garden and kangaroos are not bouncing down the streets. Funnel-webs and redbacks aren't lurking in every corner. I guess we learn from a young age to be aware. There're much more dangerous two-legged animals on the streets in London, trust me.'

She nodded. He wasn't wrong. 'So how did you come to be here in England?' She took a sip of her coffee; she couldn't really tell the difference between it and a Costa.

'Met the girl of my dreams, who was on a working holiday in Australia. I came back with her and did the same thing over here, and when my time was up, we couldn't bear to be apart. Got married. Had a handsome little fellow, but we lost Dougie real early. Got pregnant again and Julie – that's my wife – miscarried. We tried again and had our third, a gorgeous little girl called Emily, who helped gather up all the pain and gave us everything to smile about. She made it to four months. And then one day she just didn't wake up.' He looked down.

'There are no words, Jim. I'm not going to try.'

'No,' he said with a sad smile. 'We were already just hanging on by our fingernails. Emily brought us together, and then losing her just tore us apart.'

'It was similar for Jon and me when we lost Billy. But we had seven great years with him.'

He frowned. 'Shit! Seven! How did you lose him? Or would you prefer me not to—'

She gave an expression of weariness. 'No, I'm happy to shout it from the rooftops. The anger never leaves but you learn how to shift it elsewhere.' She sighed. 'He had a regular operation. A tonsillectomy, because he kept getting so many throat infections. They thought it best. There was this terrible night when he began bleeding. We took him back to the hospital and they kept him overnight to sort it out. It was all routine.'

'So what went wrong?'

'Sally Holman went wrong.'

At his confused look, she elaborated. 'A nurse. He needed a blood transfusion, and she did the routine blood test to make sure the right blood would be used.'

'Oh, no.'

'Yeah. She took the sample from the wrong child. And Billy, already compromised from the op and quite weak, was given the wrong blood type. He tried to rally, but my son lost the fight.'

Jim shook his head. 'Hannah, I have so many responses to this, but you'll have already heard them all.'

She nodded. 'None ease the pain.'

He squeezed her hand but let go immediately so she didn't have time to flinch or feel intruded upon. 'Thanks for telling me.'

'It's what we do, isn't it? Kindred, grieving parents and all that.'

'I suppose. What happened to the nurse?'

'Happened?' Hannah sipped her coffee and sighed. 'Nothing. She doesn't do nursing any more, but she wasn't prosecuted, if that's what you mean. Nor was anyone else in that chain of error.'

'Nothing?' He looked shocked.

'I'm sure she suffered in her way. I'm sure they all did, but I don't care. Between them they killed my child. It's their job to make sure patients get the right type of blood.'

'And does this former nurse have children?'

Hannah nodded. 'Yep. She mentioned them on the stand, citing her horror if it had happened to one of hers. So I presume she has more than one, but I don't know how many. Anyway, she was let off.'

Jim looked back at her with disbelief. 'She killed your child.'

'Not deliberately. What could they do?'

'Something! They prosecute drivers who are careless. It's called manslaughter.'

Hannah shrugged. 'Well, in this case the finding was accidental death, because there were so many factors. No one person was deemed capable of bearing the full blame.'

'You accepted that?'

'We had no choice.'

'I think I'd have to make someone pay.' Jim leaned back in his chair.

'Don't get me wrong, I still feel the most unholy rage,' Hannah said. 'Every day I feel rage.'

He nodded. 'But there's no channel for it.'

'Maybe.'

He sipped his coffee, watching her.

'Unless someone has lost a child, they can't really appreciate that our little boy has been sort of forgotten . . . like he was dismissed as, oh, one-of-those-accidents-and-we-must-do-better kind of thing. Except they don't do better. They can sleep at night because all the right words were uttered, all the best intentions were voiced. But what's really changed? Lots of nodding heads and stroking of beards while a mother's world is shattered.' She paused. 'Sorry, I don't mean to bang on.'

He gave a sad smile. 'I don't mind. Will you come to the meetings again?'

She shook her head. 'No. I've decided to stop. I contribute nothing, and I hate listening to all of them. It only makes me sadder, madder. I've been feeling considerably more in control recently.' She gave a bitter laugh. 'I haven't admitted that to anyone other than my ex, so saying it aloud to a stranger makes me realise I do mean it. Maybe I've turned a corner.' She shrugged. 'But I don't think those miserable gatherings are any help. Getting back into my work has been a great healer, as has finding a fitness regime, and I think just being busier is the right medicine for me at the moment.'

Jim looked like he understood. 'Can we meet again?' When she gave him a look, he raised his hands in a small defensive gesture. 'No pressure. Just a coffee or a stroll in the park with a takeaway. We can be our own support group.'

She thought on this and finally nodded. 'Okay.'

'Same time next week?'

'Don't you work?'

He laughed. 'I do. From home and for myself, so I'm the boss. So a Tuesday is fine.'

'So do I – work from home, I mean. What's your line?'

'I'm an architect.'

'I'm a freelance editor.'

'What does that involve? Corporate stuff or . . .?'

'No, real books.' She gave a small grin. 'For the big commercial publishers. It keeps me busy, focused and earning.'

'Famous authors?'

'Some. The jobs vary. I like fiction best.'

'Not much travel for you, then?'

She shook her head. 'Unless I have a meeting in the city, and those are day trips.'

'I work mostly from home too. I go into the city maybe once or twice a month; sometimes further afield. Anyway, look, we can meet close to you. Where around here do you prefer?'

Hannah was glad he didn't offer to pick her up or suggest her home. 'Hampstead Heath is probably easiest.'

'Sounds good.'

She kept it breezy. 'Okay, then. Thanks for the coffee. See you next week.'

'Should I take your number?'

'No need. Same day, same time, outside Gospel Oak Tube station, and if neither of us make it, nothing lost. No obligation.'

'That's fine.'

She saw nothing in his expression that suggested he was disappointed or offended. 'Bye, Jim. Have a productive week.'

'I'm glad we met. See you soon.' He smiled, and was gone.

The next week he met her as arranged, carrying takeaway coffees that they sipped as they walked. Their conversation felt easy and ranged further this time; she discovered he was attached to a big project in the city.

'It's been a lifesaver, actually,' Jim admitted. 'Not just good money when I most needed it, but the right distraction. I won the job just as my wife and I were parting, and it was the single shiny thing in my life. Now it's giving me the steady income I need for the next few years and the reliability that I need to be able to build my bolthole at Crouch End.'

Crouch End. Very hip, Hannah thought, thinking about one of the fastest-growing residential areas in London, which she could only dream of affording. If she and Jonathan had stayed together and only had Billy, maybe they could have afforded a home in one of the more salubrious suburbs. Nothing wrong with Gospel Oak; she felt lucky to hang on to it and Jonathan had been more than generous. He'd insisted she keep the house.

'I'll work it out, Han. I earn good money. I can rent or look to buy down the track. I move around a lot, as you know, so I don't need a big base, especially now with no dependents.' But that was before Shelley. She had the impression that Shelley came from money, though.

Jonathan had lucked out. He deserved it, for all his tenderness.

3

Sally was looking forward to the weekend after all the hype of Christmas and the extra work involved in the celebration. The children were both away on sleepovers and her husband was off playing golf with mates, despite the icy weather. It was her and the cat for the rest of the day and all of the next until early evening.

'Bliss!' she said aloud as she drove home. It was cold enough to make her toes ache, but nothing could ruin her mood. She'd kissed them all goodbye and dashed off a text message to friends who were going out for 'a cheeky night', saying that she was exhausted and would be no fun. Instead, she'd nipped down to Marks & Spencer – not her usual place for food – and had enjoyed a half-hour of wondrous grocery shopping. Normally it was a chore, and often a fight with the family to help, especially to unload the car. But this weekend she could be totally selfish in the best way. *Take care of yourself and it's taking care of the family better.* She really was weary, and she was looking forward to being lazy for the next day and a half.

Her plan was to drag a quilt downstairs and cosy up beneath it with the cat – who wouldn't be able to believe her luck, no doubt – and eat lots of delicious treats and not move from in front of the TV. She had a haul of DVDs to watch: some oldies and goodies, some she'd not yet got around to.

At Marks & Sparks she'd spent money on things she'd usually never buy, not that it would come close to the cost of her husband's golfing weekend. She had picked up cheese and bread, pâté, table grapes the size of huge marbles. She'd chosen a delicious pea and ham soup, knowing that if Marks did it, it would be tip-top quality. She bought crisps of all kinds and popcorn that was salted and some that was caramelised and one that had chocolate on it. She also bought a ready-made pasta dinner and a salad, because she had no intention of cooking, plus a tiramisu for dessert.

She'd lingered in the wine aisles and finally landed on a Spanish rioja and a merlot from Chile. She was the only one in her friendship group who liked red. Even as she was queuing at the checkout, she decided she couldn't walk out without some Extremely Chocolatey Biscuits. All her friends and family were milk chocolate lovers, so it was rare that she could cut loose with dark chocolate. Some Belgian chocolate–covered raisins wouldn't go amiss either.

So there it was. A veritable feast, and as she pulled on the handbrake of the car after pulling into the short driveway, she sighed. *Let the fun begin!*

A knock on the passenger side window startled her. A man with a beard was waving. She automatically lifted a hand to wave back but she didn't recognise him. He had a beanie pulled low over his forehead.

He opened the door and got in.

'Er, excuse me,' she said, bemused. 'What are you doing?'

'I have a knife,' he said, smiling, and looked down deliberately.

Shocked, she followed his gaze and saw a vicious-looking blade in his hand. 'What do you want?'

'I want you to drive me somewhere.'

She couldn't speak momentarily. 'Where?' she finally asked in a shaking voice.

'Just drive. I'll direct you.'

'Who are you?'

He shrugged. 'It doesn't matter. It never did.'

She didn't understand. He had such lovely, kind eyes. How could someone with such tenderness in their gaze be cruel? 'Can you tell me why you're doing this?'

'Please drive and we can talk as we move. Where I need you to take me is not very far.'

'Look, take the car,' she pleaded. 'Here's the keys. Just let me go.'

'No, I want you to drive me.'

He must be a nutter, she thought. A handsome mental case with a threatening knife in his hand.

'I will hurt you if you don't go now,' he said, sounding horribly calm.

'Okay.' She put the keys back in the ignition. 'Why me? What have I done? I have children,' she bleated.

'They'll manage without you.' He smiled.

She was found a day later on Hampstead Heath by some walkers. The timing of her death was estimated by the pathology team to be at around noon on Saturday 8 January. She was fully clothed and had not been sexually assaulted. Bracken had been used to cover her strangled body, but the walkers' dogs had discovered her. Her car was found abandoned in the car park of the nearby golf course, where her husband had been enjoying a boys' weekend.

The police had no theories for why this mother of two might have been abducted in her own car and killed not far from home, but soon enough they started to draw parallels with another death, this one in Cardiff. A lone woman, strangled in her home. The two police divisions began to quietly exchange details.

Jack kissed Kate on each cheek in greeting as she arrived at Flat White in Soho. He did not relish the idea of having this conversation, but he wanted to do it in person and, besides, the coffee was worth the trip into the city on a Monday morning.

'I'm glad you called. Haven't caught up in a while. I'm guessing something's afoot?'

He grinned. 'Two feet, in fact.'

'Ooh, mysterious. Let me get the coffees. You always pay.'

'And I'm not changing now. Flat white, latte, macchiato?'

'Just a coffee, thanks.'

'There is no such thing. Leave it with me.' He tapped his nose, then went to the counter to order, before returning to their small table in the back corner of the café. Best spot in the house. 'Love the new cut,' he said, gesturing towards her hair.

'Thank you,' she said, touching the golden bob that flicked out a little at the front. She'd kept her hair long since he'd met her, so it was quite a change.

'Very sophisticated,' he said. 'And how are you? You certainly look fabulous.' He knew Kate enjoyed his compliments, still liked to be recognised as a woman even though she worked in such tough environments, and she took care with her presentation. Today she wore slim charcoal trousers over neat ankle boots with a slouchy crew knit and a white shirt underneath. He could tell the knit was cashmere just from a glance. She'd already heaved off her heavy overcoat and a scarf the colour of a robin's egg. She had style – not always something that went hand in hand with police detectives, but then the TV shows tended to paint them all in a dim light.

'Then I'm fabulous as always,' she responded with a delighted grin.

'And Geoffrey?'

'He's good. We're good.' She shrugged, smiling. 'I want to say it's as if we never split. If anything, it's better.'

He nodded. 'Stronger. Wiser because of the time apart. You've both realised how good you are together.'

'Are we?' She was teasing him.

'You know you are. Geoff worships you.'

'As he should!' they both said together, laughing.

'And how about you? Are you and Lou . . .?'

'Still together, yes. In fact it's one of the foot things I wanted to talk about.'

She frowned and then laughed. 'Oh,' she said. 'The things that are afoot, I get it.'

'Two flat whites?' A young woman approached.

'Perfect, thanks, Skye,' Jack replied.

'No worries,' she replied, smiling back at him.

Kate shook her head in mock despair. 'You're here so much you know her name?'

'You know I am. She's having a working holiday in London. She's from Melbourne.'

'And let me guess, she—'

'Yes, she knows her coffee and how to make it,' Jack finished, grinning. 'Get that into you, Kate, and dare to tell me it's rubbish.'

She sipped. 'I can't, much as I want to. It's delicious.'

He gave a smug grin.

'So, what's afoot with Lou?'

He took a deep breath. 'Er, well . . . we're engaged.' And there it was. Spoken out loud to the one person he had not looked forward to telling. No turning back now; he would need to simply absorb the oncoming wave.

Kate blinked twice and put her coffee down. 'You're kidding?'
And then caught herself. 'I mean, *you*? Engaged? To be married?'

He shrugged. 'It happens to most of us.'

'Not to you,' she said, unable to hide her shock. 'I mean, this
is very sudden, surely?' She sounded like a parent trying to be the
voice of reason.

Jack laughed. 'Outwardly, perhaps.'

'No, Jack, not just outwardly. You've only known each other,
what, barely over a year?'

'Long enough to know how we feel about each other.'

'Bloody hell.' She was now doing her best to disguise her shock
and the flare of something else in her eyes. 'Oh, is she . . .?'

Jack frowned. 'What?'

'You know . . .' She pulled a face of embarrassment for him.

He shook his head once and smiled. 'Not pregnant, to my knowledge. Besides, she was almost as shocked as you are now when
I asked her.'

'Why? Not what she wants?'

He wouldn't let himself think she sounded hopeful. 'No, just
surprised, I think, that it's what I want.'

'On bended knee and all that?' She couldn't fully hide the envy,
but he ignored it.

'I'm afraid so. It was in the middle of a Venetian restaurant.'

'Ugh! You're so bloody corny,' she said in disgust.

'I like to think romantic.'

'And I suppose you whipped out a gorgeous ring?'

'No. The proposal was spontaneous. The moment was right. In
fact everything was right . . . the setting, how I felt, how she felt,
that second in time when the fates coalesced and pushed me.' He
chuckled at her look of disdain. 'We found a ring in Venice.'

She smirked. 'Of course you did. Romeo and Juliet.'

'That was Verona, not Venice,' he corrected in an arch tone.

'You know what I mean,' she said, her prickliness showing now. 'I mean, marriage, Jack, is for—'

'Forever. Yes, I realise that.'

'Are you absolutely sure? I'm your friend, I have to ask this – devil's advocate, blah blah.'

He'd known beforehand how this conversation would go and had been ready for her reaction; based on their history, it couldn't have gone any other way. It was playing out entirely how he'd expected, and he was glad they were nearly at the end of it. 'Never been surer of anything, Kate. She's the one.'

'Wow.' She looked down, seeming uncertain of what to say.

He had to save her. He lifted his cup. 'Here's cheers, then. I wanted you to be the first of our friends to know.'

That nod to close friendship helped. What else could she do but raise her cup too? 'To you and Lou. I hope you'll be truly happy together.'

He knew she meant it, but also that it cost her emotionally to say it. He just hoped she could accept it. 'Thanks, Kate. And maybe if I lead the charge, soon it'll be your turn.'

She gave a scoffing sound, but he suspected a more settled life with someone was exactly what Kate wanted. Her problem, historically, had been hoping for the wrong guy. But now the right one had found her again, despite her best efforts to thwart him. Geoff made her happy in so many ways. Perhaps Jack would have to give his mate a shove in the back.

'So to the second thing afoot,' he said, forcing a brightness into his tone.

'Mmm,' she said, not looking at him.

'I'm going to be on a new op and don't want to face it without you.'

She looked up. 'New op?' She frowned, the personal stuff pushed immediately to the background.

He nodded. 'Actually, it's a taskforce at the outset, which might turn into an op.'

'Go on,' she said, sipping her coffee, already intrigued.

'We think we might be facing a domestic terror threat.'

'Aren't we always, these days?' It was a jaded response and his gaze narrowed. 'Sorry, I just feel we're continually having to be wary now.' She made a glum face.

'This one's different or at least might be. I've been asked to establish what we're dealing with – assemble a team to work quietly on it – and then if we have enough evidence to convince the powers that be, we'll get a full ops team together and go hunting.'

'I've never worked counterterrorism, per se.'

He nodded. 'No, but you were attached to its command, and your experience in border control at the airport and flying squad could be enormously helpful.'

She smiled. 'I'm all in, you barely have to ask.'

'Thanks, Kate. I'll talk to your boss and have you seconded, okay?'

'Sure. When?'

'Come in Thursday; we'll have got some digs by then.'

'The usual gang? Want me to contact Sarah?'

'Please. I don't know if Joan is still working – do you?'

'You might just catch her. I know she's retiring this year but I'm sure she'd love one last hurrah. And Cam's back – he'll want this.'

'Terrific. I'd also like to get Nat, from our last op.'

'Yes, she's a sharp one. I've also been working with Hirem Kumar. He's good. Just made DC.'

'Perfect. Can you see if he's available?'

'Sounds like you've got carte blanche.' Kate raised her brows in query.

'Rowland will sign off on who I want for this, but the head of CTC will need to as well.'

'Right. Well, lots going on in your life, Jack. When's the big day?'

So she wasn't ready to let go. 'Uh, next year, maybe June, I think. I want my sister to come over with my niece and nephew, and Lou likes the idea of an early summer wedding in the New Forest, which is where her folks are from.'

'Lovely,' Kate said, her voice soft. 'Plenty of time, then.'

'Yes. Besides, I can't think about that right now – you'll see why when I brief the team. Shall we?' He drained his cup.

She'd already finished hers. 'That was very nice, thanks. So I'll see you on Thursday, then?'

'I'll message you as to where we'll meet at New Scotland Yard.' He guided her out of the door, lifting a hand in farewell to Skye, who nodded back, busy at her coffee machine with a lengthening queue. Seems they'd got there at the right time.

Outside they shivered beneath a white January sky. Winter remained determined. Kate began wrapping her thick scarf high enough to cover her mouth. 'Congratulations again,' she said, in a muffled tone, putting her arms around his neck and hugging him hard . . . holding on a moment or two longer than what would be considered just friendly. 'It's wonderful news. I'll send Lou a card.'

'She'd like that.' He might as well tell her everything. 'And perhaps send it to my place; she's moved in.'

'Lou's wasting no time, then.' Kate blushed. 'Sorry.'

He hugged her again. 'I know you are. I need you to be grown up and nice to her.'

'I will, I promise,' she said, stepping back. Her eyes were moist and she turned away quickly. 'Bye, Jack.'

'Bye, Kate.'

It sounded final . . . and in a way it was.

4

Hannah had met Jim a couple of times now, and she was more relaxed around him, to the extent that she'd realised it was sensible to exchange phone numbers after all. She knew she needed to be honest with him, though; if he was hoping for some sort of romantic hook-up, it wasn't going to happen. She'd tell him today.

It was Tuesday morning and they were catching up in Kensington Gardens in the city, because Jim had shopping to do later. Hannah had arrived via Queensway Underground station and wandered down the picturesque Broad Walk of the gardens to where Jim was waiting near the Orangery, close to Kensington Palace, two coffees in hand. It was very cold but still full of the joy of New Year that everyone else seemed to be feeling. They sat on a bench watching Londoners – and no doubt a pile of tourists, going by the phones on selfie sticks – moving in a steady stream down the wide pathway that led to gates at either end. One opened up onto Kensington High Street, where Jim would go later for his errands.

'So who are you shopping for now that Christmas is over?' Hannah asked, trying her utmost to fake the spirit of the season.

He groaned. 'I'm useless at shopping. I still haven't sent anything to my English aunt, who has always been so good to me. My parents are coming over from Australia and they'll be thrilled to see me still sober and eating properly. I'll find something for each of them too as a very late Christmas gift.'

'Well, the sales are on, so lucky you. No siblings coming?'

'Adored only child,' he said with a smile. 'It has its problems. How about you?'

She shrugged. 'I've a brother and sister, so that means nieces and nephews are always having birthdays or something to spoil them over. I reckon I'll pick up a bargain and hold on to it for that next birthday.'

'Yeah, it's good to make the effort.'

She nodded, sipping her coffee. 'Will you see your aunt while your parents are here?'

'Yeah. They're staying with her. My mother's worried look will relax over the days. I'm sure she still thinks I nip out the back and guzzle a bottle of Scotch.'

Hannah smiled for his benefit, then frowned. 'I hate this month, when everyone's got so much optimism for the year ahead.' She really could be honest with him.

'Is that when . . .?'

She gave a sigh. 'Just before Christmas. I used to scratch calendars with scissors on that day. No calendar was safe. I was once escorted by police out of WH Smith for ruining a wall calendar on display. January reminds me of the hardest time of my life.'

He gave a sad smile. 'Now you can say the date out loud and stay calm.'

She nodded. 'Not that calm. I never lose the desire to take out my rage on something, someone. But I'm learning how to focus it elsewhere.'

He frowned. 'What does that mean?'

Hannah hadn't meant to say that. 'Nothing,' she said hurriedly. 'Walking on the Heath, mainly.'

There was a brief silence. Hannah watched a red squirrel darting across the lawns towards the stand of trees.

'Hannah, can I ask you something?'

'Is it being nosy?' She gave a laugh to soften the question. 'I don't like nosy.'

He smiled. 'You can be the judge.'

'Go on, then.'

'When we first met and I'd suggested you didn't have an outlet for your existing rage, you said "Maybe".'

She stayed quiet; so he had heard that.

'And now you've said something else not dissimilar,' he continued. 'I'm just wondering what you meant.'

'It didn't mean anything,' she said, too fast.

'Just like you said a moment ago that learning how to focus your rage was nothing?'

She sighed. Held her silence.

'Sorry,' he said. 'But I'm a good listener, and you must never forget that I share similar pain and rage at the world.'

It was Hannah's turn to frown. Was now the moment to say it? 'Jim, I'm not looking for a new romantic relationship.'

He held up his hands, palms out. 'Whoa! Where has that come from?' He sounded surprised, not offended.

'Well, we're seeing each other regularly. I just thought it best to be honest early and say I appreciate your friendship, but I don't want it to develop into anything more.'

'Fair enough. I hadn't progressed to any thoughts beyond how nice it is to have a new friend. You're lovely, Hannah, really – Jonathan was barmy to leave you – but you're in no danger of anything but an understanding friendship from me. I've known real love, and I can't replace it. But I have walked in your shoes, as you have mine. It's hard to find that understanding elsewhere.'

She nodded. 'Thank you. I appreciate more than you can imagine what we have, but I want it to stay just like this . . . friendly and casual. No expectations, no pressure, nothing more.'

'It can.'

'Good.'

'But you haven't answered my question. You deflected it, actually, by changing the subject and throwing me on the back foot.'

She laughed. 'I did. But I'd promised myself we'd have this conversation.'

'And we have. So what *did* you mean by "maybe"?'

She hesitated. 'Perhaps I'll explain when I know you better.'

'You'll never know me better than you do today. We're both guarded. But we're close in other ways. Tell me what you meant. Maybe I can help.'

'I doubt it.'

'Is it a secret?'

'Yes.'

'I am excellent at keeping secrets. I take them to the grave.'

'Mmm, that's what everyone says. But my mother always said a secret shared is a secret no more.'

Jim chuckled. 'She's likely right. But I hold confidences in a vault.'

'Even so . . .'

Jim sighed. 'Shall I share *my* secret?'

She was intrigued. 'You have one too?'

He nodded, more seriously than she'd expected, given how they were toying with each other. 'But I'd prefer you to go first, because I am certain they're intertwined.'

'Impossible!' She laughed, surprised that she sounded so amused. There was nothing amusing about her secret.

He drained his coffee and carefully dropped the cup into the bin next to the bench. Then he took hers. She hadn't finished, but it was cold enough now that she was happy to relinquish it.

Jim turned back, squaring up and looking at her intently. Suddenly all the people milling back and forth faded away. It was just them. 'Tell me,' he said, almost commanding her.

Hannah swallowed. Out it came. 'You remember the spiked baby formula last year?'

He nodded. 'That was you?'

She opened her mouth and closed it again, shocked that he would immediately jump to the right conclusion. 'It was me,' she said, stunned to hear herself admit it out loud. And then the rest tumbled out. 'I was so horrified when a child was taken to hospital that I came close to killing myself that day, when the news broke.'

Jim was calm. Too calm, she thought, given what she'd admitted. 'What did you think would happen?' he asked.

She shrugged, feeling stupid. 'I was in such a dark headspace. I didn't want to hurt children. I really wasn't thinking. I found myself wandering the baby aisles in chemists and shops, feeling angry that other parents were safely happy with their children, busy choosing the right formula or which bottle teat to use. I can't really recall what I was thinking other than I wanted to be with Billy. I was just striking out.'

'I'm glad you didn't take that next step.'

She shrugged. 'Too cowardly.'

'I doubt that. I think it means that deep down you feel you have something to give to this world. Or,' he said, before she could jump in, 'perhaps you feel you need to redeem yourself.'

'I couldn't hate myself more,' she ground out in a low voice. 'I nearly did to those parents what someone did to my child. I can't forgive myself.'

'But no baby died.'

'No. Twenty-four hours under obs in hospital.'

He nodded. 'And presumably you've stopped?'

'Yes. Clean for nearly a year now.' She crossed her heart to make him smile.

'What inspired that behaviour in the first place? I mean, other than your own child dying.'

'Needles in strawberries was the beginning.' She looked down. 'That began around eighteen months ago. And the fear it produced was so impressive that I couldn't stop. I wanted others to feel that fear.'

'That was you, too?'

She nodded, horrified all over again. 'And the toxic lipstick samplers.'

He shook his head with awe.

'I told you, I have been in a sort of madness. But I've stopped trying to make people understand what my fear and horror feel like.'

'How did you stop?'

Hannah shrugged. 'Well, I knew my behaviour was unhinged, so I got some help. I was seeing a psychologist, not that I mentioned anything about my antisocial behaviour, but I certainly admitted to feeling irrational and wanting to strike out. She was brilliant, actually. And then last year I joined the support group, where we met, hoping it would add an extra layer of recovery. It didn't, but in all truth I haven't felt inclined to create that sort of terror lately. I still see my psychologist and while life doesn't really look any different, it is moving towards the opposite end of madness. I am rational at last. Whatever it was that was driving me to lash out in that way has gone; now I must learn a more academic way, perhaps, to win the public's attention. I should maybe write a book, or get on radio, TV interviews, take up politics even – anything to help kickstart a groundswell of change. I remain profoundly sad, though, for myself, for Jonathan and, of course, for our little boy. I doubt the pain will ever go, but I'm learning how to put it somewhere safe so it can't hurt me in the same way, or others.'

She saw something ignite in his eyes; she couldn't tell what it was . . . disgust, excitement or perhaps even pride?

'Wow,' was all he said for a moment, and she maintained the silence. 'I don't know that I heard about the lipstick thing, but I certainly heard about the strawberries and baby formula on the news.'

She felt ashamed, but somehow freer, having admitted it. 'I want to put it behind me. I can't wait for it to be a year, then two years, and to one day look up and think all that revolting behaviour was years ago.'

'Isn't there more?' he asked. 'The mushroom scare,' he added when she didn't answer.

'No, no. That wasn't me,' she said, making a warding gesture with her hands. 'That only happened very recently. I told you, I stopped.'

Jim shook his head and stood, pacing a few steps before returning to stare at her. 'I don't know what to say.'

'That you're horrified and never wish to see or speak with me again?' she offered. 'I understand, but please don't turn me over to the police. I'm done with it all, I promise. After Billy, and then my husband moving on with someone else, I wanted to strike out at people going about their business, all happy and jolly and unaware of the enormous pain I felt. They looked straight past me. I've thought so many times about just killing myself and doing everyone a favour but, as I said, I wasn't brave enough and I knew my family would suffer for the rest of their lives. It would be too selfish.' She sighed. 'But now you know and now you can leave. I know you'll probably feel you have to tell the police – I don't blame you.'

He sat again and shook his head, fixing her with that intense stare. 'I'm not going to tell anyone, Hannah.' He paused. 'I can't imagine the planning it took.'

'To hurt people? During that time I was doing everything by rote. I didn't taste food – I simply consumed it as fuel. I didn't feel any joy when I smiled – it was simply an expression I remembered to make for others. I might as well have been a robot. I took no interest in the future. I wished I could just go to sleep and not wake up.'

Jim shook his head. 'There's a better way to end it.'

'What do you mean?'

'Better than killing yourself. What's the point in that?'

'There's no point. But the pain ends – that was my rationale.'

He paused again before answering. 'And those who caused that pain . . . the person responsible for effectively murdering your son and then you by extension, what – gets on with her life? That's all right with you?'

Hannah blinked, baffled. 'What do you expect me to do? Kill her instead?' She felt an invisible shiver pass through her as she stared at him, her mouth slightly open.

'Would that bring you peace?'

She'd never considered the question. 'I don't know.'

'I doubt it,' he said.

She didn't know what to say. 'The woman was very sorry – she cried in court, again and again – but I hated her tears. They were pathetic. She claimed they were for Billy but I knew they were for herself and all the horrid attention she'd received and how her life would change. She was grieving for herself first and foremost.'

'Naturally,' he said.

Someone interrupted them, gesturing to the bench next to theirs. 'Er, can we sit here?'

'Sorry,' Jim said, affable and with a lovely smile. 'We're just waiting for our family.'

'Oh, apologies,' the woman said, backing off. 'We'll find another.' She urged along a child. 'Come on, darling.'

Hannah stared at Jim, and he chuckled. 'I didn't want us interrupted.'

'You're some sort of chameleon, the way you just smile when we're talking about something so serious.'

He nodded as if he'd heard this accusation before. 'Going back to our discussion. If she could be punished, would that help?'

'The authorities and general public probably believe she has been. All the do-gooders will say the stress alone has punished her enough.'

'But the care for you dried up.'

'You're right. As soon as our story faded from the news, our family's pain and loss was forgotten.'

'Meanwhile, the nurse has probably rebuilt her life and moved on.'

'Yes, I suppose she has. I wish she could experience the grief I suffer in just a single day.' Hannah looked at her hands.

'Look at it this way,' Jim said. 'You have someone you can target your rage at, and you probably have no idea how life-saving that is.'

That shocked her. 'What do you mean?'

'I mean, all I can do is shake my fist at the heavens. My babies died of their own accord . . . as if they were imperfect somehow. But your hate for the nurse . . .' He shrugged. 'It sort of keeps you sharp and alive, because your *anger* is alive. It has direction and a target. I don't think you'd swap your pain for hers.'

'I don't know,' she admitted. 'Two years ago I'd have said yes in a heartbeat, even for her to feel all of that just for a few moments.'

'And now?'

'And now I'll settle for a quiet life where my misery becomes part of me and I learn how to live alongside it without making it anyone else's problem. That's my goal now. If there's revenge to be taken, someone else can do it for me,' she said, smiling sadly. 'What goes around and all that. Maybe fate will step in.'

Jim simply nodded. 'Come on. I'll walk you back to the Tube station.'

'You don't have to.'

'I want to.'

Hannah never did learn Jim's secret. If she was being honest, she didn't actually care about it, nor did she particularly want to dig any deeper into someone else's life. Through gritted teeth, she agreed to spend that afternoon and evening with her family at her parents' home, where her siblings and their children had gathered. She had tried to wriggle out of it, but her mother was having none of it.

'Hannah, darling, we never celebrate New Year's any more, and this is a good compromise. I want us all to be together.'

'Mum, you know—'

'Yes, darling, I know very well how hard this is for you and what I'm asking of you. But still I'm asking it, because I feel that family is your only guiding star at the moment.'

Hannah sighed audibly at how romantic her mother made grief seem.

But her mother was still talking. 'When you're with us, you're distracted from what happened and sometimes even engaged with us. I'm not asking you to be festive; I'm simply asking you to be present and prepared to join in at times. It would mean everything to your father and me.'

'You both worry too much.'

'I'm allowed to – I'm your mother. And your father will be broken-hearted if you don't come. You know you're his favourite, although I resent admitting that aloud.'

Hannah actually smiled. It was true. 'I'll be there, Mum, but please don't expect me to play charades.'

'I won't. I just want you with us.'

It wasn't nearly as hard as she'd imagined, and somewhere deep in her core she found herself enjoying the youngsters in the family, with no sense of resentment towards them or their parents. That was new. The children were innocent, unaware of her loss, and treated her without the gentle gloves that everyone else did. They demanded she play with them and the youngest asked her to read a book, her new favourite. Holding a four-year-old on her lap and turning pages felt deeply wonderful and, while she couldn't say it was healing, it was a distraction, as her mother had promised.

Her father heated up the new glass room her parents had installed and they ate 'outside'. They were very pleased with what her father called the 'garden room' and her mother rather pretentiously called 'the pavilion'. Over the course of the day, it became 'the conservatory' for everyone, her mother giving in to the gentle mockery from her children.

It was lovely there, Hannah had to admit, surrounded by her parents' regularly tended garden, the lawn like stretched velvet, and she knew in the spring and summer it would be achingly pretty. Right now the rose bushes were sticks of bare promise, not a rosehip to be glimpsed. Her father and his secateurs were deadly. Her mother's eye for floral beauty could be sensed in the layout of her beds as she'd walked her adult children around the garden, pointing out where dozens and dozens – her words – of bulbs would emerge come spring.

Despite the new conservatory, it was still the garden they'd grown up in and could instantly be changed into a cricket pitch, a putting green or even a badminton court, as her father had shown his grandchildren. It seemed French cricket was the favoured game of the afternoon, with the whole family joining in and her old school tennis racquet the weapon of choice. At the bottom of the garden, two big old plum trees offered the perfect limbs from which to safely hang a tyre swing, and the children had fun while their parents reminisced nearby about the secrets and laughter shared in the same spot a quarter of a century earlier.

The smells in the kitchen were comforting and reminded Hannah of childhood. The old kitchen had been updated a dozen or so years ago and already looked outdated because her mother was so conservative in her taste. Even so, home wrapped its familiar arms around her and she could have been described as vaguely sunny during her time with the family.

By Wednesday morning, however, she was back in her own home and in a slump. Her psych had counselled her on these moments when they arrived, so at least she had some strategies to try: 'Be proactive. Recognise it and get busy on something. Distract yourself. Even a long walk will help, just to change the scenery, change the mood, change your outlook.'

She decided to take her father's pestering advice and contact the local shelter about rescuing a dog.

'A dog is a friend who makes no judgement but is always thrilled to be with you. It would lift you in ways you can't imagine.'

'It's a responsibility, though,' she said, sipping a warming cuppa in the freezing walk through his garden.

'You're not exactly a party girl, Hannah. You're not travelling either. You work from home – it's perfect for dog ownership and not only will you save a life by rescuing that life, but he or she may just rescue *you*.'

'I don't need rescuing, Dad.'

'You do, my love. You need to come back to us, and it begins by learning to love again. Hard not to fall in love with a puppy. I'll come with you if you like.'

'Let me think about it.'

Now, the phone was answered promptly. 'We've got seven right here for you to choose from,' the woman said, once Hannah explained why she was calling.

'Any puppies?'

'Not babies, no, but we have a gorgeous little fox terrier who is about sixteen weeks. He's very small – probably the runt – and fun.'

'Why does he need rescuing?'

'Er, it's a bit of a sad story, actually. He was brought into a family who were expecting their first child, intending that he and the little one would grow up together. But an accident claimed that child's life, and the parents were in no mood to raise a puppy. No one else in their circle could take him. He arrived two days ago.'

An accident. A child lost. It felt like fate. 'Sixteen weeks, you say?'

'Yes, we've checked with the vet who gave him his original vaccinations. His name is Chalky, as he's mostly white, but you can probably teach him a new one.'

'No, I like Chalky. He sounds perfect for me . . . I, er . . . I'm grieving too. We'll help each other.'

She could almost hear a sad smile in the stranger's voice. 'Sounds perfect.'

They made arrangements for Hannah to come by and do the paperwork that afternoon. It was the first time in an age that she'd felt anything close to excitement, though she wouldn't quite call it that. More like a solid step forward. She was about to dial her parents to give them the news about Chalky, when a breaking news story flashed across the TV, which she tended to have murmuring constantly in the background, more for company than anything else.

'The police have released the name of the woman found dead in North London on the weekend and are treating her death as a murder. The body of thirty-eight-year-old Wood Green mother of two Sally Holman was found on Hampstead Heath near Kenwood House. Local police have not yet confirmed the cause of death, but there are suggestions that the deceased may have been the victim of a car mugging gone wrong. We'll bring you more on that story as we hear it. In other news, the Prime Minister today said . . .'

Hannah stared at the television screen, the words of the presenter fading as the fate of Sally Holman loomed large in Hannah's mind.

Dead. Her nemesis was dead.

Killed.

How spectacularly marvellous and abominable at once.

5

Jack was on his way up to the sixteenth floor at New Scotland Yard to see Commander Barton, the head of Counter Terrorism. Jack had worked in the division previously, so it wasn't unfamiliar, but it had been a while and he hoped his rusty skills would quickly get their shine back.

The commander was expecting him. Jack was shown immediately to another office, which was teak veneer from top to toe.

'Ah, Hawksworth, good to see you again. Cuppa? I'm having one.'

'No, thanks, sir. I've had enough for the morning,' he lied. He was not taking the risk in this building.

'Right, well, Carol Rowland assures me you're the person we need on this troubling series of events.'

'I'm glad to help. Um, obviously we begin by establishing any links.'

'Indeed. There's a space already cleared for your team on the seventh floor, so get started as soon as you can gather everyone you need. I presume you'll start small?'

Jack nodded. 'Five of us, sir.'

'All vetted for CTC?'

'Probably not our youngest, DC Natalie March, sir. DCI Kate Carter and DI Sarah Jones are the others for now and probably DC Hirem Kumar. I would have asked for DI Cam Brodie, but it seems he's not available.'

The commander's assistant arrived with a tray and a pot of coffee. 'Just me, Nicola.'

'Want me to pour, sir?'

He shook his head and she departed.

The commander had scribbled down the names. 'Nicola will double-check those you've chosen for clearance. And this Natalie March, she's special?'

'Whip-smart, sir. I worked with her on Operation Stonecrop. She's young, keen, came top of her year out of Hendon.'

'Well, perhaps we can get around the rules in this instance, because I am up against enormous pressure, as you can imagine, to get this person or persons found. I had to sit through an uncomfortable call from the assistant commissioner this morning.'

'I can imagine.'

'It seems the only thing that can push these incidents out of the headlines is our failing to win the hosting of the World Cup, and now the deaths of these women.'

'Yes, I heard on my way in about the woman killed in North London. Found on the Heath?'

'Yes, terrible business. That's two women strangled now. The first one was in Wales.' The commander made a sound of disgust. 'This second victim leaves a husband and two kids. Imagine that, to kick off a new year . . . what a bastard.' He made a face as though his coffee suddenly tasted bitter. 'They've set up a taskforce to investigate. Your mate DCI Geoff Benson is heading it up.'

'He's the best,' Jack said, pleased to hear it, before shifting attention back to the case in question. 'Do we have anything at all on the series of terror cases?'

The commander shook his head miserably. 'We're all over the shop, Jack. I don't want this repeated anywhere, but the fact is we can't draw a line between any of these events other than how bizarre they are. That's the only commonality at this stage. I've put everything in here for you,' he said, lifting a thick file and pushing it forward. 'Different towns, counties, north, south, west.'

'Operation Cedar,' Jack read aloud. So the op names were now moving through trees, he thought with amusement.

'There's no helpful intelligence on this from the National Public Order Intelligence Unit. We're at ground zero. And I don't want anyone in the community spooked by similar events – it just leads to civil unrest when these sorts of things snowball. All the trouble-makers take advantage of people's fears.'

Jack nodded, knowing this to be true. So the cases were being moved from the NPOIU. Made sense. 'One more person, sir, if I may be so bold? I'd love to get Joan Field, if she can be persuaded.'

He grinned. 'Who do you think is setting up your office?'

'Good old Joan.' Jack gave a nod of thanks.

'She halted her retirement for this.'

'Oh, I didn't mean—'

'Nearly broke her neck on those heels rushing back when she found out what it was and with whom. Seems you have a mother hen in Joan . . . not that there's anyone better, I have to say.'

'I couldn't agree more, sir. She's a powerful ally in an op, and I'll thank her properly.'

The commander tapped the desk. 'All right. Get your team moving and find me some links. These mushroom poisonings have created a lot of chaos, especially since someone died.'

Jack nodded. 'Report to you directly, sir?'

'Yes. Speak with Nicola anytime; she'll organise anything you need. We're giving you and your team absolute priority on this. So I need results, Jack.'

'Yes, sir.'

Down on level seven, Jack walked in to find Joan humming to herself and setting up her desk, wearing a pair of black suede boots beneath a neat, knee-length houndstooth skirt.

'Looking dashing, Joan,' he remarked without salutation.

'Jack!' she said, sounding delighted. 'I see the new year didn't waste time in delivering something dark for you to work on.'

'It never does.' He walked around the desk to hug her. 'You seem taller?'

'They're my wedges,' she said, stepping back to show them off. 'You should see the height of the heels this year – far too high, even for this gal.'

'Elegant as always, though,' he said. 'I can't tell you how grateful I am that you're here.'

'Wild horses and all that . . .' she said, beaming at him. 'Seriously, I hoped with all of my heart that you would somehow get involved with this case – if it even is one. Do you know any more?'

'Than you? Are you joking?' She laughed. 'I was just with the commander, and you probably already know what he said to me. Everyone's at a loss, no information from the various agencies, so our first role is making sense of it all and finding out if there are any links.'

'And finding this pest?'

He nodded. 'Of course, presuming it's one person. Could be more. But yes, I assume we'll get the green light for an op but we're keeping it tight for now until we know more.'

'Kate and Sarah, I presume? I heard Cam Brodie might be coming back.'

'No, he would love to but can't. We'll start small, just us . . . and Natalie from the Stonecrop Nat and Matt team if I can persuade them to fast-track her vetting. Kate is bringing in a new DC called Hirem Kumar. He's ace, apparently.'

'Right. Well, I've set us up. I presume everyone's in tomorrow?'

'They are.' He walked a few steps further into the space where the taskforce would assemble. 'Joan, you know everything, so I presume you also know the latest in my life?'

'That you're engaged? Yes. I didn't know whether to believe it, of course.'

He looked at her with astonishment; he had been joking. 'Now, how do you know this, and through whom?'

Joan tapped her nose. 'I never reveal my sources. But I am gloriously happy for you.'

'Thank you. To be honest, I haven't had time to think on it much because I got the call from Rowland on the same day.'

'Oh, no!' She looked genuinely miffed for him. 'I know Louise is a special woman to have caught you, but how is she coping with all this?' She waved her hand around the room.

'Well, she got an ugly taste of it when we first met, and I've warned her it doesn't get any easier.'

'It will definitely get worse.' She paused. 'How did Kate take the news?'

'Are you pretending you don't know?'

They shared a smile.

'She was great, actually. Obviously I was a little worried. She was disbelieving at first, but only because I took her by surprise. She was off the back foot within moments and refocusing on this op.'

Joan nodded. 'I suspect you're being kind. But she's had years of practice. She'll do her grieving privately. Still, I have to say Geoff Benson is the best thing that's happened to her . . .'

'Again,' they said together.

Joan laughed. 'He really is. And with luck, he too will pop the question and give Kate what she needs most of all. Watch out, Jack, this will be you soon.' She rocked an imaginary baby in her arms.

He looked back at her in awe. 'Don't!'

Her amusement followed him out of the ops room.

Hannah's mind was scattered following the news bombshell about Sally Holman. But it wasn't an unfamiliar sensation, not after Billy, so she forced herself to leave the house to meet and collect Chalky as she'd committed to.

The phone rang on her way out of the door.

She wasn't surprised. 'Hi, Jon.'

'Have you heard?'

'About the nurse? Yes. Just a moment ago on the news.'

There was an awkward pause as neither of them seemed to know how to respond.

'It's suspicious,' he said.

'Just in case you're wondering, it wasn't me,' Hannah replied, blunt offence in her tone. 'Did you think that?'

'No, of course not!'

'How do you feel about it?'

'I don't really know. Shelley asked me the same thing.'

Her lips twisted at the idea that Shelley had anything to say about this. 'Well, you should know that I'm not celebrating, but deep down, I'm not entirely unhappy at the news. My psychologist insists I always be honest with myself, and while I'm ashamed to admit that, it's the truth. I'm sure by tomorrow I'll feel differently.'

'Come on, Hannah. She's left behind two kids and a grieving husband. You're not like that.'

'She made sure I had no kid and no marriage. Right now, I couldn't give less of a damn.'

'I don't believe you. But please don't say that aloud to anyone who asks, especially if the media hunt you down for a comment.'

Hannah scoffed. 'I'll say what I want about Billy and the woman who murdered him.'

'She didn't mu—' He stopped and sighed.

It was old ground. Well covered, and it didn't need rehashing again. Surely he was thinking the same.

Jon coughed. 'Well, I rang to see that you'd heard and that you were okay. Listen, Han, I should tell you something.'

'That you love someone else? I know.' She wished she hadn't lashed out like that, bitter and unnecessary, but he was still her husband. She still loved him, even if they couldn't bear being together. The wedge of Billy's death was one thing, but another person now claiming his heart was something she simply couldn't process maturely.

He was silent, she realised.

'Sorry,' she said, feeling glad she could apologise. 'I'm not very good at being your past. But I'll get to the present, Jon, I promise.'

He gave a loud sigh. 'I'm just going to say it. Shelley's pregnant.'

She let her shocked silence hang between them.

'Can we talk about it?' he tried. 'It wasn't planned.'

'She's young. You're obviously the real deal together. Why wouldn't it be her plan?' Hannah said, her tone flat.

'I just didn't expect this . . . well, not so soon, anyway. I guess I knew in my heart that Shelley would want a family, as she comes from a close one.'

'Just remember, you're Billy's father first before you're a father to her child.'

'Do you think I've forgotten that?'

'Just don't forget him.'

'How could I?' He sounded hurt. 'I've just learned how to put it away because it will eat me up otherwise. You might benefit from teaching yourself how to do the same.'

'Don't lecture me about grief,' Hannah said coldly.

'Okay, okay, I'm sorry. I would like to, um, formalise things with Shell, though.'

'Formalise? Oh, you mean marriage?' Hannah blinked as shock after shock piled on.

'She wants our child to share one name.'

'*Our* name, you mean.'

'It's been years since we parted, Han. Longer since we lost our way together. Can you give me this? Let me move on?'

'Feels like yesterday to me,' she admitted.

'Look, you already know this but I'm going to say it anyway. There is no hope for us together – we both know that – and I knew I would just waste away with misery if I didn't build a new life for myself. I couldn't bring him back, I couldn't console you, or know how to help you, or help myself. I felt useless, pointless, lost. Only time and change – new decisions – could repair that.' He sighed. 'And the change that Shelley is bringing into my life is exactly what I need.'

Hannah ignored his plea. 'How far gone is she?'

'Eighteen weeks. You're the first to know, actually – she hasn't even told her parents yet. But I needed to tell you before anyone.'

She swallowed. 'And now you have. Should I say congratulations?'

'I don't know what you should say. I don't need you to feel happy for us in order for me to be happy. I just need you to find a way to rebuild a life as I have. There's no grace in suffering.'

Hannah knew he was right even as his words stung. She really did want to try to move on. 'Will you let me know the baby's sex when you find out?'

'We already know. It's a girl.'

Her mood lifted slightly. 'That's actually a relief. I don't mean to be—'

'No, I know. Believe me when I say I was quietly relieved too.'

'Billy's sister,' she murmured, half in awe, half in despair. He would have loved to have a sister.

6

Jim Clydesdale's number flashed up on Hannah's phone screen. She smiled to herself, eager to hear his voice and pass on her news but also to have someone to talk to about emerging events.

'Hey, you,' he said affably.

'Hi.'

'What's happening in your day?'

'Two big things, actually,' she said.

'Which are?'

'I rescued a young dog from the pound.'

'Oh, way to go, Hannah! Good for you. Tell me more.'

'He's a funny little chap who looks like Snoopy. I nearly called him that, but he was already named Chalky and he knows his name so I kept it.'

'What breed is he?'

'Oh, who would know? Definitely a fox terrier, but there's a merry mix in him. He's the cutest little man. I think I'm in love with him.'

'Lucky fella,' Jim remarked. 'And what's the second thing that's happened?'

'Well, it's bizarre, actually – and scary.'

'Oh? Tell me. Can I help?'

'I don't know. I wouldn't mind talking about it.'

'Want to meet up?'

Hannah paused. 'Am I interrupting your work?'

Jim gave a laugh. 'Yes, but I love to be interrupted when all I'm doing is client letters. When I'm draughting, that's a bit different.'

'Then yes, please.' Hannah was relieved.

'Okay. Where shall I meet you?'

'Would here be all right?'

'Your house?' She could hear the surprise in his voice.

'I trust you. And I know you well enough now that you're the first person I've told about Chalky and this other thing.'

'All right, then, send me the address. I'll leave now. Shall I grab some food?'

'I can do you cheese on toast.'

'No, come on. How about a Chinese?'

'Oooh, nice. Thank you. I eat everything. I've even got a chardonnay in the fridge.'

'Even better. I'm on my way.'

It felt strange, but she had to admit it was also quite nice to be talking to someone with such ease. She didn't have to hide anything from Jim. He knew the pain. Didn't try to fix it or explain it. He just accepted she had it, like a disease. The same disease he suffered. But they weren't making each other suffer the other's pain like she and Jon had. In fact, she smiled while she spoke to him and she felt safe when she heard him answer the phone. And now he was coming over with Chinese to meet her pup and to cheer her up, perhaps help make sense of the shocking news of Sally Holman's death.

It had to be murder.

She turned the volume up on the news and listened to the headlines. They had more information.

'Police are now treating the deaths of Sally Holman in North London and Patricia Hayes of Cardiff over the New Year season as murders. Detectives are yet to link the two deaths, but they have confirmed that both women were killed by strangulation.'

She muted the TV, knowing what was coming and, right enough, an image of Barnet Hospital flashed up alongside Sally in her nurse's uniform. She had to look away, glad she got to the sound before it could reach her.

For the first time in a long time, she turned off the TV. She no longer needed it; Jim was coming over, and in the meantime she would wake up Chalky. Tomorrow, she'd get him a proper bed, but he had already made himself at home on an old pillow and blanket on the floor in the second bathroom. His happy licks and exuberance were irresistible. Her dad had been his usual wise self in suggesting she consider a dog. It felt good just to know another heart was beating in this lonely home. Chalky would need regular exercise and it occurred to her that a small house she'd seen recently advertised in Hampstead might suit them for long walks on the Heath. Perhaps it was time to leave this home and all of its memories. Perhaps even that cottage in the far west beckoned . . . the old dream. She sighed.

By the time Jim arrived, she'd laid a table. Nothing fancy, just forks and plates with some paper napkins and wineglasses. She was tempted to put the wine in an ice bucket but that would be a bit too glam, so she decided she'd simply retrieve the bottle from the fridge. The other temptation was to light a candle, but again this suggested too much – a different mood, a little too romantic. Instead she dimmed the lights ever so slightly and switched on two lamps. It all looked casual but cosy. Perfect.

He stood on the doorstep, looking pleased to see her, and lifted two white plastic bags. 'Dinner's hot.'

'And the wine is chilled. Welcome.' She stepped back to let him in. 'Here, let me take all that. Thank you for this,' she said, easing the bags from his hands. 'You pour the wine. It's definitely five o'clock somewhere.' She smiled.

'Not far off here either.'

'Sorry it's such an early dinner.'

'I don't mind. I haven't eaten all day – I've been busy, and very glad we're doing this.'

'Good,' she said, putting the boxes onto a big tray. 'Do you mind all this coming to the table?'

He chuckled. 'I don't even mind if we don't have a table.'

'Well, we do. Come on, join me.'

Behind her, he bent into the fridge, found the chardonnay and brought it over. 'Oh, this is all very nice.'

'I don't usually have company, and this gave me a good excuse to— Oh, meet my new friend.'

Jim's expression lit up as he saw the young dog scampering in, full of pleasure at another human to jump over. 'Oh, look at you, matey! Aren't you lovely? Chalky, you said?'

She nodded.

'And he doesn't know what he is, does he?'

She laughed. 'No, he's a mixed-up pup, but he's actually been toilet-trained and he doesn't try to get up on chairs or anything, not yet anyway. The couple who originally had him couldn't keep him due to personal circumstances,' she said with care, not wishing to touch on the real reason. 'I saw him the day after he came in, so it was fate, I'm sure.'

'Yes, you were meant for each other. He's lovely, Hannah.'

'I'll just get him a biscuit to chew on while we eat.'

Settled, they clinked glasses with a gust of a laugh and tucked into the food.

'Mmm, I do love lemon chicken,' she said, heaping the food onto her plate.

'So, tell me.'

'First news, my husband has got his girlfriend pregnant and now wishes to marry her.'

'Oh,' he said, watching her closely. 'You found this out today?'

She nodded. 'Yep. He rang to see how I felt about the breaking news of the nurse who was killed . . . Billy's nurse . . . which I was still trying to wrap my head around when he king-hit me with his request for a divorce.'

Jim blinked. 'Right, that's a lot of stuff. Are you asking for advice, or do you just want to talk?'

Hannah looked at him seriously. 'Tell me what you think.'

'You're sure?' He shrugged. 'Give him his divorce. What are you hanging on to your husband for?' Before she could answer, he smiled gently. 'Look, I know you want to tell me you still love him, or at least that the love you have for him is intact . . . but it can't work the way it did, I'm gathering.'

She sighed at the truth of his words.

'Do you wish him unhappiness?'

'No!' she replied. 'Not at all. He's done well. Her parents own a hotel or something in Scotland, and he's got a really good job, great pay, so they're secure. I won't use the word happy, but he sounds positive, looking forward to a new life. I do want that for him.'

'Then let him go. Here's his chance at happiness. What you've got now isn't worth anything, is it? It has no value other than it being nostalgic, and it just rides alongside pain.'

Hannah sat back in her seat. 'Gosh, when did you get so wise?'

'Let him get on. It also releases you – you'll feel differently when you're no longer his wife and someone else is.'

She gave a wry smile. 'I feel a bit of venom, actually.'

He laughed. 'Only to be expected. Let me guess, she's younger?'

'Of course.'

'Well, I don't even need to see her to know she couldn't be prettier.'

She smiled again. 'Thank you. I know you're right about the divorce. I just have to get there.'

'And with the baby,' he continued, 'it's only natural. You can't prevent it, a young woman falling in love and wanting to start a family. You did. My wife did. Don't blame her for that instinct, or for her innocent child. And he's not really guilty of anything in fathering one.'

'It's a girl.'

'Good. Billy has a sister, then.'

'That's amazing you say that,' she said, chewing on a mouthful of lemon chicken. 'That was my first thought.'

He nodded. 'As for the nurse, all I can say is, what goes around comes around.'

'Really?' Again he was echoing her thoughts. 'I . . . this has rocked me.'

'Is it because you have no target for your rage any more?'

She put her fork down to think about this. Jim had also stopped eating. He was a big man, much larger all round than Jonathan. Jim was broad and tall with a big presence. You couldn't miss him. His beard needed trimming, as did his hair, but what she had first noticed about him – and she suspected most did – was the curiosity reflected in his eyes.

His question overwhelmed her, though. Jim's bluntness was on target today. She let out a long sigh. 'I can't tell. I feel numb again.'

'Only numb? Dare I ask if maybe there's some contentment?' He waited through her long pause, then added, 'It's okay, Hannah. No one's listening but me and Chalky.'

That made her smile. 'I'm deeply embarrassed to admit I want to punch the air, but somehow it's not joy. It's more like . . . fair's fair. Childish, eh?'

She expected him to look disappointed with her but there was that flare of something again in his eyes. Yet she was none the wiser for seeing it repeated.

'Good,' he said, taking her by surprise.

'Good? Surely there's something wrong with me.'

'No, there isn't. It's very human. She effectively killed your son, and now someone's killed her. An eye for an eye, they say.'

'I want to, but I'm not sure I can look at it that way.'

'Why? Is hurting a stranger easier?'

She cut him a sharp look. 'I told you that in confidence.'

'Nothing's changed. It remains between us. Was I shocked? Did I recoil? Did I look at you differently?'

She shook her head. 'The opposite, I would say.'

He shrugged. 'Does that make you feel safe?'

'It does.'

'Good. Because it was done for you.'

Her eyes narrowed in confusion. 'What was done for me?'

'The nurse. Your call for revenge was answered.' He paused. 'You did say let someone else do it, after all.'

7

Jack hadn't spoken to Jane in an age, even though she had been such a balm when he was grieving the loss of his girlfriend, Lily. They had kept in touch – the odd phone call, a Christmas message, even a drink a couple of years back – but time had flown and their friendship was still there but filed under 'distant'. He was just wondering whether her number may have changed when she answered his call on Wednesday afternoon.

'Dr Brooks speaking.'

'Jane, hello.' There was a pause. 'Er, sorry, it's Jack. Jack Hawksworth.'

'I haven't forgotten your voice – just surprised.'

'I know, it's been a while.'

She chuckled. 'A master of understatement. Lovely to hear from you, lovely Jack. I'm guessing this is not a social call?'

He sighed. 'I could use your advice on a case.' He knew he sounded sheepish and deserved to be, given the drought of contact.

'You sound embarrassed – as you should be. And how are you?'

'I'm really good.'

'Genuinely?'

'Yes, in a happy space personally.'

'Excellent. All right, how can I help?'

He could imagine her tiny frame, curled up on her sofa. 'Thank you. I'd like to tap into your expertise. Do you have a few minutes?'

'Of course. Actually, why don't you come over? I'm always ready to help Queen and Country.'

'Well, that really is what you'll be doing. Still at Spitalfields?'

'Yes. I've got two more appointments, but how about eight o'clock? We can talk over a glass of something and graze on some things I have in the fridge.'

'Perfect.'

'Why don't you have anyone to be with?'

'I do,' he repeated and felt a pang of guilt. 'She's having dinner with some family.'

'Not invited?'

'I am, it's just . . .' It was always the same excuse, and he always felt it wasn't good enough.

'Under the usual pressure?'

'So much I think my eyes are bulging from their sockets. We've got nothing, and yet we've got so much prevalent danger.'

'Shall I chill a bottle or put the kettle on?'

'Let's share one glass of something scrumptious, but let me bring it. Red, white or sparkly?'

'Hmm. White, please.'

'Do you like amber wines?'

'I don't even know what that means, but it sounds rich in flavour.'

'The colour – and taste – will knock your socks off.'

'See you around eight, then.' He heard her chuckle as she rang off.

He checked his wine fridge, certain there was still a bottle of the Roxanich Sara Chardonnay, which he'd only discovered this year.

The simple orange label caught his eye and he let out a sigh of relief. An hour later, he grabbed the bottle, put it into a thick neoprene sleeve to keep it cool and shoved it into his messenger bag. He took his keys from the dish near the front door – a ritual he never strayed from – and set off on the near hour's drive from his townhouse in Richmond to Jane's apartment and office in Spitalfields.

When he arrived at the familiar modern building in Fournier Street that ran off Brick Lane, he pressed the buzzer, pursing his lips momentarily. This area was where his former lover, Lily, had been discovered dead. He banished the thought as fast as it had come, well practised at doing so, and instead focused on this old area of London. Once home to a market most famous for meat, it had followed in the footsteps of the other very old area of the Docklands and was now a most desirable address, with cutting-edge buildings of chrome and glass that attracted the seriously upwardly mobile. Its reinvigoration was stunning, but he was personally still drawn to all things historic and often pined for his old place at Greenwich.

Jane's voice sounded slightly tinny over the speaker. 'Password?'

'Chardonnay?'

'Perfect.' At the buzzer, he pushed the door open and entered the calm, softly lit space he remembered well. He took the lift up to her floor and, as he exited, heard her call from down the hallway.

'Hello, you,' she said, with a small wave.

He approached, noting just how petitely beautiful she was, like a doll. Time hadn't changed much, perhaps a new flash of silvering here and there in the lustrous hair that she'd pinned up with a claw-style clip. She wore a charcoal-grey tracksuit with pale pink socks and no make-up. *Now there's a confident woman*, he thought, just as he had when he'd first met Lou. Jane had a natural beauty – olive skin, dark eyes – but meeting an old lover would have prompted some to redo their hair or add a little blush or mascara. But Jane looked as though she'd been working, strands of hair loosening to frame her face, not even a whiff of perfume.

'Hi,' he said, arriving at her apartment door. She likely wouldn't suggest they go across the hall into her office, though it was technically a work visit, so he followed her inside to her living quarters. 'It all looks much as I remember it.'

'Well, it hasn't been *that* long, has it?' They regarded each other and then, breaking into smiles, fell into a hug. 'Ah yes, I remember this. It was how we began, wasn't it?'

'What do you mean?'

'You needing a hug.' She grinned.

He chuckled. 'Your memory is better than mine.'

'Like a vice,' she assured him. 'It's lovely to see you, Jack, and I have to say you haven't changed either. Still as tall and lean as I recall. And every bit as handsome.'

'A bit greyer,' he said, pointing to his ears.

'Welcome to the club,' she said.

'You look even more beautiful, Jane, and I am not flattering you simply because I need your help. You know I'm no liar.'

'Well, thank you. I don't know why, but most women over forty begin to hate what's looking back at them in the mirror. We all desperately miss our twenty-something bodies.'

This was not a conversation to pursue. 'You have nothing to worry about,' he said carefully but with honesty. 'Let me get this chardonnay open.'

Jane tossed him a corkscrew and fetched some tall wineglasses as he pulled the cork.

'Let me tell you about this rich, luscious chardonnay that is referred to as Meursault style.' He handed her a glass.

She frowned at the orange colour. 'Wow, you weren't kidding about amber, were you?'

'Go on, taste it.'

'To old friends,' she said, raising her glass. He did the same, clinking it against hers, before she sipped and frowned. 'Mmm. Wow.'

'Wow, good?' he queried. 'Or . . .'

'Wow, fabulous,' she admitted. 'Meursault as in the French region?'

'Impressive,' he said. 'This winemaker insists on organic viticulture, and these grapes macerate for a week to get this deep colour and aroma.'

Jane sipped again before saying, 'I taste oak.'

'You'd be right. Around six years in barrels to get this sort of nutty nutmeg flavour.'

'Nutty nutmeg, eh?' She laughed. 'Come on, sit with me and let's talk about why you're here.'

They arranged themselves on the sofa and Jack put his glass down, sighing. 'I am grateful for this and I don't mean to take advantage of an old friendship.'

'You're not. And so long as we keep it friendly and general, we're not stepping on any toes, I presume.'

'Right.' Jack gave her a brief rundown on the various domestic terror events.

'And you want to know what sort of person you're hunting?' Jane asked.

He nodded. 'I know they're troubled, and I think they're angry but, hell, my team's starting work tomorrow and we've got nothing to begin with, Jane. I need to find something. We don't know if this is a man, a woman or several people. We've got no nationality or demographics. It's a blank.'

She nodded thoughtfully. 'Any potential for copycatting?'

He shrugged. 'Plenty.'

'Instinctively? Any inkling?'

Jack frowned. 'Based on the facts, I'd guess it's more than one person.'

She nodded. 'I agree.'

'Why, though? I mean, I know why I think so, but I want to hear what you think.'

She gave a shrug. 'Because during the last event someone was killed. It feels different.'

'That could have been coincidence.'

'Yes, it could, but that's the difference I see. And you have to start somewhere.'

'For me it's the gap between the final event and the previous ones. The first three happened in relatively quick succession, just a few months apart, and then the mushrooms after a bigger gap. Usually individuals escalate – the events get closer together.'

'That's relevant,' she acknowledged.

'And only one of the mushroom events killed, the other didn't. Why?'

'Level of toxicity, how they were cooked, how quickly they got help . . . Maybe they never intended to kill at all, only make someone sick. Or maybe it was designed that way.'

'Designed?'

'Yeah. Maybe there was only ever one death intended.'

'That's a very blunt weapon to use when a knife, running someone down with a car, strangling them, any number of other ways of killing would ensure that one person alone died.'

'Perhaps that was the intention, though. To kill one person and cause a bit of chaos around it all with others sickening.'

Jack sucked in a perplexed breath; that was a new thought to consider. 'Let's leave that for now. If we go with the notion of two separate perpetrators, why are they independently pursuing random disruption, or indeed death?'

'Oh, Jack, so many reasons.'

'Can you wrap it all up into one parcel with a ribbon?'

She laughed. 'Do you want me to come in and brainstorm this with your team? I think they might find it helpful.'

He let out a sigh of relief. 'Would you?'

'Of course. However, let me say that some kind of grievance might be a good place to start.'

'Because of the anger within these incidents?'

'Mmm, yes. People in pain want to lash out at something.'

He was reminded of the Mirror Op. It had all begun with a random accident that set off a rampage of killings. This case potentially had echoes of that need for vengeance, although he knew not to get hyper-focused on something so hypothetical so early. But it was a place to start. The wheels of his mind felt better greased, and he was energised for having some sort of direction. 'Any chance you could come in tomorrow?'

'Oh, now you're pushing it,' she said, getting up to reach for a large diary. 'I'll probably have to move a couple of appointments. Right, if I can come in early, around nine-thirty, and be gone by ten-thirty, then . . .'

'Just give us forty minutes tops. I'll send a car to pick you up and bring you back here.'

'Gosh, you know just how to spoil a girl, Jack.' She cut him a cheeky smile. 'All right.'

'Thank you, Jane. This is brilliant.'

'Oh well, let's see what we can untangle together. Hopefully between us all we can find some sort of pathway forward. So, shop talk done, what's happening in your life that puts you in that happy space you mentioned?'

It was only fair to tell her. 'I'm engaged.'

Jane couldn't have looked more shocked, but she was even more damning than Kate. 'Really? I would never have thought you capable.'

'I don't understand why people are so surprised.'

Jane shrugged. 'I can only speak for myself. And from a psychologist's perspective, you're quite the enigma. You've had a challenging childhood that taught you to be independent and sort of distant. The one time you opened up to someone she turned out to be a dangerous woman . . . a killer. Need I go on?'

He shook his head. 'She died, you know.'

'Oh. I thought she was in jail.'

She had been. 'It's a relief, if I'm honest. I hated that she was caged up.' Before she could remind him that this woman had killed several men, he held up his hand. 'It was the kindest ending for her, given her past.'

'And then the next woman—'

'You don't have to remind me.'

'My point is, you taught yourself how to shut all that emotion away and still enjoy women but not get entangled. Who is she?'

He told her.

Jane smiled. 'I'm glad she lives in a world that is aeons away from the world you walk through.'

'I think that's what makes it work. She talks about art or history, both topics that I find enjoyable, and it means I don't have to even discuss my day to day. But she's very aware of what I might encounter and the effect it can have. She's a smart, witty, wonderful soul.'

'And I'm guessing very pretty.' She grinned.

'It's the least of her qualities she trades on, but yes, she is. Her name is Louise . . . Lou.'

'Well, I'm suddenly jealous, but I'm desperately pleased for you at the same time.'

Jack smiled. Jane was the only ex-lover that he would consider a close friend. They hadn't seen each other in a long time and yet it felt as though they caught up regularly; this was due to her attitude and easy manner. 'Is there anyone in your life, Jane?'

'I'm seeing a nice man. We're keeping our lives separate as he's divorced but loves his kids. He lives in Brighton, so it's an easy commute for both of us.'

'I'm happy for you.'

'Oh, well, it's easy, relaxed and fun. We put no parameters on each other. And it helps that he's very wealthy and can take me to extremely nice places for dinner.'

Jack laughed and so did Jane, their gazes lingering.

'I must go,' he said with a soft sigh. 'Thank you again.'

'Don't leave it so long next time.'

'Well, as it happens, I shall see you tomorrow.'

She smiled. 'And I'd like to meet her sometime. Maybe as a wedding guest?'

He nodded, amused. They kissed affectionately once on each cheek, enjoyed a short final hug and he was back in the cold, as a light shower began in the London night.

8

Jack's group had gathered on level seven under their new banner of 'Cedar' early on Thursday morning. The presence of the swear tin had been highlighted by Joan, and now everyone was awaiting Jack's first briefing.

'Thank you all for saying yes to this,' he began. He glanced at his watch. 'Any moment now, Dr Jane Brooks will be coming in. She's a forensic psychologist as well as a clinical psychologist, and she is very used to working both on cases and on helping police officers in their personal lives. I've asked her to come in this morning to help us find a way towards some sort of clarity on this case, which is presently murky at best.' He smiled. 'But first, introductions are in order. Many of you are familiar with each other, but DC Kumar, we're very pleased to have you among us. Kate tells me you're an ace operator.'

The newcomer, an Indian man in his mid-twenties, nodded at everyone, looking grateful for the friendly welcome.

'All right, it's first names in my team all round. You can call me Jack
or Chief, or Guv, or whatever feels comfy, but please not Detective
Superintendent Hawksworth unless we're in formal company.
Other than that I have no rules. Work as long or as hard as you
like, but please remember we need you alert, so getting home for
sleep, food and to see your families is vital. Your first port of call
for just about everything is Joan, because she's an all-seeing marvel.
And for all advice regarding the cases themselves, then Kate and I
are always your go-tos. Think of Kate as me in a skirt.' That made
everyone chuckle, relieving some of the inevitable tension at the
start of an op.

'Jack?' It was Joan. 'Dr Brooks is on her way up.'

'Okay, great. Ask as many questions as you want. Don't be shy,
because no query is a silly one. And sometimes the odd questions
can lead us into a whole new area of thought or activity. So be
bold.'

He heard Joan welcoming their visitor and then Jane was shown
in, looking immaculate in a neat dark suit with her familiar skyscraper
heels. Joan would approve, he was sure.

'Everyone, please meet Dr Jane Brooks.'

A chorus of salutations ensued, and she smiled at them all,
lingering on Jack. 'Thank you, everyone. I'm glad to see if I can
be of any help. And please, I'm Jane.'

Jack pulled a seat over so she could sit facing the whiteboard.
'We only have Jane for forty minutes, so let's plunge in. Here's
what we're facing.' Jack walked them through the various events.

'So chronologically, we're looking at needles in strawberries, then
the toxic lipstick samplers, followed by the baby formula scare and
then the mushrooms,' Kate summarised.

'Correct,' Jack said.

'Okay, let's get those up on the whiteboard with dates, Nat,'
Kate said, and Nat obliged.

Jack continued. 'As far as anyone knows, these are four entirely separate events, so Kate, perhaps you could plot out where these occurred on the map that Joan has kindly set up for us. What you'll see is that there is no apparent rhythm in timing, and nothing obvious that links these events geographically other than a couple having occurred in Bristol. All we know is that they were presumably designed to cause terror. Our job is to find more concrete links if they exist. And if we can, then the powers that be will throw everything at it.'

He let that sit for a moment or two while Nat's whiteboard marker squeaked behind him and Kate was busy marking up the map.

'I probably always say this at the start of an op, but time is our enemy. I know it's obvious, I know it's a cliché, but you only have to see the expression of the commander of our counterterrorism unit to know how worried he is. We can't let that get out, of course. For the moment the general public isn't scared – these incidents have *appeared* isolated – but I am depending on everyone in this room to remain discreet about what we're doing. No one, and I mean no one, is to engage with the media. We have proper channels for that. But the fact is, our country is now depending on this group of people right here in this room to figure out the next step. How to prevent any more domestic terror being perpetrated by this person or group, whoever it is. It needs to stop.' Jack looked around at their engaged expressions; they were waiting for him to lead the way. 'So let's throw it open. Anyone?'

'It's most likely to be someone with a grievance rather than a mischief maker,' Jane said, having waited a beat to let the others jump in.

Jack nodded. 'Why?' He needed her to explain so everyone could grasp the rationale she'd shared the night before.

'Because all the various events are cruel in their own ways. The first three are not necessarily life-threatening, and they didn't persist long enough to do any real damage to people, but they're certainly leaning into malicious rather than mischievous. And then the mushrooms were clearly intended to cause real harm, even if the death was unintended.'

'So not kids with nothing better to do?' Hirem asked.

Jane shook her head. 'I don't think it's likely. The brevity of each attack could make you think that, but when you look at the spread of attacks, I don't think bored kids – unless it's a gang online urging each other around the country – would cover the ground that these attacks show. That's presuming it's one party, of course.'

'Well, I can tell you that there are dozens of people with grievances and a lack of emotional control in the system,' Sarah offered. 'They're hurting and angry.'

'And probably twice as many walking around that the police don't know about,' Kate added.

Jack nodded. 'We have to think about what forces a person to take that next step, from wishing harm to doing harm.'

'As Jane said, I guess we're looking for a proven grievance,' Hirem offered tentatively.

Jane shrugged. 'Well, you've already noted people being angry. And I do agree. Let's focus on the first three events again. Someone has been deeply hurt and wants to hurt back, but perhaps has no idea how to retaliate against the person they blame for hurting them, so they lash out.'

'Why wouldn't they target the person they blame?' Kate asked.

Jane turned away from the board to face the whole group. 'Maybe it was a corporation that inflicted the original wound, such as a sacking, so there's no individual to go after. It could even be a government decision – a change in law that profoundly affected them. Or it may be an accident, or a simple tragedy – you know, a fire swept through their house and killed their family, burned everything they owned and left this one person behind with nothing. And

it was seen to be an electrical fault with their toaster or something.'
She shrugged. 'Who do you blame?'

Kate nodded. 'I get it.'

'Yes. You feel completely helpless. Lots of rage and nowhere
to spend it. So maybe then you threaten others in a way that says,
"See what this feels like." It's not directed at anyone in particular.
It's just plain fury and pain, looking for an outlet.'

Jack was grateful Jane was here to articulate this for the team.
'What else should we be considering?'

She blew out her cheeks. 'I'd imagine someone in this situation is perhaps not getting the answers they want about whatever's
happened to them or their loved ones. Perhaps they feel more
should be done; blame might have been levelled but no punishment
given – maybe someone negligent just got a slap on the wrist. They
feel helpless. They're the one bearing all the anguish, and perhaps
someone they feel is complicit is getting off lightly.' She lifted a
shoulder in a small shrug. 'That sort of thing. Those types of feelings
can lead to dramatic actions.'

Jack nodded. 'Good. It's a start. And the mushrooms?'

After a brief silence, Jane spoke. 'That feels altogether more
concerted than the other three, doesn't it?'

Jack was glad she'd raised it, but Kate frowned. 'Why do you
say that?'

'Mushroom poisonings occurred on two occasions, was it?'

'Yes. Counties apart.'

'But the timeline . . . didn't you say just a few days, Jack?'

'I did.'

'Well, I could be wrong, but the first events feel like they were
aimed randomly, at whichever unlucky people happened to buy
strawberries that day, or test some lipstick, or buy baby formula.
The mushroom poisonings happened only twice, though, and one
person died, while the others only got sick. Why?'

'Are you suggesting this wasn't random?' Sarah asked.

'There were only two occurrences, which is odd if you compare the other tampering incidents. And none of those were designed to kill, I gather, although I know a baby was unwell briefly. But in this one instance, only one person died. The others got sick.'

'So you're proposing that only one of those people was targeted?' Sarah asked, looking confused. 'How? If all four ate the poisonous fungi? How would someone make sure only one died?'

'How did the woman who died compare in height and build to her friend who only became ill?'

Sarah checked her notes, although Jack didn't think she really needed to, given her recall. 'Pretty similar. They were the same age and within four centimetres of each other's height with similar weights. The victim was slightly taller.'

Jane shrugged. 'So it wasn't to do with the efficacy of the toxin. I don't suggest it flippantly, but that's why you guys are the detectives. My role is simply to give you scenarios. Maybe only the victim was the target, not her friend, and the other couple you mentioned were just the unlucky purchasers of one or two randomly placed poisonous mushrooms.'

'Yes, well, instinct is all we have right now. We have zero to go on,' Kate said, already sounding prickly.

That didn't take long, Jack thought.

'And a link between these incidents is needed yesterday, presumably?' Jane asked, not noticing or, more likely, ignoring Kate's tone, and looking to Jack.

'CT Command all but has a gun to my head. So your best advice?'

'Pull together a list of people already in the system who have any sort of track record for hurting others in a random way. That's the obvious beginning, because they've demonstrated a penchant for it. I would recommend that you start looking a year or two back from the first event for any incidents in the general locality of the needles in the strawberries, since that was first. I'm thinking road accidents, any sort of accident, in fact, er . . . local council plans that inflict hardship on residents, that sort of thing. Anything in that time frame, in the region where they found the straw-berries, that might have caused someone to feel isolated, angry, defenceless.'

'The first event is critical?' Sarah asked.

'Yes, I believe so. If this is all one party, then we're looking for whatever triggered this person into first taking action. No longer just wishing they could strike out at the world, but actually acting on that feeling. And my experience suggests that they'd begin in their local area.'

'Right, what sort of grievances are we looking at, then?' Jack asked the group. 'Let's list them. Here, Sarah, your turn at the board.'

Nat handed over the marker and returned to her seat.

'What about wrongful accusations?' Hirem asked.

Everyone looked to Jane, who nodded. 'Definitely.'

Sarah, Kate and Nat joined in, calling out ideas for potential grievances until their list had more than a dozen items.

Jack, who had said nothing, letting the ideas rage, now looked at them, bemused. He pointed behind him. 'How do we begin to investigate all of that across the whole of Britain?'

His team was silent and he sensed a despondency already.

Jane caught his glance. 'May I?'

'Please.'

'You have nothing, really. You all know that. It's why you've been gathered here, with all your experience and cunning. Looking at that list, I would suggest you pick three things that you believe would move an otherwise ordinary person to such a cruel and dramatic response. Start there. See what you find.'

Jack heard the sighs of despair; he felt it too, but now wasn't the time to show it.

'Are we going on pure instinct now, Jack?' Kate asked, blinking. Jack could tell she was trying not to sound accusatory in front of their subordinates.

He shrugged. 'Jane's right. You are all here because you have proven to have excellent intuition. But, no, it's not pure instinct, Kate; it's informed, confident judgement. For instance, looking at this line-up,' he said, twisting to regard the whiteboard, 'it's my judgement that we're not looking at someone who was proven guilty of a crime and had a bad time in jail. That just doesn't line up with what we're seeing. Agreed?'

He heard murmurs of agreement and Sarah struck it off.

'Not a sacking or retrenchment either,' Kate offered.

'Why not?' Jack asked, for everyone's benefit.

'My instinct says if you were going to do something malicious in retaliation for a sacking or retrenchment, then you would attack the establishment.'

'They did, though,' Sarah said. 'You could view it as undermining the supermarket chain, the chemist chain and so on.'

'There are easier ways to do that, though, such as through the media. I'm on the side of the fence that says this person is targeting individuals rather than companies, even though the victims are random.' Before more could be said, Kate added, 'The actual events feel, I don't know, specific.'

'What does that mean?' Hirem asked. 'Specific how?'

Kate shrugged. 'This is way out in the furthest cosmos for being instinctive,' she said, reinforcing the word for Jack's benefit, 'let's be clear. But if I didn't know better, this feels like a woman's work.'

Jane glanced at Jack at the same moment he felt his energy kick. It was exactly what he was thinking, and he loved that he and his most trusted professional partner thought so alike.

'Bravo, Kate,' Jane said, nodding.

Kate blinked, perhaps not ready for the praise.

'Explain that more, Kate,' Jack urged. 'If it's encouraging, I happen to agree and clearly so does our forensic psych.'

All eyes fell on Kate, who looked shocked. 'Well, for me, needles in strawberries . . . it's cruel, but it's also subtle. Dare I say – and without prejudice – men tend to be a bit more obvious in the cruelty stakes, but the person who dreams up a fine needle in a strawberry . . .' She shrugged. 'I think that's a woman.'

The women around her gave soft nods.

'But I can add a bit more weight to that hypothesis,' Kate continued.

Jack nodded his encouragement.

'I've read the cases and these needles must have been put into the fruit during the middle of the day, according to the reports. If we're speaking about sheer probability, I find myself saying that a woman is more likely to be available during the day – if, say, she's a mother. And also, again, a bit sexist – forgive me – but I think if this were a bloke, he'd use iron filings or tacks rather than needles. A woman may well have grown up sewing or have needles and thread at home.' She shrugged in a sort of apology. 'And then, the baby formula and the lipstick samplers also feel like things a woman might be more likely to gravitate towards than a man. A man at the lipstick counter is more likely to stand out.'

Jack couldn't fault her rationale. 'It makes sense. If it were a man, he'd have been remembered by an assistant. We'd have some witness, or some clue, perhaps, by now. But the hundreds of women who might stop in at any Boots, at any time of the day or week – well, witnesses are going to be hard to come by.'

'I see where you're going with this, but don't rule out a man. He could be trying to get back at women in some way,' Jane cautioned. 'If he's been rejected, for example.'

Kate's mouth twisted in disagreement. 'Yes, but I say again, I just don't think a man would use needles in fruit specifically to get at women. Don't you think he'd be more likely to . . . I don't know, spike drinks or slash car tyres, unnerve them more directly? The fruit is too broad in who he affects . . . it might be a child, or a husband, or a bird, for that matter.'

'The same goes for a woman doing it, surely?' Hirem frowned, confused.

'But the *feeling* is different. You see, in my mind, a woman putting a needle in a strawberry isn't thinking about who it's going to hurt, just that it has the potential to hurt. But if we follow Jane's theory that it could be a man trying to hurt women, then he could achieve that much faster and in smarter ways than this random sort of event . . .' She blinked. 'That's my point.'

'I don't disagree,' Jane said, 'but I have to try to poke some holes in any rationale, just to make sure it's strong enough to withstand scrutiny, and especially given your time frame. It sounds to me like decisions being made today are going to send you all scrambling down specific pathways, so I'm trying to be sure the effort isn't wasted before it begins.'

Everyone now nodded thoughtfully, even Kate.

'And what about the mushrooms? Do we think that's the work of a woman, too? Is it the same party?' Jack asked.

Kate gave a tsking sound. 'That I can't say. Poisoning does seem to go hand in hand with women, historically speaking, but I'm not sure . . . Does anyone know who died? Man or woman?'

'Er . . .' Sarah flipped back through a file on her desk. 'It was a woman. Olivia someone. I don't have her full name. These are just some notes I made.'

Kate shrugged. 'I think poisoning *could* be a woman's touch, but I wouldn't bet my house on it.'

'I think if we use Kate's suppositions, then the mushrooms are the oddity in the line-up,' Sarah said, frowning. 'Because the mushroom incident has killed someone. Also needles, babies, make-up, I have to agree, sir, they do sort of go together, whereas something about the mushrooms feels different . . .'

'Go on, Sarah,' Jack said. He suspected her gut was telling her the same thing Jane was alluding to, the same thing he believed but had to find a way to prove.

'If I'm not mistaken, then the first three events happened over the course of nine months and then stopped. We've had nothing of that nature – as far as we can tell – since then. And then the mushroom killing took place just a few months ago. A gap of what . . . six, seven months? Don't these things usually get closer together, not further apart?'

Well done, Sarah. 'What could that mean?' he asked, his tone not betraying his thrill.

'The mushrooms are a different perpetrator?' Nat wondered aloud.

Jack nodded. 'Potentially, yes. And that also ties back with Kate's thoughts – if we agree with them – that the first three events *feel* female-driven, whereas this final scare doesn't necessarily have that same aura about it.'

Kate and Sarah nodded.

'So that means we have two people . . . er, parties, frightening the community at a very local level?' Hirem said, vaguely exasperated. 'Is that likely?'

'Could be a copycat?' Kate offered.

'Or a coincidence,' Nat added.

'Or they have nothing to do with each other and the mushrooms are simply a different case,' Sarah said. 'After all, someone died. Maybe they were meant to.'

Jack cast a glance Jane's way.

'All of your theories have weight,' she said, smiling wryly. 'We're not narrowing it down much, are we?'

'What about just an out-and-out psychopath?' Hirem mused.

'Or someone having a psychiatric event . . . a nutter,' Nat offered, visibly embarrassed by the term. Jack saw Jane smile. 'You know what I mean, sir, sorry.' She blushed.

'Look, I agree, Hirem, but I suspect what Jane is saying is that given the time frame and the escalating nature of this—'

'Wait! Er, sorry,' Kate interrupted. 'How do we know it's escalating if these are two different parties?'

Jane jumped on this question. 'You don't. It *could* be the same, let's say, *person* for now, who has decided that what they were doing a few years back was amateur hour and now the stakes have been set higher. Or,' she said, sighing, 'the mushrooms could just look a bit like those other crimes but be an entirely different perpetrator. But I imagine what CTC needs to know first is whether you can somehow prove they're related – or prove that they're not.'

Jack was glad Jane was keeping them on track. 'Thank you, Jane. So, everyone, we have to begin our investigation somewhere. Ignoring for now the psychopath or the "nutter", which of these grievances might make someone – an otherwise perfectly responsible member of the public – go rogue?'

They all looked at the board again.

'I'm going with death of a family member,' Kate said. 'Mirror Op told us what people are capable of with that sort of shocked grief.'

As not everyone present had been on that op, Jack quickly explained that the Mirror investigation had involved a vigilante carrying out acts of extreme violence, leading back to an original trauma.

'I'd go further, sir. I agree with Kate, but perhaps I'd say the death of a child,' Sarah offered. 'If we lean into the female aspect, then a mother who loses her child is perhaps fully capable of losing her mind.' Everyone turned to look at Sarah, who pushed her glasses back up her nose. 'I mean, I'm no mother and I don't have much experience with children, but I have a sister who suffered two miscarriages and I am acquainted with another woman who lost a child to SIDS. Both of these women admit to a sort of psychosis . . . a madness of grief.'

Jack thanked Sarah with a nod. 'Okay, let's isolate that one, Nat.'

The young DC went back to the board and started a new shortlist.

'Anything else?' Jack asked.

Hirem gave a nod. 'I think someone who has lost their business and therefore their income, their means to provide for family, is a candidate for either suicide or blaming the world.'

'I agree,' Jack said and nodded at Nat to add that too.

'Being wrongly accused of something and doing time,' Nat added. 'Going to jail for something you didn't do could screw you up.'

'Add it,' Jack said. 'Shall we work with those for now?' Everyone murmured their assent. 'And could we keep in mind accidents: fatal car crashes, pile-ups, fires, any sort of catastrophe,' he added.

The group nodded and most looked at Sarah, who would likely get that job, given the need for the careful filtering of incidents; she was the expert in the HOLMES database.

'Right. Hirem, you get to work on anyone in the last few years who has come to the notice of police or media based on a business collapse, however big or small. Sarah, let's get a list going of post-mortems of people who died inexplicably or by misadventure in the two years prior to the first event. You can widen your arc as you see fit to include children, but keep it tight to begin with. And let us use where the first case erupted, as that might be our starting point. I'll be leaning on you for those unexpected crises as well – accidents, et cetera.' He gave Sarah a firm look. 'I'm aware of the breadth of what I'm asking, so come and find me for help.'

'I'll be fine, sir,' Sarah said, already standing up.

'Nat, I'll get you working on people who were out of prison, in the right time frame, who have consistently pleaded their innocence and so on.'

She nodded. 'On it, sir.'

'Kate, how about you and I scrutinise the four events in question: talk to the police officers involved, maybe speak with the victims. You never know what might pop up.'

'Sure, but leave it with me for now,' she said. 'I need to get my head around these events. You read up and I'll make some calls – is that okay?'

'Perfect. The commander is expecting us to perform some sort of miracle, so let's not let him down. I want an update from each of you by the day after tomorrow – so you have forty-eight hours to bring to me anything you've discovered that is relevant and valuable. Thank you.'

Everyone else stood and made for the tearoom or their desks, keen to get to work. Jack turned to Jane, who was picking up her bag, but Kate had come over too.

'Jane.' She shook the petite woman's hand. 'What a pleasure to meet you at last. Jack's told me a lot about you.'

'I'm surprised. I haven't seen him in such a while, I thought he'd forgotten me,' Jane said, casting him a soft smile.

'Jack never forgets his favourites,' Kate said and before anyone could reply, she continued. 'Thank you so much for this morning.'

Jane shrugged. 'I'm not sure I was that much help.'

'You were, more than you know. It helps enormously to have your sort of expertise around, to make us work for our deductions.'

'That's exactly why Jack suggested I come in. I'm glad it helped. Truly. The person doing these things – assuming at least the first three were done by the same individual – is definitely in need of help. The fact that they stopped their antisocial behaviour is obviously import-ant, but it doesn't mean the root of the problem has gone away.'

'What do you think it all means?'

Jane considered the question. 'To me, it suggests that this person – let's say this woman – is potentially getting the help she needs, perhaps seeing a counsellor or psychologist, for instance. It could mean she's met someone who has had a positive or uplifting effect on her life. Or she might have found a new job, a new form of distraction that is aiding her recovery. She might have got married, divorced or simply shifted countries. And we can't, of course, rule out the often overlooked therapy of time, and perhaps a good network of family and friends offering support.' Jane sighed. 'All of that said, she could be a ticking time bomb who had gone quiet but has now resumed her terror, escalating into killing someone. It may not have been intended directly, but it certainly suggests someone who doesn't care about the consequences of their actions.'

'Or maybe someone else has stepped into the terror arena,' Jack said. 'Someone who isn't just scratching at the surface. I get the impression that the lipstick meddler and formula tamperer and supermarket ghost is one person, who is perhaps itching to do some damage but not willing to go all the way.'

'Someone with a conscience?' Kate asked.

Jack nodded. 'Maybe. And then along comes a different person without that final barrier of sensibility who simply doesn't care who gets hurt – or perhaps is happy to hurt others.'

Jane gave them both a reassuring grin. 'It all sounds feasible. If you had time, the kind of research—'

'We don't have time,' Jack interrupted, but gently.

'So gut instinct it has to be,' Jane said, unfazed. 'Based on as much information as you can gather. There will be a clue some-where – there always is. No one just suddenly starts behaving like this as an adult. There is always some history. But there is always a trigger, something that makes a functioning adult move into this sort of behaviour. Find the trigger and you'll feel more confident in your presumptions. The incident that killed . . .' She shook her head. 'Like you said, it doesn't add up in my mind to being the same person but again, that's just instinct talking.'

At Kate's frustrated face, Jane squeezed her arm. 'But it's instinct from years and years at the coalface, Kate. Don't ever underestimate it. Good luck.'

'I'll see you out,' Jack offered. Kate nodded goodbye, and he walked Jane to the lifts.

'She's a smart one,' Jane said, as they waited. 'Fond of you, too.'

Jack was not at all surprised by her perceptiveness. 'Nothing's ever happened between us. I've been very careful over the years to keep it professional, but she's also a great friend. I can tell her anything.'

They stepped into the lift. 'Does she see it that way?'

He nodded. 'She does now. It's taken a while.'

'Good. A friend is far more valuable in the long run than an ex-lover.'

Jack saw her to the main entrance and out to where the driver waited. He opened the back passenger door and kissed Jane on both cheeks before she got inside. 'To ex-lovers and good friends.' He smiled.

She touched his cheek. 'Stay safe.'

In a simple potting shed, sitting on a 250-square-metre allotment in southern England, a man began to shift his dark thoughts for the next phase from a loose plan to an organised timeline.

Everyone involved had to pay. That had become his creed.

He'd lost everything.

And none of it was his fault.

He would leave no one out. Everyone he could track as having a hand in it simply had to pay.

Those who knew him had stepped back, making soothing sounds that were meant to placate but only made it worse. If no one was going to help, then he'd help himself.

What he really wanted was to ensure he got as many people's attention as possible. They needed to know what this suffering felt like. They needed to know what loss meant and how profoundly it would shape someone's future days. How a lack of hope corroded your ability to look forward. How death coming early might be the easiest option.

But before he drew his last breath, people had to pay.

And they'd do so spectacularly by the time he was done.

9

The next day, Jack was leaning against the wall of the taskforce room, observing the team as they gathered for the morning check-in. There appeared to be some fresh energy in the room this Friday.

'Okay, everyone here?' Jack called.

Kate nodded at him from the back.

'Good. Right. Did yesterday's visit from the psychologist help?'

Sarah nodded. 'Definitely. Just being able to lay out our thoughts together was really useful.'

'Nat?'

'Yes, sir. I found it helpful that Jane kept bringing us back to the main question and yet allowed us to roam in our thoughts.'

'Yes, she's quite cunning. Most of all, what she's done for this taskforce is to confirm that we're actually kidding ourselves if we don't think this will turn into an op.' He won some cheers for that remark. 'But it doesn't buy us any more time.'

'Might buy us some extra hands, though?' Kate asked.

'Indeed. I am going to request more bodies now we have some specifics to investigate, but what do we have so far? Hirem, anything?'

Both he and Nat, who had seemingly pooled resources, had thinned lips and apologetic expressions.

'Plenty of drunkenness, a bit of violence – including some family violence – on various cases that link back to the loss of businesses, incomes, et cetera, guv, but nothing that stood out yet as being out of the ordinary and worthy of putting on the table,' Hirem answered. 'I'm sorry. I don't want to waste anyone's time chasing down people who just don't fit the bill.'

'You've spoken to the local teams involved in those cases?'

'Just about all of them, guv,' Hirem confirmed. 'I'll keep going, but my instincts say these aren't right.'

'Okay.' Jack deliberately kept his voice even so Hirem didn't sense any disappointment. He was a good detective, according to Kate, so Jack had to presume his instincts were well honed. 'Plough on. And you, Nat?'

'I'm drawing blanks too, sir. I've got a couple of ex-prisoners who have been quite public online about their innocence, but they're both men, both middle-aged, and nothing they've said and nothing in the reports I've read suggests they'd take steps like the crimes we're working on. I'll keep on it, though.'

'Good, okay. Maybe there's nothing to find, and we'll swing you off that line of inquiry shortly. Sarah?'

'Thank you, sir. You asked me to look at deaths dating back two years from the first event. I've got more than a dozen potentials: these are deaths of children up to the age of sixteen within quite a wide area that draws a ring around the first needle discovered. That was in, er . . . Muswell Hill at the Tesco Extra,' she said, looking at her notes. 'If I widen the circle, the numbers obviously increase. If I add adult deaths, it goes a bit exponential,' she said, pushing her owlish glasses back up her nose.

'Of the ones in the tightest circle?' Jack asked.

'I've spoken to the pathologists for nine of those, and I have the other three yet to follow up. They're all very sad stories, of course, but so far I just don't see the causes being of interest to this case. I am happy for you or Kate to go through them, though.'

Kate frowned. 'Can you give us a sweep through the nine, Sarah, please?'

'Sure. A bike accident. Two car accidents. One death from a piece of farm machinery – sadly, both parents were present. A routine operation in hospital that went badly for a child. One drowning, one asthma attack and two SIDS deaths.'

'We might cast our eyes over those, just to double-check. Let's get the other three done first, but that's fast work, Sarah, thank you. And Kate?'

'Right, I've scrutinised the four events, beginning with the needles through to the poisonous mushroom death.' She grimaced slightly. 'It's still my contention that the last is the odd one out.'

Jack agreed, but he still wanted to ensure they weren't making false assumptions. 'Tell us why.'

'It's the death. Somehow it still feels targeted, rather than accidental. I can't shake the feeling that it feels like a murder.'

'So intentional, but made to look like it was general terror?' he qualified. Jane had alluded to much the same.

Kate nodded. 'That's my suspicion.'

'As much as I respect your instincts, we can no longer rely on hunch now, Kate. I need evidence if this is where we're going to concentrate our efforts.'

'Well, let me tell you all what I've discovered, and you can get a collective view. I spoke to the officers who attended the scene at both poisonings,' Kate began. 'The first was in a small neighbourhood called Hotwells, in Bristol. The second occurred around thirty miles from there.'

'Weird,' Hirem muttered.

'Exactly,' Kate agreed.

'Why is it weird, Hirem?' Jack asked.

'In my opinion,' the younger detective said, 'if I was going to use poison mushrooms to cause mischief, then I'd work fast in one area to lower the risk of being caught, especially if I was only going to do it twice. If I planned to really terrorise, then, yes, I'd set up six or seven poisonings in various places around a few counties and get maximum attention and fear going. But only twice? It feels odd.'

'I agree,' Kate said, nodding at Hirem. 'To stop at two and spread them so far apart bothers me. It's a lot of effort for random poisoning so I think Hirem's right – if you're going to terrorise, then you'd go for broke and spread them around, or if you wanted to make a statement and only do it twice, then why risk exposure by spreading the crime so far? However, if you were being more targeted – intending to harm a specific person – then maybe you'd kill who you intended to and then try to throw a bit of chaos in by killing elsewhere, far away, using the same method.'

This was Jane's rough theory; he couldn't ignore it, not when multiple minds were landing on the same thing. Jack wanted the whole team on board and exploring this idea. 'What if the mushroom person had intended a spate of poisonings but got spooked with the death and stopped?'

Kate shook her head. 'The poisoning that killed came first. I don't think the person responsible could have been spooked, because it happened again, but this time it didn't kill.'

'Okay, give us your premise, then,' Jack said.

'I believe these two events are not as accidental or random as they appeared. And I'm not alone in this. The detectives who worked on the cases believe they are linked.'

'What do you mean?' Sarah frowned.

'I agree with their belief that if this was an accidental poisoning – a mistake by the suppliers – then surely more people would have been affected.'

'But we're not presuming they accidentally entered the system, are we?' Sarah wondered. 'I assumed we were thinking someone deliberately contaminated normal mushrooms with toxic ones?'

Kate nodded. 'We are. And if we subscribe to that intention to cause harm, do you all feel satisfied that the perpetrator chose to scatter a few poisonous mushrooms in a big supermarket's mushroom box on display, and then they also scattered toxic mushrooms in a small greengrocer's some distance away? We know the mushrooms were purchased from two entirely separate places, not the same supply chain.'

That was greeted with a tense pause.

'Let's say that we go along with this. How come only four people suffered? Those mushrooms could have been bought by anyone. I spoke to both pathologists. The woman who died had a very high concentration of the fungi in her system, while the people who got sick had far less, and one only very little. That makes sense, of course – if you ate more of the toxic mushroom, you'd be more likely to suffer adverse effects. The police retrieved mushroom scraps from each home and the remains of the food dishes that were cooked but not consumed. The couple who got sick ate a meal the wife had cooked. She bought the mushrooms from Tesco. But the woman who died was served her meal. She had not bought the mushrooms, and neither had her friend, who got sick but didn't die.'

'They ate in a restaurant?' Hirem asked.

Kate shook her head. 'No. This is where it gets interesting. The victim was eating with a friend at home. The friend is the person who had her stomach pumped and was good to go in a matter of hours.' Before anyone could leap in, she lifted a finger that suggested intrigue. 'But apparently that woman ate an identical meal. Explain that!'

No one could. They waited.

'Who cooked the meal?' Jack asked, knowing Kate was leading them somewhere.

'The meal was cooked by the victim's boyfriend. He purchased the food. He could have planted the poisonous mushrooms, bought them from the greengrocer to shift any potential blame and then cooked them with the intention to kill his girlfriend.'

The silence that met her words was filled with a tight sense of anticipation. Kate finished her tale. 'But the police were never able to speak with, meet or even learn who this boyfriend is.'

Jack frowned. 'Okay, Kate, I know you're enjoying this but spill. What happened?'

She grinned. 'According to the friend who recovered, it was a girl's night in. As a treat, the boyfriend, who the friend knew only as Peter, had shopped, cooked, served the meal and left them to their movies and popcorn and ice cream sundaes, none of which they got to, for obvious reasons. The friend rang for an ambulance when they started feeling unwell soon after the meal, and managed to vomit, which no doubt helped her situation. But while the paramedics did stabilise the girlfriend and get her to A&E, she went downhill fast and died. Peter was quite new in Olivia's life, apparently. The friend didn't have a phone number for him, and the number in Olivia's phone had been disconnected. It remains a cold case as far as that team is concerned. No other toxic mushrooms were found at the local greengrocer; I think he controlled that fully, so no one else would be affected.'

'Were the friend and boyfriend having an affair?' Sarah asked.

'No evidence to suggest it. These were childhood friends, and the guy was new. The friend who called the ambulance was newly married and from what that police unit could tell, very happy, just moved into a new home, trying to get pregnant, blah blah. She was distraught and clearly devastated at losing Olivia.'

'Why didn't we know this?' Jack asked, aghast.

'Because it became overshadowed by other things. The mushroom death was pushed off the front pages and it seems that most people, including the media, believed it was accidental, another in the series of more minor incidents like the needles, baby formula and lipsticks. Because there hasn't been another mushroom poisoning since the original two, it's sort of out of sight, out of mind. Not to the two police units, though. They've stayed on it, and they are looking for this elusive guy, Peter.'

'If Peter meant to kill her, it's an odd way to do it,' Nat said.

'But it worked,' Kate said, sounding electrified. 'He has got away with it – so far, at least. This way, he doesn't have to dispose of a body – the authorities did it for him. And he's covered his tracks well enough that no one even knows who he is. So he's out in the wild and, for now, safe.'

'Why would he kill her?' Jack asked.

Kate shrugged. 'That I can't even give a tiny clue towards. No theft, no violence, no abuse. Apparently he was handsome and lovely; she was quite smitten with him. They were together for about five weeks in total, barely out of each other's sight, and then he kills her – if I'm right – and disappears.'

'If that is what happened.'

'I think it did, Jack. I feel it in my bones.'

He nodded with a grin. 'I'll be sure to tell the commander that.'

She gave him a sarcastic smile.

'So, if we go with your theory that this Peter has deliberately killed Olivia, he took the precaution of ensuring the friend got almost none of the toxic mushrooms, and put more poisonous mushrooms in a supermarket miles away to what? Cover his arse?'

Kate nodded. 'That's what the police in those areas privately believe, as do I. And Dr Brooks was clearly alluding to the same notion. This Peter fellow risked tossing a couple into the supermarket as a distraction – and it was a big risk, it was lucky no one else died, but I don't know how much you need to ingest to die. And then most people believed it was simply another of those wicked events like the tainted lipstick samplers. I think he hid his crime among the others, but he had every intention of killing Olivia. He was there and made sure she had a potent amount of the food. He could have cooked a separate dish for the friend and only contaminated a little, or maybe he just didn't care who died, so long as Olivia did. The friend got lucky, didn't eat as much, vomited quickly, got help fast, et cetera.'

'Wow,' Sarah murmured.

Hirem gave a low whistle.

Jack ran a hand through his hair and looked at his second-in-command. She gave him a sad grin. 'What do we do with this, Kate?'

'I don't know. It's still hypothetical but, damn, Jack, I think this was murder.'

'If you're right, then we're still no further in understanding whether needles, baby formula, lipsticks and mushrooms belong in the same camp—'

'Wait!' Sarah said, startling her colleagues.

Everyone turned to look at her.

'Oh, I'm sorry, sir,' she said, looking suddenly mortified. Jack opened a palm towards her, giving silent permission for her to interrupt away, and Sarah whipped her head back to look at Kate. 'What did we say the dead woman's name was?'

'Olivia,' she answered.

'No, I know that.' Sarah sounded distracted, and Jack had to suppress a smile. Her social skills still needed some help in times of stress or excitement. 'What's Olivia's surname?' Sarah demanded, racing to her keyboard and tapping frantically.

'Uh-oh,' Jack muttered and cast Kate an arch look.

She gave him a smile of pure enjoyment. Inside these walls they were as closely connected as two people could be. He would go so far as to say there were moments when they could read the other's thoughts.

'It's not Olivia Craddock, is it?' Sarah asked.

Kate, who had checked her notes, said, 'Yes. Olivia Craddock.'

No one moved, until the stillness in the room was broken by the arrival of Joan, who looked around at her charges.

'Ooh, I'm sensing an expletive moment,' she said. 'Should I fetch my tin?'

'What the fuck?' Kate obliged, eyeing Sarah.

Joan cackled with glee and looked at Jack. 'The commander's on line one,' she said quietly.

'Can you buy me one minute, please, Joan?'

'I can try,' she said, before disappearing. He knew she'd succeed; she always did.

'Sarah?' Jack urged. 'What have you found?'

'Er, you're not going to believe this, sir . . . everyone,' Sarah said, shaking her head.

'Oh, please tell me this is turning into an op,' Kate pleaded. 'Draw us a beautiful line between the mushroom poisonings and something else in that clever brain of yours.'

Sarah pushed her glasses high up her nose and nodded. 'I told you about the cases I'd checked, including those with the pathologists who performed the post-mortems.' At Kate's urgent nod, Sarah dropped her gaze back to her notes and continued. 'Back in 2007 in London, a seven-year-old boy, Billy Parker, died in hospital after being given the wrong blood during a transfusion. He was in hospital following a routine procedure of tonsils removal, which caused some expected but insistent haemorrhaging.' She looked at Jack.

Jack knew how Sarah's mind worked and gave her an enthusiastic nod. Her ability to hold and retrieve myriad details was second to none. Everyone waited. She wasn't deliberately building the tension, as Kate had, this was just Sarah's way of retrieving and downloading the tonne of information she could hold in the clever files of her mind.

'Sarah, you're killing me,' Kate said. 'How does Olivia relate to what you're telling us?'

'I think the Olivia Craddock who died from toxic mushrooms – and who you believe was killed deliberately by this Peter – is the same Olivia Craddock who donated the blood that eventually found its way into the arm of Billy Parker and killed him.'

Jaws dropped open. Gusts of awe were expelled.

'Fuck!' Kate said.

'Bugger me dead!' Jack echoed.

Joan rattled a tin in the distance; Jack suspected she'd put a coin in there simply so she could make the annoying sound. She arrived at the room's entrance. 'That's a two-pound coin from each of you, and an extra two pounds from you, Superintendent Hawksworth, for that creative new vulgarity. Where do you get these phrases?'

'It's Australian,' he said sheepishly.

'Well, I think it should cost you a fiver, actually, for borrowing another country's profanity. Well, kids, we'll be able to have high-quality afternoon teas given how day two has started.' She gave Jack a glance that said, 'No more hedging.'

'I'll call him back now,' he said obediently.

'He'll be on line one in about thirty seconds,' Joan said, pointing to Jack's desk.

Jack walked into his office, picked up his phone and hit line one. 'Sir, sorry to keep you waiting.'

'Joan tells me something's brewing?'

He couldn't believe he was so well ahead of them. 'Er . . .'

'Don't be coy now.'

'Nothing certain, but we might have just drawn a line between the mushroom poisoning death in Bristol and the death of a child in 2007 . . . in London.'

'Good grief. Murder?'

'The mushroom death, potentially. I don't know yet, sir, but there's sufficient doubt in our collective minds to make me pursue it. And the connection is extraordinary . . . vague enough that it might have been missed if we didn't have a particularly smart and focused member of this taskforce. DI Sarah Jones.'

'Is she that strange one who doesn't smile?'

'Not strange, sir. Just hyper-focused. She is very serious about her work, but I would always have Sarah on my team.'

'Well, she's already proved why. So what now?'

'I've just found this out, so my mind is going in various directions, but maybe we can link the child's death back to the terror events.'

'And give us some motive, you mean?'

'Potentially,' Jack said carefully. He knew how much the commander wanted to go rushing to the media and get them and his superiors off his back, to prove that his counterterrorism team was up to the job, but it was early days. 'I don't think we can say anything publicly yet, sir. It's just a working theory.'

'Right.' The commander somehow managed to sound impressed and disappointed at once. 'Even so, that's very encouraging.'

'Encouraging, yes, but it all needs locking down.'

'Then lock it down, Hawksworth. Rowland assures me that if anyone can bring closure, it's you and your people.'

'We're working hard, sir, and I shall keep you fully up to speed on everything.'

'I know you will. And Hawksworth? Good job. I won't be saying anything about this yet, but you understand I need to start updating the Commissioner of Police and the media.'

'I do, sir. Give us another twenty-four hours and we'll know more.'

As he returned to the main room, Kate approached. 'Wow,' she said, still amazed by the connection they'd made. 'I wasn't expecting that!'

'We could have so easily missed it,' Jack replied. 'Can you get everyone sorted? We'll switch our attention to that old case.'

She nodded.

'How's the old chap, by the way?' he asked, meaning Geoff.

She grinned. 'Creaky and feeling his age. I just spoke to him. He's back from a run, even though he should be sleeping – he's had a series of late nights.'

'I can barely believe you're talking about my chubby mate.'

'He offered to try on my jeans the other day just to piss me off.'

Jack smiled broadly. 'He's looking good.'

'Yeah, well, I wish his mood would match. That's why he went out running in the rain.'

'He's working on those strangulation murders, I heard?'

'Yes. Father on a golf weekend, children away, mother pampering herself with a quiet couple of days at home with a lot of carbohydrates and fun stuff from Marks & Sparks . . . Terrible. Geoff says she was abducted in her own car and then found dead on the Heath not far from where her husband was playing. I hate the world sometimes.'

'No clues?'

She shrugged. 'He's feeling like we felt a day ago. He's hoping forensics and pathology might turn something up today. But those kids are coming home to no mum this week. He's just filled with rage over this seemingly senseless death. She wasn't robbed or raped. He said more details are breaking now.' She glanced at her watch. 'Hirem?' He looked up. 'Can you put the BBC twenty-four-hour news on, please?'

Hirem obliged. The news service was just powering through its headline countdown music. Jack and Kate stood transfixed as the story of the murdered woman opened the breaking news, with visuals of the police and forensics crew gathered around a small tent on a lonely sweep of land, a small copse curling around where they stood.

'That's from Sunday afternoon, when she was found,' Kate said. Geoff and his team were all over that bleak little place, though it was a few days on now and they still had no leads.

Now the newsreader explained that police were treating the death as a murder. 'The deceased woman, Sally Holman, worked in a nursing home and had been shopping at . . .'

'Sir!'

Jack and Kate looked over to find Sarah staring at them. Her mouth was open and her gaze was moving from them to the TV screen and then back again. 'What is it, Sarah?' Jack asked, signalling to Hirem, who had also looked up at Sarah's sudden excitement. Jack mimicked muting the volume on the TV remote and the report was silenced as the image of a woman came up on the screen.

'Sally Holman,' Sarah said. Everyone waited for another of Sarah's blinding moments of inspiration. She looked around at them, as if she was surprised they hadn't made the connection. 'The nurse who did the blood test and ordered the wrong blood, which eventually killed Billy Parker. She was called Sally Holman.' Sarah blinked behind her round glasses.

Jack looked again at the silent TV and the image of the woman, which flicked off almost immediately as the presenter moved to the next important news headline. 'I'm not even going to ask if you're sure, Sarah, because I know that mind of yours doesn't get facts wrong.'

'Whether it's the same Sally Holman, of course . . .'

Kate was already reaching for her phone, presumably to call Geoff. Everyone else was watching Jack.

'Two North London Sally Holmans, both in nursing, is unlikely . . .'

Sarah sighed. 'They just said the murdered Sally worked in a nursing home. This Sally' – she held up her files – 'left the hospital and paediatric nursing when the Parker case erupted. I don't know what she ended up doing, but it makes sense she would continue to use her skills outside of the hospital system.'

'Right.' Jack blew out his cheeks. 'Kate, is that Geoff? I need to speak with him.'

She handed over her phone.

'It's me.' Jack proceeded to fill Geoff in.

'You're not serious?' His old friend sounded incredulous.

'Well, if Sarah's right – and we both know she's rarely wrong – then there's a very good possibility we're going to be storming into each other's cases again,' Jack said.

10

Hannah and Jim were on their weekly 'date', this time walking Chalky, who was already very good on the lead.

'His previous owners taught him well. Shall I let him off?' she wondered aloud.

'Try it,' Jim encouraged. 'You can already tell he's not going to run away.'

'How?'

'Because of the way he keeps looking up at you. He's probably more terrified that you'll abandon him than the other way around.'

She grinned and unclipped the dog. 'Go on, sniff anywhere you like.' Chalky hesitated before trotting off, sniffing at anything and everything. Hannah noted he continued to circle back to them. 'Good boy,' she encouraged him, keen to ensure he would always keep her in sight.

They were on Hampstead Heath.

'Dogs aren't allowed up there,' Jim said, pointing, 'but if we follow the swimming ponds, we'll be fine.'

'You know the path?'

He nodded. 'Really well.'

'Of course, sorry,' she said, recalling that he and his wife had lived nearby.

'I used to swim in the ponds.'

'You're kidding! It must be freezing.'

'Oh, it is.' He laughed. 'But brilliant. I used to swim in creeks and rivers back home. Did some sea swimming, but that's got all sorts of problems in Australia, especially around northern Queensland.'

'Do you mean sharks?'

'Sharks are everywhere, and our tourist beaches are patrolled. But, no, I'm talking about the marine stingers.'

'I don't even want to know what those are. You see, everything wants to hurt you.'

He chuckled. 'Yeah, they hurt something awful. The box jellyfish and one called Irukandji are really dangerous – they can kill you. The bluebottle stings hurt a lot but after about half an hour you can usually get some relief . . . that's if you haven't swum into a pile of them. Off to hospital then.'

She shuddered. 'Ugh.'

'But the water's lovely,' he said mischievously. She gave him a push and grinned. 'It's nice to see you smile, Hannah. Changes your whole countenance.'

'Yeah, well, I can't find much to smile about, I'm sorry.'

'That's okay. If I can win one a day when I see you, then it makes me feel good.'

She stopped walking and regarded him seriously. 'I can't stop thinking about what you said.'

'About the nurse?'

He was quick; she'd give him that. 'Yes.'

'What I said or how I said it?'

'Both, to be honest.'

'I am a firm believer in karma, that's all. And part of that spiritual attitude is my belief that there is cause and effect to what you put out there.'

'Careful what I wish for, you mean?'

He shrugged. 'I suppose you could put it like that. I know you wouldn't put into words that you wanted her to pay but, deep down, you probably did at some point wish for it.'

'I don't feel like that now.' She sounded appalled. 'I . . . you know, none of the pain has gone, but . . .'

'But what?'

'I don't know. These days I just want to be left alone and for Billy's memory to be left alone.'

He gave a sheepish grin. 'I just aired the thought that your wish – however long ago it was – was granted.'

She shook her head. 'Your hard attitude has been nagging me all week.'

'The fact that I don't feel particularly sorry for her?'

'Yes, I suppose. Why don't you feel anything?'

'Well, her carelessness destroyed your family; it killed your child, broke your marriage, and essentially changed your path and that of your husband's. Whatever plans you had together, whatever dreams you imagined, they were ripped away, along with a little boy's life. And all because she was tired.'

'She was exhausted,' Hannah said, emphasising the word. 'There are days when I can find it in my heart to feel a little sympathy for her situation. It was actually the hospital's fault more than hers. But those days don't come often.'

'Is this one of those days?'

'Probably,' she said, with a shrug. 'And I'm thinking of her family now she's gone. A husband, two children . . . their lives wrecked. How will those kids cope knowing their mother was murdered so brutally?'

He nodded. 'How did you cope while your case raged on and you had to live through how Billy died, his depleted blood cells rallying to fight the invading blood?'

'Don't, Jim.'

'Sorry. I just want you to stop feeling sorry for anyone.'

'Including myself,' she said. It wasn't a question.

'Yes, but that might take a lot of time. Years more before you can forgive yourself for allowing yourself to live again. And that's okay. But Nurse Sally should now be out of your mind, and certainly off your conscience. She's gone. Someone has removed her. Let her go. Each time you let go of anyone involved in that time, you step into a stronger you.'

She blinked, taking that in, then gave a smile. 'Fighting talk. You make me feel tough.'

'You don't have to be tough, though. I'm not saying let the pain go, I'm saying put it away. Put Sally away, because she's now paid for her sin.'

Hannah sighed. When he put it like that, it made perfect sense. Plus, ever since she'd shared her secret with him, she'd felt not only unburdened by her crimes, but also closer to him. She still wasn't of a mind to start any sort of intimate relationship, but he made her feel safe in a way that Jonathan couldn't after Billy's death. He was a friend.

'I'm surprised you can be so objective about death, when it's death that has caused us both all the grief in the world,' she said. It had been on her mind for a while.

'I don't know her, so I don't care about her. It's a bit like hearing about a bridge collapsing in India. There's an immediate shock and then it passes as another piece of news captures interest. It didn't happen to me. It didn't happen to anyone I love. It didn't even happen to anyone I know, so it fades into white noise. But with this nurse's death, I do know someone affected by it, so I'm invested and, dare I say, content that this woman who caused you so much pain is gone. I'm glad, in fact.'

She gave a little sound of shock, even though she too had a sense of relief about the nurse's death; she'd said 'fair's fair', after all.

Jim shrugged. 'Call me callous. You should be thankful to the killer, because he's released you.'

She frowned. 'How do you know it's a he?'

Jim looked momentarily uncertain. 'Er, well, I don't. I am assuming, I guess. Women are rarely predators of other women.'

Hannah wanted to ask more, but her mobile phone rang.

'You get that. I'll get us a coffee,' Jim said. He sounded relieved for the interruption.

She didn't recognise the number and was tempted to let it go to voicemail, but Jim had already walked away. 'Hello?'

'Good morning. This is DCI Kate Carter from the metropolitan police. Am I speaking with Mrs Hannah Parker?'

'Er . . . yes, you are. What's happened?' Her mind raced towards Jonathan. Was he hurt?

'No need to be alarmed, Mrs Parker. I'm actually making some inquiries for a case, and I wonder if we could speak with you this afternoon?'

'Why? What's this about?'

'It would be better if we explained in pers—'

'No, please tell me now. Why do the police need to meet with me?'

The detective gave a barely audible sigh. 'It's in connection with the death of your son, Mrs Parker.'

Hannah felt her whole carriage weaken and she looked around for a bench, fearful she would collapse where she stood.

'Mrs Parker? Are you there?'

'I'm sorry,' she said. 'Could you hold on, please?'

'Of course.'

Jim was returning with takeaway coffees and could obviously see she was shaken. 'What's wrong?' he mouthed.

She beckoned and he hurried forward, throwing the coffee cups down on the ground next to them as Hannah shook her head and began to weep. 'Why . . . why are you raising this all again?' she stammered.

'I am deeply sorry. May I call you Hannah?' The detective's voice was kind.

Hannah didn't reply.

'Er, we're not sure if we have some new information,' the detective continued, 'and we'd be very grateful if you would allow us to speak with you as soon as possible.'

'It's not going to bring him back,' Hannah snarled, but without much heat.

'No, nothing will.' The detective was blunt now. 'What it might do, though, is give us some answers.'

'About his death? I know how and why he died, DCI . . . Carter, did you say your name is?'

'Yes. Please call me Kate. Look, I will explain everything when we meet. You're right, what we're pursuing is not so much about Billy dying as how his passing might be connected with another death.'

'Another death?' Hannah repeated. 'You mean this happened to another child?'

'No, no, I don't mean that. If you'll let me meet with you, I shall explain.'

Hannah paused to think, while Jim put his arm around her, handing her a serviette. She dabbed at her cheeks. 'Okay. When?'

'One-ish? Would that be possible?'

'Yes. I'm on Hampstead Heath at the moment. It will take me a little while to get home.'

'One-thirty, then?'

'That's fine. Shall I give you my address?'

'I have this one on record,' Kate said and read it out.

'It hasn't changed.' Hannah sniffed. 'Only I have.'

The detective didn't attempt any placation. 'See you soon, Hannah. Thank you.'

The line rang off and Hannah stared at it. 'That was the police.'

'Police?' Jim frowned. 'Have they caught up with your—'

'No,' she said, shaking her head firmly. 'It's something about Billy. They have some new information, but it's not about his death. Someone else . . .' She suddenly startled. 'Oh, it's probably to do with the nurse!'

Jim blew his cheeks out and frowned. 'Yes, I suppose you're likely right.'

'Yeah. She wouldn't say. She's coming to the house soon. One-thirty.'

Jim looked at his watch. 'Better get you home, then.'

She nodded. 'Will you stay with me, Jim? I mean while they're there?'

'No, love. I don't think I should. Probably best not to even mention me.'

She frowned. 'What do you mean?'

'I'm sorry. I know it sounds strange, and in any other situation, I'd be there to support you, but I don't want to get dragged into any police case. Let's first see what it's about, and if you need a support person at the police station or whatever, I promise I'll be there for you then.' He paused, noticing that her expression was still one of concern. 'I tell you what, how about I take Chalky out so you don't have to worry about him while they're there? You know how excited he gets.'

She nodded, troubled by Jim's evasiveness. 'No, it's okay, no need to take him out – he's exhausted and will sleep.'

'I'll shout you a taxi so you don't have to rush, and if you want, I'll cook for you tonight. Is that okay?'

'Sure,' she said, still wondering. Why was he so determined not to come into contact with police? 'I have to say I'm feeling a little abandoned.'

He gave a soft glare of exasperation. 'Tell me exactly what the detective said.'

Hannah repeated it as close to word for word as she could.

He shrugged. 'Listen, Hannah,' he said gently. 'I'm not getting the impression they're suspicious of you. But, yes, it surely must be about the nurse. Tread carefully.'

'Why? They know I didn't kill my child, if that's what you mean,' she said, with a firm edge in her tone.

'I don't mean that at all. But you have a secret,' he said, meeting her worried gaze. 'And we need to protect that secret unless you want to do jail time. I know you were out of your mind – I've been there. But a baby went to hospital and an adult died.'

'No, I've told you I had nothing to do with poison—'

'I know that, but they might not believe you. You don't want to give them any ammunition to scrutinise you further. Sounds to me like she's coming to share information, not to formally interview you. So let her tell you what she knows, but don't let her get a whiff that you were ever capable of the things you've done, or that you've suddenly come into contact with another grief-stricken parent.'

She frowned in new confusion. 'You and me? I don't see the problem.'

'No? They will. Keep me out of it, because that protects both of us.'

She watched him carefully. 'You sound like you're hiding something, Jim.'

He looked back at her in silence for a period that began to feel uncomfortable. 'Only my pain,' he said. 'Come on. I don't want to be involved, but I will help you when we know more. Let's get you that cab.'

11

Jack and Kate were seated opposite Hannah in a square-shaped sitting room.

'You have a lovely home, Hannah,' Kate said, admiring the tall shelves of books that lined the walls. Jack's attention was caught by the small but neat walled garden, where the lawn was enclosed by a circumference of beds housing some well-pruned roses. He could see a barbecue on a tiny paved area that had cobwebs, so it wasn't getting much use, it seemed.

Hannah followed his gaze. 'My father takes care of my garden but I'm getting more involved again. I can't wait for the dozens of daffodils he's planted for my spring. He said I need a happy garden again.'

Jack smiled. 'Nothing so cheerful as daffs.'

Kate took over. 'I could live among these books.'

'Really?'

'Yes. There's never enough time but I try and get in a couple of chapters each evening.'

'Well, we like readers. I'm an editor,' Hannah said. 'Can I offer you a tea or coffee?' she asked, standing again just moments after they had sat down.

Jack shook his head with a smile, but Kate answered. 'That's kind, but we've just had one.'

'Where's your dog?' Jack asked, looking at all the little toys and the comfy bed in front of the combustion fire. He watched Hannah's shoulders relax slightly and she sank back into the sofa. He wondered why she was so tense, though he supposed many would be anxious at a visit from the police.

'He's sleeping. He's new. A rescue. His name's Chalky.'

Both detectives smiled.

'He's good company,' Hannah continued. 'Now that I live alone, my father thought a dog would be a good friend.'

'I'd love to meet him,' Jack said.

'He's in the laundry. I didn't want him leaping all over you.'

'We don't mind,' Jack said. 'I'd have a dog in a heartbeat if my working life allowed it.'

Hannah smiled. 'I'll get him. I'll just let him into the garden momentarily and be back.' She disappeared.

'Why?' Kate asked in soft admonishment.

'See how she relaxed when the dog was mentioned? This will only help us get some answers. Nice home.'

'It is. Has a nice sort of cosy vibe.' Kate pointed to the blanket on the back of the couch. 'That is definitely homemade . . . so are the cushions. She's crafty.'

'I suspect you mean that in the artistic sense.'

Kate mugged at him. 'I do.'

Hannah returned with the dog in tow, which, as expected, leaped towards them in excitement. 'You'll have to forgive him. He's still young and needs training.'

'He's adorable,' Kate said, glancing at Jack.

He knew Kate was lying but at least she was good at it. She had never had a pet throughout her life, as far as he knew. *Oh, but wait, there is Geoff,* he thought, amusing himself.

'I'm knitting him a coat for our walks,' Hannah said, pointing towards a basket of wool next to Jack.

He looked down courteously. It was an earthy, appealing colour. 'He'll look very handsome.'

'Keeps me busy of an evening,' Hannah added, 'and what else to do with all that spare wool?'

Jack grinned. Back to small talk, then. 'I learned to knit at school.'

That made Hannah smile. 'Lots of men knit – they just don't admit to it.' She sighed. 'Our son desperately wanted a puppy. I don't know why we never got around to it.'

That was the segue they needed, and Kate leapt in, while Jack entertained Chalky, scratching his smooth head.

'Hannah, we're deeply sorry to be here and raising the subject of Billy's death. I know it must be painful.'

She gave a soft shrug. 'It greets me every morning and walks around in my dreams. It never lessens and it never leaves, so you don't have to apologise for bringing up something that's always front and centre.'

'I'm so sorry,' Kate said. 'Well, we wanted to talk to you about a woman called Sally Holman.'

Jack watched Hannah's lips thin. No, she had not forgotten that name.

'I thought as much. I heard she died.'

Kate nodded. 'She was killed,' she qualified.

Jack noted Hannah didn't flinch.

'How does this affect me?' Hannah asked, barely blinking at Kate's bluntness. She looked between them in slight confusion.

'Hannah, there are two deaths now – Sally Holman, the nurse who made the error with the blood order, and there's Olivia Craddock, who died from eating poisoned mushrooms.'

Hannah stared at them, absorbing this information. 'Olivia Craddock? I know that name,' she said, sounding breathless. Her alarm seemed genuine. 'Olivia Craddock donated the blood that was put into Billy's arm . . . the blood that killed him.'

The two police officers nodded gravely.

'You're sure?' Hannah ran anxious hands over her face and through her hair. 'But . . .'

'We're sure,' Kate said evenly, without any accusation.

Hannah let out a low sigh, as though focusing herself, easing away from the shock. 'Is there a reason you're telling me this? I don't understand.'

'You asked how Sally Holman's death affects you. *Does* it affect you?' Kate replied, which seemed to take Hannah by surprise. 'Especially now we've told you about Olivia Craddock?'

'What do you mean?'

'Well, how do you feel about Sally's death?'

Hannah shook her head. 'I feel nothing.'

'I see,' Kate said, her tone neutral.

They both waited quietly, forcing Hannah to continue.

'Am I glad she's dead? I don't know . . . Maybe. On some vengeful level I think I want to cheer. And you've shocked me regarding the other woman. I don't know what to think. I'll have to process that.'

Again, Jack and Kate stayed quiet, watching her.

She shrugged. 'I'm being honest. I don't hold the person who donated blood responsible, so of course I'm horrified she's dead, but that nurse killed my child. I'm not unhappy to learn she died. But then I think of her family, and I know her husband and kids are having to go through the same horror, shock, despair that my husband and I did. They have a long journey of grief ahead of them. And I don't wish that on anyone. So for the most part, when I think about her being killed, I feel numb.'

'Where is your husband, Hannah?' Jack asked.

'Jonathan and I separated,' Hannah said. 'It's hard for any marriage to survive that sort of grief. Ours couldn't. We were . . .' She shook her head in helplessness. 'Broken is the only word I can think of to describe it. I guess we just weren't strong enough for each other, but we both love each other, and I doubt that will change.'

'Is he still nearby?' Kate asked.

'No, he lives in Scotland now, but he often works in London.'

'And you stay in touch?'

'Yes, we do. We're really still close, in spite of the fact that he's in a new relationship. He's asked me for a divorce so he can marry her. She's pregnant, you see.'

'Oh, right,' Jack said. It was a lot more information than he'd anticipated, and he admired her directness.

Hannah gave a tight smile. 'Life goes on,' she said in a slightly singsong voice.

'And you?' Jack asked. 'Is there anyone for you?'

'No.' She said it as if it had been a stupid question. 'I mean, I'm forcing myself to get out a little more, to make friends. All the old ones – the couples we used to mix with – have fallen away.' She paused. 'I forgive them, though. They're awkward. They don't know how to be around such depthless grief. I get it. So I'm trying to connect with people who didn't know me as Billy's mum or Jonathan's wife.' She stroked Chalky's back; the dog had left Jack's attentions to curl up with his owner. 'There's a nice man I met at the grief group. We're just aching souls who can meet for coffee and talk – we both get each other's pain.' She paused again, frowning this time. 'Can I ask you why you're here, please, and asking me these questions?'

Kate nodded. 'We're all just joining dots, Hannah,' she said with a gentle smile.

Jack couldn't let Hannah know that police cases at an operational level were now potentially merging. Certainly the lines had been deeply blurred by two separate deaths suddenly being connected through Billy Parker. He had to navigate this conversation with care. 'The police have two strangled women now, and their deaths are suggesting it's the same murderer. That's very scary for the police – and obviously for the community at large. One of those victims was Sally Holman, the other a woman in Cardiff, Patricia Hayes, and now we have the Olivia Craddock link, we have to look into all of their backgrounds to try and find out what caught the killer's attention. We need to find out if all three have a link to Barnet Hospital or only two. It might help us find whoever murdered all three women.' He deliberately didn't say Billy's name in case he inflamed Hannah's alarm.

'Couldn't he just have chosen them randomly?' Hannah asked. 'It could be a coincidence.'

'Indeed,' Kate said. 'And that's the likely scenario at this point, but we don't want to miss some vital clue because we made assumptions. We have to follow through on everything, or it could cost another woman her life.'

Jack leaned forward. 'We're talking to a lot of people, Hannah,' he said. 'Making sure we leave no stone unturned. You are one of the people loosely connected to Mrs Holman and in a way to Olivia Craddock, so we are doing what we call due diligence.'

'And I'm in this frame because, what? I have a motive to kill a nurse or a blood donor?'

'That's not what I'm saying,' Jack replied firmly. 'But policing is all about information; we gather it, study it, put most of it aside, but the more we assemble, the better our chances are of finding that elusive clue. We appreciate you helping us with inquiries.'

Now it was Kate's moment. 'So perhaps you don't mind if we ask where you were on the eighth of January?'

Hannah couldn't hide her anger. 'Are you serious?'

'It's just routine, Hannah,' Jack said, trying to restore the sense of calm.

'Routine? You're a detective superintendent and she's a detective chief inspector. That doesn't feel routine.'

'How does it feel?' Jack asked.

'Well, it feels like overkill. Either that or you suspect me of something. Otherwise why send such heavyweights to see me?'

'We don't suspect you of anything,' Jack said, not sure if that was true yet. 'But, just for the record, could I ask you to answer the question, please?'

'What day of the week was that?' Hannah replied, clearly irritated.

'Last Saturday,' Kate answered quickly.

'I was working.' She explained that as a freelance editor, weekends didn't really exist. 'They used to when I was married and Jonathan had weekends off – we had a little boy who looked forward to both his parents being at home and ready to play. But these days I tend to work. Hang on, I'll get my diary.' She walked out of the room.

Jack stayed quiet, resisting the urge to check in with Kate in case Hannah was watching them or listening. Kate picked up his vibe quickly and made idle chitchat, saying that the name Chalky reminded her of her family dog as a child, who had been called Gussie.

'I had a rabbit called Snowflake,' Jack said, which made Kate stifle a laugh. She had to straighten her expression quickly as Hannah returned.

'Last weekend I was working on a book that had a tight deadline. I got it away on Monday to the publisher. You're welcome to go back through my computer records. I have Time Machine on my iMac, so you'll be able to see I was working on the manuscript most of that day. Besides, I'm sure your clever people can track my phone; it would have been here all weekend.' She went to sit down again and stopped suddenly. 'Ah, wait, I recall now. I helped a neighbour that day.'

'Helped them how?'

'Their dog was clipped by a car, and she was just back from the vet, but they had a matinee show to go to. I offered to sit with the dog, who was still very drugged and sleepy. I worked off my laptop for a few hours. I'll just write their details down, and you can check for yourselves.'

'Thank you,' Kate said, glancing at Jack.

'Do you remember much about Sally Holman from the coronary hearing?' Jack asked.

'I remember everything like a movie I can replay,' Hannah replied, her eyes flat. 'What do you want to know?'

'Did you speak to her?'

Hannah shook her head. 'I couldn't speak to anyone. But I wouldn't hold myself responsible for losing control if I had. I was there at Billy's side when the nurse gave the transfusion . . . that wasn't Sally, though. I hadn't met her until I saw her at the hearing.'

'What do you mean?' Jack said, frowning.

'Well, Sally Holman made the mistake that killed Billy. She took a blood sample from the wrong boy, and when that blood cross-matched to the other boy came back, it was put into Billy's arm. It was Annie, the nurse from the ward, who transfused Billy. She was blameless, really – couldn't have known it was the wrong blood. The mistake was made in the hour before. I never met or saw Olivia Craddock, nor the woman from Wales.'

'I see. Again, we're deeply sorry for your loss,' Jack said.

Hannah nodded wearily. 'Are you, though? Those are such easy words to say, but no one really cares. You'll forget about Billy and my pain the moment you leave this house – not that it's your fault, or your problem, but no one understands this grief unless they've been through it. My son didn't die – he was killed. But no one called it murder or even manslaughter. They called it an accident. It's certainly negligence. The hospital threw all of its resources into stalling our case and in the end we just gave up. How are grieving parents supposed to stay strong enough to fight? And what was money going to achieve anyway? Neither of us wanted money as compensation for Billy – how atrocious. I just wanted our son back.'

Jack understood where she was coming from. She'd surely heard the commiseration too many times to feel in any way comforted, or that it was more than just rote sympathy. He wished he could say something that would feel meaningful but stopped himself trying; there really were no genuine words of comfort for a grieving parent. He nodded at her to convey that her words had been heard, and then looked at Kate. It was time to go.

They stood. 'Thank you for seeing us today,' Kate said, shaking hands with Hannah.

'Did it help?' Hannah asked.

'It means we can tick a box. Catching bad guys is always in the detail, no matter how much action the TV shows depict. Most of the time we're indoors, studying information or simply waiting for information to break, as opposed to jumping into cars and screeching off. It's mostly slow work, but the truth is always in there,' Kate answered, avoiding Jack's eye – he knew why, given the drivel she had just spouted. Kate swiftly switched topics. 'That's a beautiful quilt,' she said, gesturing towards the back of the sofa Hannah had been seated on. 'Can't stop admiring it.'

'A hobby,' Hannah remarked.

'It really is amazing. I'd like that in my house. Fabulous colours.'

Hannah found a smile. 'It's a modern design, with a nod to old-fashioned leadlighting. I designed and sewed it while I was pregnant with Billy.'

'Your own design?'

Hannah nodded.

'Wow.' Kate did sound impressed. 'Do you use a machine or . . .?'

'Yeah, for some of it, but I'm a bit of a purist and I like to hand-finish all my quilts. I really enjoy sewing anyway, so it's no drudge.'

'Have you always sewn?'

'Since I was a child at my granny's side. All of her sewing gear came to me. I'm not sure what she'd make of this, though, as she tended to sew very traditional quilts and she liked using her machine, which I now own.'

They moved to the front door. 'Thanks again,' Kate said.

It was Jack's turn to shake hands. 'Here's my card, if you have any questions. We appreciate your time.'

12

Back on the Underground after walking to Kentish Town station, Jack and Kate shared a large bag of fruit gums.

'I could eat this whole bag,' Kate admitted, digging in for the third time.

'I am not ashamed to say I *have* eaten a whole bag in one sitting,' Jack replied, prompting a smile. 'Although I speak with experience when I say that's not wise – tough on the old bowels.'

She snorted a laugh. 'I lied about Gussie.'

'I guessed.'

'You didn't lie about Snowflake, though, did you?' she said, in a slightly mocking tone.

He raised his brows, all innocence. 'Snowflake was very precious to me.'

Kate broke into chuckling laughter. 'Oh, gosh, *you're* precious. Did you take him to bed with you?'

'Her!' Jack said, sounding insulted. 'You don't call a male rabbit Snowflake; you call him Yeti or something.'

That only made her laugh more.

'Snowflake was a lovely girl, and no, I did not sleep with my rabbit. Her hutch was in the shed. I loved her, though.'

'I bet. So, all right. What did you think of Hannah?'

Jack gave a soft sigh. 'Hard to read at this stage. She was extremely tense to begin with. The dog was a good distraction.'

'Yes, I noticed too. It's why I tried to finish our meeting with all that stuff about the sewing.'

He shook his head. 'I would have expected eagerness to know more, given Sally Holman shattered her life, but there was no eagerness there to find out what we know. She didn't ask after the family; she didn't ask for any more detail on how Sally died, where she died, why. For someone who privately wants to cheer at the nurse's death, she didn't seem at all interested.'

Kate nodded. 'And yet so hesitant and suspicious.'

'Well, she clearly wondered if we were lining her up as a possible killer.'

'So what did we get out of that visit, with all our terrible clichés and dreadful fibs and drivel?'

'My instinct is telling me she's hiding something.' Jack shrugged.

'Why?'

'Can't explain instinct. It just happens. There was no need for her to be so tense.'

'Oh, I don't know. Everyone is tense around police, Jack. Even cars doing the right speed limit seem to slow down if they see a squad car. It's a funny thing, but everyone seems to feel sudden guilt if a police officer looks their way.'

He grinned in acknowledgement, then selected another fruit gum and popped it in his mouth. 'Love the black ones, especially when they're soft.'

'Yes, me too. Don't steal them all.' She waited. 'So do we watch her?'

He thought about this, staring out of the window at a hedgerow that passed in a blur of green. 'I know we set out looking at community terror acts and not suspicious deaths, but if the poisoning death and a murder are connected to a dead child . . . Given we were looking for someone with the kind of rage to elicit the terror acts, we can't ignore that link. Nor can we simply overlook the fact that Olivia Craddock was killed by poisoning and the apparent poisoner is nowhere to be found. That does put Hannah Parker squarely in the frame, even if she says she doesn't blame the donor. Let's just find out more about the family . . . the husband . . . friends. Get our terrier, Sarah, on it. Incidentally, let's find out more about the nurse Hannah mentioned who actually gave the transfusion?'

'Annie,' Kate said. 'I can't remember if she mentioned the surname.'

'Hmmm, Sarah leaves you for dead.'

She glared at him playfully. 'Right, for that, the black fruit gums are all mine now.' She picked through the bag and retrieved as many as she could, stashing them in her pocket.

'Hope they get all hairy,' he said.

That made her laugh aloud. She quickly quietened herself as others looked around in the quiet train. 'I do love working with you, Jack.'

He grinned. 'So it wouldn't hurt,' he said, getting them back on task, 'to find this Annie just as a precaution, to know she's had no strange events surrounding her life lately, and no strangers in it. I'm hopeful we might be able to step away from the murder.'

'You mean that it's just an unfortunate crossover?'

'Perhaps. Although my gut says otherwise, much as I'd like to leave that to the boys and girls in Serious Crimes.'

'I suppose our events should be considered by homicide and major crime too.'

'There's going to be overlap. We can't avoid it now. It's why Carol Rowland was consulted by the head of CTC. I think he wanted an experienced team who've worked on murder previously to bring that expertise to this conundrum.'

'Okay if I ask Geoff to keep me posted on the murders?' Kate asked. 'I know he's in touch with the local teams.'

'Shouldn't be a problem. Rowland and CTC may want confidentiality – all of us staying in our lanes – but CT wants answers first and foremost. Geoff knows the drill.'

'Can you let the commander know that I'm discussing this with Geoff? I don't want my knuckles rapped because we're bleeding into another op.'

'Leave it with me,' Jack said. 'So, what's on for your Friday evening?'

Kate sighed. 'Right now, I think I'd like to curl up with a bowl of hearty soup, some crusty bread, and have Geoff crack open a decent bottle of red. You?'

'That sounds lovely. I'm going to a new exhibition opening in Soho.'

'Oh.' She pulled a face at his miserable tone. 'Not looking forward to it?'

He shrugged. 'It's performance art.'

'Ugh. I don't even know what that means and I hate it.'

Jack laughed and threw a red fruit gum into his mouth. 'In a nutshell, and really simplifying it too much, it's the artist showing us the work through movement. Something to do with vandalism. I don't really know. I shall tag along and do my best to be entertained.'

'Yep. Soup, red wine, Geoff, chocolate and a movie at home sounds far preferable,' Kate said, looking happy, and a little as though she'd chalked up a victory against Lou.

Jack smiled back in neutral.

★

It was Friday, work was over, and Annie was looking forward to the party this evening, about half an hour outside St Albans. Was it really a party? She used to go to those in her teens and early twenties. Now, in her late thirties, it was really more of a gathering at a friend's house. But there would be music and food, and most of all there would be alcohol, perhaps some marijuana – though nothing heavier, not with this group. She suspected the majority would be tucked in bed by midnight because they'd have to drag themselves to children's sport the next morning. They were not as footloose and fancy-free as younger partygoers.

The gathering was at Ash's house in Hertfordshire. She and her husband, Mike, had a large place that lent itself to entertaining. He was a landowner; though Ash still worked at the hospital, Annie didn't think she would for much longer. They were trying for a baby and shiftwork wasn't conducive to either making babies or raising them. She quietly envied Ash but was also pleased for her, hoping for much the same herself.

She was hoping that her new squeeze, Mark, might decide tonight that they should become exclusive. She winced at the thought; it sounded so juvenile even thinking it, but she'd been seeing him now for nine weeks, whenever they could find the time, and they always seemed to have fun together. He hadn't pushed her into sleeping with him; in fact he'd shown inordinate patience until she was pressing him to stay overnight. He was a nicely built man: not too muscled but not flabby anywhere. He was fit and lean, eager to please her . . . and handsome to boot.

Heaven had waited a long time to cross her path with someone like this. When she thought about the losers she'd dated before Mark, she felt embarrassed. They'd been lost and forlorn, arrogant and aggressive, distant and unreliable, needy and clingy, and everything in between but now, finally, here was a stable, amusing, kind guy, who listened to her complain and laughed at her darkly comic stories, which she usually only shared with other nurses. He carried no discernible baggage, had no past relationships that had left him wary, beyond the usual number that had fizzled for whatever reason. He seemed to be at the stage of his life – as she was in her own – to settle down with someone.

Annie didn't think she needed marriage for proof of love and commitment. She would happily live with someone, but she had always hoped to have at least one child, so at nearly thirty-seven that window was closing rapidly. Maybe Mark would offer her that chance, but if a child wasn't in his plans, that would be all right. So long as *she* was in his plan. She wanted something meaningful, with or without a child. And she really, *really* fancied Mark for the role.

Having watched many of her friends' marriages take a hammering once children came along, she thought there was something to be said for life without them, or so she'd convinced herself. She was not a born mother, that much was true, and when she pressed herself she realised that she didn't feel angry or twisted at the idea of not having children; it had just never occurred to her that she wouldn't. She loved the idea of helping to create a new generation and of giving love and security to a baby who she could raise into a good human being. Anyway, she shouldn't get ahead of herself. Tonight she'd see if she could ease Mark into a corner . . . and perhaps he might tell her where he thought their relationship was going.

But Annie never did get to ask Mark whether he saw a future for them, and she never made it to the party. Ash called twice and sent several messages that lit up Annie's phone in her bag, but the first person to read them was the police detective called to the scene in Annie's home after neighbours complained that her small dog would not stop barking. Police officers found her lying on her bed, dressed for a night out, dead.

The back door had been kicked in and the house had clearly been ransacked. Because she lived alone, police were unsure of what might have been taken, if anything, and wondered if perhaps this was some sort of bungled theft.

Only a small dog called Pixie knew that Annie Dawes had been strangled by someone she knew.

13

Lou looked at Jack in all seriousness as he set the wine down in front of her. 'What did you think?'

He took a sip of the pale ale he'd ordered, desperate to quench his thirst, and held up a finger while he swallowed at least a quarter in one gulp. 'Oh, I needed that,' he said with a soft sigh. 'Sorry.'

She waited.

'What did I think of the artistic performance?' he asked, knowing that was exactly what she meant but pathetically buying himself some time.

She sipped her wine. 'No point in saying cheers given you've already downed yours.'

'It was hot in that place,' he protested.

'Hot in here, too,' she said, looking around the bar they'd fallen into.

'Claustrophobic, then,' Jack tried. 'The atmosphere in that tiny theatre was so thick.'

'But what did you think of the performance?'

He couldn't avoid it any longer. 'Well, it's not my thing, Lou,' he finally admitted. 'All those achingly intense, arty folk, all so earnest, in anticipation of bodies rolling around in paint.'

'You didn't appreciate the symbolism?'

'No,' he said, needing to be honest with her. 'To me they were half-naked people making an arse of themselves.'

He was so grateful to her for her burst of convulsive laughter.

'Okay, Jack, that's performance art off our list.'

'Thank you,' he said with exaggerated relief. 'In return, I'll bake for you this weekend. Whatever you want.'

'Ooh, I want that soaked fruit tart that tastes like Christmas, even though December is behind us.'

'Done.'

'But it has to be homemade pastry.'

He put a hand to his chest in shock. 'Lou, who buys pastry?'

She giggled, then leaned in and kissed him softly. 'I hope it's always going to be like this, Jack.'

'Like what?'

'Funny, affectionate, silly, truthful.'

'Always, I promise,' he said, kissing her again. 'Thank you for understanding. I like exhibitions, theatre, concerts – I'll even do poetry recitals if you twist my arm. Just not the nutters,' he said, conjuring Nat's observation about the sort of people who might terrorise the community at large.

'How's the case going?' Lou asked, as though she could read his thoughts.

He shrugged. 'Oh, you know, we're still wrapping our heads around what we know and what we don't know.'

Lou nodded. 'And how's Kate?'

He sat back with a look of amusement. 'Now I know that's code for "Does she know we're engaged?"'

'It is,' she said, laughing. 'You see, that's why you're such a smart detective. You can winkle out when someone's hedging and looking for that perfect segue. No wonder you're so senior.'

'Well, yes, I told her. I thought she should know before the taskforce got going.'

'And?'

'And . . . what could she do but accept it?'

'What did she say? Please don't make me get out my thumbscrews, Jack.' Lou looked uncomfortable even to be asking, so it was obviously very important to her. In the time he'd known her, he'd chalked her up as someone who felt utterly secure within herself, and this was a rare chink in her armour. He didn't blame her.

He took her hand. 'She didn't say much, just that she felt it was fast.'

'It is, by a lot of people's standards,' she agreed, not making eye contact.

'And then while she was getting over that,' Jack continued, 'I told her you'd moved in.'

Lou met his amused gaze and allowed a smile to break.

Jack shrugged again. 'I have no secrets from Kate. And I needed her to know you are the love of my life and the woman I intend to spend the rest of my days with.' He watched her eyes mist and then water. 'Oh, please don't cry.'

Lou sniffed and gave an embarrassed laugh. 'I don't know any man who says that sort of thing. No wonder women love you.'

'How do you surmise that?'

She gave him a look of mock despair. 'The thing is, Jack, I love you. I don't care any more about all the previous women in your life, because you're mine now. But I need you to stay safe. I'm committing my whole life and future to you, so don't shorten it by taking chances or running into danger.' She stroked his face. 'I mean it.'

He knew she did, but found it hard to meet her gaze. 'This is a bit heavy for Friday-night drinks in a crowded bar as I recover from naked people rolling in paint, isn't it?'

'No, it's perfect timing. Make me a promise.'

He looked at her properly. 'I'm a senior detective and trouble is my playground, Lou.'

She was unmoved. 'When I take my vows I'm not marrying a senior detective. I'm marrying Jack Hawksworth, who bakes and talks about architecture and hums a lot.'

He let his mouth drop open. 'I do not.'

'You do. Nonsense tunes. You even make up small songs . . . about my bottom.'

Now he laughed. 'It's worth singing about.'

'Well, I love it all. I don't want any of it to stop, and so I need your word that you won't let me down by dying or being hurt by some criminal.'

Jack nodded seriously now; he didn't want to lose this closeness either, and he could promise not to take any unnecessary risks. 'I give you my word.'

She smiled. 'Good. All right, let's go shopping for fruit tart ingredients—' His phone rang. 'Oh don't, please.'

He apologised with his eyes. 'I have to,' he said. 'Perks of being that senior detective. Come on, I'll walk and talk. Lead us to Tesco's.' He answered. 'Hawksworth? Oh, hi, Kate.' He listened and his expression darkened. 'You're sure?' He nodded.

The doors of Tesco Express slid back for them and Jack followed Lou inside. 'Oh, I see. Well, let's call in all favours. I'll be in for eleven. Okay, see you there.' He put his phone in his pocket and took a breath.

'What's happened?' Lou asked with a concerned expression.

He shook his head. 'Another death,' he murmured, checking no one else was nearby. 'Nothing to do with our cases and yet potentially everything to do with them.'

She squeezed his arm. 'If you have to go—'

'No. Friday night is all ours. And we can still have breakfast together.'

'Really?'

He nodded, smiling. 'And you can cook dinner, but I shall have a winter fruit tart awaiting your highness's pleasure for tomorrow evening.'

'Then I'd better have something ready for your pleasure,' she teased.

'May I have it early? Tonight?'

'No, the wait will make it worth it,' and she took off down the aisles, giggling as he gave gentle chase.

He was glad for the distraction, pretending to just miss grabbing her, and apologising to a woman nearby who tutted that they'd nearly bumped her. He could see from the set of her mouth that anyone having fun was a nuisance to her. He felt sorry for her: this sort of childish joy was what made life worth living. If he allowed himself to think about the death of Annie Dawes, then his weekend would be as ruined as hers.

Ruin could wait a few more hours.

He kept his promise to Lou, serving her breakfast in bed before allowing her to – as she liked to put it – 'ravage his body'. He made a pot of tea. Then, rugged up in dressing-gowns, they huddled together on Jack's rooftop garden overlooking the River Thames as it slid by. They sipped from mugs, talking over where they might honeymoon. It was still a while away, but he enjoyed her musings, which ranged from the Maldives to Patagonia.

'I'm easy, Lou,' he reiterated. 'Whatever you want.'

'I'd be happy right here. I love living here.'

'Really? I was wondering if we should move.'

She frowned. 'Why? Who wouldn't want to live here, right between Kew and Richmond? I consider myself lucky.'

'Oh, I don't know. It was a bachelor house before it became a couple's townhouse. I thought you might like an old place with a garden, or perhaps to move out of London proper.'

'Jack, I love London . . . everything about it. Besides, if I was going to move away from the city, I'd want it to be somewhere overseas, not down the road. Here we have a little garden – I love what you've done with your tiny veggie and herb boxes. It's the best of both worlds.'

'I thought it was all too masculine.'

'Is that because of those lemon sheets I've introduced?'

He laughed. 'Maybe.'

'Well, it's just that the house was so neutral and I did get rid of a lot of my stuff . . . I like those sheets.'

'I like them too. They remind me of our first time together.'

She smiled. 'You ran away that time too. Do you *have* to go in?'

He nodded, his face grave. 'Someone has been murdered.'

She looked ashamed. 'Sorry. Go on, then, abandon me. I might not be here when you finish showering – I'm going for a run.'

'Be careful, it's slippery just outside on that towpath, especially under—'

'The bridge, I know. And before you say it, I do know it's the one you jumped from on your last big operation.' She gave him a salute. 'Hope it's not too gruesome.'

'Murder always is,' he said and gave her a peck before leaving to shower. 'I have to say it really was quite a leap into that cold water.'

He left her laughing.

Within an hour, Jack was seated with the team in a quiet corner of an eatery where they served a great breakfast, not too far from New Scotland Yard. The café was mostly empty after the morning rush. He was pleased to see Geoff next to Kate. 'Order away, it's on me,' he urged them.

While Kate and Nat decided on porridge with a winter compote of dried fruits in a sticky syrup, Geoff went all out with eggs and sausages with beans. These days he needed it, with his fitness regime.

'You've never looked better, mate,' Jack told him.

'You should come with me, you naturally lean bastard,' Geoff said, tucking into his sausages.

Sarah and Hirem had ordered poached eggs on sourdough, which now arrived, along with teas and coffees. Still full from breakfast with Lou, Jack went with tea; this place wasn't up to his usual standard of coffee. Until now it had been small talk, waiting for the food, but Jack got down to business as everyone ate. They knew to be quick.

'Right. Who's beginning?'

Kate looked at Geoff. 'I think Geoff should. This new murder really confirms the path we were already going down.'

Jack looked to his friend. 'It's staggering we're overlapping again.'

Geoff shook his head. 'I'm just stalking you, mate.' After the obligatory grin, he turned serious. 'Two of these murders have occurred in and around the Greater London region, the other in Wales. Initially, various local divisions had their own teams on each of the deaths but our op has taken over the lead on these cases.' Geoff looked around to ensure no one was eavesdropping. Feeling safe, he continued. 'In summary, three strangulations. No mutilation, no sexual angle and, to our knowledge, no theft or trophies. Each still had her purse in her bag. We have no motive at this point . . . and I'll be honest, we have no clue about the perpetrator, if, as we assume, it's one and the same. The women were strangled from the front; two had fractured larynxes . . . plus the expected injuries of swollen tongue, bloodshot eyes, petechial rash and so on.'

'I'm guessing no DNA?' Jack said.

'Nothing that links the three of them.'

'Why are we talking, then?' Sarah frowned, never one to mince her words.

'Well,' Kate began, cutting a glance at Jack for permission. At his nod, she continued quietly. 'The woman murdered last night was Annie Dawes.'

Sarah's eyes widened in alarm. She knew the name.

'We now have ourselves the link we've been looking for. She's the third connection.'

Sarah turned to Jack. 'So Billy Parker's death is the catalyst?'

He nodded. 'So it seems. It has to be our premise. Apart from the Cardiff victim, Olivia Craddock, Sally Holman and Annie Dawes were all connected to Billy, but we need to move slowly now, and with great care. Hirem, help Sarah lock down all details of the Welsh death. We need to know if it links somehow with Billy. Everyone, please remember, we are dealing with a grieving mother, and I have no intention of adding to her grief by opening up those wounds again.'

'They're not healed,' Kate said. 'Hannah Parker's fragile.'

'All the more reason for us to tread lightly.'

'I've got some thoughts on how we can proceed,' Geoff offered.

'Let's take it back to the office. Everyone finished?' Jack asked, draining his tea. The others scraped their chairs backwards to stand and heft their coats on. 'I'll get this and meet you up on level seven.' His team ambled away while he waited at the counter to pay, his phone buzzing with a text. He glanced at it: Geoff.

Up on the sixteenth floor of New Scotland Yard, Jack swiped himself in through the glass doors. The usual receptionist for Special Operations was not in on the weekend so he turned left, past the commander's office. It was quiet today. He glanced to his right at the major ops room, which was also silent. It was often full of people watching suspects being followed live, or armed searches being performed. It was either the proverbial hive of activity or dead silent, as it was now. Jack knew it wouldn't last.

Geoff was running the op for the strangulations from up here. Clearly he wanted to discuss something in private.

'Hey,' Jack said, as his friend met him with a grin. 'I think I know what's on your mind.'

'Hawk, I think we should fold your taskforce in with my guys as an op. We can run both investigations side by side.'

Jack agreed with Geoff's logic, but they weren't the only ones with a say. 'Counter Terrorism is only focused on the terror acts. Command will not want its taskforce investigating the murders.'

Geoff shrugged. 'It won't have to. I'll spearhead the murders, you lead on the terror acts. You're the senior across both, wherever we overlap, but we need to share information, because I know you feel it in your bones, as I do, that these crimes are linked. We can even prove it, although I suspect we're a way off yelling *bingo*.'

Jack nodded. 'I do. We'd better speak to our respective bosses.'

'Will do. I know we could have done this downstairs, but Kate has big ears and I didn't want you to feel ambushed or put on the spot. She's always ready with an opinion on everything.'

Jack grinned. 'Another reason you love her.'

'I really do love her,' Geoff said, unexpectedly serious. 'Hardly the time and place to admit it, but I need you to know it.'

'I do, mate. Does *she* know it? I know she's happier than she's been in a long while, but does she know how serious you are?'

'I'm not one for a lot of words, Hawk. I try to show it. She surely knew last time that I would never stray.'

'I don't know, Geoff. Women love to be told. Not all the time, because then we'd come across as soppy. But you're not soppy ever, so hearing it a bit more often from you is going to have a major effect on her. When did you last tell her you loved her?'

'Told her I loved her in a dress she wore to dinner.'

Jack shrugged. 'Do better, please.'

'Maybe you need to give me lessons.'

'No, I don't. Kate likes to come across tough, but she needs to feel how committed you both are this time.'

Geoff nodded. 'Speaking of commitment, I haven't even congratulated you on your good news.'

'That's because I haven't had a chance to share it with you – though I'm sure Kate did. So, for the record, I've asked Lou to marry me and she said yes.'

They burst into laughter. Jack was unsure why but he enjoyed it all the same, and they hugged on the eighteenth floor, which was usually reserved for very serious business.

'I'm proud of you, mate,' Geoff said.

'Why?' Jack laughed. 'Didn't think I had it in me?'

'Definitely not, not with your track record of broken hearts.'

'Don't start. Lou is . . .' Jack shook his head. 'Well, I can't imagine not being with her now. I love watching her, I love listening to her, I love sleeping next to her, I just love being hers.'

'Can I use those lines when I try to explain how I feel to Kate?'

Jack grinned. 'Just don't tell her you got them from me. Then she'll hate you.'

'I can't lose her again.'

'You won't. And I think my engagement has settled something.' Jack needed to say it; it had been an invisible, silent elephant between them. They both understood that Kate's feelings for Jack ran deep, even as she loved Geoff.

'You're sure?'

'Positive. To be honest, I found her wistful that day. I could be reading into it more than I should, but I know Kate pretty well and I believe that what she wants is permanency too. It's taken her a while, but my instincts tell me she's come to that precipice and wants to jump . . . marriage, family, a steady home.'

'I hope so. I'm taking her away when this is all over and I'm going to pop the question.'

Jack slapped Geoff on the back and kept his arm around his shoulders. 'Do it sooner than that, you old rogue. Don't hesitate. She loves you. She just doesn't realise how much. Come on, let's head down, they're all waiting.'

14

When Jack and Geoff arrived, the ops room quietened.

'Hi, sorry to keep you. Let's talk through what we know,' Jack said, removing his thick jacket. He got straight down to business, ignoring Kate's querying expression. It must have seemed odd for the two seniors to arrive together and late, even though everyone had left the café at the same time. 'So now we have three strangulations. Two of those deaths have occurred in London, both of them nurses . . .' He sighed, shaking his head. 'And both of those nurses can be connected not only with the hospital but also with the ward where Billy Parker died after a blood transfusion went wrong. Both of these nurses were involved with Billy's care.'

At Kate's direction, Nat had pinned up photographs of the two women above their names. Sally Holman and Annie Dawes smiled out at the room. The third strangled woman, Patricia Hayes, was also pinned up, but slightly to one side: the victim from Wales. Olivia Craddock was just being attached to the board as Jack turned to point.

'Three of these women – Sally, Annie and Olivia – as outlined, have a clear link to Billy Parker's death. Patricia is the oddity.

She was a 59-year-old teacher from Cardiff.' Jack gestured towards the map of where all the domestic terror incidents had occurred. 'We're not yet sure how she fits in but, even so, Greater London remains the key. It's where the first and second incidents of needles in strawberries occurred and the worst case of the lipstick tampering, at Boots Oxford Street – its biggest store. The baby-formula tampering occurred in Hounslow. Olivia Craddock was poisoned at her home in Hotwells, close to Bristol city centre. What do we know about Olivia?'

Nat put her finger up. 'I've collated some extra information. Olivia, went by Liv. Thirty-one. Single, but according to those who knew her had been seeing a new man for a couple of months. Apparently her donation, which found its way into Billy's arm, was her first time giving blood and she was devastated when she learned of it. Um . . . according to her best friend—'

'This is the one who ate the poisonous mushrooms too?' Kate interrupted for clarification.

'Yes. Her name is . . .' Nat consulted a file. 'Mia Dryden. According to Mia, Olivia was quite struck by this new guy, Peter, and was hopeful it might turn into something permanent. Mia described Peter as late thirties, tall, quite slim, dark hair and close beard; also as amusing, quietly spoken and generous, and seemed smitten by Liv, so Mia says.'

'He sounds perfect,' Kate said, cutting a glance at Geoff, who mugged a look in return that said *what?* Jack looked away, smiling inwardly.

Geoff cleared his throat. 'It's probably pertinent to mention here that Annie Dawes was also seeing someone relatively new. I don't have all the details yet but an early interview with her friend, the one whose party she never made it to, describes the boyfriend, known as Mark Logan, as nicely built, dark-haired, with some facial hair. According to her, he might have been just under six foot. She didn't know him well enough to comment on his personality but said Annie was quite excited about him. She put him at around forty.'

Jack looked around at the dropped expressions. 'Okay, our next urgent task is to find out more about these men. Geoff, I'll let your guys handle that, so we try not to bleed too much into each other's investigation.' Geoff nodded, and Jack saw Nat's expression falter briefly.

'And in the meantime, Kate, I want to know the full journey and processing of blood, from its donation point to how it's ordered and finds its way into someone's arm. I want to know how it went wrong when it's intended to save, not kill.'

'On it,' Kate said. 'The Coroner's Court did a thorough investigation, so I'll pull up those records as a start.'

'Sarah, can we find out everyone who was on the ward at the hospital in London where Billy Parker died? All shifts for the time he was there.'

'Do you mean from the moment of his admission for surgery, sir?'

'No, I don't think that's necessary, but from when he presented in A&E afterwards. Do this fast, Sarah. There are potentially more lives at stake.'

She nodded, undaunted.

'And Nat?'

She looked up and he could see she expected to be given a piecemeal task, as she was near the end of his list. 'I want you to organise an application for a surveillance team to be put on Hannah Parker for the next few days. I'm making you responsible for that team, Nat. And Kate, Geoff or I will sign off. But Nat, you can brief them, and you can head up the surveillance out of the ops room. We want to know where she goes, who she meets, favourite haunts. She's already suspicious of us, so they're to keep their distance and keep it simple.'

Nat seemed to grow in stature. 'Yes, sir,' she said, her face shining with pleasure. 'Er, do I join them, sir? I mean on day one, so that I can point her out, or do I brief them with a photograph and address?'

'Do we have a good snapshot from the news articles? Or anything from social media?'

'Only something old,' Kate answered. 'Her hair is blonder now, and short. She's lost weight.'

'Okay,' Jack agreed. 'Point her out for them, Nat, and then get back in here to keep tabs on the surveillance shifts – what they're seeing, offering thoughts and gathering up whatever you think is useful for us to know.'

'Thank you, sir.' Nat returned to her desk to start filling out necessary paperwork.

Jack continued. 'Hirem, can you see what you can find out about the family around Hannah Parker, please? Especially the ex-husband. Perhaps when you find him, you might make an appointment for us to meet. Keep it very casual, just helping us with our inquiries, that sort of thing. Talk to Kate first; she'll give you the angle we used when speaking to Hannah.'

'Right, sir.'

And suddenly everyone was busy. Jack looked over at Geoff, intuitively waiting. Jack gave a flick of his head and the two of them left the busy taskforce to their duties.

'Think it can work?' Geoff asked.

'So long as we can run the investigations side by side, I can't imagine the powers that be having a problem with it, especially when we show the links. It would be madness not to work together.'

'CTC's going to be harder to convince, so you go in first.'

'Okay. Listen, can we meet with the pathology team who did the post-mortems on the strangulations?'

'Sure. I'll set something up. Today?'

'Hopefully they can see us this afternoon.' Jack nodded his head towards the op room. 'They'll be busy for a full day on what they're hunting down.'

'Lovely. A boys' day out, then,' Geoff said in a sweet voice. 'I'll make a call.'

Jack and Geoff sat across the desk from Hilary Davies, the pathologist, a woman around their own age. She was Geoff's height, dressed in black pencil trousers and short black boots. Her trim figure provided a sharp frame for the clothes, but she wore her soft fabric blouse untucked and over her trousers for a shapeless look. Her hair was tied up loosely and she wore only natural make-up. Jack always noticed these things; he felt he could glean clues to a person's personality from their presentation. Hilary Davies projected the aura of a self-confident person who felt secure in her senior role. Even her glasses, which she took off now to rub at tired eyes, were rimless and simple.

Her voice was soft with a kind lilt to it. 'Sorry, detectives, we've been burning the candles at both ends. If I yawn, it's not you.'

'That's why we brought these,' Jack said, lifting a box of dough-nuts they had picked up at the train station. He grinned. 'Maybe the sugar will help? Hope there's no more than a dozen of you.'

She looked happily surprised. 'Wow. No, there's six of us on now. They will love this! I'd like to claim I organised it.'

'Go ahead,' Jack said warmly.

'No, no. I'm joking. How thoughtful. They can have that shortly. Now, tell me, how can I help you, detectives?'

'Call me Jack,' he said.

'I'm Geoff.'

'Then I'm Hilly.' She smiled. 'This is about the strangulations?'

Geoff had left a message with one of her staff. 'Yes. Thank you for seeing us at short notice.'

'Anything we can do to help solve these horrific crimes.'

Jack gave her an encouraging smile. 'Hilly, I know we can read the report, but would you please tell us about these two victims, Sally and Annie?'

'I'll tell you about all three, in fact. We are officially linking the earlier one in Cardiff – the similarities are too striking,' Hilly said.

'We thought as much,' Geoff said, and Jack nodded at him to take the lead. It was, after all, Geoff's case. 'Can you talk us through what you know, please?'

'Yes, of course. I'm guessing neither of you are squeamish, so shall we discuss with the bodies on hand?' She looked between them. 'It's probably quicker for explanation.'

'Sure,' Geoff said.

'Good. Why don't you go through there' – she pointed – 'and I'll have my team set up. Won't be more than five minutes.'

Jack and Geoff made their way to the viewing room, where they and dozens of police officers had stood before, looking through the glass into the theatre where the post-mortems were performed. They watched two gurneys arrive with body bags on them. Then Hilly appeared in scrubs, gloved, hair tucked into a cap, feet in squeaky boots. Her mask was undone and she smiled at them. 'I've got Sally and Annie here. Ready?' At their nods, she looked at her assistant. 'Thanks, Danny.'

The assistant carefully unzipped both bags, pulling back the heavy plastic to reveal the naked bodies of two women, but only to the sternum. Jack was sure this sensitivity was Hilly's doing, as he had been at many a post-mortem viewing where the whole body was on display, often unnecessarily, while the pathologist, assistants and police officers talked over and around it. He'd always felt a rush of sympathy for the victim in those situations – they were so vulnerable – though some would argue a corpse didn't need modesty. Jack had always believed they should take what care they could, whether in life or death, particularly given the violence or violation many of these people had suffered. These women's bodies and their memories belonged to others . . . to families and friends who loved and missed them.

He shook himself free of those thoughts and focused. The women looked fragile in death, particularly Annie Dawes, who was slight. Jack couldn't say why but he somehow got the sense she must have been someone of cheerful disposition in life.

'So, as you can see,' Hilly began, 'there's no need to view the whole body, because all the information we need is happening right up here,' she said, gesturing at the women's heads. 'And the same goes for our third victim from Cardiff. Each of the women was found fully clothed, no sexual assault, no tampering and minimal movement of their body after death. Where they were strangled is essentially where they were left.'

Jack nodded to Hilly to continue.

'As you know, the first victim was Patricia Hayes in Cardiff. Then, Sally Holman here. Marks on skin aren't always visible, but there were none on her.'

'So no evidence of fighting back?' Geoff asked, pressing the intercom button so she could hear him.

'None. But that doesn't mean she didn't. She might have swatted her killer's hands desperately.' Hilly gave a good impression of what that might have looked like, batting at the side of her neck, then shrugged. 'Everyone responds differently, and if he had a good grip on what is essentially a very slim neck, then she wouldn't have been able to do much. However, that's supposition, which is something I don't get involved with. I can only tell you what is supported by physical evidence.'

'What made you think strangulation?' Geoff asked.

'We didn't, at first. However, Sally's body ultimately gave up that fact through a full post-mortem. We did see the pinprick blood-shotting of the eyes at the scene, which often speaks to asphyxiation.'

Jack liked the way she wasn't using a lot of medical terminology; he knew the correct term was 'petechial haemorrhage', but she chose not to sound superior. He was reminded of the Australian pathologist he'd met in Adelaide; he'd liked her for a lot of the same reasons. These women worked with such ugliness and yet they seemed to find beauty in their victims, showing only tenderness in how they handled them. He especially liked that Hilly called Sally by her name, stopping her from becoming 'the corpse', 'the victim', 'the deceased'.

'So the pressure creates the blood-shotting?'

'Yep. It's simple plumbing,' she said, smiling, but he noticed she laid a hand on Sally's arm. 'As you probably remember from school, the arteries take blood to the brain and the veins return it to the heart to be re-oxygenated. Veins are more fragile – they're thinner, smaller. When you squeeze the neck, the arteries can still keep getting the blood up to the brain for a while, but the veins in the neck are compressed; their fragility means they are quickly blocked. There's nowhere for the blood to go. Blood pressure in the head soars and bursts tiny vessels around the eyes, the upper and lower eyelids, sometimes the forehead and cheekbones. If someone has darker skin, like the woman from Wales, you don't always see these things at the scene. It would have been during the post-mortem that the pathologist noticed the burst blood vessels. I might add that the Cardiff victim, Patricia, was found facedown, which complicates the findings, because that can also cause blood-shotting of the eyes.'

She sighed. 'Anyway, Sally sadly died a healthy 38-year-old, who'd recently had a physical at her GP's because she was wanting to take on some runs for charity, I gather, and took the right precautions. Her medical notes attest that all her vitals, from BP to weight, were excellent.' She turned back to Sally. 'There were no marks on her body to suggest drugs via needles or any other sort of bruising. Her bloods came back perfect. Her stomach contents suggested she hadn't consumed much for a few hours.'

Hilly shrugged. 'So with nothing obviously physically wrong – kidneys, liver, lungs, heart all in good nick – it meant we hunted for the less obvious. Sally was found on the Heath. It wasn't a freezing night, but it was cold and I estimated she'd been dead for approximately twenty-five hours before she was discovered, lying face upwards. There was only the start of rigor mortis in the small joints.' Hilly held up her hand. 'Fingers, eyelids and' – she drew an invisible line near Sally's face – 'jaw. Lividity was still early; her skin could blanch.'

Both men nodded.

'So with nothing obvious on the skin, i.e. bruising or scratches, I performed what we call a layered neck dissection. Heard of those?'

'I think I can guess,' Jack said, nodding towards Sally, who'd obviously had a major surgical procedure on her neck.

'We need to get to the strap muscles,' Hilly said, drawing lines against her own neck upwards from her clavicle. 'We look at the first layer, and if we find nothing, we peel those back and go to the second, then lift those and go to the third. We're looking for subtle bruising below the skin. But first we need to carefully remove the brain and drain the blood, because for us to see clearly, we need to work in a bloodless zone – a clean field, if you will. Once that is done, we have a better chance at getting more definitive answers.'

'Okay,' Geoff said. 'And you found some bruising in the neck presumably, which led you to conclude that she had been strangled?'

'With certainty,' Hilly assured them. 'With the layers carefully laid back, I could see the bruising in the neck, and the superior horn, which is the high side of the thyroid cartilage, showed a classic break at its base, which is something we see in strangulation. It can occur in other injuries, such as a kick or a punch, but together with the petechial haemorrhages'—now she used the scientific term—'and the bruising . . . that all equals strangulation.'

'And Annie Dawes?' Jack asked. 'Did she show all the same injuries?'

'Annie was found in a warm house and had been dead for about nine hours when she was discovered. I attended with the SOCO team, and her skin was already considerably darkened, lividity was fixed, rigor was at its peak. When I learned Annie was a nurse like Sally and there were no signs of sexual assault, although I am not prone to jumping to early conclusions, I decided to check for strangulation as soon as I had her back at the morgue. I could already see the petechial haemorrhage in her eyes. In Annie's case,' she said, moving over to her body, 'not only was the thyroid cartilage fractured, but the hyoid bone was also broken on one side – a sort of crescent-shaped bone here.' She again touched the right point on Annie's neck. 'It sits above the thyroid cartilage and supports a lot of structures for the mouth and helps with speaking, as well as tongue movement, swallowing, et cetera.'

'That seems rougher than Sally's death, if such a qualification could be made,' Geoff said.

Hilly nodded sadly and sighed. 'He really went hard at her.'

'You're convinced it's a man?' Jack asked.

She nodded. 'I am, based on the amount of pressure exerted, the angle, which suggests height. I should also mention that it was a front-facing strangulation in both cases.'

'Why would someone do that?' Jack asked, thinking aloud.

'I can't comment on that. It would be speculation,' Hilly said.

'Then I will,' Geoff said. 'It suggests to me, Hawk, that the killer wanted to watch the lights go out; he was possibly even talking to them as he killed them, enjoying their struggle.'

Hilly shrugged, refusing to be drawn. 'One more thing, if you're not convinced.' They waited. 'He left behind something unequivocal.'

'What?' Geoff said, shocked. 'I haven't heard about—'

She smiled, held up a hand. 'I only just discovered it, Detective Benson, because I did a secondary inspection this morning. If I wasn't seeing you today, I would have phoned you with this detail of good news.'

'Which is?' Geoff's nose almost touched the glass with eagerness.

'He was wearing gloves.' Both men frowned. That suggested no DNA or fingerprints would be available. It didn't sound like good news. The pathologist continued. 'I believe they were woolly. The weave of the knit left behind a distinctive pattern on the bruising. I didn't take a lot of notice of it at first, but it niggled, so I went back in this morning.'

'Good grief,' Jack murmured and she smiled.

'He probably thought he was safe wearing them, but he left his mark. I think they're hand-knitted gloves, because there's a clear pattern on the thumbs, which is unusual, and . . .' She paused before delivering the next sentence. 'The pattern is mirrored on the bruising of all three women.'

Jack looked at Geoff, whose mouth was agape.

'We knew there were similarities between these murders, but nothing so unequivocal.' Geoff turned to Jack. 'This is huge. This is what we need.'

'When I spotted the pattern this morning, the other pathologist and I went over our findings again together. Dr Leigh went hunting for what I had found and discovered the same curious pattern on Patricia's body. I can link these three deaths without question for you. I'm afraid you have yourselves a serial killer.'

15

'Hope this helped rather than hindered?' Hilly asked as she returned from the theatre to the corridor, bringing a smell of disinfectant with her. 'I know this isn't necessarily good news – a serial killer – but good news, perhaps, that you can link the deaths.'

'It will certainly aid Geoff's case,' Jack replied. When she looked back at him quizzically, he explained. 'These murders are commanding a full operational team led by DCI Geoff Benson here, but it's showing signs of bleeding into another operation that I'm spearheading. They're worlds apart, but we're finding some curious links that draw them closer to each other.' He kept it as vague as he could; even though she seemed entirely professional, he couldn't risk anything getting out. 'Geoff and I are collaborating wherever we can, because the lines that are being drawn are, frankly, chilling.'

'I see,' she said. 'And your case, Jack. Can these victims help with anything? Can I?'

He shook his head. 'Not immediately. But what might interest you is that the two women you have in your morgue would have been known to one another, and they do tie back into my case.'

'Wow, how confusing,' she said.

'Please don't mention that to anyone. I'd appreciate it, Hilly,' Jack said.

'Not even to my team, I give you my word.'

He believed her. 'Thank you, and for your time and help this afternoon.'

'You're welcome. And, just for the record, I'm not sure whether Annie will be the last victim. I have no evidence, of course, but . . .' She shrugged.

'You mean because serial killers don't stop?' Geoff said.

She nodded. 'Well, given what you've just told me, Detective Hawksworth, I'd be looking at how many more women have connections to your case, because that might indicate how many more women could turn up dead.'

Jack kept his promise to Lou, making the winter fruit tart as she pulled together a stir-fry that evening. She chopped vegetables and created loud hissing sounds with the wok, while he worked on his sweet shortcrust pastry. He rested it before working it into the tart tin. Satisfied, he took out the fruit he'd macerated the night before: prunes, dried figs, raisins, currants, sultanas, glacé cherries, dried apricots and dried blueberries. They were plump and smelled of the rich sherry they'd soaked in as he tumbled the mixture into the pastry and then got to work expertly weaving a lattice crust for the top.

'Last time you made that I was left wondering how on earth that lattice is achieved.'

'Now you know.' He beamed.

'Very clever. Let's get it into the oven.'

'It will need to rest for forty-five minutes after it cooks – too hot, otherwise.'

'I would wait all night for that tart,' Lou said, lifting noodles with two ladles and coating them in the sauce she'd made.

'Smells good,' Jack said.

'My chicken stir-fry and your winter tart – a match made in heaven,' she said.

They risked eating on the rooftop again, fully rugged up.

'I really do love it out here in the moonlight, that glittery water snaking past,' Lou said, sighing.

'You'll love it even more in summer, and when I grow my veggies.'

She laughed. 'Each day I love you more and more.'

'My plan is working,' he said, twirling an imaginary moustache and affecting a devious tone. 'How's your exhibition coming along?'

'It's happening slowly, but each day we inch forward. It's a big space and a lot of art.'

'It's going to get a lot of attention, you said. This is an up-and-coming artist?'

'Oh, I hope so. He is a great new talent. His work is so exciting that I have to make sure the exhibition echoes that energy. I'm enjoying it hugely, though. Haven't had so much fun in years.'

'Actually, I think that's me, not the exhibition,' he suggested, grinning.

She smiled back and took a sip of wine. 'There's that too,' she agreed. 'And you? Any breakthroughs on the case?'

Jack gave a soft sigh. 'Maybe, but invariably that break comes with various rabbit holes we have to run down. Most of today I was with Geoff at the morgue.'

'I won't ask what you were doing there and can't imagine it was fun, but it must have been great to be alongside him for a few hours?'

'I'd be lying if I didn't say I'd forgotten how much his friendship means. I take it for granted. And that's mostly my fault. I need to make more time to see him socially.'

Lou nodded. 'Start now. Why don't you invite him and Kate over for a meal?'

Jack was surprised she'd suggested it. 'Should I?'

'Yes, of course. And you should also take him up on his offer to do some things together.'

'I am not taking up his crazy running.'

Lou rolled her eyes. 'Well, find something else to do together, then.'

'You're right.' He groaned. 'We used to do so much together. Work and life got in the way.'

'You can fix that,' she said. 'Girls are so much better at this stuff. We keep in touch.' She stood to pick up their plates.

He nodded. 'All right, I will. How's next weekend for you?'

'Busy, but I can make it work if you cook. I'll tidy up, because I know I'm the messy one that's brought chaos to your neat life.'

Jack smirked. 'I had noticed.'

'You haven't said anything!'

'I don't want you to change for me. I like you exactly as you are . . . just a fraction chaotic.'

She laughed and put the plates back down, then sat on his lap and kissed him gently. 'Thank you.'

'I should be thanking you,' he said, their lips barely parted.

'For what?'

'Anchoring me. I haven't felt this needed, loved, secure, happy to get home, or as comfortable around mess since I was a child.'

She frowned. 'That makes me sad.'

'Don't be. My life hasn't been sad. It just hasn't had you in it. But now it does, and I thank the angel who cast that vixen, Gabriella, into my life and made it possible for our paths to cross that night.'

'That angel was Kate. If not for her forcing you to attend her birthday party, we'd never have met.'

He frowned. 'You're saying I owe my new-found happiness to Kate?'

'Another reason to have her and Geoff over. It will be good for her to see us together, too.'

'None of *this*, though,' he said, nodding towards her chosen seat.

'What, this?' she said, pecking him with kisses. She grinned. 'I shall be on excellent behaviour. But will she?'

'I guarantee it.'

'Kate and I could have been friends, if not for you.'

'Well, in spite of me, let's start that friendship. See if it works, because we'd make a good foursome – they're very safe company for me in what I do.'

'So long as you don't all start talking post-mortems and grisly crime scenes.'

He shook his head. 'That's for the ops room only.'

'Good. Because otherwise I'll start talking performance art,' she said, laughing when he gave a mock shiver of horror.

16

Kate and Hirem ushered Jonathan Parker into the interview room on Sunday morning. Under the guise of clerical staff, Sarah not only took his coat and outdoor things but also offered to fetch takeaway coffees. To Jonathan she might appear to be no one important, but Sarah's instincts had proven too reliable in the past. Jack, who was behind the two-way glass, observing, had no immediate suspicions about the man, who was obviously keen to be helpful, but he kept an open mind. He'd learned that in every interview they could discover something that might contribute to their case. He had thought it best to keep himself out of this conversation; as their meeting with Hannah Parker proved, it was intimidating to have such senior officers present, especially as this meet had been organised as a friendly chat to help police with their inquiries.

'I've hung up your stuff, Mr Parker. If I'm not around, just ask for it when you leave,' Sarah said, finding a rare smile as she pushed her glasses back up her nose.

'Thanks,' Parker said.

Hirem flashed her a grin and waited for her to leave. 'The stuff they call coffee here is atrocious. I thought we'd have something decent.'

Jonathan nodded. 'Perhaps we should have met in a café? This all feels a bit daunting, I have to say.'

'Sorry about the spare surrounds,' Kate said, keeping her tone light. 'And thank you for taking the time to come in and see us.'

'Well, when I spoke to DI Kumar, he said it could help.'

'Everything helps, Mr Parker.' Kate beamed.

'I was in London today anyway – I've got a meeting tomorrow – so it wasn't too hard to come by.'

'What do you do for work?' she asked casually.

'I work for Armourex, a company that sells security equipment. I'm the director of sales.'

'Oh, is that cameras?' Hirem asked.

Jonathan grinned easily. 'No, no. Body armour and the like. Things like stab vests, riot shields, special helmets and so on.'

'Cool.' Hirem grinned. 'Who are your clients?'

'Well, you guys, for starters,' Parker said in an ironic tone. 'Your riot squad, but also the Home Office, um . . . the UN,' he said, sounding like they should be impressed. Kate gave a nod of awe. 'But we also service private security contracts for people going into war zones, and then there's prisons. The full gambit.' He shrugged. 'Any operation that needs protective gear.'

'How did you get into that line of work?' Kate asked.

'Let's just say I knew the right people.' He looked sheepish. 'Turns out I'm good at it and I enjoy it, so everyone wins. Anyway, tell me how I can help.'

'We appreciate you coming in, Mr Parker,' Hirem said, sipping his coffee, relaxed and precisely as he'd been briefed.

'Please call me Jonathan,' he offered, grinning at them both.

This was going exactly as Jack had planned. 'Keep it all relaxed; we don't want him to clam up before we start talking about his dead son,' he'd said to Kate, and she'd agreed.

Hirem began. 'Well, firstly, we're mindful of raising the topic of your son's tragic death. Both of us would like to apologise up front for doing so.'

Jonathan nodded, more serious now, and took a sip of his coffee. 'No one should go through what we did. It was incredibly difficult, as you can imagine, especially for my wife . . . er, ex-wife, I should say.' He gave a faltering smile. 'We're not yet divorced, so I'm not sure of how to describe her status. Separated but friends. Do you have children, either of you?'

They shook their heads.

'I have a niece, though,' Hirem offered. 'She's two, and she lights up our family's world.'

Jonathan smiled sadly. 'Either of you married or with someone permanent?'

Again it was Hirem who fielded the question. 'I'm soon to be married.'

'Then you'll know that your partner's pain is yours, and vice versa. I couldn't separate my anguish from Hannah's.'

'Is that why you broke up?' Kate asked gently.

Jonathan nodded, looking down. 'Grief is not something that can be avoided. You just have to fucking wade through it.' He looked up, shocked. 'Sorry, forgive me.'

'It's okay,' Kate assured him. 'You lost the most precious thing in the world.'

Jack felt they were handling this interview well. Maybe the father could throw some light on why his son's death might provoke someone to hurt others.

'And more than just my boy . . . my wife too, the life we'd built.' He shrugged. 'Grief of this nature is all consuming. It breaks you.

It certainly broke us. We tried so hard to hold each other together, but there was nothing left in the end. The grief sucked us both dry. And I knew my only chance at sanity was to move away from Hannah. I didn't want our marriage to end. At first, I thought if I got out, it would give her a chance to think, to breathe, to be surrounded by family who might be able to give her more than I could.' He gave a sad laugh. 'Turns out I was right. Me leaving gave her overwhelming grief all the more space to let rip. I do sometimes wonder if I should have stayed and toughed it out for her, but Hannah disagrees. Actually, I saw her recently. She's looking good, so maybe she's slowly coming back.'

Both Kate and Hirem nodded, encouraging him to continue.

'I have high hopes that she'll find a steadier path now that a few years have passed.'

'We met her a couple of days ago,' Kate said with a soft smile. 'Hannah told us you've started building a life for yourself too.'

'I have.' He smiled back. 'I had to do something with myself, or Hannah and I might as well have made a suicide pact!' He looked away. 'Sorry, forget I said that. I wouldn't do that sort of thing . . . I suppose it's just a figure of speech to explain just how low we were feeling,' he said, 'but as much as I say I regret not sticking it out, I know in my heart we'd have taken each other down awful pathways of darkness. But being apart, we've had to work out how to survive. I've found a place to put Billy where he's always safe in my thoughts. Meeting Shelley was a surprise, so unexpected.'

'Shelley's your fiancée, is that right?' Kate asked.

Jonathan nodded. 'She's all brightness. I didn't think I deserved to find someone special again, and I'm not sure I'm giving her enough yet, but she certainly loves me and that makes me one of the luckiest men around.'

'When are you getting married?' Hirem asked.

'After the baby comes.'

'Oh,' Hirem said, acting surprised and delighted. 'Sorry, I didn't know. Congratulations.'

'Thanks.' Jonathan grinned. 'That too was a shock, and I didn't think I would be able to look forward to another child after . . . well, you know what happened. But I think she's going to bring a lot of hope and joy back into my life.'

'She?' Kate repeated.

'Yes,' Jonathan said. 'A daughter.' He looked genuinely happy.

'How does Hannah feel about that?' Kate asked.

'You'd have to ask her. She was initially shocked . . . and then, as Hannah is, she was incredibly generous and told me to go be happy for both of us, because she was struggling.' He frowned. 'Um, do you mind me asking, is all of this relevant? I mean, I really want to help but . . . this feels like a counselling session.'

When Kate and Hirem laughed, Jonathan did too. Jack knew Kate was ready to probe properly now.

Right on cue, she sighed softly. 'Actually, Jonathan, you've been incredibly open with us, thank you. This sort of background does paint a picture and you've been patient. The reason we're speaking with you and with Hannah is because of the recent death of Sally Holman. You've probably heard about it on the news?'

Jonathan nodded, his expression suddenly grave. 'I could hardly miss it. I spoke to Hannah immediately. It was a shock, especially as she was killed.'

Geoff entered the observation room to join Jack. 'Hi, mate.'

Jack nodded, not taking his eyes off the man being questioned.

'Anything?' Geoff asked.

Jack shook his head. 'Not yet. It's all been small talk, nothing we don't already know, and they've been circling. They're just closing in now. This guy is in security sales – body armour and the like. You know people in the riot squad, don't you?'

'Yep. Want me to ask around?'

'I think we should.' He nodded at the glass. 'Here she goes.' They fell silent as Kate made her first real prod.

'Jonathan, I'm sorry we have to ask this but it's a question everyone in connection with the case is being asked.'

'Okay,' he said, focused.

'Can you tell us where you were on January eighth?'

'Fuck! Am I a suspect? Sorry.'

Kate smiled. 'We asked Hannah the same question actually, not for a moment believing her to be a suspect.'

'But surely you wouldn't ask if you didn't think me or my wife had motive, right?'

'It's just due diligence,' Hirem added. 'Protocol. If you don't mind telling us where you were, then we can rule you out for further investigation and move on. It's a box ticked, mate.'

'Do you mind?' Kate asked, sounding so sincere and concerned it made Jonathan smile. Which made Jack and Geoff smile in the other room.

'She's good, isn't she?' Geoff said.

'One of the best.'

'Even I believe that tone.'

Jack grinned. 'And so does he.'

'I don't mind at all,' Jonathan answered. 'Er, let me think. That was the Friday before last, was it?'

'The Saturday,' Kate confirmed.

'Oh, okay. Um, the eighth . . . Do you mind if I check my calendar?'

'Go ahead,' Kate said.

They watched Jonathan flick back through his phone calendar. 'Yes, that's right. I had a meeting with a private security firm in Belgium and I overnighted.'

'You stayed in a hotel?' Hirem asked.

'Yes. The Concourse.'

'Thanks,' Hirem said, taking notes.

'You said you're the director of sales,' Kate said, speeding up the conversation now.

'That's right.'

'Isn't meeting with buyers a little below your pay grade?' Kate asked.

'No.' Jonathan laughed. 'I like to keep my hand in, and besides, there was a conference on. My meeting was held after a session where I was the speaker. And I should add, these buyers were directors of their companies.'

Kate nodded. 'Ahh, that makes sense. Hope you got the sale.'

'I certainly did,' Jonathan said. 'Several, in fact.'

'Perhaps I can take some details of that conference before you leave,' Hirem said.

'Sure. I can probably send you the program, if that helps?'

'Great.' Hirem smiled in thanks.

Kate placed her hands on the table. 'Well, Jonathan, I don't think we need to keep you any longer. Once again, we're grateful for your time and co-operation.'

'Not a problem. Glad to help.' He paused. 'Did it help?'

'As DC Kumar says, it just helps us to cross people off. Or tick a box – whichever way you like to look at it.' She smiled, warm, and Jack knew what was coming.

'Watch out,' Jack whispered to Geoff.

'Oh, and by the way,' Kate said, 'I hope you don't mind me asking, but how do you feel about Sally Holman's death?'

'How do I feel?' He frowned, faltering.

Kate nodded as if she hadn't noticed, waiting.

'A bit torn, I suppose. No, that's not right. I think what I mean is . . . I want to feel released. For years her name has provoked tears, rage, despair, for both me and Hannah. But since learning the news, there's no relief, no sense of release. It's just a sort of numbness.'

He paused, rubbing his face. 'I never wished her harm. Unlike my wife, I never zeroed in on Sally or laid all the blame at her feet. I think the hospital system let us down – I think I've accepted that it was staff shortages, long hours, unreasonable pressure on the nurses, et cetera, that caused Billy's death. Sally was an easy target for our fury. My wife isn't quite so rational, I'm afraid – what parent could be, when they've lost their child to such carelessness? But please don't blame her in this regard. I don't think she's capable of hurting anyone physically, even if perhaps she felt a moment's triumph at the news of the nurse's death. We're both thinking of the woman's family. The last thing we would wish on anyone is the torture we've been through, and that's exactly what they're facing now. Absolute torment for those children who've lost their mother.' He shook his head.

Kate nodded. 'Thanks for your time and candour, Jonathan. Okay to contact you if we have any more questions?'

'Sure.' He looked at Hirem. 'You have my contact number, right?'

'Right. Are you in the UK for the foreseeable future?' Hirem asked.

'Yes, yes, I believe so. The next overseas trip will be to the US and that's not until just after midyear.'

'Great, thanks.'

'I should warn you I am on the move a lot. Hate to think of myself as a travelling salesman, but when you boil it down, I guess that describes me.'

'I can't imagine we'll need to follow up. Just following protocol, as Hirem says.' Kate smiled.

'Okay, fine. And what about Hannah?'

Kate frowned in query.

'I'm sure you understand that this will have stirred up the past for her. We might be following divorce proceedings, but I still worry about her and want to know she's not . . .' He shook his head.

'Not what?' Hirem asked very gently.

'Look, in the past she's talked about suicide. I'm not suggesting for a moment that she's back in that space – I didn't sense it when we last spoke – but please tread very lightly around her. I'm sure you know what you're doing, but she's still, um, fragile.' He looked between them, slightly embarrassed. 'Sorry, I—'

'Don't be. We'll be very cautious,' Kate said. 'It's wonderful that you are both still so close.'

He nodded. 'Yes. We still share things. She told me there is potentially someone new in her life, actually. I'm happy for her.'

'Oh?' Kate said.

Behind the glass, Jack looked at Geoff. 'She didn't tell us it might be romantic.'

'Yeah, I think early days,' Jonathan replied. 'She said he's very kind, not pushy, also a bereaved dad. They met at a grief group or something. I don't know if it has any long-term potential, but I'd love to see Hannah smiling, perhaps looking forward to . . . well, not so much a new life, but a different one.'

Kate and Hirem nodded. They all stood, shook hands.

'Hmm,' Jonathan said, looking around. 'Your assistant took my coat and scarf.'

'I'll chase those down.' Hirem left to find Sarah.

'Come on, I'll walk you out,' Kate said, although she didn't move. 'So what's new in the body armour game?'

'Ah, always new tech. I hardly know where to begin. The riot gear that's coming out now, for instance, is pretty amazing.'

Jack looked at Geoff. 'Kate doesn't like him.'

'Yeah, she's keeping him back, still probing. I hope it's not that obvious to him.' He grinned. 'Why, though? She's never met him.'

'I think she privately sympathises with Hannah and doesn't think much of Jonathan as a husband. He didn't fight hard enough.'

'Hmmm. Judgey,' Geoff said, though he didn't argue.

★

Kate gestured for Jonathan to go through the door first. 'Tell me about the new body armour. What an interesting field to work in. What's so amazing about the new riot gear?'

She wanted to keep him talking; she'd learned from Jack that you never knew what else might slip out, especially once the formal interview was over. The man seemed genuine, but he hadn't ruled himself in or out during the conversation. And since both Hannah and Jonathan were saying they still essentially loved one another, she didn't believe he had done the right thing in moving out and moving on. He should have tried harder. Maybe they'd still be together – it could have been them having another child, not Shelley. Instead, Jonathan was looking at a good life ahead, while Hannah looked to be simply treading water, learning to keep her head above it so she didn't drown. It was a private opinion, though, and Kate had learned the hard way not to let it colour her attitude.

'I assume you've used vests?' he said as they walked down the corridor towards the main reception.

'Yes, of course. When we're going into any confronting situation, we wear them.'

He nodded. 'Well, then, you'd know they're not exactly comfy.'

She laughed. 'No. Especially for women. These tend to get in the way,' she said, pointing to her breasts.

Jonathan chuckled with her. 'Well, Kate, my company can now tailor a vest just for you.'

'My gosh, are you saying you offer haute couture body armour?'

'Indeed, and a perfect fit.'

She smiled, making sure she looked most impressed. 'Ah, here's your battle gear for the wintry day outside,' she said, noting Hirem's approach. 'So, can I contact you for a tailor-made stab vest?'

'Anytime.'

'Thanks again for helping with our inquiries.'

'Pleasure,' he said, and took his outdoor clothes from Hirem. 'Cheers, mate.'

Kate watched him wrap his scarf around his neck and dig in his coat pocket for a phone or maybe a beanie, before leaving.

Jack came up behind them. 'He seemed relaxed.'

'Pity he and Hannah couldn't make things work,' Kate remarked. 'It's obvious he still has a lot of feelings for her, and vice versa.'

'Grief is a monster,' Jack said. Kate looked down; she knew he had dealt with his fair share. 'Geoff's calling in some favours with people who might know him, just to get a further read. Hirem, let's get onto the Home Office Procurements, and perhaps we can tick that box and move on.'

'Good. What now?' Kate asked.

'Let's find out more about this new bloke in Hannah's life. She kept that pretty coy.'

Kate nodded. 'I was thinking just that.'

17

It had been years of grief and horror, but the despair had finally found an outlet. The idea had taken him by surprise when it erupted in his mind, building itself gradually over time until he'd just needed the final shove.

Hannah had given it to him.

She didn't know it . . . couldn't know it.

But she was the reason the killing had begun. He'd be killing another tonight.

And now he couldn't let anything get in the way of his final flourish, as he liked to think of it.

Initially he had considered using a car bomb, but as he began to hatch the plan, he realised it was too ambitious for one person to pull off alone. It would take an enormous amount of explosive to achieve what he wanted, and gathering the materials for that would be risky. To avoid raising suspicions, he would have to source his materials from a range of suppliers, which complicated matters and left loose threads for police to follow.

In the end, he settled on an incendiary device. Much simpler.

And easily transportable. He began to make a list of what he'd need.

Kitchen timer.

Cotton wool.

Fireworks.

His list lengthened to another half-dozen items and he smiled as he added 'x 2' next to 'timer'.

Then, a smiley face.

Alec Chalmers didn't know he was being followed but, as of two days ago, his new shadow had been watching his every move.

And plotting his death.

The best place to get him was after a late shift, the killer had surmised after an initial period of surveillance. The rest of London was mostly asleep at the end of Alec's shifts, certainly in his quiet street in Potters Bar.

He'd also whittled it down to the best day. The Saturday night shift was the one to target. It ended at 5 am on Sunday; at this time of year that meant tarry skies, when even the birds were not yet thinking of making their first calls of the morning chorus, so it was the right time to surprise him.

He'd worn black. Black trackpants, sneakers, hoodie and, in his pocket, a black balaclava. He followed Alec home in the car, expecting him to call into the Indian grocer, as he usually did. Right enough, he watched his prey park alongside the grocer, who was just opening the shop. This was the perfect lead time, so he sped on, parked some distance from the house, and jogged back to crouch in wait in Alec's small garden, behind the hedge. His victim wouldn't see him waiting in the darkness.

He heard a car arrive and peeped through the leaves. It was Alec. His heart thumped in his chest, adrenaline flooding through his body. It was a feeling he had recently become accustomed to, but it made him remember an identical feeling from his past. *Don't panic!* he told himself. *Remain calm and methodical. Stick to the plan. And when the time demands it, move fast, hard and confidently as you have before.*

His prey lived alone, and no pets either, so there was no rush, there would be no surprises . . . other than for Alec. He'd run the scenario through in his mind a dozen or more times.

It would work if he followed his plan.

He heard the car door open, a pause, then close. Another door was opened, presumably to grab the groceries, then closed too. A footstep or two, the beep that indicated the car had been locked and then more footsteps towards the gate. A cough from Alec. A distant bark. The first tentative call of the first bird into the loneliness. He registered it all in his heightened state of awareness. Now he heard the soft squeal of the small iron gate as his victim arrived home, no doubt tired and looking forward to a cuppa, and maybe some buttered toast, before climbing into bed. He knew Alec would be distracted, and he would use that lack of awareness to pounce.

Alec entered the small front garden. It was yet to become off-street parking, in the trend that had changed the look of neighbourhoods all over England.

Not yet, he told himself. *Stay patient and wait for the key.* Obediently, as though Alec were listening to his killer, he lifted the keys to the lock in the front door, his other hand holding the groceries and a messenger bag slung across his body. He was helpless. Oblivious.

Now with his prey's back to him, the killer rose from his crouched position and stealthily stepped onto the pathway, making sure with a quick whip of his head that no lights were on in opposite homes, no one looking out of a window and watching. He heard Alec turn the key and the soft sigh of the door giving way to its owner.

This was the moment.

Without hesitation now, he took two long strides and pushed his hands into Alec's back. Before the man could register a protest, he was on his knees just inside the door. His attacker stepped in, kicked him hard in the back so that Alec yelped and jumped forward, and then the door was closed.

Alec was now prisoner in his own home and his breathing time was limited.

But he didn't know this yet.

He was gabbling in shock – quite understandable, the killer thought, not that he cared.

'Shut up, Alec!' he said. It was spoken in a quiet voice, all the more menacing for it.

'How do you know my name?'

'Silence,' he said, withdrawing a knife from his zip pocket.

The darkness was now being diluted by the first brightening of morning and he knew Alec could see the knife well enough. He, meanwhile, was taking in the room.

'What possessed you to paint the walls this colour?' he asked.

Alec looked confused. 'The walls? I didn't.'

'Then who did?' the killer said, shaking his head.

'M-my parents did it as a surprise for me when I went on a conference.'

'Why?'

'Why what? The conference?'

'No, you idiot. Why would you let your parents do this?'

'I didn't know. I'd just bought the house. They'd contributed, so they probably felt they had a right to paint it whatever colour they chose. It's hideous, I know, but I haven't got the heart to change it and offend them. Besides, I don't have the money.'

'You won't ever need to worry about that,' the killer said, revolted by the near electric blue of the hall, made all the brighter by the white woodwork of the stairs and door. It felt like a Greek island but altogether wrong.

'Please,' Alec began, eyeing the knife, trying to sound reasonable. 'What do you want? I have a good watch and some money in my—'

'I'm not here for money or anything you own. I'm not a burglar, Alec.'

'What, then?'

'I'm the person who's going to watch you take your final breath.' He bent to pick up the litre bottle of mineral water that had spilled from Alec's grocery bag, exactly what was needed.

Alec began to cry. 'Why are you doing this? I don't understand.'

'Never mind. Go upstairs.'

'Please . . .'

'Do it, or I'll stab you here.'

'But you'll stab me up there,' Alec said, still rational, it seemed.

The killer nearly laughed. It was a reasonable objection. 'No, I won't. I'm going to give you a choice.'

'I don't—'

'Please don't tell me you don't understand again. Go upstairs or die here.'

Weeping hard now, Alec moved towards the stairs. The killer noticed Alec had wet himself with fear, so the air around them as they traipsed upstairs was thick with the smell of urine. Alec climbed with the heaviest of treads.

'Into your bedroom,' the killer said, 'and lie down.'

'What?'

'You heard.'

Robotically, Alec did as instructed, lying on his side. He was handed the bottle of water and his hands shook as he took it. 'What do you want me to do?'

'I want you to drink it.'

Alec frowned.

'And swallow these,' the killer added, pulling out a blister pack of sleeping tablets. They were a generic brand.

Alec stared at them. 'Valium?'

The killer wasn't surprised he recognised the drug name. 'That's right. It's a kind way to go, drifting off, relaxing into the long sleep. Easier than me slashing your throat, or opening an artery in your thigh or wrist, don't you think? Less messy for your friends to find. Or your parents, right?'

'Please don't do this.' Alec shook his head.

'We're doing it and we begin this moment. Choose. Sleep or slash – it's up to you.' The killer grinned, liking his phrasing and its alliteration. 'And don't even think about fighting back – I'm faster, stronger and a better scrapper than you could hope to be.'

Alec hesitated. 'Can you tell me why, at least?'

'No. I don't want to. Choose . . . I'll count to three. One . . .'

'I need—'

'Two,' he said calmly, raising the knife above Alec's body.

Alec twisted open the harmless drink that would kill him. It fizzed and spluttered a spray of water all over the bed; its topple in the hallway had shaken it up.

'You've wet yourself anyway,' the killer observed in a cold voice as Alec gave a groan of frustration. 'Right. Two at a time. Off you go.'

The striped curtains of grey and white were closed, so he switched on a small lamp next to the bed; its dove-grey shade contrasted gently with the soft charcoal walls. Really. What had possessed his parents to go with those frightful colours downstairs when clearly Alec was a neutral sort of guy? He glanced at the time. No one would think a light being switched on upstairs was odd given their neighbour worked nights. Good. Everything was going as planned.

He looked back at his prey. Tears streamed down Alec's contorted face as the first blister gave up its little yellow tablet. And then another.

'Do it.'

Trembling, barely able to get the first two pills into his mouth, Alec swallowed from the bottle.

'Show me,' the killer demanded, and Alec obediently opened his mouth; it was empty. 'Again.' Alec took another two tablets and they repeated the process. 'And again.'

'There's still time . . .' Alec pleaded.

'Not for you. Again.'

By the time the killer was satisfied, Alec had finished the bottle of sparkling water and had consumed two sheets of tablets that would relax his body into a permanent sleep. Without emergency help, there was no coming back from this.

And there would be no emergency help.

'I've just met someone nice. I had plans to travel next year,' Alec moaned. He'd be slurring shortly.

'You can travel in your dreams,' the killer said, not unkindly now, seating himself on the edge of the bed.

'Are you going to wait?'

'Of course.'

Alec closed his eyes. 'Thank you, I suppose.'

'It's not out of kindness. I want to ensure your heart has stopped.'

Alec wept briefly again. 'Can you ring my parents?'

'No.'

'Can I write a note . . . just to tell them I love them?'

'No.'

'I'm dying, right?'

'Yep.'

'So why not tell me why? No one's listening.'

That was true. And it would pass the time. 'A woman I care about is grieving because of you, that's why.'

Alec shook his head, baffled, but it was clear he was beginning to drift off. 'I didn't . . . I don't know what . . .' He looked lost and then confused. The drugs were taking effect.

'Yes, you did, and yes, you do. Go to sleep, Alec. Go to sleep for good.'

Alec's head drooped. 'Tea,' he murmured, losing track. 'So looking forward to a mug of tea.'

'Night, night, Alec.'

Alec's breathing slowed and then a snore began. His head was propped awkwardly on the pillow, but there would be no stiff neck for him tomorrow.

'You'll be stiff in every way, Alec,' the killer said softly, almost conversationally, standing to switch off the lamp, then opening the curtains and settling himself into a nearby chair.

It would be a while yet before he'd feel sure he could leave, that his man was dead and he could slip out before the day got going. He checked his watch. Yes, around twenty past six, he reckoned.

The snoring had stopped.

Now he would wait for Alec's breathing to follow suit.

18

On Monday morning in their room on level seven, Jack gestured towards Nat. 'I'm going to let Nat brief us; she's been surveilling Hannah Parker for us over the weekend. Nat?'

'Thanks, sir. Er, well, Hannah Parker leads a quiet, somewhat predictable life from the snapshot we have. She is a professional editor and works freelance for a number of the major publishers.' Nat scanned her notes, but Jack suspected she didn't need them. 'She makes regular visits to the post office and shops for groceries every other day at the local SPAR. For the whole time we've been watching, she has stayed in at night. Her family do not live in London – her parents are in Maidenhead and her siblings scattered in Hertfordshire and Buckinghamshire. She has recently acquired a dog – as you mentioned, sir – and she puts a lot of time into her pet, taking the dog for walks three times a day. The morning walk is at oh-seven-thirty, usually around the local neighbourhood. The midday walk is to a nearby park frequented by mothers and nannies with pushchairs and young children. She rarely chats to anyone, but throws a ball for the dog for about fifteen minutes. Around four, she goes for a much longer walk – about thirty to thirty-five minutes – usually making a beeline for the Heath, though she sometimes goes via the high street if she has stuff to post. Then she returns home, taking the same route daily. Mrs Parker had no visitors in the surveillance period, and rarely does, according to the neighbour I spoke to, except one. His name, we've found out, is James Clydesdale.'

Sarah interrupted with a clearing of her throat. 'Er, sorry to butt in. Nat asked me to do a cursory check into him this morning, so I haven't had a lot of time. He's Australian but lives in England. No criminal history that I can trace. He's an architect.' She nodded to say she'd finished.

Nat smiled. 'Thanks, Sarah. The neighbour said Mr Clydesdale regularly visits and they go out for walks together.'

'Did the neighbour get any sense of them being lovers?' Kate asked.

Nat shook her head. 'None. They walk alongside each other as friends might – a clear gap between them, which you don't tend to see with lovers, the neighbour said. She's never seen them hold hands, or even touch, but they're relaxed in each other's company.' She looked at Jack.

He nodded. 'Good. Anything else about this James fellow?'

'Er, only that he lives at Crouch End,' Nat said. 'We've got his ID and date of birth, too.'

'Married? Divorced? Girlfriend or boyfriend?' Kate asked.

The BBC News was on in the background, but the volume was muted. Jack glanced at the headline that was streaming beneath the woman explaining the weather; a body had been found in Potters Bar, but police were not treating the death as suspicious. He looked back to Nat as she answered.

'Obviously we weren't following Mr Clydesdale to and from his home, so I can't speak to his personal life.'

'Right,' Jack said. 'Let's find out more about him. Sarah, can you get onto that?'

She gave a nod.

His phone rang and he reached into his pocket. 'Okay, good work, Nat. A couple more days and that should do it for Hannah Parker.'

'Yes, sir.'

'Thanks, everyone,' he said to let them all get on. He answered his phone. 'Hi, Geoff. What's up?'

'Seen the news?' his friend asked. 'A body's been found. I'll be down in ten.'

Jack captured Kate's attention. Sarah was already busy rattling on the keys of her computer, searching for information, and Nat was heading out of the ops room for the surveillance suite. Kate walked over. 'What have you got?'

'Geoff's caught something in the net,' Jack said. 'He's on his way up. Another death.'

Kate blew out her breath, her face mirroring how Jack felt. 'We should be following this Clydesdale fellow,' Kate said.

'I agree. We should get him in for questioning, although I'm not ready to alert Hannah Parker that we're building this case. Just not convinced yet about her — what if she is involved?'

Kate looked at him with a dubious expression. 'You don't really believe she's killing these people, do you?'

Jack shrugged. 'No. But maybe she knows who is. If Billy Parker is seemingly at the core of this activity, that puts his mother front and centre . . . not as a murderer necessarily, but maybe she's been involved in the terrorism?'

Geoff arrived before Kate could answer, not bothering with pleasantries. 'Where's Sarah?'

Both frowned, then looked around. She was hunched over her keyboard as usual. 'Excuse me, Sarah?' Jack called.

She looked over, then stood and walked across the room.

'Does the name Alec Chalmers mean anything to you?' Geoff asked.

Jack watched her repeat the name silently. 'Yes,' she said, frowning. 'He's the blood guy who was on duty in the hospital laboratory the night that Billy Parker died. Why?'

Jack never failed to be impressed by her cognitive supremacy.

'He's also the guy found dead in his home two days ago by his parents,' Geoff replied.

'Fuck!' Kate murmured and heard the jangle of the swear tin. She groaned.

'Go pay your dues,' Jack said, before turning back to a waiting team. 'Listen up, everyone. We have a new lead.'

★

Hannah was proofreading a novel from a new writer that one of the majors had recently acquired. Her phone, on silent, suddenly lit up beside her and vibrated. She put down her red editor's pencil, brushing away some of the detritus of the rubber where she'd written something and changed her mind. It was Jonathan.

'Hi,' she answered, relieved. 'I knew you'd call.'

'Han, something really dark is happening here. Did you hear about Alec whatever his name is?'

'I know, I'm frightened.' She really was; she had been thinking about calling him ever since she'd heard the news. 'Is this killer or killers . . . whoever it is . . . Do you think they're coming after us too?'

'No!' He sounded shocked. 'Why would you say that? We've done nothing . . .'

'It's like everyone connected to Billy is being killed. Why wouldn't we be next?' Hannah argued.

'Shit.' He paused. 'I hadn't thought of us being in the frame. But why? I mean, we're the victims, right?'

Hannah shuddered. 'I can't even imagine what this person's interest in Billy is anyway. It's disturbing.'

'I have no idea either. But you can be sure if we're putting it together, then so are the police. I saw them a couple of days ago.'

'The police?'

'Yeah. It was the same Detective Carter who interviewed you, I gather; she asked me to come in, so I did.'

'Why would they want to speak with you?'

'Well, I imagine for the same reason they spoke with you. They obviously know about the link to Billy.'

'But . . .'

'I don't imagine they're suspicious of us, love. I think this is just the process. They interview everyone, mostly to get firm alibis and eliminate as many people as possible from the investigation. I mean, that's four deaths now – they can't not be making the connections we have. Don't be surprised if they want to speak to your friend, Tom.'

'Why would they want to speak to him?'

'I've just told you. They just need to tick people off. It will just be protocol, and he shouldn't worry—'

'His name's not Tom,' Hannah interrupted.

'What? I thought you s—'

'It's James . . . Jim.'

'I don't understand. Is this someone new, or—'

'No, look.' She sighed. 'I fibbed. I'm sorry. I was just trying to get you off my back about moving forward and all that. So I made him up. I wanted you to stop worrying about me and . . . oh, I don't know. It was stupid.'

'So Tom is just fiction?'

'Yes, I'm sorry. But Jim isn't. I met him after we had that conversation. It was just a chance conversation at grief group, but he's become a friend. He's safe and good company – exactly what I needed, just as you, my parents, my brother and sister . . . everyone has been telling me. We walk the dog together – you know I have a dog now?'

'Well, no, I didn't. But that's great. We always said we'd get one.'

'He's a rescue. Dad forced the issue, and I can't imagine being without him now, but that's not why I'm mentioning him. Jim looks after Chalky if I need to go somewhere, and he usually walks him with me of an evening. We meet for coffee sometimes – that sort of thing. Nothing more.'

'I'm happy you've made a friend. You don't have to sound guilty.'

'I'm not!' she said, becoming exasperated.

'Why are you angry, Han?'

'Because if what you say is correct, then they're going to want to interview Jim, I imagine.'

'Probably. Due diligence. Is that a problem?'

Hannah was worried. 'He won't like it.'

'None of us like it. What's he got to hide?'

'Nothing! I mean, I don't know,' she qualified, realising she sounded a bit mad. 'He acted strange when he heard the police were talking to me, but I can't blame him, really. He's been kind, but he probably doesn't want to get caught up in my problems.'

'Look, none of this is your problem. I don't really understand what's happening . . . our son died, and now someone seems to be picking off the people who were involved in his stay at the hospital? That's what it's looking like, right?'

'It does look like that. But how crazy,' she said, almost gasping. 'I don't get it.'

'It is crazy, but just between us,' he said, his voice quiet, 'it also feels a bit like divine justice.'

Hannah nodded, even though he couldn't see her. 'I'm not going to lose sleep over these deaths.'

'Don't say that aloud to anyone. Especially not the police.'

'I won't, I'm not daft.' She was annoyed again; did he think she was clueless?

'And I don't mean this to sound harsh, but I don't really care about Jim's awkwardness about talking to the police. I just care that you've got nothing to worry about.'

'That's, well, sweet of you.'

'It's the truth. I haven't stopped caring, you know.'

'I do know,' she said in a soft voice.

'So we've both co-operated; we told them both everything we could.'

Hannah paused. 'Not everything,' she said in a small voice.

'What do you mean?'

'I didn't tell them everything.' Now her tone was flat and dulled. She got up from the table. She really didn't want to have this conversation, but knew it had been waiting for her.

'What else is there to know?'

His question hung between them.

'Hannah?'

'I . . . well . . . I'm scared.' She began to cry.

'What's going on?'

'I've done some things . . . things that I'm deeply ashamed of. I wish I could take it all back. I didn't really mean anyone harm. I was just hurting so much, you know, in those early years. I'm not that person any more. I'm getting better at handling my pain, and I don't feel the desire to behave like that now. It was a sort of crazy time, me acting out of control.'

'Hannah, love, you need to explain.'

She paused again. How could she tell him? 'Where are you?'

'I'm here in London.'

'Still?'

'Yes, I'm working.'

'Can you come around?'

'Not immediately.' He sounded worried. 'I have meetings. How about in a couple of hours?'

She sniffed. 'Okay. Thanks. I'll explain then.'

A few hours later, Jonathan stared at Hannah in silent disbelief. What had she been thinking?

'Say something . . . anything,' she said, dabbing at tears.

'I'm too stunned. You of all people. You, who makes sure the squirrels have food in the feeders, and who volunteered for Meals on Wheels. And you've been out there hurting people?' He shook his head and stood. She reached for him, but he stepped away. 'Hannah, what the fuck?'

'I didn't actually hurt anyone . . . well, I know a child got sick, and some lips blistered and the needles could have caused an injury . . . but they didn't. Nothing really bad happened.'

'Well done,' he replied, helplessly sarcastic. He ran his hand through his hair.

She looked chastened. 'I know, I know . . . but I was out of my mind. I've stopped, I promise. I stopped ages ago. I'm so much better now. But then there was the mushrooms.'

'Hang on . . . What about the mushrooms?'

'Someone died! But that wasn't me, I swear! I had nothing to do with the mushrooms scare. You have to believe me.'

He looked back at her, aghast. 'Okay. I really don't know what to say.'

'Say that you forgive me.'

'It's not for me to forgive, Hannah. I mean, the baby formula . . . Imagine what that could have—'

'Jon, I know! I came to my senses. I stopped.'

Now he paced the room, thinking. She'd been so reckless. 'What if the police are watching you? What if they've got some sort of lead?'

'How could they? They would have found me back then, wouldn't they?'

'You've got to turn yourself in.'

'No!'

'Yes! Own up before they arrest you.'

'Don't be crazy. They were just talking to me to help them with their investigation.'

'Their investigation *into* you!' He whirled around to face her, pointing a finger.

She looked terrified. 'All right. Calm down. Let me think about it.'

'Well, don't take too long, Hannah, or you and your friend Jim are going to be marched into the nearest clink. They won't take any chances, not when these murders all point back to Billy – to us.' He sat down again but stood up immediately; he couldn't stay still.

'We aren't murdering anyone, Jonathan.'

'They don't know that, and if they're looking into us, they might already know you were behind the supermarket and chemist scares . . .' At her despairing groan, he added: '*Might,* I said. They *might* be building a case against you and gathering evidence. You yourself said they were pretty heavy-hitting detectives – ask yourself why they would send such senior people if they weren't smelling some sort of rat? No, Hannah, own up to those events before they nail you. They will go easier on you, given the circumstances.'

'Will I go to jail?' she bleated.

'I don't know, love.' He hugged her. 'You don't deserve to, given all you've had to face, but the courts may not see it from our perspective. Then again, they might see a woman who was melting down in grief. But you'll be doing yourself a favour if you own up now before they arrest you. Go on. You need to call that detective. Do it now.'

Jack was reading the full report on the latest death and realising how hungry he was. He checked his watch; Lou would be eating alone again this evening. But then he was pushing his whole team; everyone was working back-to-back days, none of them taking much in the way of breaks. He had insisted all but the seniors head to their homes for dinner with their families or friends.

'Completely different MO,' he said, sighing.

'Doesn't mean it's not the same killer,' Kate replied, looking up from her file and stating the obvious.

He made a face at her. 'I realise that, but nothing about this death connects it with the strangulations,' he said.

'Other than the link to Billy Parker. He fits with that group of women.'

'It's too much of a stretch in my mind to believe this is a coincidence,' Geoff chimed in, closing a file he had been poring over.

'You know I don't believe in coincidences,' Jack growled.

'Then he's another victim of the same killer,' Kate concluded.

Jack rubbed his eyes. They were going around in circles, but she was right. 'When can we have the full pathology report? Maybe some forensic evidence for us.'

Geoff shrugged. 'I'm pushing. Hopefully first thing tomorrow.'

Sarah came over and hovered, not wanting to interrupt. 'Hi, Sarah, still here?' Jack asked wearily.

'Nothing pressing to get home to, sir,' she said and found a smile. 'Bit more action here, though. We just got some information I've been chasing on the needles used in the strawberry scare.'

'Really?' Kate said. 'What made you chase that down?'

Sarah gave a shrug. 'We seemed to be drawing a blank on the terror acts while murders aplenty were happening, so I started to think in micro, going over every tiny detail from the original cases.'

'And?' Kate asked, intrigued.

'Well, turns out the needles that were used in the supermarket scare are not produced any more. They're vintage. Probably from the late fifties and early sixties, forensics are suggesting. I've got the brand name and serial numbers, but their age is far more relevant, perhaps.'

'That's quirky,' Jack remarked. 'How so?'

Kate looked confused. 'Couldn't they have just been picked up from a vintage shop? That would potentially throw anyone off the scent. Anyone could have bought them, right?'

'Definitely a possibility,' Sarah agreed. 'Except they're quite specialised. They're quilting needles, and what popped into my head was . . . well, when we were in the tearoom with Joan, you were telling us about the beautiful quilt that Hannah Parker had in her sitting room.'

The three senior detectives listening to Sarah held her gaze, collectively astonished, as they processed what she'd just said.

'Bloody hell,' Kate finally murmured. 'You're right. Hannah said she'd learned her quilting from her granny and that she had all of her sewing gear.'

Before Jack could even begin the instruction to get over to Hannah's house and bring her in for questioning, Hirem appeared.

'And you haven't gone home either?' Jack sighed.

'I was just on my way.' The younger man shrugged. 'Er . . .' He took them in with one sweeping glance and pointed over his shoulder. 'Jonathan and Hannah Parker are downstairs. They've got something to tell us.'

19

The Parkers had turned up at New Scotland Yard and shown Jack's card. Jack had met the couple downstairs, organised visitor passes and taken them to a sparse grey interview room in what was known as the Back Hall. He introduced himself to Jonathan and gave Hannah a sympathetic smile.

'How can I help?' he asked.

Jonathan began. 'Er, look.' He nervously ran a hand through his hair. 'We're here because my . . . um, Hannah has something to say.'

'I want to confess,' she blurted out. 'It was me. The strawberries, the baby formula, the—'

'Wait,' Jack began, taken aback. 'Mrs Parker, before you say anything else, would you like to have a solicitor present?' She needed to understand the gravity of what she was doing.

The Parkers looked at each other, unsure. 'She's admitting it, so she probably doesn't need legal advice,' Jonathan reasoned. 'Go on, Hannah. Just tell them what you told me.'

'Mr Parker, just hold up,' Jack said gently. 'We can organise a solicitor to be present for this initial interview, and there will be no cost involved. I would advise having one.'

Jonathan nodded and, finally, so did Hannah.

Jack was relieved. As much as he wanted to hear what they had to say, he had to do things by the book. 'Your interview will not be conducted here. Please wait while I make some calls.'

It didn't take much more than ten minutes to make the necessary arrangements. Kate came down to meet him. 'This is happening?' She looked as surprised as he felt.

'Seems so. Let's take her to Belgravia Police Station and conduct the interview there.'

They got the nod that the car was ready, and Kate opened the door to the interview room. 'All right, Hannah. You will be taken in a squad car down to a local police station, and the interview will be conducted there.'

'What happens then?' Jonathan asked.

Kate held his gaze. 'If you leave now, you can probably see her before her interview, in case she's taken into custody.'

'You mean I can't travel with her? She's—'

'Sorry, Mr Parker, you may not. It's protocol.'

He stared at her with so much indignation that Jack, having watched the exchange, stepped in. 'This is normal police procedure, Mr Parker. I'll travel with her; she will be safe, and I will keep her calm.'

It took another thirty-five minutes before they were seated in one of the interview rooms at Belgravia, an anxious Jonathan in the waiting area. A solicitor had arrived just after them. Jack knew and liked her. She was of Sikh heritage and had married a Welsh police profiler with whom Jack had worked on several occasions. They made a handsome couple and had two children. The boy had his mother's fine looks, and the girl had her father's infectious laugh and height.

'Hannah, this is your solicitor, Jasminda Smithson. I'll leave you both to have a talk and be back shortly.'

'Call me Jas.' The woman smiled at Hannah, then nodded at Jack.

He and Kate made a cuppa, then returned fifteen minutes later. Jack switched on the recorder, introduced himself, Kate, Hannah Parker and the solicitor.

'So, Mrs Parker, I gather you have some information on a series of domestic terror events that you wish to share.'

He watched her cast a glance towards Jasminda. 'Domestic terror,' she repeated, sounding shocked.

'It's how it's classified by the police, Mrs Parker. I am speaking to you today in my role for Counter Terrorism.'

She visibly shook at this, again looking anxiously towards her solicitor.

Jasmine nodded sympathetically now to her client. 'Be sure, Hannah. As I counselled, you are not obliged to say anything.'

'I want to. I promised my husband.'

Jack looked at Hannah. 'Whenever you're ready,' he said, with a smile of soft encouragement.

One after another she confessed to the series of scares, her time-lines and locations matching up with the crimes they knew about. Her voice was calmer than Jack expected; he got the impression it was a relief to finally share what she'd done.

'It was a psychosis,' she said finally. 'I know that now. I barely recognise myself from that time. I was overcome with rage — no other way to describe it — and while I think there's still some residue of it, I'm learning how to make peace with my loss — our loss,' she corrected, smiling sadly and briefly. Her eyes filled with tears but she didn't let them fall, wiping them away quickly. 'No one could see or hear my pain — or so it felt. Billy became a statistic so quickly. Everyone had forgotten he was a child . . . our child.'

Jack sensed Kate wanted to jump in and gave her a subtle nod.

'And you stopped feeling driven to hurt others when, Hannah?'
Kate asked.

She gave the date. It matched up with the baby formula scare,
when the child going to hospital had hit the news. 'And I haven't
felt a desire to behave like that again since. I see a psychologist and
I've started attending a grief group, and while I don't necessarily
enjoy being around all those miserable people, I feel keenly aware
now that I'm not the only mother going through such an experience. At the time it felt like it had only ever happened to me, and
I had nowhere to turn and no one who understood what it felt
like. That's why I did those terrible things.'

Jack believed her; everything had the ring of truth he'd learned
to trust.

'As I mentioned, I still see a psychologist on a monthly basis,
which I find extremely helpful. She can track my progress, and she
describes me now as a new person, different from the broken one
she met back then.'

'And you are sticking to the claim that you had nothing to do
with the toxic mushrooms?' he asked.

'My client has—' Jas began in a cautionary tone, but Hannah
interjected.

'Vehemently!' she confirmed. 'That was not me. I know I said
I really couldn't think straight back then, but I do know I never
set out to kill anyone. My intention, I truly believe, was to create
some attention because everyone had forgotten about Billy. He was
already old news within days of his death, and soon after that just a
vague memory from the headlines. And yet I was living every day
as though it was the first one without him. I lost my child, I lost
Jonathan, I lost my ability to function and then I lost my sanity,
clearly. My doctor refused to prescribe any more sleeping tablets.
Everyone was deserting me . . . except the ghost of Billy. I suppose

I needed people to know what the fear and grief felt like, but I did not put poison mushrooms into a greengrocer or supermarket, and you are welcome to check my diary and anything else I can provide to prove that I was nowhere near the locations where they occurred. I have never been to Bristol in my life.'

'All right, Hannah,' Kate said, trying to soothe her. 'Last time we spoke you said your friendship group had fallen away since you and Jonathan separated.'

Hannah nodded.

'No new friends made?' Kate probed. Jack knew she was waiting for Hannah to admit to the relationship with James Clydesdale.

'Well, I think I mentioned meeting someone at grief group? A lovely man, but we're just mates, really, I hasten to add,' she said, glancing her solicitor's way, who nodded. 'He's a gentle person who has had his own fair share of terrible trauma.'

'Oh, yes?' Kate asked.

'Yes. It helps to talk to someone who's been through a similar loss. Jim lost two children to SIDS, the poor man, but I think he and his wife suffered some miscarriages as well, so it's been a long, hard journey.' She shrugged. 'He understands better than either of you, or indeed any psych or well-meaning doctor, what I'm going through . . . what we've both gone through, though Jonathan handles it better. He's building a new life, but both Jim and I are sort of stuck, alone with our misery. I guess we've become a grief group of two. That's how he thinks of us anyway.'

'Forgive me for mentioning this, but you said it's not a romantic relationship, is that right?' Kate asked.

'Right. As much as Jonathan would like me to stay open to the possibility of starting again with someone, I'm not ready to consider any such thing. And Jim knows this and agrees; we've discussed it openly. All he wants is to be my friend. We usually meet for coffee, and we walk my new dog most evenings together. He's safe to be around, and having him there makes me feel safe on the Heath at night too. I don't even know whether I'd be attracted to him in different circumstances, or him to me. But we are good for each other, sharing our friendship . . . and our pain.'

Kate nodded. 'I can see that. And he lives where?'

'Er, Crouch End. He's planning to build a new home for himself there. I've not seen where he lives.'

'Have you told Jim about your secret activities?'

Hannah hesitated. 'He won't like me saying this but, yes, I told him everything.'

'Why won't he like us knowing this, Hannah?' Kate pressed.

'I don't really know. He was oddly quiet when I told him, and he didn't respond how I imagined – I expected revulsion, but instead he was kind. He seemed to understand my motivation and he impressed upon me that I'd stopped, and maybe that was enough.'

'Do you think it's strange that he didn't tell you to come forward to the police, or report you himself?'

Hannah thought for a moment. 'He didn't react like Jonathan did, that's for sure. I told my husband today and here I am. He was horrified and insisted I turn myself in. But Jim is really generous in how he treats people. Like I said, I expected him to push me away in horror, but he can see that I've come through this trauma, and I am no longer any danger to anyone. Maybe I shared it with him to unburden myself, in the hope he would bring in the authorities, but he didn't seem to think it was a good idea . . . He seemed to accept my behaviour as almost understandable under the circumstances. I was grateful at the time, but I do feel an enormous weight has been lifted for telling you. Whatever the outcome.'

They'd reached a natural break in the interview. Jack glanced at Jas, who gave a small nod. 'Mrs Parker, you've been cautioned and now I am arresting you under Section 38 of the Public Order Act,' he said. 'You do not have to say anything, but it may harm your defence if you do not mention when questioned something on which you later rely in court. Anything you do say may be given in evidence.'

As he outlined the offence she was being arrested for, Hannah began to softly weep. Kate summarised for the tape and clicked it off.

'What will happen now?' Hannah asked tearily. Kate held out a box of tissues and the woman took one but simply scrunched it in her hands, looking down.

'You'll be taken into custody and will appear before the magistrate tomorrow morning, I suspect,' Jack said gently.

'I'll ensure you're seen with some urgency,' Jas said. 'I have a really good barrister in mind, and we'll apply for bail immediately.'

'I have no doubt it will be granted,' Jack added.

'And then a date for your hearing will be set,' Jas said.

Hannah looked up. 'A trial?'

Jas shook her head. 'I doubt it. The police will prepare evidence and hand that over to the Crown prosecutor and if it all matches up with what you've explained, then your admission will work very much in your favour, Hannah. My experience tells me a good magistrate will likely hear your guilty plea and make a decision then.'

There was a knock, and they all stood as a Belgravia police officer entered the room. 'Mrs Parker, will you come with me, please? I'll take you to the custody sergeant.'

'I'll be right with you, Hannah, go ahead,' Jas urged. They watched her leave, and then Jas turned to Jack and Kate. 'Such a sad case.'

'Very,' they said together.

'We'll do everything we can to push for a lenient sentence,' Jas assured them.

Jack nodded. 'We'll do whatever we can from our end too.' Jas left, and Jack turned to Kate. 'So we have our culprit for three of the events, but that only heightens the problem that a killer is on the loose – maybe more than one.'

★

Kate and Jack went out to talk to Jonathan.

He stood up, agitated. 'I can't see her?'

'Not this evening,' Kate said. 'Tomorrow, I'm sure.'

'How long is this all going to take?'

'All up? Could take weeks, months,' Kate said. 'But she'll be at home, hopefully. We think bail will be granted immediately.'

'And the media?'

Kate grimaced. 'Buckle up.'

Jack thought that was harsh, and it won a hard gaze from the husband. 'Mr Parker . . . Jonathan,' he said quickly, 'Jasminda is recommending a good barrister. Take her advice – she's already highly invested in making sure Hannah is treated leniently. In the meantime, maybe organise for Hannah to move to her parents', help get the heat off her. The media's going to be all over this.'

Jonathon gave a tight nod. 'Will she go to prison?'

'Hard to say,' Kate said. 'She created a lot of panic in the community through her malicious activities. There's also the loss of business, inconvenience, the police time invested . . .'

Kate was giving him no quarter and the man's face hardened. Jack offered more hope. 'The barrister will ensure the court looks kindly upon the fact that Hannah has confessed freely, is contrite, and can probably show details from her psychologist that she was unwell at the time of the offences. The fact that she accessed all the right help will work in her favour, and, if it helps, I do believe her when she says she is no longer a threat to any member of the public.'

'Do *you* think they'll put her behind bars, Detective Hawksworth?'

'The Crown may not press for a custodial sentence,' Jack said, glancing at Kate sternly enough that she understood to back off. 'They may give a suspended sentence, given the circumstances, or maybe some community work.'

'Do you have to leave London yet, Mr Parker?' Kate asked, making sure her tone was light.

Jonathan frowned. 'Why?'

Kate smiled. 'Just thinking of the dog.'

Jack didn't believe for a moment that was her motivation.

'Oh. Right. I'd better plan to stay a couple of days, then.' Jonathan shook his head. 'I should say, no one is more shocked than I am about this. Hannah has the kindest heart; she didn't deserve what happened to her. I have to believe it's the only reason she'd do something like this . . .'

'No one deserves grief like that,' Kate said. 'But it happens, and not everyone sets out to create mass public anxiety. You're over-looking the fact that people were injured, and that baby could have died. Many more could have become ill, and that's not something the court can overlook.'

'I suppose,' he said, staring at Kate. Jack saw he was holding back anger. 'No sympathy, then?'

'Plenty,' Jack assured, 'but it's not our job to pass judgement. It was right of you to encourage her to come forward; it will help enormously when a decision is being made about her punish-ment.'

'I had no choice. I'm utterly stunned, but I knew it was the right thing to do. Um, what about this fellow of hers, this Jim?'

'What about him?' Jack asked. *This could be interesting*, he thought.

'Is he being interviewed?'

'Do you think he should be?'

Jonathan simply shrugged.

'Why would we interview him about crimes Hannah committed before they met?' Kate asked.

'Why? Because he's a stranger spending time with my wife.'

'You're separated, Mr Parker, and Hannah is capable of making her own decisions,' Kate said.

'Of course she is, but she's still vulnerable.'

'All women are when it comes to men,' she said.

Jonathan looked frustrated. 'Detective Carter, forgive me for caring enough about the woman I was married to. If Billy hadn't died we'd likely still be together.' They'd reached an awkward impasse, but Jonathan let it go. 'Look, don't get me wrong, I think this Jim guy has been good for Hannah. She hasn't had a friend for a long time, but it does seem a bit strange he didn't react to her admission as perhaps I did, or most others would.' He shrugged, looking back to Jack. 'That's why I was asking.'

'Well, we'll see. It depends if we need any further information,' Jack replied, deliberately keeping it vague.

Jonathan nodded. 'Okay, well, is there anything else you need me for? Can I leave?'

'You can leave,' Kate said. 'We know where to find you if we have any further questions.'

He left.

Jack turned to Kate. 'What was that about?'

'What do you mean?'

'Were you deliberately needling him?'

She shrugged. 'I think I was, yes.'

'Because?'

'I don't know. I'm angry that he left her. He didn't fight hard enough. Maybe none of this would have happened if she'd had him at her side – it's fairly obvious that he still loves her. So him marrying again is curious.'

Jack thought it was clear. 'What about the pregnancy . . . doing the right thing?'

Kate shrugged again. 'Just as heinous, in my book. Busy making more babies, falling in love again, blah blah.'

'That's wildly unfair.' Jack meant it. Was the man supposed to live in grief forever?

She ignored him. 'And yet he keeps hanging around her. She

said she saw him only recently and now he's back again. He must have a very understanding fiancée, is all I can say.'

'Kate, he did Hannah a favour by urging her to make the admission.'

'I agree.' She didn't say 'but', so he left it.

'Let's meet James Clydesdale,' Jack said. 'I want to know if we can tick him off our list of suspects for these murders that we now have to focus on.'

'Are we still on the case?'

'If I have any say we will be. Besides, we haven't solved the mushroom case yet, either. Go make the call and let's set up a chat for tomorrow.'

Jack was on the phone to the commander of CTC within thirty minutes of Hannah Parker being taken away for her night in custody. He used the landline to his boss's home out of politeness.

'Barton residence.'

'Mrs Barton?'

'It is.'

'It's Detective Superintendent Jack Hawksworth here. I wonder if I might steal a minute of the commander's time? I promise he'll want to hear what I have to say.'

He heard a soft sigh. 'Please make it good news, Detective. He's been in a shocking mood all weekend.'

'It is,' he assured her.

A couple of clicks later, he heard Harry Barton's voice. 'What have you got for me, Hawksworth, that has torn me away from my first evening at home with my wife in a week?'

'Forgive me, sir. I do have news. I have an admission for you regarding the various terror incidents, from Mrs Hannah Parker, the mother of Billy Parker, who died tragically due to a mix-up with a blood transfusion several years ago.'

'Bloody hell! The mother?' He sounded understandably shocked. There was a silence and then a sigh. 'We're sure?'

'One hundred per cent for three of the events. We'll do all the follow-up, of course, but everything she has admitted to during our interview lines up with the dates and details we have. She came in tonight of her own accord, and we have it all formally recorded with her solicitor present.'

'Excellent!'

'I conducted the interview, sir, and I should add that the toxic mushrooms are not part of that confession. I'm afraid that case is still outstanding.'

'Do you think she was content to admit to mischief but wants to avoid admitting to the killing?'

'That's a possibility, sir, but I have to say I believed her. She was adamant about having nothing to do with the mushrooms and is co-operating fully for us to establish her alibi in this regard.'

'So a copycat, then?'

'Possibly,' Jack said, though he wasn't convinced.

'Why did she come forward now?'

'We'd interviewed her, sir, in our initial probe, because of the recent spate of murders that link to this case. I think she was frightened. And, to be fair, her husband – they're in the process of divorce – forced her hand when she told him of her activities. It was sound advice to get her to come forward, but we were closing in anyway; new evidence had just started to point us squarely at her.'

'Jack, can I make a statement to the media that we now have a person in custody for the public acts of terror?'

'You could,' he said carefully. 'But my inclination would be to tread more safely and say we have someone helping us with our inquiries. That gives my team a chance to solidify all the evidence with checks and double-checks on dates and aspects of her admission. And we're still chasing down leads regarding the mushrooms.'

'Okay, well, that's positive enough, I suppose, especially as we know we have our man . . . or woman, in this instance.'

Jack could hear the satisfaction in Barton's voice and didn't want to let the moment pass. 'Sir, um . . . Hannah Parker was in a state of high anxiety and despair when these events took place, grieving for her young son. I don't believe for a second that she's an inherently bad person.'

'So you're saying don't throw the book at her?'

'I doubt she'd ever have done what she did had the system not let her family down so horrifically. If anything, I'd say she needs continued counselling, not prison.'

'We'll leave that to others to decide, but I hear you, and I will make my recommendations. For now, good work. You've lived up to Carol Rowland's high opinion.'

'Thank you, sir. My team is now heavily involved in the murders that link into the terror acts and so we'll continue with that – and the mushrooms. I trust you have no problem with that?'

'That will depend on Carol – you'll be answering to her. But I can't imagine she wouldn't want her ace on the job.'

'Thank you, sir, I'll let you get back to your evening.'

Jack immediately rang Carol to pass on the news.

'I can only imagine how happy the CTC commander is,' she said. 'Hard to impress Barton, but I suspect you have.'

'We got a lucky break.'

'No. I know you didn't. Your team studied the small stuff – it's always in the detail – and drilled right down and saw it when the clue bobbed its head.'

'Actually, ma'am, what we'd been picking up was the first break on the murder cases – a clear link in the pathology of all three strangulations. We really were no closer to the perpetrator of the community terror acts op until earlier this evening when Sarah worked out something outrageously smart about the needles that were used in the strawberries . . . and, if I'm honest, she wouldn't have picked up on that if Kate hadn't mentioned that Hannah Parker was a quilter who'd learned her craft from her grandmother.'

'Very cluey operators, those two. I'm impressed. So I suppose Commander Barton is breaking the news to the media right now?'

'I would think so. Can't blame him. I asked him to play it down for now, though.'

'Good. I think I can guess what's coming next.'

'Can you, ma'am?'

'Yes, I suspect there's unfinished business for you and your team.'

He smiled into his phone. 'There is.'

'Go ahead. You have my full support. Is Geoff Benson comfortable with it?'

'I believe so, ma'am. I think he's keen for all of us to keep going as we have been. We're no closer to finding the killer than we were before the op—'

'I meant with you as lead,' she interrupted. 'You are the most senior detective.'

'Geoff's a pro,' he said, meaning it. 'And, like me, he just wants this killer caught. He's the one who suggested it.'

'You say we're no closer, but it's my understanding that the perpetrator is somehow connected to Billy Parker's death.'

'It's a presumption. Each of the victims can be linked to Billy, but—'

'But neither of us believe in coincidence.'

'No.'

'Well, then you are onto something. Keep pushing, Jack.'

20

The killer looked at his list. It was all ticked off except for one final element. He smiled. The item was old-fashioned tech, but it would be effective.

He began to search online. There were none available through normal retailers, which was probably a good thing, because they'd keep detailed records, but eBay was happy to whisk him through to some providers of what he hunted: a once-common camera accessory. He hadn't seen one of those glacier-blue cubes since childhood, when Uncle Edgar would bring all his camera equipment over to the house. He was the only one in the family who could afford such gear, so he took charge of recording family events. The German Leica camera he used to bring had eventually given way to the new automatic, smaller boxes of magic, along with the modern flash cubes. Much easier to use and requiring no other equipment, they fitted directly to the cameras, especially the new-fangled instamatic ones.

But as a child he'd loved those days of the long set-up: the tripod, the big camera, making sure the 35mm Kodak film was all wound in properly. They'd take an age to sort themselves out: the women at the front on chairs, children at their feet or on their laps, looking awkward or smiling far too broadly. The men would gather behind, all in white shirts and ties. Uncle Les usually had a pint glass in his hand. A small space would be left for Uncle Ed, who would fiddle with the camera, checking the exposure or that the flashbulb was connected and ready, before slipping back into the line-up, a rubber bulb at his feet. Then he'd cue everyone: 'Say cheese!'

'*Cheeeeeese!*' they'd chorus, and he'd step firmly on the bulb, connected by a line to the camera. The change in pressure depressed the button to click the shutter and set off a flash. Its bulb was filled with magnesium filament that burned unbearably bright, meaning everyone was blinded momentarily and they all had red, mirrored eyes when the photo was developed.

His older cousin Frankie would wait until Uncle Ed was in swift retreat, back to his place, and then step on the bulb, capturing a shot of everyone looking away, not yet smiling, and Uncle Ed a blur of motion. The family would sigh, groan, curse Frankie and it would all start again.

They were funny days.

Good days.

He looked again at the seller's profile. They didn't have a very high rating, but that's what he wanted; this seller might be more inclined to shy away from any police inquiry if they weren't entirely above board. An extra layer of protection, he hoped.

He bought a pack of five old-style flash cubes from the 1970s, whose role in photography was essentially to explode themselves. With four flashbulbs around the cube, they were filled with zirconium foil and oxygen gas. Few of the millions of households that had used them with their cheap Kodak cameras would have known it, but once the zirconium foil caught alight, it burned with a brilliant brightness, and at the base of the cube was a tiny primer of fulminate – essentially a friction trigger, not unlike how a cap gun worked.

Essentially, he'd just bought five small and legal explosives for under ten pounds.

Now he just had to wait for them to arrive. Shouldn't be more than three days at worst, he thought. It was time to build what they would attach to, but first he had someone to see.

That someone was Janine Bowes. She was coming off a late shift that, as usual, hadn't ended on time, dragging on for another twenty-five minutes while she sorted out a problem for one of the patients.

Her feet ached. She was looking forward to a soak in the bath, she thought, and a nip of Scotch – her favourite tipple at any time – on this cold night. She'd have to dig around in the fridge and find something to cook, though . . . Actually, she'd frozen some pea soup last weekend. That would be perfect with some toast. She could thaw the soup while she bathed and then heat it up in the microwave while she browsed for something to watch.

'*Luther*,' she said into the darkness as she closed the door of her car and the overhead light clicked off. 'Season two . . . yippee!' she murmured to herself as she fiddled to put her key into the ignition. 'Now which Scotch goes with *Luther*? A nice fifteen-year-old Glenfiddich or a . . .'

'I prefer Glenmorangie myself,' a man's voice said, making her jump. A figure loomed out of the darkness of the back seat. Something was looped around her neck and she was pulled savagely backwards. No sound could escape, and Janine could feel her eyes beginning to bulge. She heard a distant drumming with no idea that it was her feet, desperately kicking as the man pulled harder and then harder still, tightening the sensation at her throat. She could hear the jangle of a heavy metal clasp or something banging against her headrest. She wondered whether he was using a dog's lead and, as she began to lose consciousness, also why she was wasting her thoughts on such a weird notion.

Did she die before she blacked out?

No one could know. Janine couldn't tell the police anything when her body was found the next day, slumped in the front seat of her car as the hospital staff car park began to fill up for the day shift.

Hannah had been granted bail, as expected, and she was back in Gospel Oak, at home with her husband. It all felt surreal.

'You look hollow-eyed,' Jonathan said, gently wrapping her quilt around her shoulders before placing a mug of steaming tea in front of her.

'Thanks,' she murmured. 'It's like the good old days.' It was so nice to have someone take care of her.

'Except you've moved the furniture around,' he remarked.

'When I got that new TV, I wanted to mount it on the wall, rather than have it on a unit taking up a lot of room.'

'Looks good. The whole place looks good. The garden is brilliant.'

She sighed. 'Dad took out the swing and slide, donated them to the church. He also got rid of the sandpit and reshaped all the beds. It does look lovely.'

Jonathan kept going, seemingly keen to preserve the lighter mood. 'I've only just noticed that you've finally painted the shed yellow, just as you always wanted to.'

She found a smile. 'I wouldn't call it yellow, Jon. It's really just a buttery cream. That colour is going to look really nice once the creeper grows around it. I tolerated the blue because I was growing old with two boys in my life. But then one died and the other one left.'

That deflated the mood.

'I'm sorry,' she said, grimacing. 'Thanks for taking care of Chalky for me. I just don't kn—'

'It's fine, Han. He's a lovely little pup. And I wanted to help.'

She searched his face. 'Can you stay?'

'Best if I don't. Shelley's very understanding but—'

'Do you have to tell her?' Hannah asked. 'I mean, you could be in a hotel, and it's not like we're sharing a bed.'

He gave a small laugh. 'I don't really want to start my married life with a lie.'

Hannah paused. 'Did you ever lie to me?'

He looked away. 'Han, come on. Don't do this. Why don't you try Jim again? Maybe he can sit with you for a few hours.'

'I told you, he's not taking my calls.'

'I really can't stay, I'm sorry. I'll try to come back for . . .' He didn't want to say *the hearing and sentencing*. 'I'll be back soon, okay? You're going to be all right. That Detective Hawksworth believes you have a good chance of leniency, and perhaps even a suspended sentence, he said.'

'The solicitor said the same.'

'See! That's good, right? Hawksworth has sympathy. Can't say the same for that Carter woman.'

Hannah shrugged. 'She's been very nice to me.'

'I think she blames me,' Jonathan said, scowling.

'For what?'

He shrugged. 'I don't know. Your crimes, probably – what else?'

Hannah wasn't convinced. 'I actually think she's quite empathetic to my situation. But soon everyone will know what I did. How do I live that down?'

'You could move,' Jonathan said. 'Didn't you always want to get out of London? Sell here – it's worth plenty now. Gospel Oak is the new Highgate.'

She scoffed.

'No, really. You'd get a good price. Just go . . . Brighton, like you always said, or you could even do what we dreamed together and go to Cornwall. Start over. Fresh home, fresh county, go back to your maiden name. No one will know Hannah Davison. You can change your hair, cut it short as you've always threatened, or change the colour, and bingo: you've reinvented yourself. Fuck Jim. There'll be another Jim and he won't have the baggage. Han, you're young enough to—'

She held up a hand. 'Don't say it!'

He backed off. 'Okay, okay, but the fact you've listened to me go on this far . . . Be honest. I'm making sense, aren't I?'

'It does sound nice,' she admitted with a sigh. 'I can't go through all the photographers hanging around again.'

'Then go. Let's book you a long-stay cottage now. You can take your work anywhere – why not go tomorrow?'

'I can't. They said—'

'Yes, love, you can. Let your legal team know, let the police know. You can come back up to London for your appearance, and then it's over. You can disappear. Only tell your family where you are. The publishers don't care where you work from so long as you do your job. And if you do everything that's asked of you by your solicitor and barrister, from psychiatric reports to saying yes to whatever they advise, everything will be all right.'

'What about this place?'

Jonathan shrugged. 'Easy. Lock it up. You can get your brother to sell it when you're ready, but just leave it for a few months for everything to calm down. I'm sure you could slip back to London to empty it – or your family will help.'

'What about Billy's things?' she bleated.

Jonathan gave a gentle smile. 'He doesn't need them, Hannah. Neither do you. Take his special things with you, but the rest . . . let some other child enjoy them.'

'But his ashes . . .'

'I'm not suggesting you leave those here. Why don't you take them with you, and sometime, when you feel ready, we can scatter them from the cliffs off Penzance. No point in keeping them all sealed up. His spirit's flown – let him fly free now.'

She wept for several long moments, and he waited. Finally, she swallowed her sobs and nodded. 'You're right.'

'I am.' He didn't sound glib, but heartfelt. 'Come on, let's go hunt for a place you might feel comfy in.'

She squeezed his arm. 'Thanks for being here for me.' She paused. 'I have to ask . . . what does Shelley think of all this?'

'She doesn't know anything other than I'm working down south. I'll tell her the gist, of course, but she doesn't need to know what we've planned now. She's going to her mother's next week anyway, preoccupied with baby plans, you know.'

'Yeah, I do know.' Hannah looked away.

21

The activity seemed to have gone up a notch in the ops room when Jack arrived on Tuesday. There were more people now, with Geoff's team officially joining theirs on the seventh floor.

'Like a beehive in here,' Joan said, appearing at Jack's side.

'Let's organise some sandwiches or rolls for lunch – I'll pay – or none of them will eat.'

'Leave it with me,' she said.

Jack caught Nat's attention. 'How are you going with the phone records?' They needed to lock down all the evidence supporting Hannah's confession right away.

'Hannah doesn't interact with a lot of people by phone. Regular numbers are her parents' landline, her siblings' mobiles and James Clydesdale's – oh, and her ex-husband's. There are a few calls to and from some London numbers but each one corresponds with a publisher she freelances for. Other sundry numbers I have ticked off are the dog rescue place, the local vet, her local

Chinese, a hairdresser, that sort of thing. Nothing that raises any red flags.'

'All London calls?'

'Yes, sir, apart from her parents' landline and calls to her brother's mobile.'

Jack nodded. 'Good. Let Hirem know. He's collating all the information for the Crown prosecutor. Make sure he sees everything.'

'Right.'

Joan was back. 'I thought you'd like to know that Hannah Parker was approved for bail.'

'Good,' he said, relieved. 'Oh, and can we add some pastries to our order?'

'Ooh,' Joan said, looking delighted. 'There's a new bakery nearby doing fabulous Portuguese tarts and custard doughnuts.'

'Great. Let's fill them with sugar as we deliver the news that while Commander Barton is happy with our work, Chief Rowland is now breathing down our necks.'

She grinned. 'Leave it with me.'

Jack gazed around. The room was quiet but full of earnest activity. No one was chatting socially or staring out of the window; it was heads down and busy. He walked over to Kate's desk, where she was typing furiously.

She looked up. 'Hi.'

'Let's get everyone together in . . . ten?' She nodded and he moved towards the screened-off area that served as his office.

He rang Geoff. 'Are you nearby?'

'Just about to get in the lifts.'

'Okay, good. See you shortly.'

Next, he rang Lou. 'Ms Barclay? This is Detective Superintendent Jack Hawksworth from the Metropolitan Police.'

'Oh, yes? How can I help you, Detective Superintendent?'

'Just a heads-up, Miss Barclay, that I shall be entering your, um, premises, this evening.'

'Is that so? Well, you are most welcome to do so, Detective,' she said. 'I have nothing to hide.' He could hear the amusement in her voice; he was smiling too. 'Although, I will insist on you bringing your truncheon—'

'Oops, got to go,' Jack said, still grinning. Kate was suddenly peering in at the makeshift doorway. 'See you tonight. I might be late.'

'Aren't you always?' she said, but with no malice. 'Bye, Jack.'

He looked at Kate. 'What's up?'

She gave him a look of uncertainty. 'Come and see.'

He walked back to where the team had crowded around Sarah's desk, all amusement wiped from his face.

'Sir, you asked us to compile a list of everyone working at the hospital during Billy Parker's stay,' Sarah said.

'Right.'

'We made a comprehensive list of all the nurses and ward staff that have any sort of physical connection to Billy, on the wards and in A&E. Potentially and conservatively, we're looking at forty-two people.'

'Blimey,' Jack said, frowning. 'And more conservatively?'

'We can closely link twelve to Billy, and four of them are now dead. Given the blood donor is one of them, someone who had absolutely no control over what happened to Billy, I don't think we can discount the chain of people involved in collection either.'

Fresh alarm pounded at Jack's temple. 'So how many might that be?'

Sarah pulled a face. 'The nurse who collected the blood, the team at Filton who processed it, and the—'

'What's Filton?' he interrupted.

It was Kate who answered. 'Filton is one of the major locations of the National Health Blood and Transplant Centre. The lab at

Filton is the largest blood processing centre in the world,' she began, with a look on her face that said *You should know this*.

'How many people work there?'

'Hundreds.'

He stared at her in disbelief. 'Well, the killer can't go after all of them.'

'Want a crash course in Filton?'

Jack blinked and then nodded.

'Take a seat. You'll need it.' She gestured towards an empty chair.

Jack sat down and Kate began. 'I've been researching. Filton is an industrial park on the edge of Bristol where you'll find the NHS's largest blood processing unit – of which there are several others around the country, I might add, including one in London. But this is the biggest. It's also home to the University of Bristol's Master in Transfusion and Transplant Sciences, and has suites and suites of what are known as 'clean rooms' for laboratory work. It's here that donated blood is sent from the whole region, but other sorts of donations are processed here, from stem cells to organs and other tissue. But let's just focus on blood, since it's at the core of our op.'

Kate began to pace. 'So, blood arrives at Bristol from all the donation centres from the south-west region, and products could end up anywhere in England. Even though London has its own centre, it wouldn't be uncommon for blood from Filton to end up here due to demand, which is what occurred with the Billy Parker case.' She now paused, leaning against a desk. 'Wrap your minds around the fact that Filton processes around one point three million units of blood annually.' That won a sound of collective awe. 'By processes, I mean cleans, tests for disease, and then breaks down into its components – red blood cells, white blood cells, the clotting factor called cryoprecipitate, as well as plasma, platelets and perhaps more. The blood is tested for its group, and the rigorous checks and balances mean there can be no mistake. None,' she emphasised. 'Each donation has a separate barcode.'

'So we can trace the blood that Billy was given through its processes,' Jack asked. 'That's how we know the error was at the hospital, not from the blood itself or where it was collected or processed?'

'Yes,' Kate said. 'Every unit of blood is tracked from the donor through to the arm of the person receiving that blood up to thirty days later.'

Geoff had quietly arrived and been listening. 'Fascinating, but why do we need to know this?'

Kate sighed. 'Because it means there are so many more people involved in the chain of events than we realised. If this person is casting their net as wide as the donor and we don't get to them soon, they may have dozens of names on a kill list.'

'How would they know who to target?' Jack asked.

She shrugged. 'Maybe they work at Filton or one of these huge processing centres. There are all sorts of lab techies doing the checks and balances I spoke about, working in shifts, but maybe the killer isn't interested in those nameless, blameless people. They've demonstrated that they are after everyone who had some sort of involvement with what happened to Billy – either they physically handled the blood, or were directly responsible for the chain of events that led to Billy's death. Sarah's pulled together a list of the likely people, and that's how she's got to forty-two.'

Geoff nodded. 'Too many to keep a close eye on. Who do we cover, who do we not alarm?'

Jack sighed. 'Sarah, who took Olivia's blood donation? Do we have that person's name?'

'We do, sir, yes, if you'll hold on.' Everyone waited while she looked through her list. 'Er, well, two nurses were on, both called Gail, if you can believe it. Different spelling, though.'

'Okay, Sarah, get their details, please, if you can. Let's start at the beginning. We know Olivia Craddock was targeted. Who's to say the nurse who drew her blood isn't next? I think we have to warn them.'

Kate cut him a look. He knew what she was saying: *Is this a wise expenditure of our time?* But he thought it was. 'The clues are in the detail,' he said, repeating Carol Rowland's mantra.

'What shall I tell them, sir?'

'Put them through to me and I'll talk to them.'

Sarah nodded.

'If anyone needs more info about the NHS at Filton, it looks like Kate's your oracle.'

Kate grinned. 'They sent me pictures. They can line up thirty samples of blood and tell you who had a big week of food and booze.'

'Ugh,' Hirem remarked. 'I don't want to see that, I don't think.'

'No, you don't. It will stop you eating steak and chips or greasy pizzas in a heartbeat.'

As Sarah looked up phone numbers and the others drifted back to their desks, the senior detectives got in a huddle.

'What's happening with James Clydesdale?' Jack asked Kate.

'He's coming in at midday.'

Jack checked his watch. 'Okay, and Hannah Carter got bail as we anticipated.' Over his shoulder, he caught Nat's attention. 'Does the team have eyes on Jonathan Carter?'

She gave a nod. 'Yes. He picked up Hannah from the Magistrate's Court this morning and took her home. They were both still there, last I heard.'

'Right. I'd ask you to call him, Kate, but I'll get—'

'But nothing!' she growled, before dropping her voice. 'Let me do it.'

'What have I missed?' Geoff asked, looking between them.

Jack lifted his chin towards Kate. 'She's got it in for the husband because he deserted Hannah.'

Geoff gave her a pained look. 'You deserted *me*, and I didn't turn into a psychopath.'

'Actually you did,' Jack murmured and the two friends smiled.

'Jack . . . er, sir, I don't really have it in for him. I'm sad for Hannah, horrified for what the death of their child has spawned.'

He nodded, having seen the plea in her expression. 'All right. Obviously we want to know if he has any thoughts on anyone who might be holding a grudge on the family's behalf. We have to widen our net – maybe it's one of her siblings? Her father?'

'Or him, of course.'

'Yes, we need to know his movements at the time of each of the deaths. But Kate, don't antagonise the guy, please. He won't give you anything if you do, and then I really will have to pull rank.'

She feigned an angelic face. 'Like a fairy I shall tread.'

'Geoff, perhaps you and Nat can interview Clydesdale. He's in for noon. But right now, I need to finish the briefing. We got sidetracked.'

Back with the group, Jack confirmed Hannah Parker's bail details and that the team was now responsible for gathering all the necessary evidence that supported her admission, alongside continuing to investigate both the toxic mushroom poisonings, the three strangulation murders and now Alec Chalmer's death.

'Hirem is spearheading Hannah's case, and please don't keep him waiting. Sarah and Nat, you'll do most of that legwork, but we have Josh and Andrea here, who will be extra arms, legs and voices for you.' He smiled at the two constables in their midst, joining from Geoff's team.

'We're also welcoming two detectives from DCI Benson's team. They've been working on the murders, as you know, so if anyone needs info, ask these guys – John Dee and Simon Waters. Other new faces are Janet, Lesley and . . .' he hesitated before finishing, 'er, Bill.'

Bill grinned and gave a salute.

'Please introduce yourselves to each other. We are now all officially on Operation Avon. I'll head us up, but our chief is Carol Rowland, and she's expecting a swift conclusion by what she now believes is a crack team.' That won some chuckles. 'If I'm not around, pretend DCI Benson is as good-looking as I am and treat him as me – ditto DCI Carter, who isn't nearly as good at tennis but is just as smart.' Only Kate slung him a droll look, as Geoff was finishing up on a phone call. 'All right, I'm handing over to DCI Benson, who has been leading the Avon team. Geoff?' He noticed Geoff looked grave.

'Thanks. Er, folks, sorry to hit you with this but I've just heard we have another body and it's looking awfully like our killer.'

There were collective sounds of disgust, including curses.

'I heard that, children,' Joan called out from her reception desk. 'The tin's on the desk whenever you go past.'

Jack was astonished. 'Where did this happen?'

'Last night, Barnet.'

'Shit!' The tin rattled distantly but no one smiled.

'We'd better get to the morgue,' Geoff said, and Jack nodded.

'Kate, you and Simon can handle the Clydesdale interview now. Okay?'

'Sure,' she said, casting a smile Simon's way, checking her phone. 'I've got thirty-two minutes to speak with Jonathan Parker before the interview.'

'Right. Do we know who the new victim is, Geoff?'

'Yes, a nurse. Senior Sister Janine Bowes.'

Jack looked down and stifled the obvious response. 'Strangled?'

'Same as the others, it looks like.'

'Except Alec Chalmers.'

'Maybe a man was too risky to try strangling?' Kate offered. 'Maybe the killer isn't tall enough or strong enough?'

Geoff nodded. 'Possibly.'

'Sarah, will you print off your list of all who are now vulnerable? Give everyone a copy. The conservative version. We're not taking any chances.' He moved on. 'John?'

'Sir?'

'Can you help Sarah contact everyone on that list, please. Stay calm for them, but be direct. They need to know we believe they may be followed, may be in danger.'

'Should we tell them to leave London?'

'If they can but, if not, then go to a family member's or friend's, and not to share that information with anyone at the hospital.'

'What about travelling to and from their work, sir?' Kate asked.

'Work out their shifts, Sarah. Perhaps we can have some unmarked cars on standby. Let's make sure they use underground access and exits and change their routine for the near future. I'll speak to the boss. If we can escort people, even for a few days, it might be wise.'

Both John and Sarah nodded.

'Er, sir?' Sarah said. 'The two Gails?'

He nodded.

'One's on voicemail. The other's on a shift and will be available in about fifteen minutes. I'll put her through to you then.'

'Good.'

'I can assure you, following the news of yet another potential victim,' Jack said to everyone, 'that my phone is about to ring with a demand from Chief Rowland to get this man – or woman – off our streets. Please, everyone, study the detail. As she would say, it's in there somewhere.'

22

Kate sat across from a nervous-looking James Clydesdale.

'I came as asked, but I still don't understand why I'm here,' he said, the Australian accent there but smoothed out after years in England. He was fidgeting in his seat like a child in front of a school headmaster, she thought.

Kate explained again, using the due diligence excuse. 'You are not under arrest, Mr Clydesdale, simply helping us with inquiries.'

'Inquiries into the needles in strawberries, et cetera?'

'Correct.'

'All right.' He frowned. 'How can I possibly help?'

'Well,' Kate began, 'have you been in touch with either of the Parkers in the last day or two?'

'Er, no. I haven't spoken to Hannah in a number of days, and I don't have her ex's number . . . I don't even know him to speak to on the phone.'

'Well, you should know that Mrs Parker has been arrested following her admission of being responsible for a series of domestic terror events, including those needles in the strawberries you mentioned.' He looked down. 'Which we gather you knew about.'

He gave no answer, so they continued.

'You didn't think to come forward with this information, Mr Clydesdale?' Simon asked.

Jim looked pained. 'Look, she'd stopped. No real harm done.'

Kate was astounded. 'No harm? Mr Clydesdale, people in the community were terrified. Businesses were compromised, a lot of police were involved, plenty inconvenienced. Frantic parents took their infant to hospital. And then there's the question of the death.'

Now he became more animated. 'She had nothing to do with the mushrooms − she assured me of that.'

'And you believed her?' Kate asked.

'I did. I've got to know her quite well, and my instincts told me I was hearing the truth.'

'So we have to take that as gospel, do we? Your instincts?'

He gave her an injured look.

'All right, Mr Clydesdale. Even so, you didn't come forward with critical information needed by the police because . . . you felt sorry for the perpetrator? Is that about the size of it?'

He nodded, looking ashamed. 'When you put it like that . . . Yes. I knew her sad story, and, well, I suppose I understood how someone might go sort of . . . mad for a while. She told me she'd stopped. I think she was genuinely horrified that she was responsible for scaring people, for hurting them.'

'Do you like Hannah?' Kate shifted topics.

'Er . . .' He frowned. 'That's an odd question.'

'Is it? Sorry. I think it's pretty straightforward.'

'I do like her. She's become a friend.'

'Don't friends support one another during a time of need?' she asked without any hint of accusation. She could see he knew where this was going by the slight roll of his eyes.

'Look, I've been away.'

'Do you mind me asking where?'

'No, I don't mind. I've been to Dubai.'

She sat back in her chair. 'Dubai! Wow. Holiday?'

'No, for work. I'm an architect, and I'm part of a very big project in the city. The developers wanted our team to see a building they wish to emulate . . . well'—he shook his head from side to side— 'find an echo, rather than copy.'

'And you have documents to verify your travel?' Kate asked.

He nodded. 'Of course. Hotel bookings, flight bookings, receipts from wherever you need.'

Kate didn't lose pace. 'Hannah's been calling.'

'I realise that, and now I know why, but I was too preoccupied to get back to her. This is a very big job for me.'

'Not even a message for the friend you see most evenings for a walk? You couldn't imagine she'd wonder where you were, or worry for you?'

'So now you're the friendship police? Telling us how we're supposed to behave?' Now he sounded snide.

Kate smiled. 'No, I'm just trying to establish the parameters of your relationship with a criminal who's now on bail.'

He sighed, as though weary. 'I can get very absorbed in my work. I lost one wife for being a bit absent.'

Kate glanced at Simon, communicating that he should take over. The shift was slick.

'Oh, we were under the impression that your marriage foundered for other reasons,' Simon said breezily.

Clydesdale took a breath. 'Look, how is any of this helping your investigation into Hannah's actions? I'm not to blame. I've come into her life well after the fact, so why am I being given the third degree?'

'We appreciate your help, Mr Clydesdale,' Simon said smoothly. 'We're making no accusation, but we're baffled as to why you didn't come forward with information that you knew the country was so eager to hear. Her actions have frightened shoppers, businesses and police up and down the country.'

'I know.'

'Then why?' Simon persisted.

'Because I've been involved with the police before!' he snapped. 'That's why!'

Hannah and Jonathan had found a cottage in Penzance that she actually felt motivated about, which seemed to please him.

'Just pack what you need, Hannah. It's not forever – or maybe your dream will come true and you'll love it enough to stay,' he said, giving her a warm smile. At her sad but relieved expression, he hugged her. 'Come on, I'll drive you to the station. Your parents' place first?'

She nodded. 'They're going to drive me down in a week or so. Mum says she quite fancies a few days in Cornwall.'

'Just escape it all for a while. Will you call your solicitor on the way?'

'Yes. I got voicemail on the last try, but I left her a message. She knows that I'm going to Maidenhead.'

'I'll stay here another night, if that's okay, and take off tomorrow.'

'Stay as long as you like,' Hannah said. 'Chalky and I won't be back for a while – or maybe not at all.'

At the morgue, Jack and Geoff confirmed with Hilly that Janine Bowes had died by strangulation. The post-mortem, however, didn't match the other victims who'd died by asphyxiation.

'Some sort of rope was used, about the thickness of my finger,' Hilly said, holding up her hand in an effort to help. 'It had a strange, webbed pattern to it . . . not your usual rope, not garden hose, more like a fabric of some sort.'

The men nodded.

Jack, wondering absently how the interview with Clydesdale might be going, experienced a moment of inspiration. 'What about a dog lead?'

Geoff cut him a look, immediately latching on to the idea and then looking back at Hilly.

'Yes,' she said as she considered it. 'In fact, very good, Detective Superintendent. It could well be.'

'Jack,' he corrected.

'Well, Jack, yes. A thicker sort of dog lead, one of those twisted fabric ones . . . that would be about a finger's width thick. Do you have any ideas?'

He nodded. 'Vague, but the dog lead could make sense.'

'The rope, which we'll call it for now, was tightened around her neck from behind. She was found in her car, so the killer was likely hidden in the back seat; it was still dark and she would have been tired, coming off a long shift, so I imagine she wasn't checking for a bogeyman in her car. Look, you know I don't care to work with anything other than the facts, but if we were to speculate, I suspect the killer was counting on that fatigue. They would have probably gambled that she wasn't going to be carrying gear or need to open the boot – she'd just have a handbag or backpack at most, which she'd sling into the front passenger seat. Maybe they'd even watched her come off a shift before.'

Jack nodded as she looked between the detectives with wide grey eyes.

'I'm presuming you don't need to know all the technical injuries that formed the strangulation?'

They shook their heads miserably.

'She died where she sat, scratch marks on her neck where she fought, and scuffs on her shoes and the plastic floor mat in the car where her feet would have hammered uselessly. But I do have something for you, detectives.' She gave a soft smile. 'SOCO found some woollen threads caught in the fabric of the back passenger seat, and at the top of the driver's seat.'

'The gloves again?' Geoff asked.

She nodded. 'I believe it's likely. No pattern indentation this time, but we have fibres, which are a curious chocolate and vanilla colour. If this helps, we're convinced they belong to a Ryeland sheep.'

Both men blinked in consternation.

'They're rare,' Hilly continued. 'One of the oldest breeds in England. Very few farms keep them – even fewer that might be supplying for commercial yarn.' She gave them a hopeful look.

'So if we can find the brand . . .' Jack said.

Hilly shrugged. 'You might be able to trace the purchase, I suppose. It's something.'

Geoff was already making a call as they left the morgue.

Clydesdale was shaking his head. 'It didn't matter that I was exonerated. Mud sticks. There are probably plenty of people who still believe I killed my children,' he said, a hint of anger in his tone.

'You can understand why, of course,' Kate offered softly.

'Yes, I can. I was in the house, and I was the one responsible for each child on the occasion of their death. What the media failed to report initially is that we had a lodger – my sister-in-law – who was also in the house when each child died. She was there to help out because my wife suffered very badly from postnatal depression, and we were all scared for her, for the children. Anyway, once there was that whiff of suspicion around me, it was very hard to shake. And I've been running away from that suspicion for years.'

Kate nodded in sympathy. 'I'm deeply sorry for the loss of your children, Mr Clydesdale.'

He nodded. 'I just didn't want the police thinking "There he goes again."'

'But you didn't know Mrs Parker when her son died, did you?' Simon asked.

'No,' he said. 'We've only recently met, but the media would have had a field day all the same. I'd already been through the wringer, I'd lost my children, my wife, my whole life, and, as much as my heart hurt for Hannah, I didn't want to be dragged into it all again. I'm slowly rebuilding my life and have finally found a good head space.'

Kate and Simon nodded.

'Has Hannah ever spoken about anyone who might hold a grudge on her behalf?' Kate asked.

Clydesdale shook his head. 'No. She's very close to her family, but I don't know if someone among them might be angry enough to throw toxic mushrooms into the public arena. It is the mushrooms we're talking about, right? I mean, Hannah's admitted to the other offences, you said, but as I said before, she made it clear to me that she had no part in the mushrooms that killed that girl.'

Kate hesitated. 'Yes. We're preparing a file now for Hannah's hearing and sentencing. We all hope the courts will find a lenient attitude for a grieving mother under the most traumatic circumstances, but we do need to cover our bases.'

'Hannah mentioned to me that the dead woman was the same one who donated the blood that found its way into Billy, her son. I didn't know Hannah back then to speak of who was orbiting around their family.'

Kate looked at Simon, who ended the interview. 'Thank you for your help, Mr Clydesdale. Any more trips in the near future for you?' he asked.

Clydesdale shook his head.

'Right, well, we may need to speak with you again, and if you don't mind me accompanying you home to get those tickets and receipts, that would be great.'

'Fine,' he said.

They all stood, and Kate shook his hand.

'Look, I want to help, truly, especially if it means a more optimistic outcome for Hannah.'

'Thanks,' Kate nodded. 'We'll keep that in mind.'

Kate was pleased that Jonathan Parker returned her call; she'd tried him before the interview with Clydesdale but had had to leave a message.

'Sorry about the voicemail. I've been busy.'

'No, that's all right,' she said. 'We were all pleased to hear Hannah was granted bail.'

'Yes, it's a relief. Listen, she has rung her solicitor, but I'm not sure if you'll have heard yet – she's escaped the fallout before it happens, going to her parents initially. I encouraged her to go, because she was fearing the media response and potential backlash.'

'Right. You said her parents' place initially?'

'Correct. After that, Hannah's booked a cottage in Cornwall. She's going there for a few weeks. She can work from anywhere, and we all thought that it was a good thing for her to get away. To be honest, I'm surprised I could convince her to leave the house – you know, with all of Billy's stuff there – but maybe it's a step in the right direction for her.'

'For someone who left his wife, you're being extremely caring, Mr Parker.'

There was a brief pause. 'That's not a bad thing, is it?'

'Not at all. Admirable, in fact,' Kate said, meaning it but

wondering if it was too much, too late. 'But how does your fiancée feel about you being away and taking care of your ex?'

'Shelley's a very chill person. She knows that I still love Hannah – always will – but that my new life is with her now. This is just helping someone I care about.'

'Whereabouts in Scotland is she from? It is Scotland, isn't it?'

'Er, yes. Pitlochry,' Parker replied.

'Oh, a beautiful part of the world.'

'Mmm. Her parents own a small hotel, and Shelley works with them. She'll probably take it over in a few years as they're nearing retirement.'

'Will you get involved as well?' Kate asked.

'Maybe. I'd be glad to give up all the travel, I know that much. Er, shall I give you the address of the cottage where Hannah is staying?'

'Good idea. When does she move down there?'

'She said in a week, but knowing Hannah, she won't last more than a few days at her parents'. We booked it from Friday, but it was vacant all week and I imagine she might want to go earlier. I'll text the details; I have your number.'

'Okay, thanks. Well, Mr Parker, the reason I rang was actually to ask if you knew of anyone who might bear a grudge on your behalf – yours and Hannah's, that is.'

'Oh. You mean someone who might have done the poisoning in Bristol, you mean?'

'I do,' she said. 'If Hannah's not responsible – and she swears she isn't – we still have to find who is.'

'Couldn't it just be a copycat?'

'Perhaps, but considering the person who died is connected to Billy's case . . .' Kate paused to see how Jonathan would react.

'I can't think of anyone. Have you spoken to that Clydesdale guy?'

'Yes.'

'And?'

'I can't discuss that interview, Mr Parker, but Mr Clydesdale gave me no reason to believe that he's involved in these murders. He has an alibi that we're checking, and he's been very co-operative.'

'Hmm, okay, well, he would seem the most obvious to act on Hannah's behalf. They got close quite fast, and maybe he has a past she doesn't know about.'

'What do you mean?'

'I mean she hardly knows him.'

'They see each other regularly.'

'Fair enough. But let's say he is shady, or capable of rage. Hannah may not know that yet. We don't know that he hasn't taken offence on her behalf.'

'And killed someone?'

'You asked me if I knew of anyone who might bear a grudge, so I'm trying to be helpful, that's all. And, as I say, he's got very friendly very quickly.'

'Doesn't make him a murderer, though. Why do you get the impression he's involved?'

'Yes, look, I don't mean to cast unfair suspicion, but he's the only person who is new in Hannah's life. I've spoken to him – he seems like a decent guy, but you never know. I thought he was worth looking at a bit closer, but if he's got an alibi, then good.' He sounded somewhat reassured, Kate thought, but still not entirely trusting of Clydesdale. She supposed she could understand that.

'All right, well, if you think of anything else, feel free to call.'

'Of course.'

Geoff called almost as soon as Kate ended the call with Parker to fill her in on the latest autopsy.

'Ryeland sheep?' she asked. 'You're joking.'

'We need all the team on this, and an answer as soon as possible.'

'Okay, I'm on it.' She quickly briefed him on what had transpired with Clydesdale, knowing Jack would be keen to have the update. 'So nothing that really points us to this guy, and Simon's rung to say the alibi looks solid, although we're still double-checking all the facts.'

She got everyone's attention in the ops room and gave them the news that they were now urgently hunting farms that had a flock of Ryeland sheep with a commercial yarn contract. By the time Jack and Geoff returned, the ops room felt tense with expectancy. Everyone was on the phone.

Kate looked up as she waited for someone to find some information and whispered to the men, 'Nothing yet. Sarah's almost finished her calls to the vulnerable people and—' She put a finger in the air. 'Hello again . . . yes, thank you.'

'We'd better get some pizzas in,' Jack said when Kate hung up.

'I'll organise it,' Geoff said.

Jack gestured to Kate to follow and wandered over to Sarah, who was off the phone and rubbing her eyes. 'Tired?' he asked, sympathetic.

Sarah jumped. 'Oh, no, sir. Just, um, worried.'

'Worried? What's going on?' Kate asked.

'Well, I finally got hold of Gail Prewitt. She's good friends with the other Gayle – spelt with a Y. Uh, Gayle George.' She sighed. 'Gail Prewitt said Gayle George hasn't turned up for work in a few days.'

Jack stared at her. 'Any logical reason?'

'Gail said her colleague was supposed to be going away for a week, except she'd put it off because her dog was off colour and she was taking him to the vet.'

'And?' Jack asked.

'The dog is still at the vet. They can't reach her to collect him. Gail Prewitt called by the house, but couldn't raise her.'

'Could she have gone on the trip anyway, imagining that the dog was in for a few days?' Kate asked, really just thinking aloud.

'Possibly,' Sarah replied, 'but two things. I don't know of anyone who would actually go away knowing their dog was sick, even if it was at the vet – you'd hardly have a relaxing holiday. But perhaps more worrying for us is the fact that her car is still parked in the driveway, according to Gail Prewitt. She was supposed to be driving to Hereford to stay with a friend.'

That changed everything. 'Right, let's get the local CID down there,' Jack said. 'Got the address?'

Sarah nodded.

Geoff had been listening. 'I'll send Simon down. If it's going to be what we fear, then I'd like one of ours on the scene.'

At Jack's nod, Sarah scribbled the address for him. 'I'll take it from here, Sarah. Good work.'

'Thank you, sir.' She turned back to Jack. 'There's more.'

'Go on.'

'Gail said that she remembered Olivia Craddock because they'd joked together about her being a virgin . . . as in her first time donating blood. And it was right before Christmas, so they were all singing along to George Michael, because Olivia was the last person giving blood that morning, so the unit was pretty much deserted. A real Christmas spirit, she was telling me.'

'What else?'

'Olivia spoke about wishing she had a boyfriend. It got me thinking. She got her wish eventually, because the boyfriend was the one who cooked for Olivia and her friend. Olivia died after that meal, the boyfriend never heard of again. And then the nurse, Annie Dawes, had a new boyfriend too. No sign of him either.'

Jack thought about this; Geoff had mentioned it in passing but they had nothing concrete at that stage to work with. 'Both dark-haired, if I remember correctly. If he used different names . . . unless these women had seen his ID, they couldn't know.'

'They were both new relationships. You don't tend to see some-one's passport until you know them a bit longer, and if this is our guy, then he would be deliberately concealing his identification – driver's licence, passport, any mail, probably using a second phone and so on.'

Jack nodded. 'If this tack is correct, he's seeing two women at the same time, near enough, while preparing for their deaths and probably planning the others as well . . . no easy feat. Sarah, will you please talk to Olivia's friend who got sick alongside her? And also Annie Dawes's friend whose party she didn't make it to. See what else they can tell us about this guy.'

'We did, or at least Geoff's team did.'

'Well, we're going to do it again, and compare everything we can about this guy. Get anyone you need to help you with this. Good work.'

Behind them, Hirem suddenly punched the air. 'Yes!'

Everyone turned. 'Falmouth,' he said. 'A small family farm that supplies its wool to a company called Blackburn Yarn.'

'Do we stop making calls?' Nat asked.

Kate looked at Jack, who was frowning. 'What's on your mind?'

'Blackburn Yarn,' he said, staring off as though trying to remember something. 'It's familiar.'

'Something you knitted, perhaps . . . a nice beanie for Snowflake?'

He frowned more deeply. 'Wait . . . she had that brand of wool in her basket.'

'Who did?'

'Hannah Parker.'

Kate looked at him with a much more serious expression now. 'Are you sure?'

Jack nodded. 'Positive. Remember, she was going to knit an overcoat for Chalky with all that spare wool? I saw the label.'

'Could be a co—'

'Don't even think it,' he growled.

23

Time was no longer on his side. He looked at the list of names he'd taken months to prepare. Still so many to be dealt with. They would not all meet their punisher; he had to accept this. But plenty had. It was deeply satisfying that several killers had now been killed themselves, but the net was closing in. Still, he would not let them find him until he did one more job.

The list stared back at him. One name weighed heavily. He should have killed her first, a small voice in his mind said. But dealing with Olivia and her killer blood had always been the priority in his mind, riddled with anxiety and stress as it was, though he managed to disguise it most of the time. The voice was getting louder, though. The desire to end the world around him, and himself, was getting stronger. Nights were hardest, when he closed his eyes and often toppled back into those days of death looming at every turn. What else could he do but act?

The name stared at him as though it had been highlighted in fluorescent marker, traced with glue and dusted with glitter. It sparkled off the page, demanding to be noticed, urging him to do it. Just one more.

Dr Emily Harley, Paediatric Surgeon.

The name seemed to pulse on the page in time with his own.

How, though? He would think on it. But he couldn't stay here any longer. He gathered up his few belongings and the flashbulbs that had arrived that afternoon – his luck was holding – and left the house by the back door, skipping over two fences in the darkness. He landed out on the street where he'd parked for an extra measure of anonymity . . . and safety. He hefted his small bag onto his shoulder and began to jog towards the car.

'Mrs Parker? It's Detective Superintendent Jack Hawksworth.'

There was a pause. 'Okay, look, I know I said I was going to my parents,' Hannah said quickly. 'I wasn't lying. It *was* the plan, but then I decided to just keep going all the way to Penzance, at the address that I've provided. I've already let my solicitor know, and she said it's no problem.'

'It isn't,' Jack said. 'I'm not calling about that.'

'Oh? What's happened?'

The line began to fade and crackle. 'This is a bad line. Can you hear me?'

'Yes, but you sound like you're suddenly talking from the bottom of the ocean.'

'Do you have a landline?' he asked.

'No. Sorry.'

'I'll call you back. Can you wait, please?'

'Okay.'

Jack tried again. 'Any better?' He put the call on speakerphone in case that helped.

'Worse, I think. It's a stormy evening down here.'

'Well, let's hope it holds long enough to get through why I've called. This is going to sound curious, but I have a question about the wool you had in a basket at your home. You may recall telling us you had an oversupply of it and planned to make a coat for Chalky?'

She gave a brief laugh. 'My wool, did you say?'

'Yes.'

'Okay . . . well, of all the things you might have asked, I think that's the last I'd expect. I do remember. I haven't started yet, though – a bit distracted, you might say.'

'The wool is rather exclusive, isn't it?'

'Where on earth is this leading?'

The line crackled dangerously.

'Humour me, Mrs Parker.'

'Well, it was certainly expensive, if that's what you mean. But it was a gift from an author I worked with.'

Jack squinted with concentration; it was so difficult to hear what she was saying. Sarah quietly drew close, as though sensing he might need a second pair of ears; once again, he sent up his thanks for her attention to detail.

'Her novel got to number one in the national top ten for a week. A debut, so it was quite a thing. She was grateful for my involvement, and because she loved to knit and knew I did too, she gave me the wool. As you say, it's exclusive because so little of it is produced each year. Each ball can be traced back to not only a particular farm but even a sheep, I believe.'

'Knockburn Wool from a Ryeland sheep – a very old British breed – and the farm is in Falmouth,' Jack said.

'If you say so. I don't understand what—'

The line crackled and drifted.

Jack leaned right in. 'Did you knit some gloves with that wool?'

There was a silence on the line.

'Mrs Parker?'

'How did you know that?' Her voice had a metallic timbre as the line struggled for clarity.

'And the gloves have a sort of clever pattern along the fingers, don't they?'

Again, there was silence. He was sure it was not the poor quality of the connection.

'Please, this is important.'

'It was a very difficult pattern. I must have ripped the knitting down four or five times before I mastered it.'

'Hannah,' he impressed, 'I need you to tell me who you knitted those gloves for.'

She paused. 'Why?'

'Please answer me so I don't have to send a squad car down to your cottage.'

'I've told you everything I know about the acts I committed. I've confessed, I've been arrested for my actions and I'm preparing to do my punishment. What more do you want from me?'

Jack was losing patience. The room around him had grown ghastly silent as his team began to pay close attention to the call.

'I want the name of the person who you gave those gloves to,' he said in a polite but icy tone, wondering how tinny he sounded to her. It detracted from his authority but there was nothing he could do about that.

She hesitated. 'You're frightening me, do you know that, Detective? I liked you, but I see you're like your nasty colleague who has been hounding my husband for no reason.'

Kate looked at the phone with indifference. Jack knew she was aware of how pushy she could be, but her track record was sound; she'd be heading up her own investigations soon.

'I'll ask just once more, Hannah, before I send the local CID to your place and you'll be returned to London for formal questioning.'

'I gave them to my father! Okay? Happy now?'

★

Edward Davison, Hannah's father, was sitting by the fire, sipping a glass of Scotch while he read a book about astronomy. His wife, Pamela, sat nearby on the floral sofa, a sherry within arm's reach on the smallest table from a nest of three – a wedding gift from fifty years ago.

When the doorbell chimed out the Westminster Quarters, which had always vexed him, he slapped his book closed. 'Now, who can that be at this hour? Are any of the children due to visit?'

Pamela looked up from her knitting. 'No, darling, not that I'm aware of.'

'Right,' he said, glancing longingly at his Scotch. He folded his glasses and put them alongside his Waterford crystal glass – another wedding gift. 'I'll see who it is.'

Pamela let out a small shriek and threw her knitting down, nearly upending her sherry, when two police officers traipsed into their cosy snug.

Edward rushed to her side, putting a hand on her shoulder, glaring at the officers. 'Darling, it's not the children, please don't worry. They've confirmed that much, but nothing else. Now, I insist, officers, tell us what this is about, please?'

'I'm sorry, sir, we're not privy. Detectives will be here shortly. They're on their way from London.'

'London?' He glanced at Pamela in shock.

'Yes, sir.'

'Why detectives? At least tell me that much.'

'I can't say, sir. As I said, I don't know any detail. We were asked to make contact and sit with you until the people from London arrived.'

'This is preposterous,' he snapped.

Pamela's hand flew to her mouth. 'Oh, Edward, are we sure it's not the children?'

The senior officer held a hand up to calm her. 'Mrs Davison, it is not about your children.'

She glanced at her husband. 'What have you done, darling?' she bleated.

'Oh, don't you start, Pam. You're with me nearly every moment of my days and nights, what do you think I've done except gardening and walking the damn dog?'

She stifled a sob. 'I'll get some tea.'

'Yes, why don't you?' he said wearily. 'Just enough for four, though, Pam. They've got to be at least another hour and a half away.'

Hannah tried calling her parents, but without success, due to the storm; it seemed the landlines were down, and neither of them were likely to answer their mobile phones. Her mother refused to use hers, while her father only took his if he was leaving the house, otherwise both stayed on permanent charge in their bedroom. Each of their children had attempted to explain the folly of this but couldn't change their parents' habits.

'I don't want to be contactable all day,' her father had grumbled. 'I spent a lifetime working and now I want some peace.'

She didn't blame him, but not being able to contact who you needed when you needed them was vexing.

Next, Hannah tried Jonathan. Although the call connected, it went to voicemail.

Finally, she tried her brother. The connection was poor, but at least they could hear each other – just.

'Slow down, Hannah. This line is atrocious.'

She explained again.

'So what if you knitted him gloves? How ridiculous.'

'I know, but a detective superintendent from Scotland Yard is hardly going to have a conversation about wool without good reason, is he?'

'No, I suppose not. What on earth do they think Dad's done?'

'I have no idea, but I'm stuck down here in Cornwall because the weather's so bad. Can you get over there?'

'You mean tonight? I'm going to Switzerland tomorrow, Han. It's not a good time.'

'Please, Ben. Dad's blood pressure will zoom, and Mum will just bleat and cry and get all anxious.'

'Right,' he said. 'Get off, then, so I can go. It's going to take me until ten to get there.' He sounded exasperated, but Hannah knew he'd make an effort.

But Hannah's brother didn't make it in time. He called her back to report that two police detectives had already been and gone before he arrived, taking Edward with them in an unmarked police car.

Ben was met by his mother, red-eyed from crying and beyond relieved to see her son, whose arms she collapsed into.

'They didn't say anything,' she said, weeping. 'Just that he was going to be helping them with their inquiries.'

'How ridiculous. This is all connected with Hannah, surely?'

'I don't know, darling. Let me put the kettle on.'

It was his mother's answer to all woes.

'The father?' Kate couldn't believe it.

Jack had sent Hirem to get pizza for everyone, a welcome diversion while they waited for news from Geoff and John, who'd been the ones to go and collect Hannah's father, but it was late now, the remaining slices cold.

'I'm not buying it,' she said. 'He's seventy-four.'

Sarah shrugged. 'He's got motive, I suppose.'

Jack shook his head; he agreed with Kate. 'A senior man killing six people much younger than him, all the planning, all the meticulous surveillance that it would have taken to gather information on each victim to know when to strike . . . It's oodles of work. Would he have it in him?'

'Geoff said Davison is incensed. And he believed his rage to be genuine. The man's a university lecturer.'

'Well, I guess we'll have a much better idea soon. How far away are they?'

'Still at least an hour.' Jack looked at his watch. 'Send everyone home, Kate. We need them fresh for tomorrow.'

'Are *you* going home?'

'I think I will, for a nap, anyway. I want to be focused as soon as Geoff has finished with Mr Davison.'

'Okay, then I'll do the same,' she said.

'Not waiting to see Geoff?' he asked.

She yawned. 'No. I'm cold, hungry and tired. I want a hot mug of cocoa and, like you, a couple of hours' sleep and I'll be back to full tempo.'

They looked at their watches.

'See you at five?'

'Bring me something delicious,' she warned. 'It's your turn.'

He grinned, giving her a salute.

Jack got home and rang Carol Rowland, who he knew from experience answered her phone, no matter what time of day or night, with the same alert voice. It was inspiring.

'Sorry to disturb you, ma'am.'

'What have you got for me, Jack?'

'We're bringing in Hannah Parker's father, Edward Davison, for questioning. The interview will be done tonight.'

'The father? Have we evidence?'

He told her about the gloves.

'Impressive. Bruising inside the throat?'

'Deep inside, ma'am, beneath several layers of skin, tendons, et cetera. I need to get a look at the pattern she used but they're distinctive bruises, the forensic pathologist said. Hannah Parker admitted to the design having a distinctive pattern on the fingers, so I am feeling confident they're the ones the killer wore, especially given we've traced the wool.'

'Who's conducting the interview?'

'Geoff Benson and John Dee. They're a crack team. It's Geoff's case; I doubt he'd let anyone else handle this.'

'Okay. I'll wait to hear more first thing tomorrow. Good work and goodnight, Jack.'

He took a five-minute, hotter-than-normal shower and crawled into bed next to a warm, sleeping Lou, who mumbled a welcome.

'There's ice cream in the dustbin if you're . . .' She never finished her sentence.

He laughed quietly to himself, enjoying the gibberish that she spoke in her sleep. It was one of his favourite discoveries about her.

And then he closed his eyes and tried not to think of innocent folk being strangled.

Kate ended her call with Geoff. She was already at home in her pyjamas, sipping the cocoa she'd promised herself. It was never quite as good as it tasted in her imagination, she thought, but still enjoyable.

'Did he ask for legal representation?' she'd asked.

Geoff had chuckled. 'Well, when I asked him if he wanted it, his response was "You're damn right I do, Detective Benson, and when this is over, I'm going to sue," or words to that effect.'

'I'm sorry we've all deserted you but Jack thought it best if the whole team got some shut-eye so we can tackle a big day tomorrow, plus he knows you'll be all over the interview.'

Geoff yawned. 'Yeah, I rang but it went to voicemail. I texted and he said acknowledged, so I know he's aware we're now in Belgravia nick, although he did say in his message that there's ice cream in the dustbin if I need it.'

'Is he losing it?'

Geoff laughed. 'I'm sure I'll find out tomorrow what it means.'

'I'm going to bed.'

'Wish I was there too.'

'No action here, I'm afraid. Just me in my PJs.'

She heard him chuckle again before she rang off. By the time she returned they'd have maybe twelve hours left to hold him and find enough evidence to formally arrest Hannah Parker's father.

Her phone rang again, and she answered without looking properly at the screen, assuming it was Geoff again.

'No, I won't iron your shirt for tomorrow,' she said, yawning.

'Detective Carter?'

'Er, yes, sorry, who is this?'

'It's Jonathan Parker. I'm so sorry to ring you at this time.'

'It's okay. What's happened? Is Hannah—'

'Hannah's fine, I think. I haven't spoken to her, but I saw her safely onto the train to her parents'.'

'She's not with her parents, Mr Parker.'

'What?'

'I said—'

'No, I know what you said. Sorry, where is she?'

'She carried on to Cornwall, apparently. We spoke to her there. The weather's pretty bad apparently, so it wasn't a good line. She didn't ring you?'

Parker gave a sigh. 'Ah, she did and I missed it, but when I called back I got her voicemail. It makes sense if there's no coverage. I'm glad she's there anyway. I think it will help her state of mind.'

'I don't know about that,' Kate said. 'Some new evidence has erupted and it meant we needed to talk to her.'

'New evidence? About the community scares?'

'No. About the murders that connect back to your son.'

'I don't understand. Is Hannah suspected of—'

'No, nothing like that,' Kate said quickly, 'but I can't say more.'

'That's fair enough, but that's why I was ringing . . . about the murders, I mean.'

She frowned. 'What do you want to tell me?'

'Well, it's not what I can tell you, but something I want to show you . . . give you, actually. I did try phoning Detective Hawksworth, but his phone went to voicemail.'

'What do you want to give us?'

'It's going to sound bizarre, but if you'll humour me . . .'

'Go on.'

'I was at Hannah's for a couple of nights, as you know. I leave tomorrow to go back up to Scotland, but while she was packing to leave, two parcels were delivered. Um, I didn't tell Hannah about them in that moment of arrival – she was so addled anyway. And then I forgot about them until now.'

'What makes you think the parcels are important?'

'Well, both are addressed to James Clydesdale using Hannah's address. They're from two different senders.'

Kate blinked into instant alertness, already stepping out of her comfy slippers and reaching for fresh clothes to put on. 'So Hannah doesn't know this?'

'No. But on the way to the station, I did ask her if she'd ever let anyone else use her address. She looked at me as if I was stupid.'

'Did you open them?'

He hesitated. 'I did, yes. I know that's not right, but I don't trust him, and I don't want him around my wife any more. Certainly not after opening them.'

'What was in them?'

'Kodak Instamatic flash cubes.'

A mental image immediately came to Kate's mind, from being a teenager on camp, trying to take night photos of her school pals sitting around a fire, toasting marshmallows. 'You mean those blue things?'

'Yes, good recall.'

'And why exactly should you be troubled by old-fashioned, out-of-date camera technology, Mr Parker?'

'Detective Carter, I was in the army and did my time in Northern Ireland. My main job was as a bomb detector . . . you know, car checks, that sort of thing.'

'Okay.' She frowned. 'What do the flash cubes signify?'

'Firstly, no one today uses them. Why would he need them? He's ordered these from eBay.'

'Maybe he's a collector?'

'Detective, please.' Parker sounded impatient. 'Let me quickly explain.'

'All right.'

'Even though no one uses a Kodak Instamatic any longer, they can be used quite cunningly to detonate something. I know, because I've seen them wired up for that purpose.'

'What?' She felt a chill creep down her body and flicked her phone onto loudspeaker while she hurriedly got dressed.

'Yes. All you have to do is wrap them in cotton wool. Attach them to a simple relay circuit and a timer. The cubes are coated in magnesium, so they burn fiercely and set the surrounding cotton wool on fire, which in turn can ignite something much bigger, far more flammable.'

'Like what?'

'Oh, like the stuff in the other parcel for instance . . . loads of fireworks containing potassium nitrate sulphur, charcoal . . . another way of saying gunpowder. And to me that means—'

'A bomb,' she finished. *Shit.*

'Well, an explosion, definitely. It could potentially set off some-thing bigger. I'm not saying it is a bomb, but I'm suspicious of this gear – I'm afraid my training kicked in – and think you guys need to see it, have it, possibly as evidence . . . I don't know. I could probably leave it at—'

'Where are you?' Kate cut in.

'Still at Hannah's house. But leaving in a few hours, at daylight.'

'Right. I'll be over shortly. Have these parcels got paperwork with his name on them?'

'Yes.'

'Excellent. Don't touch them any more.'

'I'll wait for you, Detective, and thank you. I'm, er, relieved.'

Kate took a final swig of cocoa – now lukewarm – and then, not wishing to interrupt Geoff's interview or disrupt Jack's sleep, wrote a quick note and left it on the floor just inside the door.

'You can't miss it, Geoff,' she said and blew it a kiss.

She made sure she had her phone, tucked a credit card into her pocket, grabbed her ID and keys and left the house. She noticed two streetlights were out, throwing her section of the street into darkness. Weird. Usually it was well lit, and all the lights further away were still on. No time to think about it; she hurried to her car, now deep in the shadows.

As she touched the driver's doorhandle she was suddenly flung hard against it before being bundled around to the back of the car. A strong hand clamped around her mouth to cut off her yell and a knife was held at her throat.

'Open the boot!' came a harsh voice.

She was still processing what was happening, noting her hand was in some pain. She'd have a bruise, no doubt.

'I said open the boot, or I'll slit your throat and you can bleed out here.' It was a man's voice.

She flicked the button and the boot opened.

'Get in,' he growled, but he didn't wait, shoving her hard and kicking her legs out from under her until she toppled into the cavity facedown. 'Scream and I'll stab you. I'll also wait for your boyfriend and slit his throat too.' As she wriggled onto her side, he pulled out some gaffer tape and cut off a length. 'Over your mouth.'

She obeyed, ignoring the dull pain in her hand, and he then made sure the ends were safely pressed down on her face before snapping a pair of handcuffs onto her wrists. She stayed calm but inside she was all rage.

'Not nice to be bullied, is it, Detective?' he said mockingly, and slammed the boot shut.

Then Jonathan Parker gunned the engine of Kate's car and took off into the night.

24

Jack woke with a start and looked wildly at his phone. It wasn't quite five, and next to him Lou snored gently. He smiled, leaned over and kissed her head gently.

She stirred. 'Oh you're not leaving, are you?' she murmured as she stretched one arm over her head. 'It's so early.'

'Have to. Pointy end and all that.'

'I could use a pointy end.' That made him laugh, and her too, and she woke up a bit more. 'Go on then, abandon me.' She yawned.

'I'll bring you tea before I leave, if you like.'

'I'm not cooking until you guarantee you'll be home for a meal.'

'Don't cook,' Jack said. 'Let me take you out somewhere.'

'Ring me later.'

When Jack returned from the shower, she had fallen asleep again. Ah, he remembered, it was Wednesday, Lou's day off. Normally she was up for an early morning tea, some yoga in winter, rather than a run. No wonder she was being so sleepy. She was also being very understanding. He needed to make it up to her. Although she'd enjoy the cuppa, it hardly touched the surface of the making-up that was needed. He smiled to himself; he knew what she'd love. He'd ask Kate – she'd know which one to order.

Whistling in spite of the early hour and the job ahead, he made a pot of tea, smeared some butter and Marmite on toast and ate one piece. He took the other to leave next to Lou with a mug of tea, which he covered with a saucer in the hope it might stay hot for her. He bent and kissed her cheek.

'Going now. Tea's hot but it's very early, still dark.'

'You're hot in that sweater.'

'Bye, beautiful.'

'Call me,' she mumbled, 'and Jack?' Her eyes were open. 'Stay safe.'

'Always.'

And then he was striding to the train, which would get him in fast at this time. He'd beat Kate, given they'd agreed to meet at five.

When he got to the ops room, he wasn't the first there, though. Geoff was, looking haggard.

'Don't tell me you slept here?' Jack groaned.

'One minute I was awake and just thought I'd sit here a moment and call Kate, and the next I must have just gone to sleep.'

'She's not going to be happy.'

'No. I left a message – she was probably asleep. I'll go have a shower and see if I can brighten up, and then I'll give you the rundown.'

'Right. I'll make you some tea. Actually I'll nip out and get us some coffee and you some breakfast.'

'I do love you, you know that, don't you?' Geoff said, blowing him a kiss.

When Jack returned, Geoff was showered and in a clean shirt, still looking sleep-deprived but fresher for his effort. He fell on the coffee and toastie.

'Thanks, mate.'

'Kate in?' Jack asked, checking his watch.

'Not yet. I thought I'd wait for the bollocking so she could do it face to face, rather than being a coward and ringing.'

Jack laughed. 'Oh, morning, Sarah. You're early.'

'Couldn't sleep, sir.'

'No?'

She frowned. 'Something's bothering me.'

'Uh-oh,' Geoff said and moved away to finish his breakfast.

'Tell me.'

'I was going over the material I've prepared for Hirem's file for the Crown prosecutor's office. Something's not adding up.'

Jack waited.

'Jonathan Parker lives in Scotland, now, right?'

'Correct. Pitlochry, Kate tells me. Nice place.'

'His is one of the few numbers that regularly rings Hannah Parker's number or vice versa.'

'Yes. And?' He waited, wondering where Sarah was headed.

'Sir, I've tracked every single call between them for the past six months, and they're all calls within the London metro.'

Now Jack frowned. 'That can't be right.'

She shrugged. 'It's what the records say.'

'In six months?'

She nodded. 'So I was just looking up McPherson in Pitlochry.'

'And?'

'There are gazillions of them, but only two McPhersons who own a pub or hotel or guest house, and they're not the family we're seeking. They also haven't heard of a Shelley McPherson and family. Seems a bit strange.'

'Keep looking,' he said, frowning deeper.

Nat had arrived ridiculously early too. 'Morning, sir.'

'Do me a favour, Nat. Get Jonathan Parker on the phone, can you?'

Geoff returned. 'Want me to brief you now?'

'Yes. Just a sec.' Jack looked at Nat, phone pressed to her ear, and she shook her head. 'Voicemail?'

'Yes, sir.'

'Okay, try a couple more times and let me know if you reach him.' To Geoff he said, 'Let's go over here.'

They moved to a quieter corner rather than Jack's office, as he wanted Nat to be able to catch his attention.

'So Edward Davison maintained his innocence and his fury at us bringing him in.'

'And the gloves?'

'He remembers Hannah giving them to him, but he has no idea what happened to them.'

'What do you mean?'

'He never wore them. Hated them apparently but couldn't tell his daughter because she'd taken the time and trouble to knit them specifically for his birthday. He found them itchy, he said. To be honest, Hawk, I believe him. I don't think this is our guy – he's a former university lecturer, a warder at the church, volunteers at the local Meals on Wheels, and he assures us his wife is quite needy and they're together most of the time. He gardens and is grandfather to several children, and he says he doesn't have time to go about murdering people.'

Jack looked back at him baldly and Geoff returned a disparaging look. 'No, I didn't accuse him outright, but he's no bunny and seemed to cotton on fast as to what we were questioning him about. It's not like the murders are lost on this family; they all know each one points back to their Billy. Despite his threats, he's refused a solicitor for now, because he's adamant the questions are futile.' Geoff sighed. 'But I think he's threatening to sue down the track. I know the clean-living guy may have a dark side – it wouldn't be the first time – but all my instincts tell me that while Davison may have motive, he's not motivated. I had a squad car drive him home last night.' He held up a hand. 'I know you probably wanted to question him again, but it would have been a waste of your time. He is not the one we're looking for. And he said he would ask his wife if she knows what happened to the gloves. John's taken him and will call.'

'Right,' Jack said, his own instincts trusting Geoff's; his friend was one of the smartest detectives he knew. 'We wait to hear from John, then. You'd better ring Kate. She and I were both coming in for five.'

Geoff nodded and picked up his phone to dial. Jack left him to his call and wandered back to Nat, looking at her in query.

'Nothing, sir. Keep getting voicemail.'

'What about you, Sarah?'

'I've exhausted all the Scottish accommodation houses I can find listings for.'

Jack sighed, looking around the room. All the others, except for Kate and John, had now trickled in. It wasn't yet six; they were keen.

'Either of you heard from Kate?' he asked the women.

Both shook their heads.

Geoff returned. 'She's not answering.'

'Not like her.'

'You try,' Geoff murmured, 'in case she's got the hump with me because I didn't come home.'

'Get everyone together, will you?' Jack dialled and the call immediately went to voicemail. 'Hey, Kate, it's me. Call in, will you? We're all wondering where you are. I have an almond croissant waiting for you,' he fibbed, needing to lead his thoughts away from the creeping worry tingling at the back of his neck. 'Sarah, can you track Kate's phone please?'

A few moments later, Sarah found him staring out of the window waiting for news. Geoff had disappeared to grab a coffee, claiming he needed to get some air.

'Sir?' Jack turned her way, unable to hide his worried expression. 'No signal from Kate's phone. We've pinged it, tried to turn it on even, but we're getting nothing, which means the sim and battery have been removed.'

He simply nodded as tendrils of fear began to take form and link hands deep within.

Kate had spent the most uncomfortable night of her life, handcuffed in a potting shed or something similar, going by the mushroomy smell of the floor she was curled up on.

Parker had spent the last few hours busy at something, which she now deeply feared was some sort of incendiary device. Lying, she told him she needed to go to the bathroom – she just wanted to get a look around and a sense of where she might be, but perhaps this was also a good time to get him talking. He hauled her up and took her outside. With light just breaking over London, she realised she was on a set of allotments.

'What, you want me to go right here? Isn't there a proper toilet somewhere?'

'No one's here, and I won't look. It's this or you hold it.' He pushed up the sleeves on his bright red hoodie impatiently; Kate wondered why he'd worn such a noticeable colour when he needed to fly under the radar. Or maybe he simply didn't care if he was caught.

'How do I do this handcuffed?' she asked. Her hand still throbbed.

'I don't know. You'll work it out.' He tossed her some tissues. 'Get on with it.'

She did, filled with horror at the indignity, but was grateful she'd chosen trackpants with a stretchy waistband.

He pushed her back into the shed when she'd finished.

'Ouch!'

'Shut up!'

'Is this how you spoke to Hannah? How you speak to Shelley?'

He laughed. 'You sad fuckers. Shelley doesn't exist.'

Kate blinked in the low light. That was a surprise. 'Why make her up?'

'To protect Hannah.'

'How does a lie protect her?'

'I suppose it doesn't matter you knowing, because you're going to die, Kate Carter. Do you know why?'

She shook her head.

'Because you're a bitch, and you disrespected me. Did you think I didn't hear your sarcastic tone, or see how you regarded me? Your boss did. He shut you down. Men are always going to shut you down because you have a smart mouth and a shit attitude.'

His words stung. Jack *had* shut her down. She had overstepped. But then she would argue that she'd been right, hadn't she? The notion was of very little comfort right now, though.

'I wanted Hannah to think I'd moved on, so she didn't worry about me,' he said. He had his back to her but she could see enough to note some wire and small pliers. 'I wanted her to feel free to start a new life of her own, but I knew if I was still around, single, moping after our marriage, she'd always feel dragged back into the past. This way I gave her freedom from me and, when she felt ready, from Billy.'

'When exactly did you decide to become a murderer?' Kate asked.

'The night my son was killed . . . the night my marriage died . . . the night my wife changed forever.'

'And does the killing make you feel powerful?'

'No.'

'What's it about, then?'

He chuckled. 'Let's call it enrichment, shall we?'

From her corner on the floor she stared at him. 'Enrichment?'

'People have to learn what loss feels like, Detective. It's far too easy to just move on from someone's loss without giving a second thought to the fact that their life is now on a totally different trajectory – changed, never to return to how it was. And grief cuts very deep, you know. Everyone who had a hand in all the processes that led to Billy's death felt sorry – they said so – but words are easy. *I'm sorry for your loss*,' he said, in a mocking voice. 'However, after the coroner's inquiry they all slipped back to their lives and their ways, didn't they? Only we were left with Billy's memory. Do you think nurses aren't still required to do unreasonable shifts? Or do you imagine that the hospital has instituted a new process where two nurses double-check each other's decisions? No. Of course not. It was all fake sorrow and fake promises to fix the broken system, no real action. Someone else will die – perhaps another child – and everyone will shake their heads and say there should be better processes, but we keep repeating the same mistakes. Meanwhile, families are ruined. Families like mine.'

'And you think you're enlightening them by murdering people?' Kate asked.

'I could hope but, frankly, right now I'm just taking revenge.' He shrugged. 'I've seen a lot of ugly death as a soldier, but I never thought death would reach out and take my beautiful, innocent son, especially not just because someone was overworked and tired. So now I'll punish everyone I can.'

'What are you doing over there, Jonathan?' She nodded towards the contraption he was tinkering with.

'I told you.'

'No, you told me what those materials that arrived at Hannah's house could do.'

'And they're going to do it.'

'How?' she asked.

'Wait and see. There! I have to go out now, Kate.' He stood and came over to her. She thought for one wild moment he was going to kill her, then and there.

He laughed. 'Not yet,' he said, as though he could read her mind. 'No, I'll save you for the finale. Then those who love you can suffer.'

Kate didn't show her fear. 'They'll find me.'

'Who? Hawksworth?' Parker laughed again, sounding demonic. 'Not where I plan to have you, but it will be fun watching him and his fellow Keystone Cops in full panic.'

'You were the boyfriend, weren't you?' Kate said, a jigsaw piece falling into place.

'What?' he replied, checking that her cuffs were still firmly around her wrists, and reaching for the gaffer tape.

'Olivia Craddock's new boyfriend and the new partner in Annie Dawes's life – that was you.'

He smiled. 'I hated them. Sleeping with Olivia Craddock made me physically sick. Luckily I only had to do it twice. As for Annie – I couldn't bring myself to go that far. After that, I didn't bother befriending the people I wanted to punish. I just followed them, learned their routines, and found my moment to strike.'

'They didn't recognise you from the trial?'

He shook his head. 'I wore a beard, and people see what they want to see.'

'Tell me,' she said quickly, as he bit on the gaffer tape to rip off a piece that was destined for her mouth. 'The murder in Wales?'

He gave her a smug look. 'Collateral damage. I needed to confuse the police and keep them busy chatting across divisions to buy a little time.' He gave another shrug. 'I picked her at random.'

The monster. 'You didn't know Hannah was going through her own version of revenge, did you? That's why you didn't come across as suspicious to us – you seemed so shocked at your ex-wife's behaviour.'

'I *was* shocked. Horrified, to tell you the truth – more than you can imagine. And I couldn't bear that I was going through what I was in order to get that revenge and keep her clean, so to speak, and then she'd gone and done that!' He paused, shaking his head in disbelief. 'I made her give herself up, because I figured the courts would go a bit easier if she confessed, grieving mother and all.'

'Do you think you'll get away with it, Jonathan?'

'When I'm finished, I'll probably drive my car off a cliff or jump in front of a train or something. I have no desire to live. I've seen too much. But, for now, they're no closer to me, are they? Unless, of course, you told someone you were coming to meet me?' Now he stared at her.

'I didn't have to. They're already onto you.'

He snorted a laugh. 'No, they're not.'

'You made one error, Jonathan, and I'm telling you, Detective Superintendent Hawksworth is tracking that error right now. He probably already knows it's you and will be putting out an APB. You'll be found before you can do much more damage.'

She enjoyed her moment of triumph, but it fled when he smiled. 'What mistake was that?' he asked.

Kate shook her head to say she wouldn't be sharing that with him, but when he raised his fist, she spoke. 'Your gloves, you dumb bastard.' She had the irrational thought that Joan would be having a field day if she could hear her, but Kate needed him on the back foot. 'He already knows it's you.'

'Well, just for that show of disrespect, I will be visiting your boyfriend – Geoff, isn't it? I was going to leave him alone, given I'll be hurting you – punishment enough for the guy, I'd imagined – but maybe I'll hurt him, maim him in some way so he'll always know it was your fault. You'll be long gone, of course.'

She gave an animal sound of anguish, then muttered, 'What a monster Billy has for a father.'

He punched the side of her head and Kate collapsed back against the concrete floor, seeing sparkles, only just aware of him leaving. She was alone, handcuffed, in the dark.

Jack was updating the commander at CTC, letting him know that Hirem Kumar had finished compiling the file on Hannah's confession. Everything lined up.

'Her bank records show those train and Tube tickets were purchased and we have CCTV footage of a woman in a yellow beanie on the train platform leaving for Brighton on the day of that scare, and on two other occasions. Hannah has told us where we can find the beanie, and DC Kumar is going over to the house to collect it.'

'Excellent, Detective Superintendent Hawksworth.'

As they ended the call, Jack found Geoff lurking nearby. 'No word?'

Geoff shook his head. 'I'm worried.'

'Can a neighbour go and check at your place?'

'I was thinking the same. I'd go myself, but—'

'But what? You stayed up half the night and kipped in a nasty Scotland Yard chair. Go.'

'I'll shower and change while I'm there.'

'Ring me when you get there, would you?'

Geoff gave a salute and left in a hurry.

Jack was giving the morning briefing. 'Last night we interviewed Edward Davison, father of Hannah Parker, who was the original recipient of the gloves we're now seeking. We're waiting on a call from John that might shed some light on where they ended up.

If we can find the current owner, we might get this bastard. Sarah, have you got that photo?'

'Yes.' She stood to attach a blown-up photo of the curious bruising pattern found on the women who were strangled.

'Sarah's been hunting knitting patterns, and we think we might have found either the one used or something very similar. The gloves are likely to look a bit like this,' he said, pointing to the second image that Sarah was putting up. 'As we know, they're going to be that chocolate colour, with light flecks that come from the Ryeland sheep—'

'Oh, shit! Sorry, guv,' It was Hirem, looking suddenly shocked.

Joan rattled her tin from the reception area. They barely reacted any more, so common was the occurrence, but each continued to pay their dues when they walked past her.

'What is it?' Jack said.

'The gloves,' Hirem said, pointing. 'I've been so busy getting the file ready for the Crown prosecutor that . . . well, I've been focused on the—'

Joan was suddenly among them. 'I'm sorry to interrupt, Jack, but it's John Dee on the line. He says it's urgent.'

'Hang on, Hirem.'

'Line one,' Joan said.

Jack snatched at a phone and hit the extension. 'John?'

'Sir. Mrs Davison has remembered what happened to the gloves. She thought she'd sent them to the church jumble sale, but I'm about fifteen minutes out and she's just rung me to say her son-in-law found them in the bag when he offered to take it down to the church and he asked if he could have them. She agreed, but only if he promised to keep it a secret from Hannah. They were just separated around then, she said, so he'd said that wouldn't be hard.'

'Jonathan Parker?'

'Yes, guv. Talk later.'

Jack stared at the phone receiver for a beat, then looked back at Hirem. 'The gloves?' he said. 'Were you going to say Jonathan Parker?'

Hirem nodded. 'Yes. One dropped out of his coat when I fetched it after the interview.'

The expletive that Jack released cost him five pounds and morning tea for everyone. Joan took great delight in collecting his debt.

'I hope it was worth it,' she said, with a wry smile.

'I am going to nail that bastard,' he said, dropping still more coins into the tin.

'Better make that six pounds,' Joan suggested.

Jack's phone rang. 'Geoff? What's the news?'

'Hawk . . . something's wrong.'

'What do you mean?' It was a daft question given he already suspected that something had gone awry with Kate's plans; Geoff was simply confirming it.

'There was a note.' His best friend's voice was shaking. 'She obviously got a call last night when she got home and went out again. The note says she didn't want to interrupt my interview or disturb your much-needed sleep, so she headed out alone to meet him.'

'To meet who?' Jack asked, pleading to the universe that Geoff was not going to say the name he dreaded.

'To meet Jonathan Parker.'

Jack banged Joan's desk with his fist, startling her.

'Why would she go alone, Hawk? And while I don't think he's especially danger—'

'Mate, stop!' Jack almost shouted.

'What?'

'We've just discovered Parker's our man.'

The silence was so heavy it felt like a third person breathing down the line.

'The gloves are his?' Geoff asked.

'The gloves, yes. All his calls have been made from London, not Scotland, or anywhere else for that matter. Sarah can't find this guest house owned by the McPherson family in Pitlochry. And I've just realised something else. He has consistently pointed us towards James Clydesdale and said they'd spoken, yet Clydesdale denied he'd ever met or spoken with Parker.'

'So he's got Kate?' Geoff said dully. 'Why?'

Jack shook his head. 'She baited him a few times, but—'

'She may already be dead,' Geoff said, his voice breaking.

'Geoff, listen, if he wanted her dead, he'd have killed her and left her for you to find.' There was silence and then Geoff cleared his throat, as though composing himself. 'Right?'

'Yep.'

'So he has her, but we're going to find him and get her back.

'Without her, Hawk, I won't be able to—'

'You won't be without her. We're going to get her back,' Jack said firmly, in a choked tone that was simmering with anger; it was one his colleagues didn't often hear.

25

In Parker's absence Kate was speaking to herself firmly, impressing upon herself that inactivity was the same as cowardliness. No one was going to come and save her unless she found a way to help herself first. Geoff would have likely read her message by now, and would hit the alarm button when he didn't hear from her. Jack would mobilise people, but he wouldn't know where to direct them.

Who could guess at this strange place?

Don't be a defeatist, she berated herself. *Think!*

She hauled herself to her feet and took stock. She was definitely on some sort of allotment, and although she could see two people in the distance, they were unlikely to hear her screaming for help, especially with gaffer tape plastered to her mouth. She considered trying to break a window with her head, but that thought passed quickly. Even if she succeeded, they might look up but would probably pass it off as a cat or something. They were a long way off to make sense of an odd sound like that. Instead, she focused her attention on what Parker had been doing through the night.

There were two contraptions. She didn't understand them, with their complex wiring and assorted bits of metal and plastic, but they looked dangerous, like trigger mechanisms, and he had already proven repeatedly that he was a man who followed through on his plans. She had no doubt that Jonathan Parker was serious in his intention to cause harm . . . but where?

The more she thought about it, the more she felt certain it had to be Barnet Hospital in North London, where it had all begun. Given Parker had been picking off as many in the chain that had contributed to his son's death, it seemed plausible that he would also want to attack the facility responsible for it. It made sense. And Jack would get there in his reasoning too . . . but he needed to know it was Parker.

How would he know?

Their only clue was the gloves. Had she seen Parker with any? She closed her eyes to think. No, she hadn't. But there was that time during his first interview when Sarah had hung up his outdoor clothes. Had he worn gloves? Had they missed an opportunity? She desperately wanted to see them in her mind's eye, but she was reaching for the impossible; she had not seen them. And then she recalled watching him leave the police station. He'd been digging in his pockets for something, hadn't he? She'd presumed it was his phone and had turned away, but what if it was gloves? Had Hirem seen anything when he fetched Parker's clothes? Had Sarah spotted one, perhaps? If anyone had, it would be her.

She sighed with frustration, tears prickling her eyes.

Please, please. Don't cry! Doesn't help. What can you use here and now? Look around.

She did. After more than ten minutes of searching, hampered by the handcuffs, she found her phone on a shelf in a tin that had once held canned peaches. She managed to manoeuvre the tin off the shelf using her nose and chin, all the while praying that her phone wouldn't break when it ultimately fell onto the floor. *Amazing what can be achieved when you're desperate*, she thought, letting out a manic laugh.

When the tin toppled onto the floorboards, the glass screen of her shiny, prized iPhone cracked but didn't shatter. Alongside it lay the battery and sim. How would she speak, even if she could jump the hurdles ahead of assembly and actually dialling?

The gaffer tape had to come off. Rubbing her cheek repeatedly against the wall of the shed, the side of the desk, the door, she managed to lift a corner. *To hell with your complexion, keep going.* Her face hurting now, she continued to rub until the tape had rolled back enough that she could move at least half her mouth. It would have to do. No more time wasting. Parker could walk back in at any moment.

She took several slow, deep breaths. Her life now depended on bringing all her years of experience to the fore. She had to find intense focus and she had to remain calm despite the fear that wanted to engulf her. *You're a police officer. You're a senior detective. Prove your worth now!* She could see Jack and Geoff both nodding at her in her imagination; both of them encouraging her to save herself. She had great dexterity and flexibility. She could do this. All the years of yoga, and gymnastics when she was younger, had helped her to remain supple.

And one more thing. Her nickname at school was Louis. Or King Louis to be more precise, from the old Disney animation of *Jungle Book*. Even Kate had found it amusing that her long, elegant arms, which she had always been privately vain about, became a source of affectionate teasing from mates comparing her to an orangutan who loved to dance. *Lovely extension*, her early ballet teacher had claimed, referring to how beautifully Kate could position her slender arms; later as a gymnast those long lines once again had helped. And it was no doubt why goal attack was her key position in the school netball team; her reach was brilliant.

She would use that reach now. One more deep breath.

Kate pulled her knees tightly towards herself and then shifted to sit on her hands. There was no way to break free of the cuffs. Her only hope was to somehow contort herself through the loop of her arms using her suppleness to wriggle through the hoop of her own body. She felt the prickles of perspiration as she began to slowly manoeuvre. She knew she could do it; the only thing that would stop her would be Parker's arrival or her own fear. She couldn't control one but she could certainly banish the other.

Do it! Geoff said in her mind. He loved her arms, kissing the length of them. Tears leaked at that thought. He would do that again.

She eased one way, then the other. Her shoulders began to protest and her wrists were rubbing raw beneath her but she found a level of concentration that she didn't know she had, where all outside sounds and all thought disappeared. Her ears began to ring with the intensity of her focus as she brought her arms beneath herself and around her toes.

Kate had no time to even celebrate as she had to get on with assembling the phone swiftly. She wiped her eyes with her bound hands, sniffed and set to. Kneeling now, she realised there was another hurdle to jump. How was she going to open the little hatch on the iPhone without the special tool that released the lock mechanism? Pushing off her knees, she went to the table, searching in vain for anything that resembled a pin of any kind. Her gaze roamed hungrily across the litter of Parker's work. Surely there was a safety pin or at worst a good old paper clip; she'd seen that used successfully.

Nothing. With a deep growl of frustration, she pushed some of her hair that had loosened back over her ear so she could see properly and her fingers touched her metallic teardrop earring.

The earring! 'Yes!' she squealed, immediately pulling it from her lobe. She stared at it, then closed her eyes with private triumph. Not wasting any further time, she pushed the end of the earring into the hole on the side of the phone and wanted to shriek with victory as the little drawer popped open. She pulled the other earring out and put both in her pocket – he wouldn't notice, she was sure – and with trembling fingers she put her sim card and battery into the phone, closed the back and switched it on. Mercifully it was almost fully charged because she'd plugged it in the moment she'd got home.

She found his name and dialled Geoff. 'Please, please,' she whispered.

It didn't even ring but went straight to voicemail. She gave a low gasp of anger. Out of battery, probably; she was always giving him a hard time about operating on too little power. 'One day you'll desperately need it, and you won't have any,' she could hear herself saying.

That day had come.

Without her permission, fresh tears began slipping down her cheeks, dropping onto the phone in splashes and running into the cracks. She hit the number she knew would answer immediately. She took a beat to compose herself and sniff back those tears. She needed to sound strong.

'Kate! Where?' Good. Jack wasn't wasting time on the most obvious raft of questions or expletives that she was still alive.

'I'm in some kind of potting shed, I suppose. About three by two, pretty old. Allotments somewhere, a few people around but not many. Must still be London, because we only drove for about twenty minutes.'

'Direction?'

She had tried to pay attention to the turns they'd taken. 'If I had to put money down, I'd say north.'

'Okay.'

'Jack, it's Parker.'

'We know. He owns the gloves.'

She didn't waste time on the energy it would take for recrimin-ation. 'He's building what looks to me like two incendiaries, not that I know much but I did a rudimentary course years ago when I worked at the airport.'

'Right. Are you hurt?'

'I'm all right, but he assures me he's going to . . .' She couldn't finish; her chin was wobbling and she didn't want him to hear her voice cracking. 'Jack, I hear a car. Bye.' She clicked off, Jack's voice distantly imploring her to wait. She had to get the phone back in the tin. She realised she would never be able to take it apart again and get it back onto the shelf, and she had to hide the fact that she'd spoken to someone for a few moments as he'd be able to check, so, in a moment of madness, she got back on her feet, glad for all that strength training that ensured she could do this move swiftly and smoothly. Without hesitation she smashed the heel of her sneaker into the already broken glass of her phone, then again, and again, using all her weight. Then she kicked it madly around the room, feeling out of control. She checked through the window; he was getting out of the car. One more thing to do. She did her best to roll the duct tape back over her mouth, pressing her face against the wall. It was only half successful, but it would do.

When Parker opened the door he found his prisoner propped against the wall, her face red from rubbing and the tape he'd applied looking ragged at one end, although her mouth was still covered.

He made a tsking sound. 'What have you been up to, Kate?' He ripped the tape off her face, intending it to hurt, and she gave him the sound of pain he wanted. 'Oh dear, look at the state of your cheek.'

It was only then he noticed the phone in the corner of the room. He grabbed it, quickly noticing how badly broken it was, but the fact that the battery and sim were now missing – inside the phone instead of lying next to it – wasn't missed.

He tried turning it on. Mercifully, it refused to obey. 'What's happened here?'

'Did you think I wouldn't look for it?' she said, shrugging.

'I meant to take it with me. But I can't imagine what sort of gymnastics it took.' He laughed unkindly. 'Look at you. Almost freed yourself. But the door's padlocked, and even slim you couldn't get out of that window. So who did you call?'

'I tried my partner and he went to voicemail. And of course I tried Detective Superintendent Hawksworth and he too went to voicemail. And then you arrived so I took out my frustration on the phone.'

He tsked again. 'After all that effort. Did you leave messages?'

'Just that I'm on some allotment somewhere. I had time for nothing else.'

'Why destroy it, then?'

'You clearly don't understand frustration.' She feigned a look of despair. 'I was so enraged I trashed it.'

He laughed again, this time with delight. 'Temper, temper, Kate.'

'Go to hell! None of this is going to end well for you, no matter what happens to me.'

'Oh, fighting words,' he crowed. 'Well done! Do you think I care what happens to me? I've been in hell for years. When you've been through what I went through in Northern Ireland, only to escape it and find sanctuary with my wife and child and then have that shattered too . . . Well, let me assure you, I want it to end but I'll take the bastards responsible for Billy with me.'

'With a bang?' she snarled, hoping to keep him angry. If he lost control, he might reveal more than he intended to.

'Yes. Congratulations, you've worked it out. I knew you were a smart bitch. I'm going to see that hospital go up.'

'What, with that?' she said, sounding derisive as she nodded towards his small contraptions.

'You're thinking too small, Kate, but don't worry. These are just incendiaries to create a much, much bigger problem.'

He slammed the door open and disappeared for a minute before he came back, this time pushing another person into the shed ahead of him. 'We won't be here for long. They won't find us in time.'

Jack stared at his silent mobile, the line dead, a taut silence around him as everyone waited.

He became aware of their stares: people needing direction. 'Joan, can you ring Geoff, please.'

'Immediately,' she said, looking uncharacteristically anxious.

He looked at his team. 'Jonathan Parker has Kate. She believes she's being held in some allotments, and her best guess under the circumstances is North London. We need to draw a circle from Islington of about twenty-five minutes in a car driving in the early hours of the morning, so next to no traffic. See what you get. I want everyone on this now. If we can find Kate, we can find Parker and vice versa.' He took them all in. 'Parker has threatened to kill her. We know he's more than capable of that. So time is not our friend.' He turned away to signal for them to hop to it.

Joan was back. 'Line one.'

Jack picked it up. 'It's me.'

'Don't say—' Geoff said, warding off his greatest fear.

'She's alive. I spoke to her.'

Geoff gave a sound like a wounded animal. 'She called me, but my phone was dead. Where is she?'

Jack told him what he knew. 'Where are you?'

'About fifteen minutes away.'

'Geoff, I need you sharp.'

'Sharp enough to cut this guy's throat, Hawk.' He sounded determined.

When Geoff walked in, Jack gave him a brief squeeze on the
shoulder. 'We've got some thoughts.'

'Okay. Hit me,' Geoff said.

'Sarah?'

'Sir. Right. Between us all, we came up with more than twenty
possible sites. But we've narrowed it down to three.'

Geoff frowned. 'Why?'

'We took in isolation, number of users, access for cars, number
of sheds and potential for privacy, sir,' Sarah said.

'We have to hedge our bets,' Jack said to Geoff.

His friend was pale, his hair still damp from his shower, but there
was no doubting he had clicked into full investigative mode. He
nodded and, not waiting for Jack, gave orders. 'John, Simon, let's
get squad cars to all these places immediately. No sirens, and lights
to go off on approach.'

The men jumped into action immediately.

'Nat,' Jack said, 'get onto Hannah Parker and ask if she knows
about an allotment that her husband might have had. Sarah, any
more information on the guest house in Scotland?'

'Nothing. If you don't mind my saying, sir, given what we've
learned, this is likely just a cover story. I see no calls to Scotland
on his phone records.'

'Right. Hirem, get onto his company, Armourex, is it?'

'Yes, sir?'

'Find out everything you can from them using the excuse of your
file for the Crown prosecutor.'

'Right, guv.'

'Sarah, Geoff, with me, please.' He led his two senior detectives
back into his office.

★

Kate stared at the trembling, tear-stained woman that Parker had dragged into the shed.

'Kate, meet Emily. She's the paediatrician who helped to murder my son.'

Emily shook her head and wept again.

'Shut up, doctor. I think it's a good lesson if your children learn to live without you. A good, hard lesson.'

'Jonathan, this is madness,' Kate began.

'Be quiet! Emily, this is Kate, a nasty, bossy, arrogant detective who has been following all the wrong pathways and missed the obvious one. She'll die alongside you before her precious colleagues work out where we are.' He gestured to the floor. 'Both of you sit there. We don't have long.' He waggled a finger at Kate. 'I just can't trust that you didn't get onto the Keystone Cops before you destroyed that phone, so I'm going to bring my plans forward.'

Kate began to object and, just to show he wasn't messing around, Parker lifted what looked like a pipe and without any further warning, hit the back of the paediatrician's knee. She went down, letting out a scream of pain.

'Ooh, that had to hurt,' he said without sympathy. 'Now you see, Kate, each time you open your objectionable mouth to make a smart comment that you think might outwit me, slow me down or put me on the back foot, I will hurt her more. You're both going to die, but she'll die a bloody, aching mess.'

Kate nodded. 'Okay, okay,' she said. She'd got the message.

'Now, ladies,' he said, far more conversationally, 'let me do my work. It should only take a few minutes more and then we'll be on our way.'

Sarah was at Jack's side. 'I've dug into his background, sir, and you're right. He's ex-army, spent a lot of time in Northern Ireland. A bomb specialist.'

Jack's expression fell; that made his foe infinitely more dangerous.

'And since he now works in high-end security products, I imagine it hasn't been too challenging for him to acquire what he needs.'

'Okay, thanks, Sarah.' Jack rubbed his temples.

'One more thing, sir. He left the army due to PTSD.'

Jack nodded. 'That fits. Right. Forgive me, Geoff, for what I'm about to express, but it has to be said that if Parker wanted Kate dead right now, he would have killed her where she stood, hidden away at home in Islington.' He watched Geoff swallow but also nod. 'Instead he's taken her, which means he has plans, because I can't imagine Kate is easy to keep quiet or still. She's already phoned us, which hopefully he doesn't know about.'

'Her phone's not answering. Goes straight to voicemail,' Geoff said, his tone dark.

'So he's turned it off or destroyed it.'

'I tried to trace it while you were talking,' Sarah said, 'but she just wasn't on long enough.'

Jack told them about the explosive material.

'So he's building a bomb?' Geoff asked.

'Kate said there were two explosive devices. They're small, so I feel they're obviously going to set off something bigger.'

'Has to be the hospital.' Geoff frowned.

Jack nodded. 'My thought too. So let's work out how he's going to do that.'

'Two explosions?' Sarah said. 'Maybe one's for Filton, where Olivia Craddock's blood was processed.'

Jack looked daunted. 'It's a good thought, but how would he control one in Bristol and one in London?'

'He could use a timer?' Sarah offered. 'But I have no idea how that works.'

'Let's find out, shall we? Geoff, get the bomb squad involved.'

Geoff stood to go and make the call, looking relieved to have something to do.

'We need to warn the people in Bristol, sir, just in case,' Sarah said. 'I know it's a hunch, but it's an informed one. He can't be there yet, so we can have security tightened everywhere while we try to learn more. He might have set up a bomb in Bristol before he got the London explosives ready.'

'Yes, good. I'll leave that with you. My worry is that he could already be at the London hospital, though, with Kate and whatever ghastly plan he's hatched. I have to phone the chief. Brief the others, will you? And let me know urgently about those allotments.'

She left as he was dialling Carol, who listened without interruption before finally speaking.

'What do you need, Jack?'

'Geoff is getting the bomb squad, ma'am, but short of that, I just need arms and legs.'

'Whatever's required.' She paused. 'What do you imagine he's thinking for Kate?'

Jack didn't want to answer because that would mean airing the thought that had been knocking on the door of his mind for the last twenty minutes.

'Sorry, I shouldn't—'

'It's okay, we have to think like this or we're not doing our job,' he said, sounding more composed than he felt. 'Kate disliked Jonathan Parker for some reason and—'

'For *good* reason, I'd say.'

'Yes, as it's turned out. I think the feeling became mutual. I don't believe he was just playing at the role of concerned husband. I think he's actually still deeply committed to Hannah, and has been pretending to be someone else for her benefit. So while I thought Kate's interview – and I have listened to it – was handled sensitively, there was a souring between them on subsequent meetings. I think

Kate found him insincere because he left his wife when Kate believed she needed him most.'

'That's highly subjective.'

'It is, and I did suggest she cool her attitude a little. I think he knew she was baiting him, though. I know we try to get a rise out of someone in interviews, get them to spill something they may not have intended to, but I didn't think it was helpful at the time. That said, Kate perceived a wrong note in him – something I wasn't tuned in to. Either way, he plans to punish her for treating him with what he likely considered was disrespect.' Jack paused, before delivering the line he wished he didn't have to. 'I think he plans to kill her, ma'am, in a way that satisfies his ego somehow.'

There was a momentary silence before she spoke in a hardened tone. 'I expect you to prevent that death, Jack, at all costs.'

'If it takes my last breath, ma'am.'

26

Kate had put her arm around Emily, who was presently inconsolable.

'Do you know where we are?'

'East Finchley,' Emily said between crying gasps. 'I have children. Three of them.'

'They're at school?' Kate murmured, trying to get Emily talking to distract her. Parker was making trips to his car, coming and going. He was clearly preparing to leave.

'Yes . . . yes, they are,' she said, her breath slowing a little.

'Then they're safe.'

'No. He said he'll kill all of them if I don't do what he says. My youngest is just five.' A fresh sob escaped her.

'We'll get him before he can do anything to your family,' Kate assured her, though she didn't wholly believe it.

Emily shook her head. 'I trust him to carry out his threat. I'll do whatever he asks. He promised me he would not hurt them if I do exactly as he wants. I have to. They're my children. Do you have any?'

'No, er . . . not yet,' Kate said, and somewhere deep it hurt to admit. Would she ever get the chance?

'You can't know. You can try to imagine, but you can't understand. I will do anything to keep them from harm.'

'And what is it that he wants you to do, Emily?'

'I don't know. He didn't say.'

Parker barged back in, suddenly sporting a convincing beard. 'Be quiet, you two, murmuring over there in the corner. It's no good plotting, Kate, or trying to persuade Emily to listen to you. Emily knows full well what's at stake here, don't you?'

She nodded.

'So follow my instructions and your children, unlike my child, will be guaranteed their safety.'

'You're a heartless bastard, Jonathan,' Kate snarled. 'Your child dies because of an accident so you threaten to kill other children? What kind of father are you? And you're supposed to be an army veteran?' Now she gave a snort of disdain. 'You're a weak, snivelling coward who hurts others.' She was pushing him, but it was the only weapon she had right now.

'I lost my son!' he yelled.

'And don't we know it!' Kate snapped. 'He's gone. He's dead. But I didn't do it. She didn't do it. Her *children* certainly didn't do it. Life and its ugliness happened, Jonathan. Billy's death was tragic. Tragic! But much as you want to blame people, it was an accident. A terrible, horrible, turn-back-time, wish-it-never-happened accident that Sally Holman would have regretted for the rest of her life if she'd been allowed to live it. She was a good nurse by all accounts – no, a great one. She was so dedicated to her patients that when her superior asked her to stay back after a long shift, she couldn't say no because a child was involved. A child who had already been through enough. No one wanted to scare him by pushing more needles into his arm. So they got their best on the job. Sally Holman was the queen of paediatric needles – she could get a needle into the arm of a child with so little fuss that her praises were sung by paediatricians and parents.

'But she was tired, Jonathan. She was exhausted, in fact, after a double shift that the hospital shouldn't have expected from her. And then it asked a little more and she said yes because she was a damn good nurse. You know this. And then she made an error . . . it was the perfect storm . . . two boys with similar names, similar ages, similar procedures and in the same ward. Fuck me! Why couldn't anyone see that at the time?' she said with deep frustration. 'The potential for error was ripe . . . and it happened. An accident. And now six or more people are dead because you will not accept that Billy could have had any number of accidents, from a hit-and-run driver to falling down and hitting his head. We all walk around vulnerable each day, and we protect our children to the best of our ability, but accidents do occur . . . they occur every day to the innocent. Billy was an innocent, but so were Sally Holman, Alec Chalmers, Annie Dawes, Janine Bowes, Olivia Craddock and Patricia, that poor woman in Cardiff who died simply to give you cover. Stop it now, Jonathan. Just stop! Billy is not coming back, no matter what you do to the world.'

He stared at her for a few seconds, then clapped slowly. Her cheeks burned even more.

'Great speech, Kate. Go fuck yourself! Get up, Emily.'

'No, please!' the paediatrician bleated.

He hauled her to her feet awkwardly and she gave a gasp of pain because her hands were cuffed and her knee was clearly injured. 'You are going to do everything I say, remember? Or you know the consequences. If you listen to Kate, here, you know I'm not lying.'

'What do you want me to do?' Emily asked, barely holding it together.

He opened a bag he'd carried in. 'I want you to put this on.' Parker lifted a vest of sorts from the bag and Kate closed her eyes with despair. She knew what he was going to ask Emily to do. 'Put this on,' he commanded. 'And then we go. Up on your feet too, Kate, and don't take your time, or I'll hurt Emily again.'

Emily looked at Kate, who couldn't meet her gaze, desperately hoping her colleagues had narrowed down the allotments that allowed car access in North London. She had to hope Jack was racing through all possibilities and would land on East Finchley quickly.

At least she'd got the part of London right by saying north.

Everyone was staring at the names that had been written up on the board: Bells Hill, Gordon Road, East Finchley.

'So these are our best guesses?' Jack asked.

'Yes, guv.' Hirem ran through the rationale for whittling down all the allotments in North London to this trio.

'And the most likely of the three?'

Hirem gave a shrug, then glanced at Simon and John, who both sighed with discomfort at having to choose. Jack knew it was a stab in the dark at this point.

'Right. Onto phones and get hold of whoever administers those allotments – let's see if we can find Parker listed as a member.'

People moved at Jack's command.

Geoff walked back in and joined him, staring at the board. 'East Finchley,' he said, looking thoughtful.

Jack looked at him in query.

'It's really not that far from our place. It's also quiet, bounded by woods, private gardens and more allotments. The area is cut through by two streams, which makes it even quieter. It has plenty of sheds and, best of all, allows access to cars. Before you ask, I know this because my dad had an allotment there when I was a kid. It's pretty much perfect for Parker's needs, in terms of secrecy. Of course, if this is his hideout, he likely used a false name. Is it worth wasting the time looking into all the records?'

Despite his calm tone, Jack sensed the deepening anxiety in his friend. He'd walked in these shoes and understood.

'You want to gamble?' he asked softly, his own tone neutral.

'It's where he'd choose – I can feel it.'

Jack made his decision. 'Sarah,' he called. 'Check with the squad cars standing by. Let them know we're on our way. Hirem, you go to one, and Simon, you lead the other. Geoff, you get down to East Finchley.' He looked at them sternly as they quickly gathered what they needed. 'No heroics, lads – this guy is desperate to finish whatever he's started, and he won't hesitate to hurt, maim or kill – and we have no idea what weapons he has. Everyone stay in touch via Sarah.'

'Coming, boys?' Geoff said to the two remaining men from his team, John and Bill. He had a murderous look in his eye.

'Geoff?'

'Don't, Hawk. I know.'

Jack nodded and let him go. He would have to trust his friend not to beat Jonathan Parker to a pulp if he found him.

Parker bundled Kate into the boot again. It was a different car to hers. This was a sleek German car with a private numberplate. It had to be Emily's.

'Try anything, Kate, and Emily suffers, do you understand?'

She nodded and he slammed the boot shut. The car, whose boot would have gladly closed with little more than a click, probably resented such treatment, she thought, feeling around in the dark with her sneakered foot for the tail-lights.

Meanwhile, she heard him shoving Emily into the back of the car, telling her to get on the floor. 'Don't so much as raise your head to look out, or it's a black mark for you. Two of those and I'll kill your youngest, Eddie. I know where he goes to school. I suspect your nanny – Rose, isn't it? – will pick him up today as usual. And she won't be spooked by me. I'll tell you why later. Pay attention to the rules.'

Kate, trying to decide if she could kick out the back lights in this strongly built car, heard a whimper and winced. That poor woman. Kate hoped she'd keep her head down.

As soon as they were in motion and she was sure they were within traffic, she began her efforts. Not nearly as easy as they made it look in films, she thought, as she kicked repeatedly, using every ounce of her strength. That was all she had right now. It took her most of the journey to finally break through, only to discover her foot was too big to fit through the hole she'd created. A toe then. She shoved the tip of her sneaker through as far as it would go and wiggled it for as long as he kept driving. Would someone see it? She didn't know, but she had to try.

On the road, behind a silver Audi in the next lane, an eight-year-old was riding in the back of her mother's SUV. She hadn't gone to school today because her parents had decided on a midweek break at their holiday home in Wendover. Next to her, her new brother gurgled in his car seat.

'Are you on the road?' her mother said, on a call via the Bluetooth.

'I'll leave the office in ten, I promise,' her father's disembodied voice said into the car. 'Kids okay?'

'All loaded and happy. Ollie is sleeping, but Flora would like to say hello. Go on, Floss.'

'Hi, Daddy.'

'Hi, darling. You looking after everyone?'

'Yes,' she said in a droll tone, as though weary of taking care of everyone in the family. 'Are you driving near us?'

'Very soon. I'll suddenly catch up in my fast car and wave next to you.'

She giggled. 'Daddy?'

'Yes?'

'In the car next to us, I can see a foot poking out of the boot and it keeps moving.'

'What?' her mother said, laughing. 'What are you talking about, Flora?'

'There.' She pointed. 'Look.'

Her mother peered to their right, glancing back and forth as she tried to confirm what Flora was saying. 'Bloody hell, Hugo, she's not lying.'

'What do you mean?'

'There's a foot poking out of a broken light at the back of a car . . . an expensive Audi driving next to us. Hang on.' She sped up slightly. 'There's just a guy driving. He's got someone in the boot, I'm sure of it.'

'It's probably a joke.'

'Maybe. But what if it isn't? What if he's kidnapped a child or something? I don't want to spend the next four days wondering if I should have done something.'

'Then pull over and call the police. Do you know where you are?'

'Yes.' She told him.

'Make sure you get the numberplate.'

'Okay, I'll call you back.'

'Mummy, the foot's wiggling again.'

'I know, just hold on while I call someone.' She took a breath and dialled quickly, not bothering to pull over.

'Emergency, which service, please?'

'Er, the police.'

'Connecting you.'

'Police emergency,' a new voice answered.

'Hello, this is Isabelle Wilson.' She gave them her exact location. 'My daughter noticed that someone is in the boot of a silver Audi.'

The woman on the other end was all business. 'How do you know this, madam?'

'Whoever it is has smashed out the left car light and we can see the toe of a sneaker constantly wiggling.'

'It's happening again,' Flora called.

'Can you read the car's numberplate, please, madam?'

'I can, yes.' Her mother recited it.

'Can I have your phone number please, Mrs Wilson?'

She dutifully gave it, and sighed.

'Right, I'll put out a notice to cars in the area. We'll find it, Mrs Wilson, thank you. You can continue your journey.'

Flora wriggled with excitement. They were going to save the person in the car!

Jonathan Parker, oblivious to the fact that a squad car was now heading in his direction, started making the twists and turns that would take him into Barnet and its hospital.

He could feel the frisson of excitement taking hold. Here it was finally: the gallop to the finish line that he'd been planning for years. He'd probably had some luck on his side – he'd got much further into his list than he had expected. It still irked him that he couldn't get them all, but taking the paediatrician hostage and using her car to deliver everything to the hospital was a masterstroke.

He wished he could have made a car bomb and blasted half the hospital away, or at least damaged it sufficiently to require its demolition, but, if his luck held, he might still make a magnificent statement.

Should he call Hannah to say goodbye? No. It would only upset her, and potentially alert police to where he was. Best to stay off the phone and away from the woman he loved; they would surely be in touch with her already. The gloves were his mistake, Kate had said, though he didn't know how. He'd thought himself cunning to use the knitted gloves for the strangulations and abductions; he couldn't imagine how they had connected them with him. It bothered him that he'd somehow overlooked such an important clue, giving himself away to his hunters. He would ask Kate – torture it out of her if he needed to – if he had the time.

He could see the hospital now. With this car, he could use the paediatrician's parking spot. It was perfect. Underground, no cameras. No one within the hospital staff and security would think anything odd.

27

Nat and Sarah looked at Jack, awaiting further instructions.

'How are we going with the bomb squad?' he asked.

'Detective Benson told them to be in touch with you, guv. They're waiting to be told where to go.'

He shrugged. 'For now, we wait. But good that they're ready. What else? Got a lead for me, Sarah?'

She looked hesitant. 'I'm not sure, sir. We had Emily Harley on our vulnerable list – she's the paediatrician who performed the tonsillectomy on Billy Parker. I just took a call from her husband.'

Jack's internal alarm bells began to jangle. *Not another body, please.*

'Apparently, his wife is not answering her phone, and no one seems to know where she is.'

'And what do we know?'

'She left her house this morning to drop her youngest at school, and her husband dropped off the two older kids. She was seen by other mothers and the teacher on playground duty – Emily spoke to her because her son has a slightly sore throat, and she didn't want him making any of the other children sick. She said they were to call if it got worse, but not before noon because she had two surgeries scheduled. But she never arrived at work. She's missed those two surgeries and hasn't contacted anyone. The husband's a banker in the city,' she said, scanning her notes, 'and he's understandably worried because Emily is pedantic, according to him, about not being late. He said she would never miss a surgery, short of some sort of emergency with the kids, and they're all fine. There have been no road accidents reported this morning between her home and work or the school where she dropped her son – I checked,' she finished.

'Where were those surgeries scheduled?'

'Barnet Hospital, sir.'

Jack knew in his gut this was the place. 'Right. Nat, tell the bomb squad to meet us at that hospital.'

'Where should they rendezvous?'

'Until Parker makes his move, we can't know exactly where they'll be needed, but I'd rather not alert him that we're there, because he'll flee or he may hurt Kate. As long as his plan's still alive, I suspect she is. Sarah, you'd better contact the director of the hospital or whoever has overall charge, and I'll speak to them. Parker likely has Emily Harley, so now we have two hostages,' he said, not allowing the thought that Parker might have already killed both women. 'We have to consider evacuation,' he said. 'I'll let the commander know.'

There was CCTV all over London; cities throughout the UK were increasingly being watched with a lot more capability than ever before. But right now, Barnet Hospital had no closed-circuit cameras installed in its staff area car park, other than at the entrance.

Jonathan Parker already knew this as he swung the Audi into the car park, following Emily's directions to her reserved space.

'Perfect,' he said. 'Well done, Emily. You can sit up now.'

She did exactly as she was told, eyes no longer wide but sunken with the fear of what was ahead. The vest she wore probably told her enough about her fate, he thought with satisfaction.

'Emily, I'm going to show you something now, and I want you to concentrate on it.' He pulled out his phone and showed her pictures of her three children from weeks earlier as they were coming and going to school, to ballet lessons, to swimming lessons and so on.

As her eyes welled with tears and she broke down once again, he said, 'I didn't show you this to upset you, Emily, but simply to remind you of what's at stake here. I want you to ask yourself what you value more . . . your life or the lives of your children?' He raised his brows. 'I'm guessing that, like every other parent I know, you'd choose your children. They're precious, aren't they? I wish I still had my child, but we know what happened to him. This hospital happened, and I would like to obliterate it. But what I don't want to do is hurt any other children, so I'm going to ask you to use the lift, enter the hospital, go to the wards and have them evacuated, as quickly as you can. I suggest you start with the children's wards, but you can warn whoever you want. I will give you thirty minutes − not a second over − from the time I see those lift doors close.' He paused and looked at her in mock despair. 'You need to stop crying, Emily. It's not doing anyone any good, and it won't save you or those innocents in there. If you pull yourself together, you can save a lot of lives, including the lives of your own babies. I know you're a good mother. I actually know you're a good paediatrician and a brilliant surgeon.'

At this she looked up, choking back a sob.

He nodded. 'I know you meant Billy no harm. And I mean your children no harm – really. But just as you could walk away and get on with your life after Billy died, I can certainly get on with what I have to do if your children have to die. I promise you, Emily – and I need you to believe me – I will not hesitate to kill them if you fail.'

She mumbled behind her duct tape. What was she saying? He ripped it off.

'I won't fail,' she insisted, repeating it over and over until it became a blended string of words.

'Shut up!' he said.

She did, staring blankly at him.

'I am counting on you. It's not complicated. Go into the hospital and have it evacuated as best you can, but don't leave. I want you standing in the same ward – you already know which one – and you must remain there. Do you understand?'

She nodded.

'If anyone tries to make you leave too, you threaten them, okay?'

'Okay,' she repeated.

'If you do as I ask, your children will never come face to face with me. They will grow up safe, with your husband and your family and friends.'

'But no mother,' she said, her tone flat, no query in it.

'I'm afraid not.'

'Is that what you would have liked for Billy?' she asked suddenly, as though awakening from a fugue state.

Parker hadn't expected that. 'Pardon?'

'Is this what you'd wish for your son – that kind of torment and trauma throughout his life?'

'He has no life!'

'I did not take it.' She met his gaze head-on. 'My skills gave Billy a chance at a much better life, without constant sore throats and problems. What I did took his pain away.'

'You ordered the blood that—'

'Would have helped him. He was bleeding, Jonathan, and I wanted him to have a swift and straightforward recovery that a top-up of blood would have given him. I did nothing wrong. I did everything right. His operation was routine, and it went perfectly well beneath my hands.'

He stared at her, all but shaking with rage. 'He died because you ordered the blood.'

'He died because of human error that was not mine. I ordered the correct type of blood. It wasn't my fault the wrong blood type was administered. But you have now murdered everyone involved with that blood.'

He shook his head. 'Not everyone.'

'Killing me is pointless.' She spoke softly.

'Killing you is a means to an end – I want the hospital to suffer.'

'Then have it evacuated with a bomb scare and blow it up yourself. Blow yourself up with it!'

He laughed. 'I didn't know you had it in you after all the blubbering. But it's time for you to move.'

'I won't do it.'

'You will.'

'The police will stop you.'

He laughed unkindly. 'They won't, you know. Look, Emily, this has been fun, but now you must go ahead and do as I've asked.'

'No.' She shook her head. 'I'm not going to help you with this . . . this sick plan.'

He sighed heavily and picked up his phone again. 'I want you to look at something else,' he said, flicking through until he found the photos he wanted. 'Here, recognise this?'

She peered at the small photo and gave a sharp gasp.

'I thought you might. Now, I've rigged your children's shed – where they keep their bikes and sporting gear – to go off at the touch of a button. I know your middle son likes to hang out in there with his mates. If you refuse to go now, I'll wait until around five this evening – I think that's football practice, isn't it? Michael will be looking for his muddy boots, so I might be able to send *him* to his maker at least. With some luck, one of his siblings might be nearby and catch some of the blast.' He waited a beat. 'How're you feeling now, Emily? Still feisty and defiant? Or are you resigned and compliant?' He grinned. 'Didn't mean to rhyme on you.'

She blinked several times. 'If I go in there, how can I trust you to do as you say?'

'You can trust me to blow this fucking hospital as high as I can – and you along with it. And you can trust me to keep my word. Once you've kept your side of this bargain, I'll keep mine. I really don't want to have to hurt your children.'

She took a deep breath and nodded. 'What about Kate?'

'Well, I can't wait to stop the racket she's been making in the boot. I have plans for her too, not too dissimilar to your fate.'

'But she has nothing to do with Billy!'

'No, but she's annoyed me enough that she can die for her trouble.'

Emily met his gaze again. 'Not so honourable, then. Killing as you please.'

'As I please, yes! Get going now, before I tire of this, or I'll just kill you where you sit and go deal with your kids.'

She nodded, resigned.

'Okay, let's get out of the car calmly.' He opened his door, stepped out and opened the back passenger door and helped her out. He checked the vest he'd adapted. 'You're good to go. Now, don't you try anything. I can hit the trigger at any time. Go and save some lives. Hurry.'

She began limping slowly, robotically, towards the entrance.

'Faster! Remember, you only have half an hour from . . . now!' he said, clicking the timer on his watch.

Kate could not follow the conversation inside the car; the voices were too muffled. But she did hear the doors open and close, and then she heard Parker, closer now, saying the words 'half an hour'. She let out an involuntary but mercifully quiet gasp and then the boot shot open.

Jack . . . Geoff . . . we've only got thirty minutes, she cast into the universe.

Parker ripped off the duct tape. 'If you scream, I'll taser you,' he said, showing her his handpiece. 'Now, get out.'

'Where—'

'Shut up and do as you're told, or I'll blow Emily sky high before she can evacuate any of the wards.'

Kate clambered out of the boot awkwardly. 'I hope you burn in hell, Jonathan,' she said, unable to think of anything more worthy to say to him.

'I'm sure I shall for my sins. Come on.' He was holding a backpack in one hand, but pulled her arm with the other.

She thought momentarily about fighting, but with her wrists still manacled she was no match for him. 'Where's Emily?'

'Cute. She was worried for you too. She said goodbye,' he said, pushing her along. 'Don't dawdle, Kate. He won't get to you.'

'Who?'

'Your handsome policeman – Hawksworth.'

'Can't imagine what he'll do when he gets to *you*.'

'He won't.'

'Oh, he will. He always gets the bad guy.' Kate wished she felt as confident as she sounded, but she knew Jack would do everything in his power.

'Superman, eh?'

'No. Just a much better human being than you,' she said as he shoved her through a door and down a flight of stairs. 'You don't rate as a man, Jonathan.'

'Oh, really? How do I rate?'

'Badly, in my opinion. More like a neanderthal. Do you want more of my opinion?' Perhaps, if she unsettled him, he'd make a mistake.

'I sense you're going to share it anyway. So sure,' he said, pushing her again. Another flight of steps. They seemed to be entering a basement.

'Given what you're up to, I'm guessing you're ex-army.'

'Bingo.' He grinned.

'But not successful there. I'm thinking you had to leave. PTSD?'

He shoved her forward again, saying nothing.

'Bingo,' she echoed, sneering. 'That explains plenty.' She decided to continue pushing her luck. 'So there's PTSD and the depression that goes with it. Add that to the death of Billy, plus the disinte-gration of your marriage, and I'd say complete failure has turned you into what you are.'

He pulled her around to face him. 'And what's that?'

'A weak bastard,' she said, almost spitting. 'A soulless monster. And Detective Superintendent Hawksworth loves catching monsters, although you've told me you're not trying to get away are you, Jonathan? But you know what? No matter what happens to me or Emily, you'll be forgotten. You'll just be the father of a little boy, tragically lost in a terrible accident, who turned out to be a killer. You've tarnished the memory of your beautiful child. Good job Billy didn't have to see what his useless, cowardly father has become.'

At that, he shoved Kate so hard she found herself sprawled on the concrete, both knees screaming in protest. All she could see were bright lights behind her closed eyelids; her knees, breasts and nose had taken the brunt of the fall, without the use of her hands to break it, and the pain was bright and sharp.

'Don't you fucking dare talk about Billy like that!' he warned.

'Why? Because you might kill me?' she said from the cold concrete. 'I'm not scared of you,' she lied, shaking inwardly. 'You couldn't make it as a soldier. You couldn't make it as a husband. You didn't make it as a father. And you blame the world for all your problems. Hannah is at least facing her punishment.'

He shook his head. 'Only because I made her.'

'I wonder what she'll go through when she discovers she was married to a cold-blooded murderer. You failed her in every way, didn't you, Jonathan? When you lost Billy, Hannah needed you to stay; she needed you to be strong for her. She needed someone to fight for her, to keep her sane through the toughest of times. Instead you left her and then you lied to her, putting her through more trauma, thinking of you with another woman, having another child. Ugh, you're despicable.'

'I did it for her, you bitch!' He was yelling now.

'No, you didn't. You did all of this because you're weak and you can't face what life has thrown at you. I don't wish your loss on anyone, Jonathan, but there are plenty of other grieving parents out there who help each other find a way through, and there are war-torn, weary soldiers who don't become monsters. You are just pathetic, so go on. Get on with it, this grand finish you're planning. I'm done with you.'

It certainly felt good to be so defiant, but the triumph didn't last. It began to leach out of her fast as she watched him break into a cage surrounding a row of what she presumed were oxygen tanks. He yanked her over to it and re-cuffed her, this time to the cage, making the bruise throb again. She had to squat awkwardly and then sit on the cold concrete, her hands bound tight behind her.

'Let me explain what's going to happen to you now,' he said. 'In each of these tanks is oxygen. The hospital uses it for the operations they perform, including during my boy's tonsillectomy. Increasingly, hospitals are using liquid oxygen tanks, which would make things much harder, but that's oxygen gas in there' – he nodded at the tanks – 'and it's highly flammable. So I'm going to give it a helping hand. I'll damage the valves over here, and when some of the gas escapes and I press the green go button on this phone' – he held up a mobile – 'then this smart little incendiary I have here – built cunningly from camera flash cubes – is going to explode and then ignite the gas, taking you and as much of the hospital as it can with it!' He laughed as he removed the contraption from his backpack and hung it around her neck.

She tried to struggle but it was hopeless.

'Best of all,' he continued, 'when I send the message through this phone, I suspect your pretty head will blow off first. Your friends – especially the handsome detective who was so kind to my wife – will find it, all battered and no longer the lovely Kate they remember.'

She looked away, unable to think of anything cutting or remotely defiant. Still, she was determined not to give him the satisfaction of crying or screaming. Silence. That was what most exhibitionists hated. And Jonathan Parker was craving attention in his small, pathetic life for all of his hurts.

She wouldn't provide it. She would turn inward and think about all that she was about to lose.

28

'I've got the hospital chief on the line,' Sarah told Jack. 'Line two, sir. His name is Les McCartney.'

Jack picked up the handset and pressed two. 'Mr McCartney?'

'Yes, what's all this about?'

'This is Detective Superintendent Jack Hawksworth from Scotland Yard, Mr McCartney, and while I don't wish to create unnecessary alarm, we have reason to believe that a man with a grudge against the hospital might be planning to do it harm.'

'In what way?' The man sounded rightly shocked.

'I'm afraid we can't be sure, but we're taking this threat very seriously. We believe he may have a bomb.'

There was a frigid silence on the other end.

Jack felt obliged to fill it. 'I am recommending that we evacuate the hospital, Mr McCartney.'

'Detective, you make that request sound so straightforward. Have you any idea of what might be involved in taking that action?' He sounded incredulous.

'Yes, sir, I do understand the magnitude of what I'm asking, but the alternative is terrifying to contemplate. I wouldn't suggest this if I didn't think the threat was entirely credible.'

'Sorry, Detective – just a minute. Yes, what is it, Amanda? Can't you see I'm . . .' The man moved away from the phone so Jack couldn't hear what was being said. A moment later he was back. 'Detective Hawksworth?' The hospital chief spoke with an entirely new tone.

'I'm here,' Jack said.

'I've just been told that Dr Emily Harley, a paediatrician who works at this hospital, has walked in wearing some sort of strange vest, and she's yelling at the staff to evacuate the hospital. She says she's wired with a bomb.'

Jack closed his eyes for a beat. It was happening. He needed to give concise direction. 'Right. Clear the hospital immediately, as best you can, Mr McCartney. The Met's Army Explosive Ordnance Officers are already en route – if you hear us talking about EOD or XPLOs, it's the bomb squad that we're referring to. I'm mobilising our people to help you with the evacuation.' He glanced at Nat, who was standing nearby, and nodded. She didn't need any further instruction, moving straight over to Joan, who was also keen to help, and both immediately jumped onto phones.

'I can't believe this,' McCartney said, clearly in shock. 'There are people in surgery right now; others are in chemotherapy, still others too sick to move right now.'

'We're on our way, sir. In the meantime, do whatever you and your staff can to get everyone who is able out of the building.' He rang off, and immediately his mobile rang. It was Geoff. 'Anything?'

'We were right about East Finchley. Found his shed and evidence of his bomb-making. I also found Kate's phone smashed to bits. I've already told the other units to stand down and await further instructions.'

Jack told him what was happening at the hospital.

'And only the paediatrician being used for this?' Geoff asked.

'So far. No news about Kate. Get everyone to the hospital,' Jack said. 'I'll meet you there. Hang on, Nat's got something.' He put Geoff on speakerphone and nodded at her.

'Sir, I've just heard through our channels that a squad car was sent to chase a silver Audi in north London, because another driver on the road noticed a foot wiggling out of the back rear light. Someone in the boot, in other words. They've had no luck hunting down the car.'

Geoff gave a choked laugh. 'Sounds like my girl.'

'And that car was moving in the general vicinity of the hospital,' Jack said. 'I still feel that's our best bet.'

'I do too.'

'See you there, mate.'

On the way to the hospital Jack briefed Commander Barton as the case once again returned to Counter Terrorism Command.

'So I've heard. Thought we'd put this threat to bed,' the commander growled. 'And now two people abducted, one of our own to boot.'

'We couldn't know the murders would become a domestic terror threat, sir,' he said, filling Barton's angry pause.

'So it's back to us.'

'Yes, sir. XPLOs and fire brigade should be there any minute.'

'And where's DCI Benson?'

'On his way, sir.' He explained about the East Finchley allotments.

'Right. Jack, you'll have all the help you need. Get this done.'

The phone rang hot. This time it was Joan. She'd had too much experience on operations to waste time with salutation or small talk or even why it was her who was bringing this information.

'The silver Audi belongs to the paediatrician. Parker abducted her in it.'

'Right. In the boot?'

'I have no idea. Why do you ask that?'

'I'm hoping the foot wiggling out of the broken tail-light belongs to Kate. She would think to do something like that.'

'Jack, I'm not telling you how to do your job, but just in case your head is swimming, you'd better warn people that with a bomb threat, the communications towers will likely cut their access to mobile phones.'

'Haven't forgotten, but thank you.' He was grateful she had his back, even though his mind actually tended to achieve its finest clarity under the worst pressure. He was more likely to lose his keys or forget a name when he was moving through a quiet day at the office reading cold case files. Still, he was grateful for her care. 'All our phones should work in the square kilometre around the hospital, even if no one else's do.'

'Good.' Joan paused. 'Bring her back, Jack.'

'I intend to.'

Nothing more needed to be said; neither of them dared to believe she was anything but alive.

When he got to Barnet Hospital, the ops team had arrived and Jack immediately got them organising cordons around the potential bomb site. 'Nat, one hundred metres and three hundred metres, you know the pack drill. Hirem, get all roads closed off.'

Nat and Hirem nodded, and they moved off.

'John, can you mobilise an evacuation of surrounding homes and streets?' John didn't even pause to nod, simply touched a finger to his temple in acknowledgement and moved away to get busy.

Geoff arrived as the bomb disposal team did. He had a spooked, faraway look and his skin, normally full of colour from outdoor exercise, had a pasty hue. Instead of its usual curl of soft amusement, his mouth was stretched into a thin line. Jack could feel his friend's despair. He was experiencing identical fear, but he owed it to Geoff to keep that well hidden.

The bomb disposal team wasted no time leaping from their van and pulling out all the necessary equipment. The head of the team lifted a hand to the two detectives as he approached. 'Geoff. Long time no see.' They shook hands; it was clear the men knew each other well.

'Ben,' Geoff said, his voice tight, 'this is Detective Superintendent Jack Hawksworth. Ben Wright,' he said to Jack.

'I know you by reputation, of course, sir,' Ben said with a brief smile.

'Jack is fine,' he said, shaking hands.

'Right. What have we got?'

Jack briefed him on what they knew. 'A doctor from the hospital is inside, wearing some sort of vest covered with explosives. The bomber, Jonathan Parker, has given her thirty minutes to get as many people out as possible, she says. The hospital triggered its evacuation protocols about' – he checked his watch – 'seventeen minutes ago.'

'Right. Do we know anything about the device?'

'Devices,' Jack corrected. 'Kate said there's two. One on the paediatrician, and the second, I'd guess, would be for Kate.'

At Ben's confusion, he said, 'He's got DCI Kate Carter.'

Ben cut a grave look towards Geoff. 'Do we know where?'

Both Jack and Geoff shook their heads.

Jack elaborated. 'He used the paediatrician's car to get into the hospital easily. No one has spotted Parker or DCI Carter yet.'

'Right, well, my lads will go in now and see what we're dealing with. Could be a timer, could be a phone signal. We'll be getting the gold sign-off for cutting mobile access,' Ben said.

'I can leave that with you?' Jack asked.

Ben nodded. 'I'll speak directly to the commander at CTC.'

'Stay in touch with Geoff – he's going to be co-ordinating my team.'

Ben glanced again at Geoff, who wasn't looking at either of them, a dazed look in his eyes. 'Are you sure, sir?'

'I am,' Jack said firmly. 'Have you got our numbers?'

'Yep, and I presume you're both in the twelve to fourteen range?'

Jack nodded, confirming that their phones would not be affected when the mobile network was switched off to the general public.

The XPLOs leader turned and began loping back to his team.

'Good luck,' Jack called. He looked at Geoff. 'You take control now, mate.'

'Why?'

'Because you're tuning out.'

Geoff gave a guilty sigh.

Jack clapped him on the shoulder. 'You're on the job, and I need you to focus and give clear instructions to our team. All right?'

Geoff nodded, looking embarrassed. 'Where are you going?'

'I want to follow a hunch. Besides, the commander asked me about you. You can't become a bystander. They're looking to you now,' he said, pointing, as he saw various members of the ops team moving in their direction.

Kate sat, unable to cope with all the thoughts scattering through her mind like a plague of insects. She decided she'd talk, rather than holding the silence. And for the first time today, she decided she'd talk to Jonathan Parker as another human being with frailties and sorrows, rather than as the enemy. She had nothing to lose right now.

'I meant to compliment you on your beard,' she began.

He looked at her, slightly surprised. 'Theatrical quality. Is it convincing?'

'It is.' She paused. 'How long have we got?' she asked.

'Fifteen minutes,' he replied. She was surprised he'd answered so readily.

'I'm sorry it's come to this,' she said.

He was leaning against the cage she was attached to and looked at her, raising his brows. 'Wow, that must hurt to say.'

She shrugged. 'Not really. If I'm going to die, I'd rather do so knowing my final words were not full of hate and despair.' She could see he wasn't ready for this more sombre mood; perhaps he preferred her fighting him. She held his gaze. 'And I do want to say that I am genuinely and deeply saddened that you and Hannah lost Billy the way you did . . . that you lost him at all, in fact.'

He swallowed. 'He was such a great kid.'

'Hopefully out of this horror some change might come in how hospitals are run.'

'Yeah. I doubt it, but I will hope alongside you for the same. For me, now at least, it's been about revenge. I don't know how to change the system – we thought the court case would make a difference but nothing really changed.'

Kate nodded in sympathy. That's what Hannah had said. 'Did you enjoy killing?' she asked, giving another shrug to say she wasn't judging. 'It's not often I get the chance to ask a murderer that sort of question.' She gave a chuckle and he joined in.

'How come we can be so friendly now?'

She tilted her head to one side. 'Imminent death does that. So go on, answer me.'

He looked down. 'No. I hated myself each time. As I prepared, I was filled with a righteous vengeance that I convinced myself I was allowed to feel. That carried me through, but after each death I wanted to vomit. I would feel sick for days. But I had to just keep going. I've got nothing else, Kate. I've lost everything – this hate is all that remains.'

'I'm sorry about that too . . . I'm surprised the army didn't offer more help in your earlier days, when you were part of it and obviously suffering.'

'Soldiers don't want to be seen to be weak. Well, they didn't back then, anyway. It's a bit more open now. People don't feel it's a failure to talk about the horror or the effects it has on you.'

'Are you planning to go up with me, then?' she asked, taking a weirdly bright tone. 'Should we hold hands and blast into the ether together?'

He actually laughed. 'You're probably good fun on a night out, Kate, when you're no longer a detective and being a ballsy bitch.'

'That's true. To be honest, I was sort of looking forward to settling down into a different role.'

He stared at her. 'What do you mean?' And then, before she could answer, he guessed. 'Motherhood?'

'Yeah, marriage, starting a family – all that I've denied myself for too long. I never did have good timing, though. Looks like I've just missed my window.'

He stared at her, the pause lengthening until he finally spoke. 'To answer your question, no, I've just decided that I am not going to die with you. I've realised I need to say goodbye to Hannah – hear her voice one more time, tell her how sorry I am and that I've always loved her. I don't want her to feel responsible or guilty about this. I've made all my own decisions in sound mind – it's not on her.'

Kate nodded sadly. 'I'd respectfully question the sound mind, given all you've faced, but fair enough.'

He paused again, regarding her seriously. 'I'm sorry you've been dragged into this.'

'It's my job.'

'Not to die.'

'No,' she said with a sigh. 'Not quite ready for that.'

Kate looked down, wondering if there was any way out of this, and then looked up as she heard a metallic sound against the concrete. She couldn't see anything in the shadows.

'That was the keys to the handcuffs. You were never part of Billy's death, Kate, so as much as you've angered me, I'm giving you a fighting chance. If your friends get here in time and can find the keys and unlock you, then good luck.'

'How do you control the bombs?' She frowned, desperate to know as much as she could, just in case her team did get to her.

He grinned. 'The bomb on Emily's vest is a fake. I never did want to hurt loads of people, especially children. But these tanks I want to explode, mostly to demolish the hospital or at least trigger a need for demolition. But you, you can suffer a different tension . . .' He held up a phone. 'Once I push this button, it's over.'

'Gosh, and there I was thinking we'd reached some sort of friendly plateau.'

'We had. Your keys are over there somewhere. You might still make it. Bye, Kate.'

She swallowed her fear. 'Hey, do you even know where Hannah is?' It was a last-ditch attempt to know where he was headed, again, just in case.

He spun on his heel and looked back at her. 'She's in Cornwall, remember. I helped her arrange it.'

'Well, you'd better hurry, because Jack Hawksworth will be on your tail.'

He shook his head. 'He'll be too busy trying to save you. Now, I've given you your very own countdown in my mind before I press the green button, but I'm not telling you how much.'

'Oh, go on. Be a sport,' she said, giving him a teasing smile she really didn't feel.

'Okay, then. Proper sport that I am, I'm giving you an hour.

That's more than you deserve, but you were nice at the end, so I'm rewarding you for that. Bye, bitch.'

She blinked, watched him walk over and kick the keys into the dark shadows of the basement. Then he pulled on a white lab coat and was gone.

29

Jack had to think objectively now. He found himself standing alone next to the silver Audi, the scene already taped off by his team. Parker had driven it in and sent the paediatrician into the hospital alone. How had he got her to co-operate? A doctor, who'd pledged to do no harm . . . It couldn't simply have been the bomb – if she thought she was going to die anyway, he didn't think anyone, let alone a clinician of her standing, would walk that bomb into the hospital to hurt more people, even if he had given her half an hour to get most of them out.

No. It had to be more. Parker would have had to frighten her sufficiently to overcome her sense of duty, override her own fears. He quickly dialled Joan.

'Jack?' There was so much hope in her voice.

'Joan, can you get on to Emily Harley's husband? I don't care what he's doing, he needs to have his children picked up and taken away from school, right now.'

'Okay. What do I say?'

'That they're in danger and we need to get them to safety. To his parents', her parents', a friend's, I don't care, but away from their home and away from school. Ask if they have a nanny – they're a busy, wealthy working couple, presumably, so they may have help at home. Don't let the children be picked up by the nanny – make sure it's the father and they all clear off.'

'Dialling now,' she said, and the line went dead.

He pressed in on his thoughts. *Come on, Jack. Forget Kate, forget the people at risk, and think like the bomber.*

He racked his mind for where he would zero in on if he wanted to create the most harm. Given that Parker had allowed Emily time to evacuate as many people as possible from the immediate area, he figured the bomber was now in a mindset to do damage to the hospital building itself; he was no longer interested in hurting individuals – other than the hapless paediatrician and Kate.

Explosives meant widespread damage to everything in its range.

His mind roamed. Parker had sent Emily in through the main hospital entrance. An IED going off there would achieve alarm and panic, but it wouldn't do the broader damage he believed Parker was after. The former soldier and grieving father was making a statement; he wanted to be noticed. He wanted the pain of his family to be understood, remembered, never to be repeated for any other family. He was punishing the system, the government, the public at large in order that they take heed. So a suicide bomb would hurt, maim some if they hadn't evacuated, but surely . . . surely he had a bigger plan.

What *was* the second device to be used for?

Incendiaries, Kate said.

So, fire. He was going to create a small explosion to trigger a fire to do what . . . burn the hospital down? No, that wouldn't work. Maybe damage it enough that it would need demolition. Yes . . . that would suit his plan to wipe out everything that had had anything to do with his son's death.

But to achieve that sort of destruction, he'd need to fuel a fire of some magnitude. Where would he get that sort of fuel? Petrol? No, he couldn't have brought in enough, and Emily's car had been checked for explosives and cleared, so it was no car bomb. Even with Jack's limited knowledge, he knew the car would need to be rigged with a lot of explosives anyway. He couldn't have got that much, and it would have taken time, more men to rig it. No, he was being more subtle, though not so subtle that fire crews could deal with it . . .

No, no . . . Parker needed something huge and explosive to bring down a significant part of the building. What, Jack demanded of the universe, would do that?

Hospital chemicals? But they would be stored inside under lock and key, Jack thought, and to use them, Parker would have to be inside. If he was, then his plan was already underway, and Jack couldn't accept that. A chemical fire could also be dealt with by a fast fire crew; they were already here and ready to go, awaiting instructions. Parker would have anticipated that.

If not chemicals, then what?

Oxygen! Nitrous oxide, carbon dioxide . . . the gases used in surgeries. Oxygen would help other materials ignite easily. If the tanks could be damaged, exploded somehow, they'd be perfect for getting a major fire going.

They didn't keep those tanks in the hospital wards, and Jack didn't have time to search all corners outside the building. He rang Geoff.

'Hawk?'

'Can you quickly reach the hospital director or anyone senior?'

'Yes, hang on.' He heard Geoff walking and then talking. 'I've got one of the surgeons here, but we're moving everyone out as fast we can. What do you need?'

'Ask him where the hospital's oxygen tanks are kept. I need a precise location.'

He heard Geoff ask the question and the man say he wasn't sure but he thought Esther would know and she was 'over there' helping move patients.

'Are you Esther?' Muffled voices. Then Geoff was back. 'They're in the basement below the staff car park. Apparently there's only one entrance, and it's hidden in the northern corner.'

'Thanks. Get Ben to phone me urgently.'

'Jack—'

'Do it, Geoff.' He rang off. It felt vicious to cut his friend off, but he didn't want to talk about Kate or whether this last-ditch idea was worthy. It was all he had.

Jonathan Parker had joined the slipstream of hospital evacuees, even helping to load a patient on a stretcher into an ambulance and then offering to take a patient in a wheelchair onwards while a grateful nurse helped others.

With his beard and white coat, together with the stethoscope hanging like a cliché from one of his pockets, he felt he looked the part. In the confusion, it was working, anyway. He pasted an expression of harried concern on his face and began issuing instructions to other people so as to look busy and doctor-like, taking charge. Within moments, he was part of the great mass hurrying out of the hospital and following police orders.

Once he was clear of the main grounds, he asked someone else to take the patient in the wheelchair, as he was going back to get others out.

'Be careful,' the woman said, and he smiled at her sadly, as though being heroic was the only approach he knew.

But as soon as she turned, he melted into the crowd and then made his way to its edge. Once he'd reached the cordon that the police were insisting everyone stay behind, he pulled off his white coat and continued to retreat. In the chaos he was able to get out into the street. He quickly pulled off the hoodie he wore, turned it inside out and pulled it on again. Not wanting to draw attention by running, he began to walk as fast as he could to the closest Underground.

His target was the train to Penzance just after 11 a.m., which he reached well in time; it had taken nearly forty minutes on the Underground via the Northern Line to King's Cross, changing there to the Metropolitan Line to Paddington Station. There had been a hold-up but he remained calm. There was another train an hour later – a direct – but he just wanted to get on his way so no wily detective could trap him at the mainline station. At Paddington he bought a ticket to the far west.

The beard itched. Anyone looking out for the pillar-box red hoodie he'd worn this morning, if Kate was able to give a description, would perhaps look past the dull gunmetal grey he now wore. The beard, the glasses he'd donned and now a cap, to hide his hair, would add the extra layer of disguise that might just work long enough.

He planned to enjoy the five or so hours of train travel to see Hannah again. They would be the last peaceful hours of his life, he was sure. After that, he didn't know what might happen. But he was not going to jail.

Jack moved quietly down the concrete steps, not wishing to alert Parker to his arrival, if indeed he was even here. Although Jack didn't have to hunch over, he was aware of the low ceiling height.

'Hello?' came a voice he recognised.

As his eyes became used to the dimness, he saw her. 'Kate,' he said, feeling a distant giddiness.

'Jack!' She gave a gulping sob. 'You need to leave.'

He was at her side in a blink. 'How rude. I've only just got here.' He took in the contraption hung around her neck.

'No, really, you have to get everyone out of here. He's—'

'Shhh, Kate. Quiet now,' Jack said, settling himself next to her and holding her close. He rang Ben first. 'I've found her.' He gave directions.

'On our way. The first one was a hoax.'

'What?'

Kate looked at him sharply and he held up a finger.

'Yep. Looked the goods but it was make-believe. He's playing with us.'

'Did it have a timer?' Jack asked.

'No. It gave the appearance of being phone-activated.'

That bastard. 'He would have known the protocols. He's ex-army. Too smart. Ben, this one has a timer. It's ticking down.'

'With you in about one minute.'

Kate was leaning against Jack's shoulder. 'You smell so good. So safe,' she said. 'Jonathan Parker smelled of sweat and fertiliser and guilt.'

'Where is he?' Jack asked, searching her for signs of injury.

'He's gone. About thirty minutes ago. He wanted me to see the timer so I knew how long I have. But this is phone-activated – he has control.'

'How could we miss him?'

'He had a disguise. Dressed himself as a doctor before he left and he's wearing a beard and a red hoodie.'

Jack nodded. 'In the chaos it would have been hard to pick him out.'

'Jack?' Kate's voice was different somehow. He understood she was scared, but this was something else.

'Mmm?'

'I think I'm pregnant.' It was as though a small bomb had ignited in his belly. 'Don't tell anyone, especially Geoff. I'm frightened for it. I never knew how much I wanted it until Jonathan Parker put me in that boot and began to take it away from me.'

'I promise you, he will not take your child.' Jack kissed her bent head. 'I promise.'

There was a clatter of boots and suddenly four men arrived in the space.

'Jack, you need to leave,' Kate began.

'I'm not—'

'You are, sir,' Ben cut in firmly, checking the handcuffs used to secure Kate to the cage. 'Your rank doesn't work here. Detective Carter knows the rules. So do you.'

Jack blinked and shot a look at Kate. 'I'll be just upstairs.'

'You'll be back at the one-hundred-metre cordon, sir. One of my men will escort you there,' Ben said. 'What have we got, Barney?'

'Well, let's just lift this off her neck so I can look at it properly. Carefully, now,' Barney said to another of the team who bent at Kate's other side.

Jack quickly explained that the timer was simply a scare tactic for Kate's benefit.

'Still here, sir?' Ben growled, glancing around at Jack. 'Please don't make me have to spend more time—'

'All right, all right! Kate . . .'

'Just go. Go get that bastard. He's on his way to Cornwall to see Hannah. And by the way, the keys to the handcuffs are somewhere in the darkness over there.'

'You could have said something,' Ben said, grinning at her; Jack knew he was keeping her calm. He felt a rush of respect for these men who risked their lives in such a relaxed manner, even though everyone was on high alert, fully focused and without any true relaxation.

'Jack,' Ben cautioned. 'My guys will find them. Go, or I'll make you.'

He cast one last look at Kate, feeling like a lifetime of conversation was being conveyed in that glance.

She gave a sad smile and nodded. 'Me too,' she said, her chin wobbling as she let her composure slip. 'Go find him. I'll be fine. We'll be fine, won't we, boys?'

None of them responded, all of them intent on what they were doing, whether disarming the incendiary or searching for the keys. Ben glanced at him, in no mood to ask again.

'Ben, you get her clear of this thing,' Jack said. And then he took the stairs three at a time and burst into the car park, running.

30

Jack rang Joan. 'Found her! She's not out of trouble yet, but we're on it.'

Joan knew not to interrupt or ask questions.

'Geoff and I are hunting Parker. Simon and John have taken control at the hospital. The paediatrician is safe, the evacuation continues, and all the emergency teams are moving through their protocols.' He stopped.

'The Harley family is also safely away from central London,' Joan said. 'Where are you headed?'

'Cornwall. He's going to Hannah. Lights and sirens on, so please warn all the usuals. They may want to track him from a distance once he reaches Penzance. He's got more than a good half-hour's headstart on us, but unless he's stolen a car, he must be on a train from Paddington as that's where the direct service leaves from. It will take him five hours minimum. We're just going to get there first. Simple as that.'

'Right. I'll get busy. Keep us posted.'

Jack hung up. Geoff was driving.

'You've got a wild man look, mate,' Jack said.

'I'm the better driver and you know it. Ask my old man.'

Jack laughed, surprised Geoff was capable of any jest at this time; it was a favourite anecdote: Geoff, at fifteen, totalling his father's pride and joy. It was the arrival of the police – as Geoff's father assured Jack at each retelling of the story – that so frightened and impressed his teenage son that he decided to join the police force.

'No, Dad,' Geoff usually replied. 'It was about girls. Girls fall for uniforms.'

Despite the flashing lights and whooping siren, Geoff was becoming frustrated by the slow-moving traffic.

'Keep your cool. I want to call Hannah. I just hope she can hear me above the racket.'

He saw a grimace of a smile as Geoff finally persuaded the slow car in front to shift lanes. Blue lights worked, but if there was heavy traffic, they still had to be patient for cars to find a way to give them space. Nevertheless, where a moment ago it felt like gridlock, with slight shifts to the left or right and some closing of gaps, they were finally beginning to weave through the busy traffic fluidly. They were moving north on the A1081, heading for the South Mimms interchange on the M25, Jack presumed, before they linked with the M4 interchange near Heathrow and heading westbound from there on the M4.

'We can swap driving anytime.' He didn't think Geoff should drive all the way. Better to share the journey and achieve full focus behind the wheel, especially at this speed.

'I'll go to Exeter and you can take over from there.'

Jack's phone rang. 'It's Ben,' he said to Geoff, who tensed in anticipation. 'Hawksworth.'

'It's me,' said a familiar voice, slightly shaky but otherwise still composed.

'Kate!'

Geoff looked over briskly.

'I'm putting you on speaker. Geoff's with me. Go ahead.'

'Hi, boys.' Her voice was soft. 'Geoff, you okay?'

'I am now,' he said, a catch in his throat.

Jack wished he didn't have to share this intimate moment.

'Where are you both?' Kate asked.

He let Geoff talk. 'At speed, racing to the M4.'

'Wish I was with you,' she said.

'Go home, Kate,' Jack instructed.

'Are you kidding? No way. The guys have done their stuff – no further threat – but there's chaos here. We need all hands on deck, and besides, I'm so amped up with adrenaline I need to be busy and distracted.'

'Are you hurt?' Geoff asked.

'No, nothing that won't heal,' she said, and both men glanced at each other, not believing the bravado. 'Listen, Jack. I forgot to thank you for finding me.'

'I followed my nose.' He didn't need to impress anyone and was feeling such huge relief that he didn't want to discuss it. 'Ring Joan, would you? She's having kittens,' Jack said. 'In fact, if you won't go home, it's probably best you get back to base and co-ordinate things for everyone. That includes briefing the commander. He'll be happy to hear your voice. Listen, we have to go. I need this line open.'

'I'll phone them both, but I need to sort out a few things here. Drive safe, you two. Good luck. See you tonight, Geoff.' She rang off first.

Geoff sighed and ran a slightly shaky hand across his face.

'You all right?' Jack asked.

'I'm really good now,' he assured him. 'And really fucking angry, so Parker had better watch out.'

Once they cleared the Heathrow choke of traffic and broke out onto the M4 to hit the fast lane, there was no stopping them.

★

On the train, Parker was beginning to relax, having eased out of Paddington, and the train reached its comforting rhythm. He was in a two-seater with no one next to him, though that could change when he switched trains at Plymouth. But for now, he could lose himself. He pulled out the burner phone that would detonate the device around Kate's neck, unless she'd experienced a miracle.

Could he do this?

He wanted to.

Killing Kate broke faith with the plan he'd conceived soon after Billy's death: Kate was not involved with Billy's murder. But then so had killing the woman in Cardiff, although he'd made his peace with that. She was necessary so that the rest of the plan could work . . . and it had. Her death had bought him the time he'd needed.

Kate, as much as she'd angered him, was never meant to be part of it, although she and her team were trying to stop him from putting the final piece of the jigsaw in place. Ruining the hospital to the point where it would require demolition was necessary – Kate or no Kate. He'd given them time to evacuate as many people as they could, even planting a fake suicide bomber to make them act faster.

Now that he thought about it, he should have handcuffed Emily to the oxygen tanks and sent Kate in wearing the dummy bomb vest. She wouldn't have cried or carried on like Emily. She would have barked orders and got more people out, he was sure. And then he could have happily pressed the send message and blown up Emily. Why hadn't he?

Because you were never convinced Emily meant your boy harm, that's why, an internal voice said. *You only wanted her to suffer the fear of the potential loss of her family . . . her life.*

He nodded to himself.

Don't do it, the voice said. *For Billy's memory, don't kill Kate.*

But his mental state was dark and that bright voice couldn't cut through. He blinked once and then hit the button.

Would he hear the explosion from here?

It didn't matter.

He'd carried out the threat. Made good on his promise.

Jack was on the phone to Hannah – they were under three hours away. It had taken an hour or so for her to answer. She'd been walking her dog along the coastal path, she explained, and hadn't taken her phone.

'What's going on?' she asked now.

'Are you at home?'

'I'm in the cottage, if that's what you mean.'

'Alone?'

'Yes, other than Chalky,' she said, sounding baffled. 'Why?'

'Your husband is coming to you, we believe.'

'Jonathan? No. I don't think so, he's—'

'Listen to me, Hannah,' Jack said. 'Jonathan is a killer. He has been picking off anyone connected to the death of your son – from the woman who gave the blood that was wrongly put into his arm to the nurse who made the initial error.'

There was a brief silence and then she spoke, her voice full of disdain and disbelief. 'No, Detective, you don't understand, Jonathan is—'

'He abducted DCI Kate Carter and tied her to the oxygen tanks at the hospital where your son died, threatening to blow her up. He also put a vest containing bomb material around your son's paediatrician, Emily Harley, and forced her to walk into the hospital. Perhaps you've seen or heard the breaking news?'

'I have but no, no, no . . .' she repeated anxiously. 'This is a mistake.'

'No mistake, Hannah. I was there. We believe he's coming to you in Cornwall.'

'To kill me?' she asked, sounding suddenly terrified.

'No! That's the last thing he wants. He's been trying to keep all danger from you, and that's why he was so shocked to learn that you were behind the community threats and insisted you give yourself up. He knew the law would go gently on you. But your husband has been on a mission, Hannah. He is determined to make the others pay for the loss of Billy.'

'He . . . suffered PTSD; he left the army in—'

'We know. We also know he's an explosives expert.'

'Jonathan saves lives,' she argued.

'Not any more. I think he has a death wish, Hannah. I think it's best you know that.'

'But he's getting married, he's got a baby on the—'

'All lies, Hannah. His fiancée doesn't exist. The baby is a fabrication. He's been living around London, keeping a very low profile since Billy died. He does work for Armourex, that's no lie, but we suspect that was a means to an end.'

'I can't believe this.' Her voice shook. 'Are you sure?'

'One hundred per cent. We have physical evidence against him. He's responsible for all those deaths you've heard about that tie back to Billy . . . and this is why. He tried to direct our attention towards your friend, who did seem suspicious for a short while, but James has been ruled out. Jonathan abducted Detective Carter – Kate – and had her tied up, along with Emily Harley, at his allotment in North London before he took them to the hospital this morning.'

'Are they safe?'

'Yes. Just. He threatened Emily's family, which is how he coerced her into doing his bidding. Kate was probably not in his original set of targets. She was critical of him, and he probably believed she might endanger his cause or get in the way, and he didn't know what to do other than drag her into his plan, to shut her up and buy himself time.'

'What's going to happen?' Hannah asked, her tone full of dread.

'Well, we know he's coming to you, most likely by train, so we'd like you to leave your cottage,' Jack said. 'Do you know anyone else in the area, somewhere you could go?'

'No.'

'That's all right. Will you trust me, please, Hannah?'

There was a long pause. 'Unhappily, but yes.'

'Thank you. I'm going to send some local police officers to you urgently, and they will get you to safety in . . .' he looked at Geoff.

'St Ives,' Geoff murmured

'In St Ives,' Jack confirmed.

'And do what?'

'Keep you safe for a day. Check into a hotel – we'll cover it – and have a meal. I won't say sleep, because I doubt you will. Just stay away until you hear from me again.'

'Okay. What are you going to do?'

'I'm going to take him into custody, Hannah, for the deaths of far too many people, and for the terror threat he posed today. But I can't have you complicating matters.'

'He won't let you take him. If it's true that he's done all of this—'

'It's true, Hannah.'

'Then it means he's slipped back into the psychosis that he experienced when he left the army. The PTSD was really bad. He was facing the threat of explosives every day of his life. He was the bravest of the brave apparently . . . and then he broke.'

'I understand, but—'

'Do you, though? Are you going to kill him?'

Jack felt saddened that she would think such a thing. 'We're not armed, Hannah. We have no intention of hurting Jonathan, but we do have to bring him into custody. If Jonathan decides to become violent, then he will be treated in the same way that we treat any violent criminals. He will be stopped by the means at our disposal.'

'I can well imagine how this works, Detective. You'll probably have armed marksmen.'

'Yes. If Jonathan is armed, how else are we supposed to protect ourselves . . . or you?'

'I don't want him killed.'

'No one does. But he's a serial murderer, so he doesn't show the same respect to anyone, and the last time I spoke to her, he had my colleague strapped up to an incendiary device that he intended to blow up, along with half of Barnet Hospital. He doesn't seem to care much about life, Hannah. You've met Kate. You know how sympathetic she is to your situation. I've had to listen to her arguing on your behalf.' There was an awkward silence. 'Do you want Jonathan out there, in this confused, reckless frame of mind? He's at the point now where anyone who gets in his way is a potential target. How would you feel if a child got in the way of his vengeance? He has openly threatened Emily Harley's three children, promising he would kill them if she didn't do as he demanded.'

He heard Hannah sob on the other end. *Good!* She needed to be shaken out of this frame of mind.

'He's trying to get to you,' Jack continued. 'I don't know why – maybe to explain, maybe for penance, perhaps just to hear the reassurance of your voice. I just don't know.'

'I do. If he knows you're hunting him, then it's to say goodbye.'

'Frankly, Hannah, I don't care about his rationale right now – I just have to stop him. Let him say goodbye to you over the phone.'

'I don't mean that sort of goodbye.'

Jack swallowed. 'Well, that makes him even more dangerous, especially if he has any sort of thought about taking you with him.'

She gasped; he must be finally getting through.

'Please do not be at your cottage. We can't protect you if you refuse to co-operate.'

There was no more to be said.

'All right. I'll wait for your people?'

'And please don't phone him in the meantime.'

'What if he phones me?'

'Don't answer it.'

'I can't ignore him!'

'I'm asking you to do just that. But, Hannah, either way, do not under any circumstances tell him where you're going or that we've spoken. You will be endangering lives if you do.'

'I won't answer,' she growled.

He wasn't going to risk giving her more time to think or reconsider. 'I want you to get your keys, your handbag, perhaps some overnight gear and be ready to leave.'

He waited; he could almost hear the voices in her mind accusing her of treachery and then the more sensible voice of reason . . . the voice of self-protection.

'I'll be ready in ten minutes.'

'Good. Give me your address.'

She recited it to him. 'It's the last cottage on the cliff before the coastal pathway takes over and becomes reserve.'

'They'll find it. I'm sending them now.' Jack rang off and immediately contacted Joan.

'I've been in touch with all our people in the west. And I heard from Kate. Never been so relieved to hear a voice.'

'How's she doing?'

'Oh, pretending all is fine and taking control down at the hospital. She'll be here soon, she said. How are you, Geoff?'

Jack smiled; the all-knowing Joan just presumed she'd be on speaker.

'I'm angry, Joan, although I won't use the language I used earlier.'

'No, because I'd be obliged to fine you to keep things fair, although between us I feel very sure I could forgive you, given the circumstances. She's putting on a brave front now, but I think the reality of how close she came will only bite later. You'll need to be vigilant.'

'I will.'

'Thank you, Mother,' Jack said. 'We'll keep you updated.'

'I've just sent you details of the head of Special Branch at Exeter. Hope that's arrived? His name is Graham Patterson. I have also recently got off the phone with the traffic control rooms along your route. They all know you're coming through at speed and taking appropriate steps.'

'Excellent.'

'Oh, and Jack, we've tracked down that blood nurse, Gayle.'

Jack looked at Geoff with relief. 'What happened?'

'Two dogs at the veterinary clinic with the same name. One called Rocket, the other called Rock, but both answer to Rocky. One of the admins gave us details on the wrong Rocky, who was in fact picked up that day. I know this is too much information,' she said to make him smile. 'But Gayle and Rocky are both safe and sound. All Sarah and I can think of is that when her sister took ill, she drove off into the night. She told her supervisor, but no one told the other Gail for days.'

'Well, I'm just glad she dodged him, whether or not she was in his sights. Thank Sarah as well, would you?'

'I will. Stay safe, you two.'

Jack ended the call. 'Right, I'll just call Exeter,' he said.

'Graham Patterson,' a gruff voice answered.

'Jack Hawksworth here, sir.'

'I heard you two were coming through. CT Commander has just got off the phone too.'

That meant Kate had spoken to him. 'So you've been briefed.'

'Yes. We'll get the bastard.'

'Can you urgently send some people to the address I'm about to give you, please?' Jack told him what he needed and passed on the detail Hannah had given him.

'And take her into St Ives, you say?'

'We'll cover overnight accommodation. Somewhere nice, so she's not tempted to leave it,' he said with a grim smile.

'I presume you want my people at the cottage too?'

'Yes.' Jack trusted Geoff with his life, but he wasn't sure he trusted him with Parker's in this moment. He couldn't say that, of course. 'I think we should have local officers to help.'

'Inside or outside?'

'Both. Everyone is to remain concealed until we reveal ourselves, or if for some reason we don't make it before he does, and it's safe to do so, then arrest him. Be assured, he's psychotic and unpredictable, capable of anything.'

'Armed?'

'He might be. He's ex-army, so he's no stranger to firearms and he works in security.'

'I'll send a local firearms unit. They can conceal themselves until we know more. Is he carrying explosives? I'll need to send XPLO in from Plymouth.'

'The house will be safe, but I don't know what he's planning. My colleague only sighted two devices, but you might want to take precautions.'

'Leave it with us.'

Parker awoke with a start, surprised he was capable of sleep today. He had been dozing for nearly four hours, and it was enough to feel recharged. He'd dreamed of Hannah and Billy – they'd been a happy family. It had felt so real, but he'd experienced similar dreams so many times that he knew not to trust it. He'd taught himself never to trust any situation where he was with his wife and child, because it didn't exist.

Now he sighed, wondering if the bulletins were sharing breaking news of the explosion in North London. Poor Kate. Had she got away? Probably not. It really should have been the paediatrician who went up with the oxygen tanks, he thought again. He stared out of the window for another hour or so, imagining various scenarios and what he would do after talking to Hannah. He'd never let himself think beyond the hospital explosion until now.

'The next station is St Erth and then Penzance. Passengers to St Ives should alight at the next station and take the branch line to St Ives. I repeat, the next station is . . .'

His heart felt lighter at the thought of seeing Hannah. Despite all his angst and despair from the army through to the death of his son, he had done a couple of things right. One was marrying Hannah, and the other was avenging Billy's death in the only meaningful way. Would she understand? There was so much to say, and he wanted to say it to her in person, not on the phone, and certainly not from police custody.

The cottage sounded so perfect. They could probably go for a walk. Could she forgive him? He doubted it, but he needed to explain, try to make her understand before it all exploded across the news channels and newspapers. Would she comprehend his drive? That's all he wanted, for her to see that the depth of his despair matched hers, because he knew she'd always wondered. He could never show it; he'd needed to be the strong one. While Hannah had raged and sobbed and shown her grief, he had become silent, but the rage had festered and found a way to unlock his feared companion.

Jonathan knew he was walking as the other Jonathan now. His psychiatrist and psychologist had explained his psychosis, teaching him to recognise the signs, recognise the thoughts that would lead him to that dark place. They both thought he was much improved, and had agreed that, while he still needed to take his medication and keep seeing them, he was sufficiently recovered to have some clarity to look ahead. They'd eaten up the story about Shelley, the engagement, her pregnancy, along with Hannah and everyone else.

It was so easy to fool people. Armourex considered him one of their key executives. They had such big ideas for him, but they were just a means to an end. And it had all gone to plan. He should be congratulated. A smile played at his lips – did the other passengers think he was demented for his amusement? *Who cares*, he reminded himself . . . *no one cares*.

There was just this final part now.

And, unlike his usual modus operandi, he had no plan for it.

Would he escape? How? He couldn't see it. A boat, maybe?

Would he die in a hail of bullets? Possibly. Not in Cornwall, though. Not unless Kate had got free and told her mates. British police didn't rain down ammunition unless special ops were called in. Had they had time? Did Cornwall even have that capability? He figured they must, given the new way that the force was having to reorganise itself for terror threats. But Hawksworth and his crew would probably do their best to bring him in alive, to make him answer for his sins – not that he ever could. Nor did he want to. He didn't need the country's judgement . . . or its pity all over again. The country hadn't given him justice, so he'd meted it out. And that felt good. It also felt complete.

Would he kill himself, perhaps? He didn't know, but there was no fear in this regard – he was sure of that. He gave a shiver; he felt like he was being shadowed. But by someone loving. Was it Billy?

Dad, come with me. We can play some football. You can teach me how to do that sideways kick with my heel. We used to laugh when you did that, remember? Let's laugh together again, Dad.

Billy! He was here. Jonathan could almost feel his son's hand in his. Still small, so trusting, so much potential.

Am I going to die, Billy?

Just come and play.

He found it curious that this murky answer made him smile. His only plan now was to tell Hannah the truth and that he'd never stopped loving her . . . or Billy. And that he couldn't live without either of them.

So maybe, once he said farewell, death was the answer. To be with Billy.

Decision made.

He saw the signs for Penzance passing by as the train slowed at the platform. He joined the other passengers and stepped off the train with a feeling of closure that he'd never previously felt. They'd arrived at the southernmost station in all of England. For some reason they hadn't driven into the main shed but had moved to the terminus on the only open line, where a stone plaque welcomed passengers in both Cornish and English. It was usually used for what was known as the Night Riviera Service, which brought lots of holidaymakers if they took the overnight service leaving London Paddington and waking up at the seaside of the Cornish coast.

Evening was drawing in. Jonathan blew on his cold hands, shocked by how fast the temperature of the day had dropped, and began dialling Hannah while he waited in the small taxi queue.

31

Everyone was in place.

There was no tree cover near the isolated cottage, but evening was pulling itself closely around the tiny hamlet, the light fading fast, so the armed unit had concealed itself behind some bushes to the side. An XPLO unit was ready, just moments away, parked in the driveway of one surprised but co-operative neighbour at the bottom of the rise. This was in case Jonathan Parker was carrying any final explosives, hoping to go out with a bang and perhaps take Hannah with him.

Jack, Geoff and two other officers were inside the house, glad of its emptiness. Jack spotted a manuscript on the table and realised he'd interrupted Hannah's work, which perhaps explained some of her reluctance. Manuscripts always had deadlines, didn't they? Maybe this one wasn't so urgent, so she'd left it behind. He wondered what sort of novel he'd tackle if he ever tried to write one – it was a fun thought, but he realised his mind was wandering dangerously. He focused again, noting the sound of wheels on the gritty road seconds before they saw a taxi roll up the driveway.

'Silence, now,' Jack warned unnecessarily. He was convinced he could hear the heartbeats of his colleagues. None of them knew what they were facing. Had Parker come here to take his wife with him? Away? To their deaths? Into hiding? For one last dinner? Jack couldn't guess.

Standing behind the curtain, with no lamps on in the cottage, he could see Parker illuminated by the taxi's headlights; they threw a halo around the killer in the falling light of the evening. Jack heard him say something to the driver and then a friendly 'Cheers, mate,' before the taxi driver lifted a hand in farewell, reversed in a tight semicircle and rolled away down the hill.

Parker paused in the driveway. He was obviously a little confused by the lack of light; perhaps he expected to be greeted by a golden glow from the windows of the cottage. He glanced up at the top rooms, and Jack hoped no one was peeking out. He couldn't see Parker's features to guess at his thoughts and prayed no one in hiding on the outside suddenly stepped on a twig like in a B-grade movie. He shook the thought away. They were pros and could wait for long periods like statues, and indeed move silently when needed.

Parker waited.

They waited.

It was tense.

'He knows something's wrong,' Geoff whispered.

Jack nodded, resigned, realising it wasn't going to be a straightforward ambush-style arrest, as he'd hoped.

'Hannah?' Parker shouted.

The two detectives looked at each other. 'Let me handle it,' Jack said, his voice hushed.

'You're the boss,' Geoff said, but he sounded dangerous.

'Hannah?' Parker yelled again. 'It's me. I tried calling. Are you there?'

Jack was aware of the two police officers tiptoeing forward from the back of the house, sensing things were about to happen.

He waited another couple of beats to counsel Geoff.

'Kate's bruised but alive,' Jack said quietly. 'We want Parker unharmed and nothing on us to say we didn't follow strict protocol, so he can pay for what he's done. So no going rogue, all right? And one more thing.' He was going to say it, but just as the words were forming, he remembered that it wasn't his place to speak of Kate's suspected pregnancy, and doing so could set a wedge between the couple. It would take too much explaining, that he knew about the potential pregnancy before Geoff did.

'What?' Geoff asked when Jack still hadn't spoken.

Jack held his gaze. 'She needs you now more than ever. You're no good to her suspended from work or living with regret. I'll handle him.'

Geoff let out a breath through his nose like a long-held sigh. 'Right. Let's not let him get away, then.'

Jack relaxed slightly. 'Let Patterson know to close in slightly and cut off his access.'

Geoff moved deeper into the house and softly gave orders as Jack walked to the door and opened it. That was the signal to the team outside. High-beam torches switched on from various points, instantly alarming Parker, as they were meant to. Twilight had surrendered to dusk but was yet to give way to night. So they could all still see well enough, if not in detail.

'You bastard!' Parker said, easily recognising who had opened the door. But he didn't linger for a conversation, cutting diagonally backwards, running for the coastal path, faster than Jack had imagined Parker might move.

'Don't shoot,' Jack shouted. 'Let me talk to him.'

Jack gave chase but realised he couldn't match Parker's speed. He could hear the heavy footfall of Geoff coming up fast behind him.

Jack was slimmer and taller, but Geoff's fitness as a trail runner showed as he overtook him and soon put distance between them. All Jack could do now was follow his friend's retreating back and the beam of light from the torch he'd grabbed from one of the officers.

He couldn't let Geoff catch Parker and risk his friend having a blood rush. Jack redoubled his efforts, feeling like his lungs might explode. But he came to an abrupt halt about eight metres from the cliff edge next to Geoff. His first thought was relief. Geoff had restrained himself from acting how he must have wanted to. The professional in him had overridden all the emotion, because Jack was convinced Geoff would have easily run his prey down, but Parker had backed away to stand near the cliff's edge. Jack knew they both now needed to keep a safe distance and not spook the guy.

Jack, breathing hard, heard others arrive. The air was charged with a fresh tension, and no one could mistake the sound of metal and weapons being drawn. They waited. They'd clearly been told that the senior guys from London would make the decision, and even Patterson was standing by, quietly watchful.

'Put your hands in the air, mate,' Geoff said, his breathing already back to normal, privately vexing Jack.

'Where's Hannah?' Parker snapped. He too was out of breath, but Jack didn't doubt his volatility.

'Safe,' Geoff growled. 'She's with the police. Now put your hands up, Mr Parker, or these gentlemen nearby may become impatient.'

Jack was deeply relieved to see Parker lift his hands. Torch beams immediately flashed up to check they were empty.

'Jonathan, are you armed?' Jack asked, trying to not sound out of breath and failing.

He shook his head. 'I'm not wearing anything explosive, if that's what you mean?'

'I do. And weapons?'

'None. Gave those up in Ireland. I do have a knife, though.'

They all heard a metallic sound as a switchblade flicked open, which had presumably been concealed up a sleeve.

'Keep your arms in the air,' Jack warned. 'I suggest you throw down the knife. Not everyone here is as trusting as I might be.'

Parker defied him. 'Don't come any closer, Hawksworth.'

'I won't move,' Jack assured him.

'So Hannah gave me up?' Parker asked, sounding incredulous.

'No,' Jack answered. 'That's Hannah's problem. She's still defending you, even though she's shocked by what you've become.'

Parker nodded slowly. 'I just wanted to say goodbye.'

'She's waiting to hear from you. Desperately keen, in fact, to talk to you,' Jack tried.

'It's too late.'

Jack breathed out, deliberate and slow. 'Jonathan Parker, I'm arresting you . . .' he said firmly, but with care, telling him why he was being arrested and read him his rights. 'Now I need you to toss the knife away.'

'That ground isn't safe,' Geoff murmured for Jack's hearing only. 'You need to bring him forward.'

'Jonathan, drop the knife, please, and take a few steps towards me.'

Parker shook his head. 'That's not going to happen.'

'Here we go,' Geoff muttered.

Jack felt everyone's tension rise to full alert again as weapons were raised in the shadows.

'Why not, Jonathan? Just a few steps.'

'So you can bang me into handcuffs?'

'Mate, there's nowhere else to go. Please, let me take you into custody and I'll make sure that you can talk to Hannah. You'll be able to see her—'

'You think I want her to see me like this? No. I realise now, it was never in the plan, Detective Hawksworth. I probably always knew how it would end. I think I even knew it back when I was in Ireland. It's the only way.'

'That was a long time ago, and you had seen bad things. You weren't thinking clearly,' Jack said, his voice calmer than he was feeling.

'Yeah, you're right. The terrible thing is, once I did start to see things clearly, I needed to put them right. Those people killed my son.'

Before Geoff could say it, Jack did. 'Detective Chief Inspector Kate Carter did no such thing.'

Parker shrugged. 'Okay, Kate's what we call collateral damage. It was a pity she had to die. I know you two were close.' He smiled, and Jack forced himself not to overreact, cutting a sharp look Geoff's way.

He could see his friend shaking with the need to run at Parker, to take him out. 'Well, if you feel sorry about it—'

'I do actually,' he said, with a small gust of a laugh. 'I broke the rule for her. I gave her a chance.'

'Well, maybe I can make you feel a bit better about that,' Jack said, gently but not sympathetically. 'Kate is safe.'

'Blow me down, and there I was trying to blow her up!' He laughed and clapped once, despite the knife in his hand.

Everyone shifted position at the odd sound, and Parker quickly raised his hands again.

'Sorry, I know, I know. Arms up, lads, although if I got rid of this weapon and lowered them, are you just going to gun me down here in a hail of bullets?'

'Parker,' Jack warned.

'What?' he demanded.

'Don't test them. If you make them nervous—'

'You mean like if I reached into my pocket?' He began to move his hand, smirking.

'Is that what you want Hannah to hear? That you died here, a coward's death, because you couldn't face what you'd done? Do you want her to not only deal with her grief about Billy but now you as well, covered in blood outside the Cornwall cottage she dreamed of living in?'

That seemed to halt his amusement. His features straightened and his hands went up once again. 'I don't wish Hannah any further harm.'

'Then come with me now,' Jack said.

Parker shook his head. 'You're wrong, Hawksworth.'

'Wrong about what?'

'About there being nowhere to go,' he said, sounding strangely sad in his triumph as he turned and jumped into the blackness.

'No!' Jack leaped forward helplessly, but it was too late. He heard flesh and bone meeting an unyielding column of cliff that had taken millennia to form itself for this moment. Parker himself made no sound.

Jack ran to the edge but was pounced on by Geoff. 'He's gone.'

Geoff pointed his torch over the edge, where they could see Parker lying lifeless on the rocks below, his limbs fractured and ripped, twisting his body into a strange form, his head hanging at a near right angle, which suggested his neck was broken.

Geoff hauled Jack to his feet; he hadn't even realised he was on his knees.

Patterson broke the silence. 'You did your utmost for him, Hawksworth,' he said in a fatherly tone. 'You stayed calm, stayed focused. No one could have done more in trying to persuade him to come in.'

'He clearly had a death wish, sir,' another senior officer said.

'I agree,' the head of Special Branch said. 'He had no intention of being taken into custody.' He sighed. 'I'll get all the right people down there. We know this landscape. Do you want to come back with me to Exeter?'

Jack nodded numbly. There was paperwork to fill out and phone calls to be made. Carol Rowland would need to be called, and Lou was no doubt waiting impatiently for news. There was Kate, too, of course, but he would leave her to Geoff. And he needed to call Joan. She'd kill him herself if he didn't ring in at whatever time of the night to confirm that he and Geoff were safe and their killer had been stopped.

As he climbed into the car and Geoff took the wheel once more, he replayed the scene again and again in his mind. Could he have done anything differently?

Geoff followed Graham Patterson's tail-lights for a while in silence before he broke it. 'I know what you're doing.'

Jack looked up. 'You do?'

'Yep, thinking on repeat how you could have said something a different way, or moved faster to stop him, or handled it from another angle.'

Jack sighed. Geoff keenly understood because he had been there before. No two situations were the same, but they tended to add up to the same thing in Jack's mind: that he'd somehow failed the person who injured or killed themselves, or forced police to injure or kill them, rather than be taken into custody.

'It might have gone another way,' Jack tried.

'How? We waited. We didn't spook him. He ran and, yes, we chased, but we kept our distance, as we've been trained.'

'I was impressed you did,' Jack admitted.

'I was too.' He gave a grim chuckle. 'What I wanted to do was run straight up to him and push him over the edge. Instead he did us all a favour.'

Jack sucked in a breath, glad conversations like these were never recorded.

'You know, mate,' Geoff continued, 'life in prison would have been nasty for him after what he did. All sympathy for him and his child would have disappeared once they found out he'd murdered innocent people, threatened children, tried to blow up the hospital. Nowhere for him to hide in there. Better off where he is; no more suffering.'

Jack knew Geoff was right. 'I'd better call Chief Rowland. Can you go in and start the documentation with Patterson?' They were approaching the police headquarters in Exeter.

'Sure. I'll call Kate quickly too.'

'There'll be some kickback from this emotionally for her – I think Joan's right on that score.'

Geoff nodded in the dark as they pulled into the car park.

Jack remained outside in the cold a little longer, speaking to his chief.

'That's messy, Jack,' she said, after listening to his abbreviated report.

'I'm afraid so. We tried, but he'd already made up his mind.'

'The media will gobble it up.'

'They're sending a team down immediately for that reason, I'm sure. Perhaps by the early hours, the scene will be cleared.'

'And you had witnesses to corroborate all that went down?'

'Yes, ma'am. Plenty of others standing with us, including the head of Special Branch here at Exeter.'

'Graham Patterson?'

'Correct.'

'He's terrific. I've worked with him. Straight talker, good operator.'

'Exactly how I'd describe him, ma'am.'

'Good. I had a vision of having to explain why one of my detective chief inspectors pushed a man we were trying to bring into custody over a Cornish cliff.'

'Geoff Benson was never in doubt, ma'am. He knows where the line is.'

'I know, Jack, but with his partner held hostage and nearly blown up beneath a hospital . . . I have to confess I was worried until I heard from you.'

'Now you can get into a hot bath and then have a lovely sleep, ma'am.'

She laughed. 'Really? At nearing ten?'

'Never too late for a bath, ma'am. It's what I shall be doing if I ever get home, vanilla-scented bubbles and all.'

She chuckled, and it was a pleasant sound. 'Drive safely, Jack. Get back to that fiancée of yours, and then come and have a coffee tomorrow afternoon so we can go through everything.'

He was glad she didn't see him wince and made sure he put a smile in his voice. 'Looking forward to it.'

EPILOGUE

London, ten days later

Lou breezed into the kitchen just as Jack closed the oven door, bringing with her a gust of fizzy freshness.

'Mmm, you smell as beautiful as you look,' Jack said, pulling her towards him and kissing her cheek, inhaling the perfume. 'Is that the one we bought in Venice?'

She nodded. 'I know it's a bit bright for a wintry night, but I love it.'

'It smells like morning in Positano. All citrus and sunshine.'

She laughed. 'You should write a perfume column.'

Jack leaned back against the kitchen bench, suddenly wistful. 'Do you know, I'd love to write.' He thought of the manuscript on Hannah's cottage table; somewhere deep down, the idea had excited him.

'Then write. You don't need permission.'

He smiled. 'True.'

'What would you write?' she asked.

He shrugged. 'A perfume blog, a travel column . . . a novel.'

Lou blinked at him. 'Are you being serious?'

He frowned, thinking before he replied. 'I've worked full-time since I was sixteen. I've had the odd holiday but'—he sighed— 'I don't have a lot of time for outside interests. You've arrived to fill up a big part of my life, but when I sat there next to Kate in the underground car park, worrying about a bomber on the loose, I did start to wonder about the future.'

'In what way did you wonder?' She didn't make light of what he was saying, didn't try to soothe him with affection; she simply covered his hand and squeezed it.

'Whether that sort of tension and chasing down the bad guy should be my only dimension.'

'Jack, you haven't told me what happened down there, or in Cornwall, and I know you barely give me more than a third . . . no, a quarter of the truth when you do allude to whatever your current case is. I probably learn more on the six o'clock news than you provide.' As he opened his mouth to respond, she held up a hand. 'No, it's okay. Truly, I'm not sure I want or need to know the danger you're in. Forgive me for preferring the bliss of ignorance. But there has to be balance. I know that sounds like a cliché, but it makes sense to want to be recognised for more than your work ethic and achievements. More dimension in your life will round you out, and I suspect it will make you feel lighter at times.'

'Well, I feel sort of weightless around you,' he said, smiling at her. 'Especially when I come home and you're there snoring in my bed . . .'

She slapped his arm playfully.

'No, but in all seriousness, I feel content. I'd like to add more of that sense of lightness, though – spend more time with you, spend more time doing things other than reading cold cases, hunting criminals and—'

'I don't need convincing,' she said, leaning against him. 'But if you can persuade yourself, you'll do it.'

'What exactly would I do, though?'

She smiled. 'Take a long, long break and do something that pleases you. Write, paint, take pottery classes . . . We could get a dog! You could do some more lecturing – you said you enjoyed it.'

'I did.'

'You don't have to give up police work. But unless you're gunning for an even more senior role that takes you into management, then I think Detective Superintendent is plenty high enough. You've achieved so much in your work, Jack. If you don't think you'd become bored, then I have to tell you I'd love to come home to you in your pinny and a hot meal each evening.'

He laughed, delighted at the image. 'Barefoot and pregnant.'

She gave him a sideways glance. 'No, that's for me. And it's something I'd like very much, but not if you don't want—'

He hushed her with a soft kiss. 'I've never really seen myself as a father, but I know you'll make the best mother a child could have. Together, I know I could be successful . . . we could give a child a wonderful life of love and laughter.'

Lou smiled. 'I know you mean that, but I wonder if you'll still feel like this after your next meeting with Chief Rowland, with whatever she has up her sleeve for you.'

He grinned. 'You'd be surprised how pragmatic – and even caring – she is. She hides it, but she has a vast sense of duty of care. I think she'd encourage me to take a leave of absence.'

'Are we doing this?' Lou asked, looking incredulous. 'Shall we buy the cottage in Devon or the farmhouse in Brittany we've talked about and just go and live for a year or two?' She sounded ridiculously excited.

Jack could see the sparkle in her eyes. 'I'll talk to Carol.'

Lou gave a squeal of pleasure and wrapped her arms around his neck. 'I can't believe it! You deserve this.'

'We deserve this,' he corrected, as the doorbell sang its funny tune. 'Do you know how much I hate that?'

'Yes,' she said, pulling away. 'It's why I programmed it to do "Old MacDonald". Shall I get the door?'

'Why not, your legs are younger than mine,' he quipped, and Lou disappeared, returning with Kate and Geoff, pink-cheeked from the pinch of the night.

'Mmm, something smells nice, Jack,' Kate said, kissing each cheek.

'Hello, you two. It's boeuf bourguignon – that's er, beef stew to you, mate,' Jack said, shaking Geoff's hand and reflecting his grin. 'You all good?'

Geoff nodded.

'Right, as it's a cold night and we're having beef, we're going straight into the reds apparently,' Lou said. 'But much as I fancied a merlot, Jack insists we drink a burgundy.'

'It's where the dish hails from,' Jack began. 'Did you know—'

'Nope,' Kate said, waggling a finger. 'No lectures tonight. No history, no architecture, no bloody etymology of words. We want laughter. Do you have a whoopie cushion, Lou?'

That made everyone smile.

'Here, Geoff, you can pour,' Lou said, dragging him over to where they'd decanted the wine.

Jack smiled at Kate, then touched the bruise on her cheek. 'Ouch.'

She put her hand over his before he could take it away. 'This is nice,' she said. 'Thank you for having us over.'

Jack took in her expression. She was letting him know he didn't need to worry any more about her feelings for him. 'We'll do more of it. How are you?'

They both knew the question was loaded.

'It was a false alarm,' she said, not wasting any time pretending. 'I was simply very late.' She glanced over at Geoff, who was laughing with Lou. 'He doesn't know. Best we don't . . . you know.'

'I do. You sounded pleased, though, for a moment.'

She nodded. 'Felt very excited for a moment.' She shrugged. 'Maybe next time.'

'I was worried he was going to do something very stupid in your honour, you know. But he held it together.'

She nodded. 'Thank you for keeping him safe.'

'Open up to him, Kate. He worships you.' That was all Jack could say.

'What are you two whispering about?' Lou said, arriving with two oversized glasses for them. A modest amount of wine gleamed from their bowls.

'I was just telling Kate I might be taking some extended leave.'

Kate was quick to catch on, always in tune with him. 'It's a good time of life to make that decision,' she agreed, eyeing Jack, subtly communicating her shock. 'In fact, you've stolen my thunder. I was thinking much the same myself.'

It was Geoff's turn to give Kate a wide-eyed look of surprise. 'When were you going to mention that?'

'Just did. Jack simply unlocked my thoughts. I think it's time I took some time for us . . . for myself.'

'Okay . . . is this for real?'

She gave a shrug. 'Yes. After the last close shave, definitely.'

Geoff barely took a breath. 'So marry me.'

Jack and Lou gasped with pleasure and stepped back.

'What?' Kate began.

'Just say yes, for heaven's sake,' Jack said, sounding vexed.

Lou poked him in the ribs. 'A girl needs to think on that sort of thing, Jack.'

'Thank you, Lou,' Kate said, blushing furiously.

'*Have* you thought on it?' Jack said, making everyone laugh nervously.

Kate ignored him, staring at Geoff. 'This is what you want?'

'More than anything . . . more than Jack's beef stew, even,' he said, as his belly grumbled hungrily, breaking the spell. 'Kate, you never have to wonder about how I feel about you. It hasn't changed since the day I met you.'

Jack turned away, and grabbed an envelope that was sitting on the kitchen counter. He scrawled three letters and an exclamation mark – *FFS!* – then held it up.

Kate laughed tearily as she saw it. 'Yes,' she said. 'Yes, Geoff, let's make it official and start a family and become normal people.'

That brought loud cheers from Jack and Lou. Geoff pulled Kate towards him and hugged her, then kissed her, both of them teary now.

'Right, wait!' Jack said, looking at Lou, who had moist eyes too. 'Put the burgundy down. I think we need a celebratory drink.' He put his glass on the table. 'Down,' he encouraged again, at everyone's loud sighs. 'We can drink that with our delicious meal – you won't regret waiting – but let's get some champagne going. The four of us really do have things to celebrate.'

As he turned to the fridge to find the bottle that was chilling in its depths, he felt a fresh sense of weightlessness overcoming him. It was a genuine rush of happiness and overall wellbeing, which he hadn't felt in a long, long time . . . or indeed ever.

ACKNOWLEDGEMENTS

As I write this in late 2024, the demand for blood in Australia is at a 12-year high and plasma at record levels. A Lifeblood campaign is asking for 100,000 Aussies to become donors. It's a wonderful gift of life. This book acknowledges and thanks all the people who donate the gift of life regularly.

This book took me to the amazing blood laboratories at Filton near Bristol in the UK and I risked train strikes and go-slows to get there. I must say, I have only admiration for the Brits, who are terribly patient through this sort of upheaval. All the hassle was worth it though, and I'd like to thank Tanya Hughes, scientific consultant from National Health Service Blood and Transplant for her generosity in taking me through the incredible facility at Filton. It is mind-boggling. And try though I might to work out a way to sabotage the blood process – which was my first inclination for this story – Tanya had an answer to all my cunning ideas. In the end we both decided – I'm sure much to her relief – that I would have my crime occur beyond the walls of Filton, where human error is far more plausible.

Thanks to Cindy Barfoot and Mike Walker in Poole for helping with the blood transfusion details in the right timeframe for this story. It would have been easy and wrong to presume that I might remember how it worked from my last donation, but that was recent. Some things don't change, but a dozen or so years ago when this story is set is a long time in medicine, and so having Mike's detailed notes was not only essential but such a blessing.

To my good friend Margo Burns, thank you for putting me onto Dr Sam Boase, a paediatric surgeon in Adelaide who took great delight in helping me with the surgical side of removing tonsils in young children and the potential complications – in the right time frame once again. You rarely use all that you learn from experts when crafting the final story, but having the right research and background at one's fingertips adds a wonderful layer of security and authenticity, for which I'm so appreciative.

Isobel Exell put me on to Daphne, former secretary at the East Finchley allotments in London, who helped out with the query I was chasing. Great to have your input at just the right moment.

Dr Karen Heath, forensic pathologist, I just love working with you and how your mind works for my stories! For *Dead Tide* Karen came up with the most extraordinary fact that I simply couldn't leave out of the book; it was a true story from a case she had worked on. Once again, when I was casting about for a hidden truth that only a dead body under the most intense scrutiny would deliver, she came up with an incredible idea that I latched onto immediately. My apologies to the people in Burnside who were having breakfast around us during that meeting as we both get very excited over post-mortems.

Jack Hawksworth couldn't have achieved what he has without the input of former senior detective Mike Warburton from Scotland Yard. He has kept me on the straight and narrow, never allowing my imagination to get the better of police protocols and authenticity. I am incredibly grateful.

Heartfelt thanks to Pip Klimentou, who has read every novel I have ever written before anyone else gets to see it. Her no-nonsense, love-it-or-hate-it approach is a blissful addition to getting the characters and pacing right.

I have a long-suffering family who indulges my time at the keyboard and my weird and wonderful research trips. I'm always striving for fresh settings and fresh themes, even when there is a serial killer involved. This means I could be anywhere from a lonely football pitch in West London or a beach in a far-flung country town, to the mortuary of a pathology unit. It is always a wild and wonderful ride into the research for a Jack Hawksworth story and thanks to my husband, Ian, for never batting an eyelid at where the next adventure is going to take me.

My publisher is equally generous – thanks to Penguin Random House's sales, marketing and publicity teams for their fabulous support but especially to my editorial partners, Ali Watts and Amanda Martin, who work hard alongside me to make sure each Jack outing is the best it can be for the reader.

Booksellers around Australia and NZ, you are gold. A big *mwah!* for being excited about the latest Jack Hawksworth.

Fx

BOOK CLUB NOTES

1. In what ways have the cases of Jack's past helped to influence this current case?

2. How has Jack changed since meeting Lou?

3. 'No one understands this grief unless they've been through it.' Is it ever possible to forgive someone for their crimes due to personal circumstances such as grief? Why or why not?

4. There is no doubt that technological advances in medical science are helping to save lives, but in what ways can they be deadly in the wrong hands?

5. Whose responsibility is it when negligence leads to injury or death – an individual's or an institution's – and why?

6. In what ways do Jack's team members complement his policing style?

7. 'You should be thankful to the killer, because he's released you.' In what ways has Hannah been released through the story's events?

8. Kate is thrust into extreme danger. Which of her qualities help her in this situation and which hinder her?

9. What would you have done in Geoff's shoes, when faced with the scene on the cliff top, and why?

10. How do you think the killer was able to fool everyone for so long?

11. If you have read the previous Jack Hawksworth books, in what ways do you think Kate has changed?

12. What do you think might be next for Jack and his colleagues?

Read on to see where it all began in
Bye Bye Baby,
Jack Hawksworth's first story

1

Jean Farmer took the call, and regretted instantly that she'd been the one to pick up the phone. She knew the Sheriffs and hated that she would now have to ruin Mike's night out at the Castle Hotel with the news from Lincoln Hospital.

'How serious is it, Sister?' she asked.

'Not as bad as it first appeared, I'm glad to say,' the nurse from casualty explained. 'We're sending her home, but she was crying for her dad and I promised Mrs Sheriff we'd call him.'

'What exactly should I tell him?'

'Simply that his daughter has been involved in a sporting accident. The wound to her arm is quite deep, but the bleeding has stopped, and it has been stitched and she'll be fine. Just ask him to get home immediately, please. Mrs Sheriff is on her way there with their daughter now, and both of them are quite upset.'

'Okay, will do. Thank you, Sister.'

Jean put the phone down, grabbed one of the staff just going off duty to hold the fort at the front desk for a couple of minutes, and headed to the dining room. Mike, in high spirits, and a group of work companions sat at the long table near the window.

She touched his shoulder.

'I'm so sorry to interrupt your dinner, Mike, but we've just taken a call from the hospital. It's Susan.'

'Su—' Mike Sheriff put his pint glass down clumsily. 'What's happened?'

Jean saw some of the colour drain from his face as alarm overrode the alcohol's effects. 'I don't want you to worry but there's been an accident,' she started. Mike had pushed his chair back and was on his feet before she could say much more. 'Mike, hold on.' Jean grabbed his arm. 'It's all right. Susan's fine, I promise. She's hurt her arm apparently, but she's okay. I've just got off from speaking with the sister on duty in Casualty.'

Mike appeared to be sobering fast. 'I'd better go.'

Jean nodded. 'I said we'd get you on your way immediately – but head home rather than the hospital. Diane's on her way back to Louth now.'

'I'm sorry, everyone,' Mike said to the teachers around the table as he gathered his things together. 'My mobile! Some bastard stole it today.'

'It was probably that toe-rag, Wilkins,' one of the others piped up. It was John Buchanan, a bitter sort. 'He's the school fence, I'm sure of it.'

She gave Buchanan a pained expression because she knew the Wilkins family too. And they were fine – their children were allowed to run a bit wild but they had good hearts and Georgie Wilkins was unlikely a thief. She returned her attention to Sheriff. 'Mike, you're most welcome to use a phone here; call on Diane's mobile as they're travelling now,' she said, ushering the bewildered man away from the table and towards the double doors that led past the bar.

'She doesn't have a mobile either,' he said, frowning. 'Never needs one.' Jean stayed quiet. 'Sorry again. I'll settle up tomorrow,' he slurred slightly over his shoulder to his colleagues.

Jean answered for them. 'That's fine. Now listen, I don't think it's a good idea for you to drive,' she said. 'Let me call you a taxi.' She squeezed Mike's arm reassuringly, then called across to the barman. 'Dave, just keep an eye on Mike for me, will you? He's a bit unsteady, just had some bad news. I'm ordering a taxi – he's got to get home urgently.'

The man nodded. 'Righto. I'm just checking through this after-noon's delivery, but that's fine.'

'Thanks. I'll be right back. Two minutes, Mike, okay.'

And that's when I grabbed my chance. I'd been playing it by ear, so couldn't squander this opportunity with the woman now out of sight, the barman preoccupied and, best of all, Mikey intoxicated enough to be compliant. Both of the staff had seen me, but what's one more tourist in the bar of a popular hotel, and I'd gone to some lengths to disguise myself by wearing a false beard, a hat and a loose coat. Besides, I was enjoying the musty, gentle fizziness of a pale ale after so many years of living abroad. I sipped at it slowly, letting the familiar flavour sluice away the fear; killing time before the real killing began.

It was hard to believe the moment of redemption had arrived. I'd watched Mikey for weeks, watched the whole Sheriff family going about their business. The first time I'd laid eyes on him I felt as though all the breath had been sucked from my lungs. For the past thirty years he and the others had loomed in my thoughts as monsters, and yet here Mikey was now, middle-aged and so harmless-looking.

I shook myself free of the unexpected sentimentality. I would go through with it – there was no doubt about that. The deep wound that he and the others had inflicted upon me all those years ago had only pretended to heal. Beneath the scab of the new life I'd built, the injury had festered.

Now, with the fresh pain of loss tearing me apart, that old fury had spewed forth in an angry torrent. To lose our perfect child, lying so sweetly in his cot as if gently sleeping, his tiny six-month-old body still achingly warm, had sapped every last reserve of my strength. It was the end of my marriage too, the end of a happy life with Kim which had sustained me over the past couple of decades. I rued the day I'd suggested that starting a family would complete us. Now we had lost two daughters to miscarriage and our precious boy to some inexplicable string of letters. 'SIDS,' the doctor had said gently, although it had explained nothing.

I had done everything to make my life work; to walk in the light rather than dwell in the dark. No one could accuse me of bemoaning my past and yet it seemed the horror of my teenage years was never to leave me. And there he was, one of the perpetrators, about to pay for the events of his own past. I took a final sip of my beer and felt a rush of adrenaline spike through me as I began my performance.

'Thanks. See you later,' I said to the barman, who was busy counting crates and ticking off sheets of paper. He didn't even look around.

I concealed myself in the corridor that led to the toilets and watched through the glass of the door as the receptionist led Mikey out of the restaurant and into the bar. He looked shaken, a bit unsteady on his feet, no doubt helped along by the beer and wine he'd enjoyed during the evening. The woman said something to him, her hand squeezing his arm, then called out to someone – presumably the barman – and left Mikey alone. He swayed slightly in a daze.

I seized my moment and pulled off the coat, hat, beard and stuffed them into the backpack I was carrying, before I re-entered the bar quietly. I pasted an expression of slight bafflement on my face, then grinned. 'Mikey Sheriff?' I called softly, contrived disbelief charging my words.

Sheriff stared at me in confusion. I could understand why. Unlike me, he hadn't changed much at all. Greyer, paunchier, those dark-blue eyes even more hooded than I recalled, but there was no mistaking plain, duck-lipped Mikey Sheriff of three decades previous. That he had won the heart of any woman was a surprise.

My luck was in: the barman was nowhere to be seen, Mikey no doubt already forgotten in his need to get on with his work. I slapped the man I was going to kill on the arm. 'You don't recognise me, Mike? Come on, you used to call me Bletch!'

I watched his confused gaze as the nickname from so many years ago registered. 'Bletch?' he repeated dumbly.

I nodded, still holding my smile.

'It can't be,' he went on. 'Not A—'

I couldn't risk him naming me publicly. 'Is something wrong?' I interrupted. I knew I had only seconds now before the woman from the front desk returned.

Sheriff didn't even notice the clumsy shift in topic. Instead, he groaned. 'My daughter's been involved in an accident. I have to get home. They're calling a taxi.'

'I wouldn't bother,' I said. 'I've heard there's a delay of about forty-five minutes.'

'In Lincoln?' he said, aghast. 'I can't imagine it.'

I nodded. 'There's some convention going on. You can try, but I was about to head off anyway. I'm happy to take you home. It's probably far quicker.'

I took his arm and guided him to the side door, keen to get him out the building before the receptionist returned. Help came from an unexpected quarter. A youngish woman – the housekeeper, I assumed, from her clipboard and name badge – entered through the same door we were making for.

'Hello, Mr Sheriff,' she said, then sensed the atmosphere and looked to me. 'What's going on?'

'Help me outside with him, please,' I said. 'He needs some air. He's just received some bad news.'

To my relief she didn't ask any more questions, just took Sheriff's other arm and helped me bundle him into the cold November night. The chill air slapped us in the face. Worried it would sober Mikey up, I quickly explained to the girl what had happened. 'So I'll run him back to Louth,' I finished. 'Thanks for your help.' Behind Mike's back I made a gesture to indicate that he'd had too much to drink.

She caught on fast and turned to him eagerly. 'Mr Sheriff, listen. Give me your car keys and I'll move your car – the red Vauxhall, right? – into the staff car park. It'll be safe there. You don't want to be picked up by the police, do you? Why don't you let your friend get you home safely?'

Friend? I had to stifle a smile.

Mike obviously shared an identical thought. 'Bletch?' he repeated and fresh confusion clouded his face. 'My friend?'

I threw a look of sympathetic concern to Emma. 'It's been a while, Mike. I'm not surprised you don't recognise me.' I gave a shrug. 'When Mike knew me, I was as big as a house.'

She didn't seem to know what to say to that; I was clearly the reverse now. I kept talking, kept moving, drawing Mike towards the car park.

'No one's told me how badly my daughter is hurt,' Mike slurred. 'I need to ring home.'

Emma spoke to him firmly. 'Mr Sheriff, get in your friend's car and go home. It sounds as if they need you back there straight-away.'

I could see she was about to ask me my name. 'Whoops!' I said, pretending to catch Mike as if he'd staggered. 'Come on. Let's get you home, champ. Your family needs you.' I looked back at her. 'I'm sure Mike will ring to thank you himself.'

She gave a grin. 'No need to worry. This is my last night here and I was just knocking off. I'm headed overseas for a year, doing an exchange.'

The angels were smiling on me tonight.

I hustled Mike quickly into the car park, all the while making the right sympathetic noises.

I bundled him into my van, locked his door, then jumped into the driving seat. I pulled a bottle of water from the glove compartment. 'Here, Mikey, drink this.'

'What is it?' he murmured.

'Just water. You need to sober up. Drink plenty and we'll see if we can't get you a coffee on the way home. That will help wake you up.'

'Where's Jean? I must thank her,' Sheriff mumbled as he unscrewed the cap. 'Is it really you? Fat Bletch?' he continued, a note of awe coming through the alcohol. 'It can't be. You look so different, so thin. Amazing.'

'Everyone looks amazing through slightly pissed eyes, Mike,' I said, pulling out of the car park. 'But I'll take the compliment. I work out, keep myself fit.'

'I can hardly believe it's you. I would never have recognised you.' He yawned.

'You could say I've reinvented myself along with the new body.' I grinned at him.

He paused then; no doubt the memories were crashing back,

closing in around us. No amount of alcohol could fully block those horrors.

'I don't know what to say,' he admitted, and I felt a small stab of admiration that he at least said that much. 'What can I say that can —'

'Nothing, Mikey. Nothing you can say will change it.' I held his abashed stare. 'So don't try, eh? It was almost three decades ago.'

'No, but —'

'Please, don't. I never allow myself to think about it, let alone talk about it. If I can bear it, you can bear not to discuss it, eh?' I gave him a friendly punch, but he looked like a startled deer, ready to flee. 'Keep drinking,' I said. 'We have to sober you up.'

I watched as he tipped almost half of what was left in the water bottle down his throat. It was enough; I could relax now.

'What are you doing here, anyway?' he said. He was concentrating hard on not slurring.

'Work,' I answered brightly. 'It's such a beautiful city and that cathedral at night – wow! I was just having a beer at the hotel and planning to drive around and enjoy all these fabulous old buildings and landmarks in the dark.'

'A long way from Brighton,' he murmured, leaning against the window.

'Too right,' I replied quickly. 'Drink the rest. You'll feel better shortly.'

'I feel worse. I was coming good, but now I feel blurry again. I don't want to be here with you. It's embarrassing. I feel awkward and ashamed. Please don't behave so generously towards me. I don't want your pity and I don't deserve it.'

I smiled in the dark and watched him give another big yawn.

Mikey was mine.

* * *

Powered by Penguin

Looking for more great reads, exclusive content and book giveaways?

Subscribe to our weekly newsletter.

Scan the QR code or visit penguin.com.au/signup